A Fairy-Tale Ending

A Fairy-Tale Ending

Book One of the Charming Tales

JACK HECKEL

HARPER
VOYAGER
IMPULSE

An Imprint of HarperCollinsPublishers

Once Upon a Rhyme copyright © 2014 by John Peck and Harry Heckel.
Happily Never After copyright © 2014 by John Peck and Harry Heckel.

EPub Edition AUGUST 2015 ISBN: 9780062420688
Print Edition ISBN: 9780062420695

10 9 8 7 6 5 4 3 2

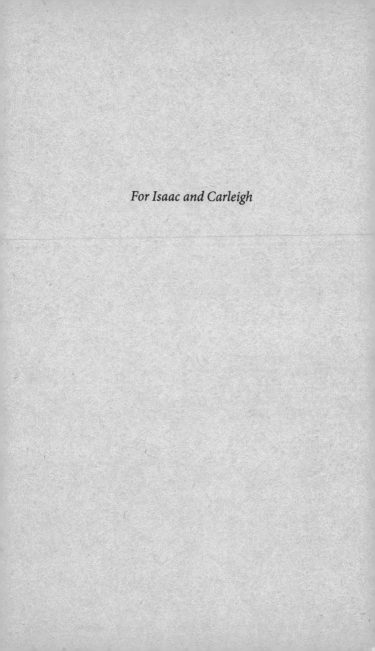

For Isaac and Carleigh

The Kingdom of Royaume and Environs

North Mountains

West Mountains

East Mountains

South Mountains

The Great Northern Forest

Grandma's Cave

Winds to the North

Quiet

King's Hunting Lodge

Marshal's Bridge

Three Goats

Scoundrel's Bridge

Three Bears Cave

Gooben Pastures

The Cooked Goose

Castle White

Blue Lake

Cottage of the Seven Players

Beast Manor

Blue Hills

Quaint

The Dwarf Cave

Winds to the East

Rapunzel's Tower

Modest

Raging River

Rapunzel's Estate

Winds to the West

Tiny Trees

Prosper

Pickett Farm

Winds to the South

Dragon Tower

Volume I:
Once Upon a Rhyme

Beneath the dragon's sleepless vigil
In endless sleep shall the maiden stay.
Awaiting there her true love's kiss
To sweep at last her curse away.
—FROM "THE DRAGON'S TALE"

Prologue

The Great Lady and the Strawman

THE DRAGON FLEW just below the clouds. This was her first night free after a long winter's slumber, and her hunt had been disappointing—nothing but a few stray cows and one fat deer. In the old days, the valley had been rich with prey, both human and livestock. The villagers had grown more clever, though, hiding both themselves and their animals in underground cellars when she came, and shooting at her from their holes with steel-tipped arrows. She had half a mind to return home, but it had been a long winter and the spring had woken in her an unyielding hunger. So she drifted south on the winds and circled hungrily over an outlying farm. What she saw was not promising. The farm looked derelict and deserted.

A sudden chill ran along her spine. She looked across

the horizon and saw that to the east the sky was beginning to lighten. During her hunt, she had allowed herself
to forget her curse. Now she felt its pull. The fairy's enchantment was drawing her back to that damnable tower
and her sleeping prisoner. An uncontrollable rage welled
up, and she rent the darkness with a jet of superheated
ichor. The caustic liquid unique to her breed crackled
with a white-hot light as it boiled the night air.

Even before the fireball faded, the cold night bit
deeper into her bones. It would be weeks before she
would be able to stoke her fires again, feel truly warm,
and her skin crawled at the thought of spending it locked
away with the half-sleeping princess. Resentment hissed
through double rows of ivory teeth as she turned back to
the south, to the mountains that lay beyond the night-
darkened fields. She would be home in an hour, well
before dawn and the magically imposed curfew. With
her front claw, she unconsciously fingered the key. It was
always with her—the fairy's little joke—hung around her
neck by a golden chain, a constant reminder of her imprisonment.

The fairy. Her mind cast back to the night the fairy
had come to her, wooed and flattered her, tricked her
into this dull servitude. She felt the anger building again,
then realized her talon was clutching the key violently,
squeezing it, trying to crush it. She sighed and let go.
The key settled against her scaled breast. As a burden it
was nothing; but as a brand, it galled and irritated her to
distraction.

How pathetic I have grown, to dwell and rage at something as fleeting as a fairy curse.

The forest at the far edge of the farm was passing beneath her when some ancient sense made her look back. *Movement.*

Two figures, the heat of their bodies radiating incandescently, moved like shooting stars through the dark ocean of the night-cooled corn. One raced ahead of the other, but then the lead figure stopped suddenly in the middle of the field allowing its pursuer to catch up. She watched as they crouched low to the ground so the cornstalks engulfed them. Hidden as they would have been to normal eyes, their bodies shone in the darkness—a pair of flickering candles exposed by her supernatural senses. Perhaps there was time for one last kill. She smiled a predator's grin and flicked out her forked tongue, tasting the wind. Folding her wings, she pirouetted on the misty ether and dove. The ground rose rapidly to meet her, and, at the last possible moment, she spread her great wings and immediately felt the pull, almost painful as her wings beat against the heavy air. Her body traced a soft arc through the sky and she leveled off, passing a few feet above the top of a timber fence marking the far edge of the field. Silent as the wind, only the whisper of the corn marked her passage as their tasseled tops brushed against her underbelly and bent in rippling waves before her.

Normally, she would have tried to flush her quarry into flight to enjoy the chase, but the sky to the east was brightening even more now, and with it the invisible strands of magic that kept her tied to the black tower were starting to tighten. The kill would have to be quick. She fixed her gaze wholly on the body-shaped embers that grew larger with each beat of her wings. She was already anticipating the crunch of the bones in her talons and the taste of hot blood in her throat.

Without warning, a man wearing a battered cloth hat loomed out of a crop row ahead of her, arms stretched wide. She had a brief impression of the thing's crude, almost grotesque, leering face before her body, reacting instinctively to the threat, rose to avoid the creature.

Have you become a crow in your old age that you would flee at the sight of a straw man?

With a malice born of anger, she forced her body back into the attack and down onto the top of the scarecrow, crushing it. She never saw the warning glint of steel from the pitchfork carelessly propped against its straw body. The metal fork and two feet of the handle plunged deep into her body. In an instant, she lost strength in her right side and her wing dropped, useless. She bellowed in surprise at the sudden pain and tried to slow her descent, but the tip of the crippled wing caught one of the deep furrows of the field and she cartwheeled headfirst into the ground. The wing snapped as the weight of her body crushed it beneath her, the painful sensation incidental to the burning agony in her breast.

Unable to stand, she rolled onto her back and, clutching the shaft of the pitchfork with her talons, ripped the hateful thing free. With a glance of disgust, she threw it into the field. She sighed with relief. With nothing to seal the wound, hot blood welled out of the ragged cut and began running in great torrents down her side and onto the flattened stalks below. She heard the hiss and pop of the corn and smelled the smoke of the fire before she felt it as the drought-dry husks, fueled by her own super-heated blood, burst into flame. Recognizing the danger, she made an effort to stand but hadn't the strength. She collapsed back onto the ground, breathing heavily in the rising smoke. Never before had she felt such weakness.

Is this how I am to end my days? To die in some field, like a common worm?

She gave voice to her bitterness, screeching her hatred of the world, its echo rebounding in the narrow valley. As silence returned, her rage was replaced by a sudden and unexpected calm. She smiled. The enchantment was lifting. Reaching up, she tore the golden key from around her neck and let it drop. At long last the bond to the sad little princess was severed. With a bittersweet sigh, she stopped struggling.

Settling her head into a fold of the furrowed earth as the fire licked around her body, the dragon gazed across the field at the edge of the rising sun. At least this moment—this last sunrise—would be hers alone, and she would be warm. She smiled. Flames rose up, consuming her, and spread outward through the field like a receding tide. The stars faded in her eyes, and Magdela the Great passed from the world.

Chapter 1

Fairytale's End

ONCE UPON A time in the kingdom of Royaume, a land of modest prosperity, on a hill of green, stood a shining castle of white where lived the aged widower King Rupert. Though he had been blessed with a son much admired by his subjects, he took little joy in the young man and was, in his waning years, lonely and morose. Not that he had always been so.

In his youth, he had fallen deeply, even poetically, for Princess Rosslyn of the house Mostfair. She was a lady of rare beauty and rarer virtue. They might have made a timeless queen and king, but on the very day that they were to be betrothed, Rosslyn fell gravely ill and died. Rupert was lost, but he was also the son of a king, and being the sole heir to the throne he had his duty. After what was thought a suitable time of mourning by their parents, Rosslyn's sister, Gwendolyn was put forward as a replacement.

Gwendolyn was, by many accounts, even more beautiful than her older sister and, after a brief courtship, she and the King were engaged, the date of the wedding set. But Rupert was, for a second time, accursed. This time by a dragon. Driven by a petulant fairy's curse, the Great Wyrm appeared in the sky on the eve of the wedding and carried Princess Gwendolyn off to its tower stronghold.

The origin of the dragon is, to this day, a bit of a mystery. Though not profoundly so for Rupert's kingdom, unlike many of its more sensible neighbors, had not yet consigned magic, or magical creatures, to the pages of fairy tale. Trolls, giants and hags were constantly lurking about in their dark forests, bashing people on the head and trying to devour naughty children. Most of these beasts were more nuisance than real danger, unless of course you were a greedy child or a disobedient child or a petulant child or an overly curious child or a child whose woodcutter father had fallen on hard times—the point being that for most adults in Rupert's kingdom, the creatures were not much of a worry. The one exception to this rule was the dragon, which, while having retired from kidnapping nobility, took to descending at the end of every winter to burn villages with an unseemly glee, gobble up cattle and peasants with equal relish, and generally make a menace of itself.

Rupert, having a great deal more political acumen than strength of arm, never quite worked up the nerve to face the creature, and, after a long period of mourning, he married another. She bore him a son. But while this queen was fair and of high birth, she was also of poor health, and died while the Prince was in his infancy.

The mood of the kingdom was undeniably bleak. Another lady fair had passed, the dragon remained, and given Rupert's unwillingness to slay the beast, most of his subjects had lost hope that they would ever be freed of its scourge. Worse still, at least in the minds of the more romantically inclined, and those that lived in places far distant from the path of the dragon's periodical destructive rage, was that the dragon still held the beloved Princess Gwendolyn captive, trapped in an enchanted, endless slumber. Then, a month after his wife's passing, the King addressed a throng of handpicked well-wishers in the flowered courtyard of Castle White, babe in arms, and made the startling announcement that their savior had come.

The news ran like wildfire through the kingdom. Prophecy had ordained that the King's son, Prince Edward Michael Charming, would slay the Wyrm of the South and free the kingdom from its curse. There was rejoicing throughout the land, if a bit premature, as the boy was naught but six-months old and the dragon had on the previous evening eaten the entire town of Two Trees.

Still, no one could be blamed for a bit of early celebration. And so it became a matter of faith that when the time was right, Prince Charming would ride forth, slay the dragon, wake the fair maiden of the tower keep with love's first kiss, and return to claim his father's throne.

That at least had always been the story, told and retold countless times to wide-eyed children around the embers of bedtime fires. But in a narrow valley of farms a week's ride to the south of the glimmering castle, the faith of two of those formerly wide-eyed children in the "happily ever after" part of the Prince's story was being sorely put to the test.

The "children" in question were Elizabeth and William Pickett—brother and sister. And the resemblance was unmistakable. Both were tall, though Will stood a head higher than his sister. Both had thick reddish-brown hair, Liz's running more to red and Will's more to brown. And both had the handsome if not exactly pretty features that always marked a Pickett in these parts—high, soft cheekbones, a thin straight nose, and large bright eyes.

Not that Liz and Will were still children. He was fully twenty summers, and she five years more—old enough that he was considered a most eligible bachelor, while she was branded by the ladies of the village an old maid. To be fair, Liz had never had much time for romance. Their parents passed away when she was only fourteen. Barely out of pigtails, Liz became the young matriarch of what was left of the Pickett estate: a few dozen acres of clay-packed dirt and the family home.

Not that the Picketts had always been so poor. At one time, the family had enjoyed such prosperity that her grandfather's father founded, and named, a nearby township: Prosper. A name the town had failed to live up to almost immediately.

The demise in the family's fortunes, though, had

really begun when their grandfather became obsessed with growing oversized beanstalks. Ultimately, he lost most of his land and riches, earning the family a reputation for madness. A reputation confirmed by their father's insistence that their fortunes would be restored as soon as his flock of geese started laying golden eggs. The townspeople took great relish in preying on his gullible nature, swindling him of what was left of their money. Destitute, the family was shunned from society, and Liz and Will, by the very fact of being Picketts, were marked as "odd."

And now, all that remained of the Pickett family fortune was burning before their eyes.

Standing on the crumbling stone wall of their well, Will and Liz watched in disbelief as the flames danced and raged through the last stalks of their spring corn. Around them the field was covered in ash and a heavy choking blanket of smoke. Matching hazel eyes watered as a breeze whipped the noxious fumes around them. But what held their collective gaze was not the burning corn, or the desolation of their home—it was instead the bulky silhouette, still rather vague in the gray light of dawn, of the Great Wyrm of the South, the dread dragon of fairy tale.

Liz was the first to stir. She pried her slender hand from her brother's calloused grasp, wiped sooty palms down the front of her equally sooty apron, to dubious effect, and lowered herself carefully from the wall. The smoke was heavier here. With a muffled cough, she wrapped a handkerchief about her mouth, tying it in a neat knot behind her neck. Then, gathering the length of her hair in both hands, she twisted it into a bun and stabbed it violently into submission with a long wooden hairpin.

She stared up at her brother with a frown. He was still atop the wall, a bucket in his hand and an all-too familiar blank expression on his face. *Gently now*, she reminded herself. *He—we—have both nearly been killed by a dragon.*

"Are you *coming*, Will?" she asked as evenly as she could.

Liz paused a moment to let him gather himself, but to no effect. She pursed her lips in irritation. "I don't think the bucket will be much use, Will," she said too brightly, the affected sweetness sounding fake even to her. "There's nothing left to burn, so there's nothing much to save."

Still, Will did not seem to hear, transfixed as he was by the contents of his leaky bucket. Liz groaned, reached up, pulled the bucket from his hands, and dropped it down the well. Will looked at her with an expression of stunned surprise. Then she put her hands on her hips in an unconscious mimic of their mother and said flatly, "Don't stand there gaping like the village idiot. Let's go see what became of the bloody great beast."

Will mumbled something that sounded like *bucket* and *talking frog*, but Liz's patience was at an end. She glared at him coldly until at last Will stuttered, "I—I swear . . . I . . . I'm not making this up."

They both stared at each other and sighed. For twenty years, Liz had been Will's sibling, eleven of which she had been, for better or worse, like his mother, and had still never figured out how to live with each other in peace. As usual, Liz broke the silence. "You do realize that there's a dead dragon in our field, don't you? I would have thought *that* might pique your interest."

"Normally, yes," he said, and made a helpless gesture with his hands back down the well. "But that frog was really something."

Liz threw her hands in the air in silent despair and stalked off through the smoldering crops toward the dragon's body, cursing her brother, fate, and dragons with equal vehemence.

To approach the dragon's body, Liz had to climb down into the massive trench the beast had cut in the field as it fell. She followed the ragged scar and shuddered as she saw that it was aimed like an arrow right at the spot in the middle of the field where she had caught Will after his mad attempt to draw the dragon away from the house . To distract herself from the memory of those terrifying moments, Liz began a careful inspection of the dragon's body, tracing the outline of one of its massive wings as she walked toward its head. This close to the beast's body, the air smelled of burnt dragon flesh, and she pressed the handkerchief tighter against her mouth to cover the choking stench.

With her eyes watering, she at last reached the dragon's massive snout, and stared into the creature's face. To be sure, it was a horror. Hundreds of ivory white teeth like butcher's knives jutted from the thing's mouth, and thousands of plates that met in raised razor-sharp rows covered its body, running along the dragon's length, growing as they went till they formed high armored ridges along its back. But, despite the vicious talons and the spiked tail, there was something very human about the creature's expression. Its eyes were closed, and bathed in the light of dawn, its face seemed almost peaceful. She ran a hand over the rough scales around the nose. The dragon was still warm; it could have been sleeping.

"Lucky . . ." Liz muttered.

She paused, her hand still outstretched, and considered the word. It was wrong, but she knew that was exactly how she felt. The dragon's troubles were over. Hers, on the other hand, had only begun. She turned about and surveyed the smoking landscape. Their home was a shambles, their crop, their only source of livelihood and sustenance, was gone. The village, with as little comfort as it might have offered them, was also likely destroyed. The excitement of the early-morning terror was gone, and Liz found herself staring at the dragon and feeling nothing but a profound emptiness.

"Why us? Why now?" she asked the dead beast. This was not how the story went. There had been no noble steed in white, no prince, no flashing sword or gleaming armor. There would be no castle on a hill, no happily ever after. This was not how it was supposed to end. All they had was a ruined farm and this ruined corpse. Anger filled the emptiness in her heart. She screamed: *"It isn't fair!"* and, with each spoken word, she hammered with her fists at the dragon's corpse, though its sharp scales cut into the soft flesh of her knuckles.

Before she had landed a half-dozen blows on its stone-hard head, Will was at her side. He threw his arms around her and drew her away from the body. Her anger turned to great wracking sobs. She collapsed into his arms, and out came a rush of words.

"It's gone . . . what little we had is gone. Everything we've worked for . . . and for what? Now all we will have is . . . is . . . hunger and misery. It would have been better if we'd stayed in that field and burned."

She knew she was being emotional and selfish and maudlin, and all the other things she hated in other women, but she could not help it—it was all true. She pulled away and looked up at him, her tears painting white lines in her ash-covered cheeks.

"What will we do? We have nothing left—nothing."

The last she spat out like a curse and then rocked back on her heels. It was hopeless. She let her body go limp, her eyes stared out unseeing at the gray stillness of the smoky morning.

There was a long moment of silence during which Liz, for perhaps the first time in her life, thought nothing. Then Will spoke. "We could go rescue the princess."

Liz was no longer crying. Instead, she was angry. She pushed his hands away and stood stiffly. *So, his answer to this disaster is to tell me a fairy tale? He is his father, and his grandfather, and his great-grandfather all over again.*

While she played this monologue out in her head, all she could manage was *"What?"*—which, even to her own ears, sounded ominously low.

Perhaps grave muttering shook Will, because when

he replied, it was with significantly less confidence. "We could go after the princess . . . it's . . . I mean . . . now that the dragon is gone it shouldn't be too hard."

Maybe he was trying to be amusing, but Liz was in no mood, and she had too much experience with the men of her family to assume that he was anything but serious.

"What princess, Will?"

She was happy to see beads of sweat form across his brow as he answered. "You know the one in the 'Dragon's Tale.' The—the one Mom used to read to us."

"There is no princess, Will!" she shouted, her anger spilling out unchecked. "The story was just *that*—a story! If this is the 'Dragon's Tale,' then where is Prince Charming? Where is his shining blade and noble steed? Where is our happily—"

Liz stopped herself too late. Will's eyes narrowed with understanding, and she felt a mixture of embarrassment and anger paint flashing red across her cheeks. Now he knew she'd also been thinking of the fairy tale. Will got to his feet, bit the nail of his index finger and, with eyes locked firmly on the ground, said, "Just because the cock don't crow doesn't mean the sun didn't rise."

Liz pursed her lips and glared at her brother. He loved those *country* expressions, and she hated them. Their mother had been Lady Pickett, their great-grandfather had been an advisor to kings. Much as it was their only source of sustenance, they were not farmers, and she would be damned if she let her brother lower himself. She started to say just that, but Will held up his hands in a gesture of peace and said quickly, "All I meant to say is that just because our field is gone doesn't mean there isn't a princess."

Liz was momentarily speechless. He actually thought he was going to be allowed to go looking for a princess. He could not be that foolish. She would not *let* him be that foolish. She would not let him ride off on some mad quest and repeat their father's and grandfather's mistakes.

She stepped forward and, despite the difference in height, endeavored to loom over him as she had done when they were younger. "Do you think this is a joke?"

She gestured widely around at the devastation, her voice rising to a shout. "This is not *a bloody fairy tale, Will*. That mad beast just destroyed our home. And what about the village? How many of our neighbors, our friends—your girl, Gretel—are in that thing's belly? Prosper may be gone. Our home *is* gone. There is no happy ending here. And for God's sake, stop biting your nails!"

Will dropped his hand from his mouth, but then the line of his jaw set stubbornly. "You and I both know that everyone in that village will be fine. They have their stone cellars and their watch fires and their bowmen and . . ."

He threw up his hands and without another word brushed past her, striding across the blackened field toward what was left of the house. She stared after him. Was that it? Then fear rushed through her. What if he rode away and left her here alone?

She called out, "Will, I'm—I'm sorry I yelled."

He stopped several paces away and bent low to the ground. She rushed after him and, reaching his side, gently stroked his back. "I—" Her voice broke again, "I shouldn't have said that about staying in the field. The only thing that matters is that we are alive and together. The rest we can figure out. I know this is hard for you to accept, but the 'Dragon's Tale' is just a pretty fable made up to help children sleep. There is no princess, there is no curse, there is nothing but a stupid, mindless, blood-thirsty beast that managed to get itself killed! And . . ."

She stopped as he rose and slowly turned toward her. He was holding something out to her. There dangling from the end of a broken chain was a golden key. It was a four-toothed affair, a little longer than his hand, with writing etched on its surface in spidery script. Liz raised her index finger cautiously, as if afraid it might vanish at her touch, and traced its length. The words written there came straight from the book she had read and reread since she was a little girl.

> *This key shall be my curse's mark.*
> *The maid shall sleep,*
> *The wyrm shall watch,*
> *Bound link-by-link by magics dark.*

The story was true? The blood pulsed in her ears until the world was a soundless roar. How long she stood there looking at the key, but seeing instead images of a gallant knight and a sleeping maiden and a high dark tower, she did not know. There was a sense of time passing, but if it was a minute or an hour she could not have later said. Finally, though, she heard Will's voice, and the meaning of what he was saying shook her from her reverie.

"See, I was trying to tell you the whole time. I saw the key glimmering there in the dirt when I ran over to pull you off the dragon. I'll take Grey and the cart up the mountain pass. I figure it should take one week— four days up and three days down—and if I don't come back with the Princess, you go to town, show them the dragon, and tell them to go to the castle to send someone after me."

Panic pushed away all thoughts of the key and the fairy tale. Her brother was seriously suggesting that he go rescue the Princess from the dragon's tower. Unbidden, their mother's voice came back to her. *He has too much of his father and grandfather in him. His head is full of adventure and glory, and if you do not keep his feet solidly on the ground, it will be his undoing, just as it was theirs.* Liz dropped her hand away from the key and squared her shoulders. She watched his eyes grow guarded and tense. *Good*, she thought. *I must make him see reason. I must be practical—hard.*

"So, let me get this straight," she said with as much scorn as she could muster. "Your plan, the one you spent the last half-minute thinking up, is to take our only horse up into a notoriously dangerous mountain pass to find a dragon's lair, and rescue a princess that may or may not exist?" He opened his mouth to respond, but she gave him no chance, and instead quickened the tone and meter of her lecture. "Will, did you look at that key? It's solid gold. Even if it isn't, it must be worth a fortune, more than this family has had since Grandfather went mad trying to buy those ridiculous magic beans. If we melt that key down, no one could trace it back to the dragon, and we would have enough money to—"

"Now wait a minute," he interrupted. "Grandfather just had a little bad luck with the phase of the moon. If he had been any kind of a farmer, he'd have planted in the waxing moon so the seed would sprout under the full moon. You see the important thing about beans is—"

Liz put her hand on her brother's chest to silence him. "Will, try and focus on the issue at hand. Please."

His eyes grew cold, and she knew she had said the wrong thing. He straightened his back so that he stood at his full height. She was suddenly very aware of how tall he was. "I am focusing on the issue," he spit. "I'm thinking about a girl trapped up in a dark tower, Liz. I'm trying to ignore your suggestion that we become . . . I don't know what—thieves? Tell me, Liz, what are we supposed to do, leave her there to rot?"

Liz turned her back to him. Her voice quavered as she answered his question. "No, of course not. But—"

"But what?" he asked impatiently.

But what? she asked herself. In her mind's eye, she saw the flowing pennants, glittering armor, and Prince Charming on his horse. She felt a pang of something in her breast, and tears began to spill down her face. This time when she spoke her voice had lost all of its authority. "But what about the Prince? The Prince is supposed to rescue the Princess. I also remember the story, Will," and she closed her eyes and recited the lines she had read so many times: "'And the Prince regarded the maiden fair—a pale flower in enchanted slumber preserved. And on bended knee did he lower himself to her, and lip to lip, breath to breath, with love's first kiss did he awaken her heart from its timeless cage.'"

She wiped at her eyes with the back of her hand and then snapped her finger under his nose. "What about all that? There's nothing in the story about a peasant waking the Princess! Prince Charming is the hero. Prince Charming wakes the Princess. You might not even be able to."

Liz knew that seeing any woman cry made Will intensely uncomfortable, so when he mumbled something incoherent about artistic license being responsible for some of the inconsistencies, she let it pass. She knew that a debate over literary device would not resolve anything. Eventually, his speech ground to an awkward halt. They stood in another of their too common silences.

Surprisingly, this time it was Will that broke the spell. He placed the key in her hands and said, "But, we are here now, and if we can save her, then that is what we should do. How can we condemn her to another day of sleep in those cold mountains?"

The thought of the Princess lying like a corpse in some forgotten tower sent a chill through Liz's bones, and she shook her head to be rid of the vision. He smiled down at her, and Liz knew from the expression that he had seen her thoughts in her expression.

"Look, I'm not saying I believe in the whole story," he said in a reassuringly measured tone. "Like you said, the Prince wasn't real, but if that kiss part is real, and the Princess doesn't wake with the key, then I'll just put her in the cart and deliver her to the castle so the Prince can do the rest. But think about it, if we bring the Princess back, then, well, then no one can deny what we've done. We'll have written ourselves into their story, and if that's not worth a king's ransom in gold then nothing is."

Liz cocked her head to one side and studied him curiously, holding his gaze with her own. There had been something in his voice when he'd mentioned the kiss that made her pause. He blushed under her examination and dropped his eyes, and in an instant she knew the truth. This was not about duty or honor, it was about the Princess.

He gathered himself and asked, "If we let the Prince do it, then what?"

Will kept talking, though Liz hardly noticed his words. She may not have gotten her prince, but Will still saw a chance to get his princess, and how could she blame him for wanting to make the attempt? Jealousy and fear tugged at her in equal measure, and she knew she must let him go.

"Maybe they will give us some coin out of their grace," he was saying. "But maybe they won't? This is our one chance . . ."

She did not trust her own motives. If she forced him to stay, which Liz knew she had it in her power to do, how could she ever know that she hadn't done so, in at least some measure, out of pettiness? Somewhere in the distance a church bell pealed its silvery tone, which meant the town had survived. Her eyes raised at the bell's call and drifted to a low grassy hill at the far end of the field. Though it was obscured by smoke, in her mind's eye she could see quite clearly the little circle of graves lying there. She had dug their mother's grave herself. If she let him go would she be digging Will's also; if she let him stay, what then for him and for her?

"For whatever reason," he said in a voice bursting with earnestness, "after all these years of beating us down, fate has literally thrown us the key to our own destinies."

"Fine."

"So, there's no point in— Wait, what?" His eyes widened in shock.

"I said, *fine*."

He stared at her for a moment, mouth open, "You mean . . ."

"I mean—" Her voice broke again, and she forced herself to look up at him without crying. "I mean you can go and fetch the Princess, if that is what you want. But"— and she waved a finger at his chest—"but no playing the hero, William."

"I don't—"

"Yes, you do," she said seriously. "I was sure I'd lost you when you ran out into that field, and I never want to feel that scared and empty again."

"The plan was to draw the dragon away from you and the house," he mumbled.

"My point exactly," she said dryly. "No more heroics."

He mumbled something that might have been a yes.

"Promise," she pressed.

"Yes," he said with an exasperated sigh and a shrug.

She studied his face, which had that irritatingly stubborn set to it again, and sighed in reply. She doubted his promise meant anything, but she also knew there was nothing more she could do. She forced her doubts and fears aside. The course was set. He would be Will, whether she wanted him to or not. Besides, now that the decision had been made, her mind could turn itself to more practical considerations. She glanced over at the dragon's body. Knowing the townspeople as she did, if they found it before Will got back, they would take it to Castle White themselves, and take the credit for the creature's death and whatever reward came with it. Will would have to deal with that.

"Good. Now figure out some way to keep the dragon's body hidden, and by then I should have lunch ready."

"How am I supposed to hide a dragon?" he asked in a voice bordering on a whine.

She shrugged. "Your plan. Your problem."

With that she plucked the key from his hand, dropped it into the pocket of her apron, and turned back to the manor house. A pall of black smoke was still rising from its collapsed roof. She turned about and looked at the ruins of the other out buildings. Her eyes settled on the sole surviving structure. "It looks like the barn managed to make it through. We'll eat there."

Fear was creeping back into her heart. Knowing that another emotional outburst was coming if she lingered, Liz turned and walked away. From behind her she heard Will call out, "I guess I could bury it . . . or something?"

Liz shook her head at the impracticality of such a plan as she passed the dragon's immense body, but at least the work would keep him occupied and out from underfoot.

By the time Will had finished covering the dragon's body with a mound of dirt and burnt cornstalks, it was midday and the sun, now sitting like a squat toad above the treetops, was baking the blackened field. In that time, Liz had somehow managed to turn the barn into a home, cook lunch, and pack for him; and as the sun set, they loaded the last of his provisions into the old wooden cart behind, Grey, their mildly annoyed swayback nag. She placed the key in Will's pouch and his badly burnt and mottled pitchfork at his side. In the back of the wagon, she had loaded two weeks' worth of jarred food and about three dozen somewhat moth-eaten wool blankets she'd found in an old chest in the hayloft.

He looked so young sitting behind the reins, and she felt the tears she had been fighting all day trying to rise again. He smiled warmly and, in his most reassuring voice, said, "You don't have to worry about me. I've been up in those mountains plenty of times hunting. I know where the old road to Dragon Pass starts; and if you go one ridgeline over and the day is clear, you can almost see where the beast lives—lived. I'll return with the Princess—if she exists. Then we can hand her over to the Prince, collect our reward, and forget the whole thing."

Liz frowned and shook her head. "I don't think it's going to be that easy," she said. And then thought to herself, *If this really is a fairy tale, then it's never that easy.*

Will laughed and gave her a wink. "Come on. What could possibly happen, Liz?" She looked at him sternly. If he noticed, he ignored her. "Don't work too hard while I'm gone," he said in a voice ringing with humor. "You've got to have a nice complexion for when we visit the King. Maybe we can get you married off to a nobleman so you won't be so much of a burden to me."

Aloud, she clucked with disapproval, but inside she smiled. Liz had never seen her brother so happy. The truth was whether he was fighting cornstalk trolls with his toy sword as a boy or jousting the straw man on Grey when he was older, he had always wanted to have one chance to be the hero, and this was it. She put on a stern face that was only ruined by the upturned corners of her mouth.

"Now, don't go being cheeky with the Princess. You be polite and show her that our family has a bit of breeding— that we weren't always a bunch of ignorant dirt farmers. And comb your hair before you wake her up. You look like the scarecrow. I'll run and get you a brush."

Will stayed her hand as she turned to go, bent down and kissed the top of her head. "Quiet now," he said. "She's not going to care what I look like. Now let me go, long goodbyes make for long journeys."

With this last—annoyingly homey—admonition, he click his tongue and gave a little rattle on the reins. Grey snorted once and then plodded forward, jerking the big iron-rimmed wheels of the cart into a slow roll toward the forest road and the distant mountains beyond. Liz stood in the barnyard amid the restless chickens watching him go, a little knowing smile on her face. As he disappeared into the woods, she whispered a blessing on the heavy night air: "Good luck, dear brother. May your fairy tale come true."

Chapter 2

Love's First Kiss

DEEP IN THE cursed Southern Forest, an ancient road twists its way up through cold gray mountains to a narrow jagged pass. At the top of that pass, buffeted by cruel winds, stands a tower of jet-black stone. There lives the dread dragon. Few foolish or unlucky enough to journey on that dark trail have lived to tell the tale, for dangers most foul haunt the way. Dire creatures only mentioned in the darkest of fairy tales prey on hapless and lost travelers, and the very land itself is accursed and twisted with evil.

At least that's the way the story was always told, but Will found the journey did not quite match the drama of the book. The road to the abandoned tower was easy to find, and in surprisingly good condition. The weather also held in his favor, with a cool breeze and no rain to make the path the least bit treacherous.

Because of the fair roads, favorable weather, and a distinct lack of danger, Will had plenty of time to consider his quest. *It certainly seems to be going well*, he reflected as he watched the leather reins slap across Grey's back in rhythm to her plodding gait. *I'm making good time, and have plenty to eat.* Although, the thought of another night of pickled carrots and beets made him shudder.

"Still, all in all, I can't complain," he said quietly to the horse's backside.

The thing was he wanted to complain. He didn't know what he had been expecting, but this wasn't it. He wanted some . . . adventure. Nothing truly dangerous mind you, maybe a troll on a bridge he could bamboozle, or a two-bit rogue he could best. Something, anything, he could brag about when he was older. The biggest danger so far was that he might fall asleep at the reins.

He rounded yet another of the seemingly endless rocky points along the path and a sudden gusting wind buffeted him. He had passed out of the tree line early that morning and, this high up, the air was bitingly cold. Will started to pull on his cloak and was still tangled in the folds and bends of the garment when the horse stopped. Will stuck his head out of the thick wool and frowned in annoyance. He shook the reins a bit and clucked his tongue. She stood, refusing to move, her mane streaming out to the side under the stiff wind.

He raised his head to look around. They were at the top of the mountain pass. On a ridge a few hundred feet above his head he could see the outline of a tower—*the tower*. A trail wound down and back and forth across the cliff face and ended at a set of well-worn stairs that emerged on the path from a crack in the cliff a few yards from where Grey had stopped.

"There's a girl," he said brightly. "Liz always did say you had more sense than me—not that you should tell her I said so." Grinning, he lifted his pitchfork from the back of the wagon and fed the old horse a handful of oats. "Well, Grey, I'll be back in a bit, let's pray, with a princess, let's hope."

And with that, Will began up the narrow stone path. It rose with many a back and forth up the cliff face to a wide ledge above. When he finally made it to the top and the tower was in full view, Will couldn't help recite a line from the "Dragon's Tale" aloud:

> *"Desolate is the high pass and dark is the*
> *tower to which the dragon flew;*
> *Therein to lie evermore was the princess,*
> *Gwendolyn, cursed—*
> *A white flower entombed in a prison of cold*
> *black stone."*

He compared the real thing to this literary vision. "Talk about artistic license," he said with a shake of his head.

Perhaps in another life the structure had been more imposing, but now it was little more than a jumble of considerably weathered gray stones rising about fifty spans into the air. The roof was a skeleton of half-rotted timbers that met in a lopsided spire. The only break he could see in the walls of the structure was a large open balcony near the top. A hedge of wild rosebushes had devoured the base of the tower in a riot of small but brilliant red and white blossoms, partially obscuring a rusted ironbound gate. He fingered the golden key in his pouch. *Let's hope this pretty bauble fits the lock, otherwise I've come a long way for nothing.*

Will made his way to the base of the tower, and was relieved to see that, though massive, the gate had partially rusted away. Using his pitchfork as a scythe, he pushed his way through the roses and into the chamber beyond. He found himself surrounded by stagnant darkness. He froze, grasped his pitchfork firmly, and waited for some sound that might signal an attack, but beyond the dying echoes of his own passage, there was nothing. As his eyes adjusted to the weak light, the vague contours of the chamber began to take shape; and from the looks of it. no one, not even a dragon, had set foot in the place for years. The floor was covered in a thick layer of dust and a blanket of decaying leaves, rose blossoms . . . and bones.

He moved into the room, the leaves and bones snapping and crunching under his feet. The light from the open gate behind him began to fail, and he was drawn toward another faint glow filtering down a vast sweeping stair that hugged the tower's curved outer wall and disappeared through an opening in the cobwebbed ceiling. He put a first foot on the stair; his heart hammered in his chest so hard it was painful. Will suddenly realized that he was not afraid, he was excited. He was actually in the dragon's tower. He was in a fairy tale, rescuing a princess, no less. He grinned and paused, to catch his breath and calm his nerves before continuing. The staircase was wide and the stairs even; and as the light above his head grew brighter, Will gave up any attempt at stealth and began taking the broad stairs two at a time. So it was at a near run that he broke through the thin layer of dusty webs at the top and emerged from the gloom into the blinding light of the chamber above.

He blinked against the midday sun streaming through a large opening in the wall directly across from him. Unlike the abandoned level below, this upper chamber was light, airy, and obviously well used. A random assortment of tapestries and sheer curtains lined the walls. They were rippling in a breeze blowing unhindered across the room, through the balcony's open door. Will wiped the cobwebs from his face and, inhaling deeply, caught the subtle hint of rose rising with the air from the bushes far below.

He moved into the middle of the room, onto a patchwork quilt of overlapping rugs. A few suspiciously impressive tears in the wall hangings and a dragon-sized area of worn carpet in front of the balcony's threshold hinted at the identity of the room's owner. He frowned and looked about. Where was the Princess? There was no obvious sign of another room or indeed any exit apart from the stair he had come up, and for a moment Will worried that he was the fool his sister thought him to be.

That there *was* no Princess. But something didn't feel right. Scratching his head he considered the size of the room. It was true that the tower tapered as it rose, but this chamber seemed too small. He watched the tapestries lining the walls of the room moving with the breeze and smiled.

There must be a door hidden behind one of these.

He began walking in a clockwise circuit from the balcony, tracing his hand along the tapestries and feeling the hard wall behind. He considered the presence of the hangings as he went, and what it meant about the dragon. In every telling he'd heard, a fairy had conjured the dread wyrm from a piece of the night sky and sent it mindlessly out to do her bidding. In the tale, it was always the fairy and some unknown slight that motivated the curse. Sometimes it was that in choosing to marry Gwendolyn, the King had, in the mind of the fairy, betrayed the memory of his true love. In other tellings, the fateful act was the King's mother's failure to invite the fairy to the wedding. But here was a beast that collected tapestries? Will was wondering at this, and about what the dragon had really been like, when the solid feel of stone suddenly vanished beneath his hand. He stopped. Here was an opening in the wall.

He examined the hanging that concealed the opening. It depicted a scene of a young maid surrounded by dark trees, a serpent entwined in the trunks encircled her, mouth open. Was the creature talking with her, or was it about to devour her? The artist left it an open question. With a shaking hand, he pulled the hanging back. A small alcove was revealed, no more than two strides wide and four long. A stone bier about waist high filled the antechamber and cradled a resting figure in white. Thin windows—really no more than slits set high in the wall—illuminated the space, bathing the white form in a soft glow as dust motes captured in the rays of light danced like tiny glittering fairies around . . . *the Princess!* Will caught his breath. The sudden realization that the she was not only real, but lying perfectly preserved a hand-span away struck him with the force of a hammer blow.

He wet his suddenly dry mouth and stepped slowly forward, letting the tapestry fall back into place behind him. The Princess was clad in a flowing translucent, shimmering shift of pearly white. Will's eyes traced the contours of her body beneath the thin cloth, then quickly lifted his gaze to her face.

She was beautiful, to be sure. But more than that, she was the fairy-tale princess come to life. Her hair was fair; in the glowing light, it sparkled and, like a curtain of spun gold, flowed down around her body, perfectly framing her face. A subdued blush of pink subtly colored the apples of her otherwise pale cheeks. It was her lips, though, that drew his attention. They were a deep-deep red, the hue of the rose blossoms flowering outside the tower—and he recalled with a sudden rush of warmth that, in the tale, it was only love's first kiss that awakened her. Enthralled, he bent down toward her—and slapped his hand hard against his thigh, coming to his senses.

Don't be a fool, William Pickett! If Liz could see you . . . well, be thankful she can't. And Gretel, what would she say?

Will actually thought about the question for a moment, but came to no answer. Women had always been a bit of a mystery to him. *And now you think you're ready to kiss the Princess. The Princess! What are you doing?*

He stepped back and leaned his pitchfork against the wall. "All right," he groused aloud, "now what?"

Looking closely at her, he noticed a thin gold chain looped around the Princess's neck. He examined it, bending till he was inches from her. As he got close, he caught the scent of a beautiful if faded rose. He wondered, *How is it that girls manage to do that? Leave me unwashed two days and I smell like a goat.* He shook his head to chase away the thought and stood up again. Whatever was at the end of the necklace was hidden in the girl's clasped hands. From what he could see of the chain, though, it looked like the twin in miniature of the one that had held the dragon's key. With delicacy, Will grasped the chain and slowly freed it from her grasp. Raising the object into the light, he saw there was a tiny lock with words engraved on its golden surface in that now familiar spidery hand:

> *Locked in sleep shall the maiden lie.*
> *Locked in dream her mind,*
> *Locked in grief her heart,*
> *Till love's first kiss does the key apply.*

Will gazed dubiously at the tiny lock, comparing it in his mind with the oversized dragon's key. "So, a kiss it is."

Gently he laid the lock back on the sleeping girl's

breathless body. Though his course was clear, still he hesitated, chewing on the side of his forefinger and thinking.

It's just a kiss, Pickett. You've kissed Gretel plenty of times, why should this be any different? Besides, it probably won't even work; after all, you're no Prince Charming.

Will remained unmoving, gazing at that perfect face. Now that he was here, he felt totally inadequate to the job. "You have not come all this way not to try," he said in a stern scolding voice, and then added silently, urgently, *Kiss her.*

Giving himself no more time to think or doubt, Will tenderly rested his lips on hers. Even before he could rise, the lady's lips parted against his and with a gasp he felt her draw in his exhaled breath. He and watched as the color deepened in her cheeks, her pallor giving way to a healthy soft pink. He hovered there above her, mere inches away, and watched mesmerized. Her eyes fluttered—but did not open—and he started to step back, but she murmured in a soft whisper that sounded half plea and half prayer: "Rosslyn, Rosslyn, I was such a fool."

Then she was quiet. The steady rise and fall of her breathing still there, but little sign that the kiss had done much of anything. The Princess lay sleeping on her stone bed as she had for all these years. Will sunk low, to the stone floor, and sat back on his heels and scratched his head, then asked the sleeping girl, "*Who* is Rosslyn?"

He stood there for some time watching her breast rise and fall, hoping for further word or sign. There was no other movement, though her color was a little better and her features had improved subtly. Will wanted to give her time, to see if his kiss would work, but he knew that outside the day was passing to evening. The light in the little room was beginning to fail, and he needed to make it down the cliff with her before dark.

"I guess Liz was right. I'm no prince," he murmured. "I'll have to carry you out."

This created a new complication. He had not noticed before how sheer the Princess's gown was. He stared, blushing and debating where to put his hands.

"Yet another practicality the fairy tales never spoke of," he muttered. "I'm sure I'd remember if the Prince in the story had remarked, 'Oh, my beloved, though I appreciate your charms so fair, take you now my cape so that you do not catch your death in the cold mountain air.'"

Then the solution came to him. In a flash!

"A cape! Yes, I need a cape. Every prince has a cape."

He turned to the wall hanging covering the opening to the chamber and ripped it down. Dust flew from the ancient cloth. He spread the tapestry on the ground, turned to the Princess, closed his eyes, took a deep steadying breath, and in a quick motion lifted her into his arms. He crossed the few steps, lowered her onto the middle of the drapery, and wrapped her body in the heavy cloth.

"Well, it may not be dignified, but I think we'll both be able to manage the journey now." Then he picked up his bundle, which was surprisingly light, and started down the stairs, forgetting his old pitchfork. The only thing in the kingdom that could rightfully claim credit for slaying the dragon had been left behind.

After picking his way back through the darkness of

the lower level to the tower door, Will paused, considering the long thorny tendrils of the rosebushes. "This'll no doubt hurt, but you wanted to be the hero."

He turned his body so she was shielded by his own and pushed into the narrow space he had made in the bushes earlier that morning. Struggling, he forced himself through the tangled branches. The thorns cut deeply into his flesh and the twisting tendrils ripped and pulled at his hair. Only when he was well free of the last of the vine and into the clear ground beyond did he allow himself to lay the girl gently to the ground.

He felt the blood dripping from his face and regarded the tears in his shirt and the bloody stripes on his arms and body. He wanted to stop and tend them, but the sun was now sitting just atop the mountains. He still had to make it down the cliff. Will checked to be sure the Princess had made it through unharmed, then, wincing, he picked the girl up again and began the painfully slow trip down the treacherous path.

In the failing light of evening, he at last reached the road. Under the horse's baleful gaze, he hastily swept aside an assortment of half-filled pickle jars, layered the back of the cart with all but one of his sister's blankets, and delicately set the Princess atop them, and used the last to cover her. Exhausted, he eyed the thickly padded bed, dismissed the idea as improper, and crawled beneath the wagon.

The next morning found him studying the sleeping princess over the edge of the cart's side wall. She still slept, but at some point in the night she had shifted, if ever so slightly. Encouraged by this new sign of life, he gave Grey a pat on the nose. "Let's get back home, otherwise we'll have Liz up here after us."

The trip back to the farm was as uneventful as the journey up. During the day, he told stories and sang songs to his sleeping passenger as they meandered down the sun-dappled road to the valley below. The Princess slept the whole way, but otherwise everything went according to plan; and on the afternoon of the seventh day of his journey, William Pickett rode into the valley that held his family's farm. But as he came into sight of his burnt field, Will knew that something had gone terribly wrong. The mound, so painstakingly built in the middle of the field, had been partially excavated and a flock of ravens fluttered here and there feasting on the exposed flesh of the dead dragon. He flicked the reins and made for the barn at a trot. Liz emerged at the sound of his approach, stared hard at the wagon for a heartbeat, then raced across the dusty yard toward them, kicking up the hem of her skirts as she ran. Will pulled Grey to a stop as she leapt onto the sideboard of the cart and wrapped her arms around his neck. "Will! You made it, you are back!"

He returned her embrace for a moment, then pulled away. "Liz what's the matter? What's happened?"

She reached her hand up to touch one of the scratches that ran across his cheek. "Will, what happened to you? Are you all right? Are you hurt badly? Was it a bear . . . or a troll?"

He pulled her hand away from his face. "I'm fine. Liz, what happened to the dragon?"

Her face paled. "It was that trollop, Gretel," she said, adding unnecessarily, "your cow of a girlfriend. She came down with her folks the day after you left and started asking me about you. I sent them off, but her father was looking at the mound and I could see he was suspicious, and . . . and then . . . well . . ." She glanced over her shoulder at where the dragon's body lay and sighed. "They came back two nights ago—about a dozen of them—everyone of *importance* in the village, I think. I tried to stop them, but they dug it up . . . they . . ."

He'd never seen her at a loss for words like this. He turned to look at the dragon's grave again. Something was wrong. No, something was missing. "What did they do, Liz?"

Her voice shook with anger, "Oh, it's awful! They took its head, Will. They've put it up on the town green. They sent for the King's man to discuss reparations, a reward for having slain the beast."

The youngest Pickett had always been slow to anger, but now his rage boiled over. *Those bastards think they can steal this from us!* He pulled his sister onto the seat beside him and, with a flick of the reins, turned Grey onto the road that led to town. The old horse champed at the bit and shook her head in protest, but he drove her on—hard. When they reached the center of town, it was at a full gallop. He reined Grey viciously to a stop, white foam blowing from the old horse's mouth and sweat slicked across her back.

There on the green, in front of the church, a tall pole, really the lower twenty feet of a denuded tree, had been firmly planted into the ground. Mounted atop was the severed blackened head of the dragon—empty eyes staring lifelessly out over the village square like a grotesque maypole. Around the base of this macabre monument, a group of children played and chanted an old nursery rhyme. Without a word, Will grabbed his ax from the back of the cart and stormed toward the dragon's head. The children scattered like leaves blown by a high wind, their screams echoing across the village. Will ignored them and began chopping at the base of the pole.

The shouting children and sharp sound of the axe in the still afternoon drew the townspeople from the buildings that surrounded the green. For a few of the ax strokes they stood there, stupidly watching as the boy hacked at their monument. Then, as one. they surged forward, shouting for him to stop. But as they got closer, the mob slowed and then, again as a single body, shuffled to a halt. William Pickett no longer looked the part of the placid farm boy they had always known.

After a dozen blows, the pole came crashing down, the monstrous head of the dragon jarred loose from the sharpened end and tumbled to the ground, its eyes staring back into the gathered crowd. Will leapt atop the battered trophy, ax in hand. He looked out over the faces of his neighbors. He hadn't cared that these people had swindled his grandfather. He had ignored that they had ridiculed his father and shunned his mother out of decent society. This was the last straw.

When he spoke, the anger in his voice burst like a thundercloud. "There was a time when I might have stood on this green and celebrated the death of this monster with all of you, but that time is past. For too long the people of this village have taken advantage of my family. I am William Pickett; it was in our field that the dragon died, and my sister and I alone paid the price for its death—and we alone will claim its bounty."

At his words, a fat man in a florid costume of brocade and velvet stepped forward. Holding a lace cloth to his mouth and nose against the stench of the gory head, he opened his mouth to speak but no words came out. Instead, his eyes bulged for a moment and he swayed on his feet. In fact, Will noticed that every face in the crowd had turned slightly and was staring at something behind him and to his right. He spun around, ax still clutched in one hand. The Princess stood in the back of the old cart. The evening sun sparkled in her golden hair and silhouetted her body through the sheer gown. Despite her state of undress, she dominated the little gathering. Her sky blue eyes—he'd just *known* they would be blue—surveyed the square with a detached coldness. He frowned a little, though. Animated now by the force of her personality, the Princess's face showed a regal rigidness, making her more beautiful than pretty.

Then she spoke: "Noble sir, slayer of the Great Wyrm of the South, I am the Princess Gwendolyn Mostfair. For thy deeds, I give myself to thee, for as thou art my savior so am I thy bounty." Her voice rang like a bell, but the words were delivered in a monotone, almost like she was reading from a script. With the speech finished, she lowered herself to her knees, and bowed her head.

Will Pickett stood, eyes wide, the dragon's head forgotten, and stared at the woman in front of him. His mind was blank. He could not move. He could not speak. Behind him a woman fainted, from the sound of the moan he thought it might be Gretel. In the confusion, the fancy man slipped quietly away. The frozen moment stretched on uncomfortably. It was finally broken by the Princess. She raised cold blue eyes and with a cross expression said, "Well, how long are you going to keep me kneeling here? I do hope you're not a mute."

Will opened his mouth, but his mind could think of nothing to say and so he closed it again. The Princess stood and, putting hands to hips, shouted, "Don't stand there like a pack of imbeciles, someone say something. And for God's sake someone bring me something to wear, can't you see I'm half naked?"

Into the awkward silence that followed came the thunder of hoofbeats. King Rupert's representative to the Southern Valley galloped out of Prosper and north toward the castle. Whether Will wished it or not, word was already spreading across the land.

The dragon was slain, the Princess rescued. The kingdom had a savior. Prince Charming, it was not. His name was William Pickett of Prosper.

Chapter 3

Towers, Trysts, and Trials

AS EVENTS UNFOLDED to the south, the Prince of the Realm, a man so aptly called Charming, who had been raised from birth to believe himself to be nothing less than legend, had chosen not to spend this day, or the week before or even the last few years, questing for the dragon. Instead, he had escaped the castle to dally with a lovely lady of noble birth renowned for her extensive golden tresses.

Such a distraction was surely his due. Quests and dragons could wait awhile for Prince Charming, particularly as his first duty on killing the dragon would likely be to marry Princess Gwendolyn, which truth be told, Charming found rather distasteful. She was his princess, he supposed, but she had also been his father's princess.

Though he would have little choice, as he could not risk disappointing his father, the King, it was an unpleasant thing to think about. So he didn't. He would spend his time on other conquests of the heart until duty called.

And on this day, what a conquest! The lady truly had spectacular hair, and once she had undone her intricate braids, he had to swim in a sea of soft gold to reach her. They had chosen one of her family's older and little-used towers for their tryst. It was of the classical style, with a single heavy wooden door at the base and single great window carved into the uppermost chamber. At the moment, the sun was streaming through this window, framing him perfectly as he embraced the lady on a low settee.

> "As I touch your fragrant golden tresses,
> I am moved by your inner beauty."

He silently congratulated himself for using couplet. As a true student of the art of romance, he knew that there was nothing that could win the heart of a maiden better than a powerful couplet. The women who surrounded him in the court always cooed and sighed when he chose to grace them with his poetic flourishes. He gave a quick glance to the mirror in her bedroom to make certain he looked as dashing as ever.

She cleared her throat and spoke in a tone that suggested she was repeating herself. "What about my inner beauty?"

He closed his eyes and paused, as if enraptured. It was now time to add rhyme.

> "Such a vision of loveliness as you,
> Leaves my tongue lost while my heart
>   speaks love true."

He waited for the inevitable sigh and, of course, for her to throw herself at him. She placed her hands on his silk doublet and pressed close against him, literally enfolding him in her tresses. "Did you just say you love me?"

He opened his eyes and smiled weakly. "Um . . ." he started, then realizing he wasn't in couplet, he quickly turned his head and gave a cough. Gently, he removed her hands and, careful not to become too entangled in the somewhat alarming volume of hair that spilled across the room, strode to the window. The Prince visibly paused, as if overcome by the moment, something that she could only take as a true sign of the depth of his spirit. Of course she wanted to hear love in his words; he could hardly blame her, but he had to bring her to understand. Prince Charming had responsibilities, and not just to Princess Gwendolyn. Given his natural charms, it would be selfish of him not to let as many women as possible enjoy them. He gazed out across the folded land so that his profile would be lit most advantageously by the sun's brilliance.

> "Alas, duty has its calling and its price,
> So may the memory of today be nice."

Certainly not his best, but this simple creature would be mesmerized.

"Duty? What duty? Do you love me?"

Things had escalated, surprisingly so. Was the lady mad? He was Prince Charming, and while this was a lovely tower, and her family was not without means, the stonework was chipped and the forest green curtains and bedding were out of date, having been woven in his not inexpert estimation at least two years or more ago, when heavy brocade fringes were still in fashion. It was archaic. He wet his lips and inhaled deeply, filling his chest. He outstretched his right arm.

> *"I hunger for thee till I have had love's fill,*
> *But as to the morrow, thou shouldst not*
> *speak shrill."*

It was a bad day. His meter was varying terribly.

"Shrill?"

He sighed. He never should have bothered speaking with her. Better to be silent, look sensitive, and kiss women whenever they opened their mouths. It was clear that this one had little understanding of his and her relative positions in the world, and the meaning of the word *tryst*.

"My Prince," came a hiss from somewhere below. He was annoyed. He had asked not to be disturbed, but he reflected that this interruption might prove to be perfectly timed. Though he often resented his father, the King, for appointing such an obnoxious old man as his squire and bodyguard, in this case, his servant might just prove helpful. The voice returned, this time as a low gravelly rumble. "My Prince, you are needed urgently."

Now was the time to win her. He looked back over to the window, leaned out, and peered down at the top of the red balding head of the squire. Making sure to school his face to a stern countenance, the Prince filled his voice with a tone of deep condemnation. "Squire, you forget yourself. The lady and I have courtly matters that we are discussing. And for a man of chivalry, there is nothing more important in this entire world than paying his due respects to a lady."

The grizzled old squire stared up at him with that hint of disrespect that reminded the Prince once again that he needed to have the man sacked. "Though I'm sure your . . . discussion with the lady is of utmost importance," he said with barely disguised disdain, "I think you'll want to come down and hear the news I bring from the castle."

"And so I shall," he said, this time real anger coloring his tone, "when we are done and perhaps the sun has set on a long day, but for now, you shall remember your place and wait. Now! Go! And never interrupt me and this lady again." He turned his back to the window and found her smiling. The straps of her dress had made a strategic retreat and her shoulders were now bare. Definite progress, but the thought was cut short by the throaty roar of his damnable servant.

"THE DRAGON IS DEAD!"

A sudden rush of blood went to his head and he swayed on his feet as those words echoed in his mind. Something had gone terribly wrong. Whoever this long-haired woman was in front of him—the stress of the moment having driven her name fully from his typically impeccable memory— didn't matter. That was his dragon to kill and his legend to be sung by minstrels until the end of days. He steadied himself and then dashed back to the window. *"What?"* was all he could muster, and even that took effort.

"It's amazing, there's a body, the Princess is rescued, and he even brought the head of the beast back to the King. Word is spreading across the land, the whole kingdom is singing his praises."

"That's not possible, the kingdom is supposed to sing about me. Who is he?"

"He's a peasant. I think his name is Tim . . . no . . . Will . . . William?"

Charming had lost his voice. He raised his hand for the squire to wait. He needed to get out of the suddenly claustrophobic chamber. "I must away," he told the lady.

"What about nothing being as important as speaking with a lady?"

She was obviously irrational with disappointment, and normally he might try to soothe her and, yet, the dragon was dead. He had no time to waste. This was a plot. Yes, that was it; it was an illusion, a deception, a chimera, a glamour meant to delude the people. Vile sorceries had to be involved. He brushed past the lady, stumbled through the grasping strands of her hair, and tried the door. It remained unmoved. He cursed as he remembered that he had locked the blasted thing against unwanted intrusions from the crone that looked after the place. He turned back to the lady . . .

Lady? . . . Lady?

Damn, he could not think of her name, the stress of the moment having driven it from his typically impeccable memory. If he could not woo her with words he would simply have to act. He took a step toward her and nearly fell over as her hair wrapped itself around his ankles like a snare. He grunted as he pulled tangles from his feet. "I must away! Where is the *key*?"

"I don't know. Somewhere in all this." She gestured helplessly at her tresses, spread like waves across the floor and over the furniture.

Her hair was everywhere. The enormity of it all engulfed him, yards and yards of golden locks. He needed the key, but given that her hair seemed to be covering every surface in the room, he thought he would have better luck searching a haystack for a single straw.

"Fine," he said perhaps a bit too curtly. "My apologies, but I'm afraid I'm going to have to open this door the hard way." He reared back on his heel and gave the door a resounding kick. The thick oak registered not even a quiver, and he barely managed to suppress an unprincely yelp as a sharp pain shot through his foot and up his leg. He limped about the room biting his lip against the curses that threatened to erupt.

"Are you okay?" she asked.

Of course he wasn't okay! His dragon was dead! He supposed *his* princess was in another's arms!

Still he had to be as courtly as possible despite that, or perhaps because, this lady was clearly unable to grasp the significance of the tragedy unfolding before them. "I must away. I have to depart for the palace with all due haste. That was my dragon. Do you understand? I have to get out of here!"

"We're trapped," she said much too happily.

"Are you coming, My Prince?" shouted the squire from below.

Charming was feeling strange, flushed and hot, and not from lovemaking. He ran a hand across his forehead, inadvertently mussing his perfect hair. He took a deep breath and steadied himself again. *I am Prince Charming; nothing is beyond my talents*, he reminded himself. He calmed himself and turned back to the lady.

> *"Do not give me false hope,*
> *But tell me that you have a rope."*

He smiled. He had regained couplet.

"Surely, you're joking. A rope? I would not have thought you were into *that* sort of thing," she said with what might have been mockery had it not been directed at him.

He stared at the woman and her cursed hair, and quite suddenly an idea formed in his head. Discarding couplet altogether, he shouted (though she was right next to him), "My lady, I need your hair! The kingdom needs your hair! Just twist it and it will be long enough for me to descend to the ground below."

"Oh, I'm sure it's long enough," she said in an acerbic voice, "but there is no way—"

He cut her off.

> *"Dear Lady, do not be slow,*
> *Throw your tresses out yon window."*

He had regained couplet. She would do anything for him now.

"Are you mad!" she said in disbelief.

He could delay no longer; explanations had never been his strong suit anyway. He grabbed as much of her hair as he could carry in his arms and hefted it out the window. The lady jumped up and held out her hands.

"Your Highness, stop! It won't support your . . ."

He interrupted with a bit of hastily conjured doggerel:

> *"Alas I must swiftly away,*
> *Cherish the memory of today."*

With that, he grabbed two thick handfuls of hair and leapt out the window. There was a shriek from above, and then he hit the ground and his already injured foot collapsed beneath him from the force of the impact. He tried to cover his scream of pain with a whoop of victory as he fell to the ground clutching his ankle.

"My Prince, are you all right?" the squire called, rushing over.

With a grimace, Charming rolled to his feet, or rather to his one good foot. He forced a weak smile as he hopped toward his horse. "Just a bit of dashing bravado and derring-do on my part. We must away."

"I've never seen hair like that," said the squire. A large

mass of blond strands had fallen to the ground beside them and lay in a tangled clump.

"Doubt you will again," muttered the Prince as he mounted. "Let's go. She was remarkably unmoved by my couplets."

"Hard to imagine," offered the squire with an unnoticed roll of his eyes.

"My hair!" shrieked the lady from the window of the tower. "My beautiful hair! You madman! You fiend!"

Charming winced under the increasingly colorful curses that rained down from above. He looked to the squire and whispered, "You don't by any chance remember her name, do you?"

"Rapunzel, My Prince," the squire said in a stunned whisper.

"Rapunzel, of course." Charming cleared his throat.

> *Rapunzel O fair maid, please hold,*
> *I will send you hair spun of gold.*

He doubted she heard him amid her hysterics, but duty demanded the attempt be made. He looked to his squire and shrugged. "Let's away." In a moment they were galloping long the road to Castle White. "So, what has happened?" he asked.

"Sorry, Your Highness, but all I know is that the Princess was rescued by a peasant, the dragon was killed by a pitchfork, and your father is praising this young man as the great hero of the age. And . . . and—" The squire suddenly stuttered to a stop and began intently studying the road ahead.

"There is more. Out with it," Charming commanded.

"Understand, Your Highness, that this is only rumor, but . . . well . . . I've even heard it said that perhaps elves exchanged you with the true Prince of the Realm as a babe—and you are of peasant . . ." The squire's voice trailed off again as the Prince's face turned an unpleasant shade of magenta.

"Treason, blasphemy, heresy," he shouted aloud. "What is wrong with people? How can they possibly doubt me? I'm Prince Charming!"

How the squire would have answered the Prince will never be known, as in his outrage, Charming had dropped the reins of his steed and stood in his stirrups, arms upraised in a dramatic gesture. Upon doing so, he promptly struck a low branch with his forehead and fell backward out of his saddle. It was an experience completely foreign to him, as he had never fallen at the lists in tests of chivalry. Then, the back of his head struck the crushed gravel of the road, and he stopped thinking altogether.

Chapter 4

At First Sight

CHARMING BECAME AWARE of the interplay of light and shadow and the sounds of muffled voices. He thought that he saw the castle with its gleaming white towers, billowing banners, and deep red pennants, but it was all topsy-turvy, as if the world was upside down. Then he had a hazy recollection that the dragon was dead and thought that perhaps the world really was upside down. Time passed in fits and starts. Then he heard the voice of a lady of high rank, which he identified because it held that particular tone of command that would brook no disrespect.

"Move aside, don't any of you know how to care for a wound?"

Charming became aware that his head felt like it was

aflame, and there was a hot wetness trickling down the side of his face.

"We are waiting for the Royal Chirurgeon, milady," came a woman's voice.

"Why would you wait for a chirurgeon? And the name is Liz. Elizabeth, if you need it. I may not be a chirurgeon, but I know how to attend a wound to stop it from swelling."

Suddenly Charming felt a blessed coolness on his burning forehead, and he smelled the comforting scent of lavender.

"Milady, that's the Prince," came yet another voice.

The Prince opened his eyes and gazed on a most lovely woman. She did not have the alabaster skin of the ladies of the court, but instead was faintly kissed by the sun like a beautiful flower. A perfect set of auburn tresses fell across her shoulders, and her hazel eyes were gentle and kind, and, for just a moment, the Prince's heart stuttered and he felt something deeper than mere attraction. He had time to wonder what this feeling was, then her eyebrows raised and she pulled back.

"You're Prince Charming?" she asked with a mixture of uncertainty, surprise, and something else.

She blurred, and the Prince blinked away the double image of her, and croaked:

"The Prince I am, Tis plain to see.
And who art thou, fair lady?"

He was proud of himself for having attained couplet in his condition, and he followed the verse with a smile, which, though dashing, was marred when he winced in pain. He raised himself upright, resolved not to show weakness in front of the lady, and then stood and steadied himself against the wall. He was somewhere within the castle proper, but in poor quarters.

With a shock he realized that this was the room of some servant, a terrible insult. It was that damned squire of his. It was just the sort of thing the man would do. Well, he'd gone too far this time! He'd have the warped little brute thrown in the dungeon for this. Yet, despite his anger, he could not help but feel the fire in his blood ebb as he gazed on the face of the Lady Elizabeth. He took a moment to pose and try to recall her from the lists of nobility.

He prided himself on knowing all of the names of the nobles in the land. In fact, his memory for names was legendary. Obviously with the occasional failure such as with Lady Rep . . . Rap . . . Well, whatever her name had been. Oddly, this Lady Elizabeth was also unknown to him.

He was in the midst of composing another line of verse in her honor when she snapped sternly. "What do you think you are doing?"

The serving women gasped. Taken aback, the Prince nearly dropped the hand supporting him, and he had to recover quickly to prevent falling. The look of disapproval she was giving him should have infuriated him, but it had such authority that he suddenly felt rather small. *No one had ever—* Then in a great rush, he felt his righteous ire coming to the fore. He was Prince Charming and she, this *Lady* Elizabeth, was not a lady of the court. He had never seen her before, nor heard her name in the lists. Despite her grace and dress, she must certainly be of lesser birth. And he had blessed her with couplet! Yet she dared to speak to him in such a manner. He clenched his left hand on his hip and found the strength to remove his other from the wall and raise himself up to nearly his full height, though the room tilted ever so slightly.

The woman Elizabeth looked around at the other women and dropped her gaze slightly. "Sorry, Your Highness, but please get back in bed."

Despite her efforts, she didn't look the least bit properly intimidated. Then her discipline broke and she laughed, and it should have made him even more angry, but it was really a most pleasant sound, and he found himself fighting the desire to make her laugh again. He was at a loss for words, which was really an unknown condition for him.

The woman, Elizabeth, reacted for him, finally mastering herself by biting her lower lip and smoothing her skirt with her palms. "Please lie down before you hurt yourself, Your Highness. You can barely stand."

She might have meant well, but he would not be ordered about by a—a woman. "Stand aside," he commanded, and he thought his exit redeemed a bit of his former dignity as he pushed past to the doorway. The other ladies scattered before him like doves on a parade ground, and he wobbled unevenly into the hall beyond.

As he emerged from the room, Charming saw his unctuous servant leaning against the far wall of the passage.

The squire's eyes bulged and he rushed to the Prince's side. "You damned foo— I mean, Your Highness, you can't be up yet. You nearly took your head off on that tree. You need to be on your back not strutting around the halls." He turned to the woman Elizabeth, "Why can't you women do your bloody job? Didn't I tell you hens to sit on him if you had to till the chirur—"

Liz cut him off before he could finish. "You sit on him! He won't listen to reason. If you ask me, he's acting like a complete—"

"SILENCE!" Charming shouted. "I have had ENOUGH!" His head was pounding. He swiveled to face his squire and nearly collapsed from the effort. He took a couple of deep breaths to gather himself. Finally, his head cleared enough for him to focus. "I will deal with you later. That you would dare . . . put me down here . . . with the servants . . . instead of bringing me to my own quarters . . . borders on treason! I should have . . . have you put in the stocks for a week!"

The Prince reflected that his admonishment would have had more effect had he not needed to pause every couple of words to catch his breath. Still, if he had not brought the squire to his knees, at least it had quieted him. Charming used the time to orient himself toward the Great Hall. He was in a servant's passage in one of the outer hallways in the eastern wing of the castle. The Prince took a deep breath and steeled himself for the inevitable confrontation he would have with his father, the King, and the charlatan who was deceiving his kingdom. Charming marched off, as steadily as he was able, past the suits of armor, shields, and crossed weapons that lined the walls.

The movement seemed to break the squire's silence, because he shuffled along at his side pleading, "But, Your Highness, I brought you here so no one would see you. I mean, look at the state you're in. You are always so bloody particular about your appearance, and—"

Charming was deeply engaged in composing a stunning speech denouncing the dragon-slaying fraud, and so paid no attention to the man. Besides, at this point the gnarled hobgoblin would say anything to save his skin. Then he passed one of the open windows and was stunned at the sight. The pennants and the personal crests of knights from across the realm lined the open courtyard. A great feasting table was being set with silver platters laden with meats and fruits of every description. Every surface in sight was being festooned with flower garlands, and there in the center of it all a sculptor on a ladder was chiseling the features of an oafish-looking fellow out of a block of marble.

Charming stopped and nearly collapsed as the world tilted violently in response to the movement. He reached out an unsteady hand and caught himself against the window casement. He turned to the squire, "Wait! Squire, what were you saying? What is going on?"

"That's what I was trying to tell you, you. Your Highness. The King has proclaimed a week of celebration. There is to be one of those damnable balls. The whole court is either already here or will be as soon as they receive word. There's more silk and feather walking around the palace than in all the houses of ill-repute in all the kingdom combined."

The Prince felt his head swim. He doubled over, gasping again for breath. "This is a plot! A plot to usurp me! Mark my words!"

The soft but firm voice of the woman Elizabeth interrupted his tantrum. "Your Highness, please calm down. There is no plot."

He took a deep breath. He decided to dispense with civility for once, not to mention couplet. "I am Prince Charming. This is my kingdom. There is a villain here who is perpetuating a terrible lie for foul ends, and I am going to put an end to his charade. You, Lady Elizabeth, whom I have never before seen in the courts, are unknown to me. While I appreciate your concern, I have a kingdom to save from a lout and liar." He made this speech in his most commanding voice, giving the merest hint of the anger he felt. The woman would probably be reduced to tears, but sometimes even chivalry had to give way to necessity.

He was quite unprepared for her reaction. Her cheeks flushed bright crimson and her lips thinned almost to nonexistence. As her hands clenched at her sides, she stepped up to him, much too close for his comfort, and looked him right in the eye.

"I'll tell you who I am. I'm the sister of William Pickett, whose pitchfork pierced the Wyrm of the South through the heart. I did not see you around when the dragon was burning up our village, and I don't remember you saving me with your noble steed and flashing blade and bright pennants." She paused and smoothed her skirt, then continued. "Or the Princess either. What I do remember is listening to fairy tales about you when I was little, and I'd rather not have you crack your skull open staggering through the hallways in a misguided attempt to discredit my brother. So, will you please lie down"—she paused for another breath and then added—"Your Highness?"

No one had ever talked to him like this. Had the world gone completely mad? He tried to think of an appropriately devastating response, but all he found in his head was a dull throbbing roar, layered over with the lovely smell of lavender that seemed to follow this woman, and the happy sound of the children outside singing, "The dragon's dead, the dragon's dead." So, he said the only thing he could think of.

"No."

He turned and shambled as quickly as he could toward the Great Hall. Behind him his squire pleaded with him to stop. This was a dream, or perhaps a nightmare. Yes, a nightmare. She was the sorcerer's sister so, of course, she would want to stop him, and of course she would be immune to his charms—charms that would cause any ordinary woman to swoon. Most likely his initial misguided attraction to her was some devilish enchantment meant to ensnare and distract him from his noble purpose. She'd likely also put a spell on his weak-minded squire. Given the man's lack of breeding, it would have been child's play.

He saw the towering doors of the Great Hall ahead of him. He picked up his pace so that he rushed through the crowds and burst into the chamber at a half run. Everyone in the Great Hall stopped, mouths agape, nobles, courtiers, guards, and servants alike. Momentarily, the swirling pageantry of the court, the mingled perfumes of the ladies, the clashing velvets of the costumes, the echoes of whispered entreaties, overwhelmed his reeling senses and he skidded unsteadily to a halt on the polished floor. But standing there on the inlaid white marble, beneath the vaulted ceiling of the Great Hall with its alcoves of statues and suits of armor and the family crests dating back centuries, he felt a surge of strength. This was his home. He was dimly aware that people were shuffling into the hall behind him. They must have realized that their prince, their savior, was here, and that things would be set to right.

The King rose from the throne, resplendent in his blue and gold robes, his white beard catching the light from the high windows above and the great crown glittering here and there with the reds and greens of inset rubies and emeralds. Worry was etched across his face. Yet it was not his father, the King, who drew his attention, but the man standing beside his father, the King, a lanky, slouching buffoon with brown-red hair that sat in a great unkempt mass atop his head. It had to be the usurper. How anyone could believe that this lout was a hero, a dragon slayer, was beyond the Prince.

"You!" he shouted, marching forward and pointing accusingly as the crowds dispersed nervously to the edges of the Great Hall.

The peasant looked confused. "Me?" he said, turning

his head from side to side, then pointing at his own chest. The man swallowed and, looking uncomfortable, lifted a hand to his mouth as if he were about to bite his nails.

"Yes, you!" shouted the Prince again, continuing to advance on the dais. The fraud was clearly unmanned knowing that his deception was revealed.

King Rupert leaned forward and whispered something into the man's ear. "Oh," the pretender said as his face widened into a big goofy grin, "Um . . . yes, Your Highness, I suppose I was the one that rescued the Princess." He made a clumsy bow and rising said, "Well met."

In the shock that followed, Prince Charming stumbled, nearly lost his balance, and had to windmill his extended arm out until it found a column. His father, the King, walked over to the peasant and clasped the man's hand. Then he looked at Charming with a warning glance.

"Edward," he said sharply, "this is Lord William Pickett, newly appointed Protector of the Realm and the Dragon Slayer. And I see you have met his sister, Lady Elizabeth Pickett. Now, my son, what has happened to your face?"

This *Lord* William smiled even more broadly and offered the Prince an arm to brace against, which Charming of course refused. "Yes, um, Your . . . Royal Maj— I mean . . ."

"Your Highness," Lady Elizabeth whispered from behind Charming.

Will blushed and said, "Your Highness, forgive me, but it looks like you tried to shave with a badger."

What were they talking about? He was Prince Charming. The Prince looked around and caught his reflection in the shining chest plate of one of the suits of armor. It was a horror. His face was a mass of black-and-blue bruises, a large _un_princely knot had erupted just above his forehead, and dried blood sketched brown-red trails from the disheveled mess of his hair to his jaw.

His handsome face was gone. This was all a plot, Rapunzel, the tree, Elizabeth, William, all meant to ruin and disgrace him before his subjects. Never had he felt such rage. He reached for his sword, but it was not at his side. He looked up to the dais and then to the suit of armor standing at his side. The mailed glove on the suit clasped a sword. He charged the armor, leapt onto the raised pedestal that held it, and grabbing the hilt of the weapon, wrenched it free.

A clamor of voices filled the Great Hall, a woman screamed, and he looked back at _Lord_ William. He stepped down from the pedestal and pointed the sword at the man's chest. "Now, William, I shall give you the salute you deserve."

"No! Don't—" came the voice of Lady Elizabeth, who was rushing between them, arms outraised. He saw her look of terror, and a cold chill shot through his body. Then, for reasons unknown, he hesitated.

In all his years, Prince Charming had learned many things, studied with the finest tutors in literature, learned multiple languages, mastered the skill of song and verse, accomplished himself as a fine swordsman and rider, developed an understanding of the intricacies of siege warfare, and memorized the diplomatic etiquette necessary for hundreds of courtly encounters. Yet he had never spent time studying how the many suits of empty armor throughout the castle stayed upright, or even how they were supported in the slightest. What any of the castle's many servants, who had the onerous task of cleaning and polishing them, would have told him is that without the sword to balance the weight of the plate armor, the suit would collapse. And, true to this inescapable physics, the suit of armor behind the Prince swayed—and as the echo of the word *deserve* was fading from the heights of the vaulted arch of the ceiling, the armor gave way, crashing down weightily from the pedestal where it had stood onto the Prince's already battered body.

There was a shock of pain as the armor struck, followed by the loud clang of metal on stone. These initial insults to his person were followed by a sense of stopping, very suddenly, as his head bounced off the marble floor. In that final instant before everything went dark, Prince Charming knew that somehow nothing would ever be quite the same again.

Chapter 5

A Timely Stitch

WORD SPREAD FROM peasant to prince, manor house to tavern, village to hamlet, in the gossip of the women and the songs of the minstrels, from one end of the kingdom to the other—the dragon was dead. And with these happy tidings the people were, for the first time in nearly a generation, at peace. Indeed, many of the most inveterate curmudgeons noted that good cheer had spread like a plague across the land. Peasants whistled like dwarves as they worked, merchants and tradesmen greeted their customers with smiles that bordered on the sincere, and the nobles took to dispensing alms even when not under the prejudicial eye of the clergy. Festivals and feasts, large and small, were held on the greens and commons of every township. Even in Prosper, the townsfolk forgot their lost chance at collective glory and embraced a more lucrative trade: tourism. The eyes of all, though, were now on Castle White, for the King had announced a Royal Ball, the first in many, many years, to celebrate the kingdom's new hero, Protector of the Realm and Dragon Slayer, Lord William Pickett.

And on that night, the castle shone with a splendor unmatched in its long history. Every suit of armor, now anchored in place by order of the Prince, was polished to a gleaming brilliance. Every pennant atop the pinnacles of the tall towers snapped with the crispness of new linen. Every flagstone of every hall, the great and the small, had been scrubbed to a mirror finish. And every chandelier, candelabra, and lantern that could be found was lit until there was not a dark corner anywhere in the vastness of the hold and the night seemed utterly vanquished. In his Royal Chamber, Prince Charming stood in front of a full-length mirror, critically examining his costume, a sublime green doublet and matching demi-cape. He trusted the Royal Tailor implicitly, and considered him the only man in the kingdom worthy to discuss important matters of fashion. In some ways, the Royal Tailor was as close to a friend as the Prince had, but the traitor had abandoned him tonight to attend to William Pickett. Charming felt his absence keenly. Everything had changed since the Picketts had arrived, and for the worse.

Just this morning, as the Prince was regaling the Duchess of North Northingham with a story about his hunting exploits, and casually admiring her substantial bosom, he had noticed Lady Elizabeth standing behind him. The surprise at seeing her so close at hand made him fumble badly with his introductions; and by the time he recovered, the ladies were tittering at him in a most undignified manner. To make matters worse, the duchess and Lady Elizabeth fell into a highly unorthodox conversation about the barbarity of fox hunting (of all things!) and he found himself being dismissed like a pageboy. He flushed again at the memory, and stood looking at himself in the glass, bemused at the magical way Lady Elizabeth had of bewitching and embarrassing at the same time.

A light knock at his door interrupted his attempted reimagining of that conversation in which he was equal parts suave and witty. The Prince realized it was probably one of the many women of the court wishing to gain early entry into his graces. It was inevitable really. Why deny a lady such a pleasure? He prepared himself for couplet, raised his arm, and, with special emphasis on being charming, gave his best "Come."

To his surprise, his father opened the door. His Royal Majesty had adorned himself in his finest blues and golds, touches of purple accents, and a cape of finest sable. The older man raised his hand for quiet as though hushing a crowd, which was odd, as they were alone, then gently shut the door behind him. In a manner more befitting a gossipy serving maid than the Lord of the Land, he smiled broadly and laughed as he clapped his son on both shoulders. The Prince noticed that his father, the King, appeared years younger and seemed happier than he had ever been. In fact, his manner was so out of character that it left Charming momentarily speechless. Since Charming's youth, his father, the King, (whom he could never think of without His Royal title) had always been so stern and exacting with him. The sudden realization that it was likely the dragon's death that had made his father, the King, so happy cut Charming in a way that he did not fully understand or wish to explore. He was trying to come to grips with this new version of his father, the King, when awareness struck again that he had missed quite a bit of the speech and that his father, the King, had reverted to his more familiar, if not more comforting, regal self.

" . . . I'm sorry, but you do understand, don't you, my son? I had no choice in the matter. I have always had to hold you to the highest standards, to present you as the model of honor. While I understand that the *incident* with Lord William at the court wasn't entirely your fault, it was certainly a grave breach of protocol. Couple that with the fact that your behavior of late has been, well, let us say, frivolous, and the fact is I was facing open revolt from the court if I had not conceded the point."

He was not sure how to respond, so Charming merely said, "I know full well that the dragon is dead." His diplomacy tutor would have been pleased with his response.

"Exactly, and as Lord William was the slayer of the dragon, certain considerations must be made. I just wanted you to be forewarned so you could prepare yourself."

The King, his father, leaned in close and lowered his

voice. "I'll make the announcement at the ball tonight. You must be ready. The whole court will be measuring you against Lord William. If he is seen as the better man—"

"Impossible," Charming blurted. He was not sure what the King, his father, was talking about, but the mere idea that the Pickett could ever be considered his equal was absurd.

The King frowned briefly at this, but then smoothed his expression. "That's my lad, always up to a challenge. Now, I want your word that you will treat Lord William as befits a true hero of the realm. You know, I think the two of you could become good friends. The Pickett family history, after all, is quite remarkable . . ."

The Prince stopped listening again. An idea had formed in his head, an idea worthy of his political acumen. If he *were* Will's best friend, then he would be close to the man, better able to manipulate, control, and ultimately reveal him as the failure and the fraud that he was. In the middle of this scheming, he realized that his father, the King, was quietly staring at him, awaiting a response. "Yes, Father, I quite agree. I was rash and not in my right mind when I first met"—he paused, then forced the name from his lips—"Lord William. I had suffered a rather nasty fall that day and certainly owe him an explanation and my royal apology."

His father, the King, nodded and patted his shoulders again, "I am pleased that you have taken this so well. I know that it cannot be easy, and I am *proud* of you, son."

"Thank you, Father. With your leave, I shall see about Lord William and make certain that he is well prepared for the ball."

The King waved with a flourish and flowed through the door and down the hall with a jaunty step, which Charming found unseemly.

LORD WILLIAM PICKETT, Dragon Slayer and newly minted Protector of the Kingdom, had never felt this out of place and uncomfortable. He had been standing for three hours while an army of men pricked him with pins, measured every inch of his body, and rubbed him with oils of such sweetness that he felt nauseous. Of course his sister had told him stories about being in the court, which had been told to her by their mother and father, but the reality was more horrifying than could be imagined. He had never dreamed that nobles could be so peculiar.

"Why are you so tall?" asked the Royal Tailor for the fifth time that night, "And please stop slouching. You're making this much more difficult than it should be."

Turning slightly, Will mumbled a halfhearted apology and, in doing so, was rewarded by a half-dozen miniature stab wounds from the pinned-together suit—and then, without a knock, the door flung open, the tailors gasped and stood back, and Prince Charming entered with a flourish. The man tried to strike a pose, but the door rebounded and hit his side with a loud thunk. Will couldn't fully suppress a chuckle. The Prince flushed red and, teeth clenched in a frighteningly insincere smile, advanced toward him. The man was wearing a complicated green outfit that was alarmingly tight in the crotch. He waved his arms at the tailors as though shooing flies.

"You are all dismissed, I have need to confer with the—the Lord Protector for a moment."

Despite the orders, the tailors, transfixed by the developing tableau, did not stir. The Prince gave them not a second's more consideration as he turned his full attention on Will, who, with a start, realized that the Prince was examining him much like he himself might examine a buck before loosing an arrow. When the Prince spoke, the tone was strange—not quite condescending but something similar.

"I'm afraid I must have made a terrible impression on you when we first met. I want to"— the Prince's voice trailed off as he adjusted the collar of his tunic— "apologize." The Prince offered his hand.

Will extended his in return, but the Prince was already now busily removing an invisible speck from the cuff of his sleeve. Once again words failed Will and all he managed was a lame, "That's all right. I'm sure it happens to all of us now and then."

The Prince smiled, but it was a thin smile, the kind of smile that on his sister's face would have made Will's mouth go dry. "Yes, well, we really should be friends. What other man in all the realm is more worthy of sharing my company than a dragon slayer?"

"Well . . . um . . . Prin— I mean, Your Highness, that would be fine. I'm sure it would be nice to have someone that could show me the ropes, so to speak. I really do find all this"—he gestured helplessly at his half-finished outfit—"a bit much."

"My good Lord Protector, may I call you Will? It would be better if I could call you Will, if we are to be friends.

"Well, that would be fine . . . um, Edw . . . I mean, Your Roy . . . well . . ."

The Prince laughed. "Call me Charming. All my friends do."

Will was puzzled because this was what everyone called the Prince, friend or no, but since the Prince seemed perfectly at ease with this resolution, Will just nodded mutely.

This seemed to satisfy the Prince, because his smile dropped and he turned to the tailors, still gathered in rapt attention at the spectacle of the two men talking. With a flush of irritation, he snapped, "Well, finish dressing this . . . hero. We have a ball to attend! Will," he said, turning back again, "I will await you in the hallway."

As soon as the door closed behind the Prince, the tailors sprang at Will like a swarm of demented bees, hurrying to finish his clothing with little regard for their subject's safety until, with all the pricks he suffered, Will wondered if the beaded red dragon woven onto the front of his tunic was actually decorated with drops of his own blood.

When they finished, the weight of the outfit, and its tight fit, made him feel terribly uncomfortable. Not for the first time since he'd arrived in the castle, Will found himself longing for the fields he had cursed for so many

years. As promised, the Prince was waiting for him outside and gave him a thorough look-over, almost like he
was buying a horse. Will could not help but feel self-
conscious and bit his lip.

"No need for that," suggested the Prince, "they put
enough color on you. You were trying to redden your lips
there, weren't you?"

Will shrugged, confused. He didn't want to say anything that might sound dumb, but he *was* alarmed. Had
someone painted his lips without his noticing? He kept
surreptitiously wiping his face on the back of his sleeve
to see if it was true.

The Prince shrugged. "You'll do. Follow me, friend.
We will make our entrance together— and how the
women will swoon!"

Will raised a finger, ready to ask if that was the reaction they were looking for, but the Prince was already off,
striding forward without a backward glance to see if Will
was following. Will tried to figure out where they were
going, but every passage looked the same to him and he
soon felt lost. Finally, they rounded a corner into another
of the endless and rather overly ornate halls and came
onto a balcony overlooking a vast space. Below him, the
Grand Ballroom was a swirling kaleidoscope of color,
sound, and smell that overwhelmed the senses. Silks and
rich velvets draped the chamber from its peak down to
the furthermost corner. Chandeliers rose toward the
heights of the ceiling, giving the impression of stars blaz-
ing above. Flowers of every description and color were
arrayed about the room—on the tables, woven about

the columns, scattered across the entryway. The nobles and honored guests themselves added to the spectacle, each one decked out in the finest of their finery. As they moved, the gleaming marble floor mirrored the dancers and guests until it seemed like there were two balls, one above the floor and one beneath.

The scene struck Will dumb. And he realized that he was standing there, eyes wide and mouth agape, like some know-nothing hayseed. Common sense told him to watch what Charming was doing; but when he did, he was surprised to see the Prince also staring in amazement—not at the entire room but at a point somewhere near where the thrones were set. He followed the man's eyes and saw Liz dressed in a formal ball gown.

For a heartbeat, he thought that Charming was looking at his sister, but then noticed that, just past her, was Princess Gwendolyn talking to the King. It must have been the Princess who amazed Charming. She had been locked in her rooms since arriving at the castle, and Will thought she must have spent the whole time getting ready for this evening. None of the fine ladies, in all their dazzling gowns, could match the peerless beauty of the Princess. Her dress was a complicated arrangement of silver and gold layers that served as a perfect complement to her fair skin and those crystalline blue eyes. There were also obviously some supports in the dress because her, well . . . *they* were displayed in a stunning, not immodest, manner. He sighed in admiration.

"She is a vision . . ." uttered Charming, letting his words trail away.

"Yes, the Princess is prett—beautiful," said Will.

Charming blinked and shook his head slightly. "Who? Yes . . . yes, the Princess. The Princess is beautiful. Indeed, she is. Yes, of course, that is inarguable."

"Um, Charming, will we have to dance?" Will asked.

The Prince looked at Will. "What? Oh, of course we dance, Will. The ladies await our presence. You'll learn these things."

The Prince straightened his coat and ran a practiced hand through his hair. How he did that without mussing it up was a mystery to Will, who himself would have wound up with little more than a tangle had he made the same attempt. Will looked at the Prince and then out at all the gathered nobility, and felt a flutter of guilt in his stomach. It had been building all day, but he could not ignore it any longer.

This is wrong, Will thought. *Everyone is here to honor you for slaying the dragon, but it was an accident! The scarecrow is more a hero than you are. You don't deserve this.*

These thoughts and doubts were not new. They were yet another version of what Will had been wrestling with since the King's man had returned to Prosper and summoned him to the court. Initially, he had consoled himself that his little omissions were not real lies, were not really hurting anybody, but now he realized that he had hurt someone—Charming. The Prince might be a conceited, vain, insufferable fellow, but that didn't mean he didn't have feelings. In fact, sometimes it seemed to Will that Charming had enough feelings for three men. Regardless, seeing the way the Prince looked at Gwendolyn, Will knew the only right thing to do was to tell him the truth. Charming had to know that he might still be her true love, whatever it cost Will personally—even if it lost him the Princess.

Will squared his shoulders and cleared his throat. "Charming, I'd like to talk to you about how the dragon died. You see, it was impaled by my pitchfork bu—"

Charming raised his hand, stopping Will in midsentence. The Prince looked suddenly ill, like he might vomit. He was shaking slightly and kept pursing his lips. "Will, a true hero does not speak of his victories or his glories. He has others do that. I know that you wish to share the story of your triumph, but you must master the desire. Never, no, never talk about yourself or your deeds, instead let the bards tell the tale for you."

"But, Charming, they don't have the story right."

"Now, now, Will . . ." Charming paused and took a deep breath, then exhaled and continued. "That is something called artistic license. The legend may differ in parts from what really happened, but you should let them recount the tale as they choose. I do appreciate your desire to share your adventures with a man equal to your . . . *heroic* bearing. Trust me, I know how hard it is to find an equal, but I would hate for you to appear vain. We will not speak of it again. Understood"—the Prince coughed slightly—"my friend?"

Will didn't really understand, and he didn't really think the Prince understood, but he could tell the man was not feeling his best, so he said, "Yes." *Nobles are very peculiar.*

The Prince took a moment, and seemed to physically gather himself. *"Now* is the time for our entrance," announced the Prince and, without further preamble, strode grandly to the top of the ballroom stair, gesturing impatiently with his trailing hand for Will to join him.

The Prince struck his most regal pose as he looked down the sweep of the stair to the ballroom floor. With Will standing beside him, the contrast between their qualities could not have been more striking. While the Royal Tailor had, admittedly, worked a wonder on Will with a dramatic white-and-red costume, the lout was clearly out of his depth. He stood shuffling his feet, and, well, he was biting his thumb. It was shameful.

Charming reflected that this should be a moment of triumph, but he could not enjoy the moment. He felt such a flutter in his chest, and the lump in his throat, that he feared the entire assembly could see his distress. He was distracted. No, it was more than that. He was bewitched by Lady Elizabeth.

Will tried to say something again, but Charming would not shut up about the damned dragon and chose to ignore him, which was easy—because, for the Prince, all the spectacle in the grand ballroom had shrunk to a single point atop the throne platform where the Princess and Lady Elizabeth stood flanking his father, the King.

Lady Elizabeth was a vision. She wore an almost ethereal blue gown of such magnificence that he wondered if it had not been spun by fairy magic. She outclassed every other woman in the room, including Princess Gwendolyn; and from the glares the women of the court were giving her, and the frantic pace of their fluttering fans, it was clear that they knew it also.

He tried to convince himself that it was an enchantment spun by magics dark and nefarious, but his mind would no longer allow the self-deception. The truth was that ever since these peasant siblings had arrived, events had twisted around them in a way that defied the natural order. He steadied himself. Tonight he would—he must—reestablish his position. Once Lady Elizabeth, and of course the Princess, had seen his mastery of all the courtly arts, they would be helplessly drawn to him. He smiled. Then, with a start, Charming realized that a hush had fallen over the multitude. Will had already begun descending the stairs. A crowd of luminaries rushed to greet him below. Charming had been left behind. The evening was beginning badly.

One of the heralds, a man of much size and volume, proclaimed in a booming voice easily heard over the music, "Lords and ladies, we are now in the presence of the Lord Protector, the Slayer of the Dragon, Champion of the Realm, William Pickett *and*"—the cheering and applause nearly drowned out the mighty herald, and the Prince barely heard—"Prince Charming."

The Prince strode regally, if a bit stiffly, down the stair. A throng of ladies was swarming Will, and Charming was left outside their fluttering circle. He could feel the color

rising in his cheeks. These outrages were unthinkable—
nay, unimaginable. As the dread specter of another social
defeat loomed, Charming's breath came quicker, his head
began to spin, and he realized that he was on the verge of
fainting. He had just begun to sway when a rough hand
grabbed his arm and pulled him to a quiet spot beneath
the stairs. It was his squire. Why the squire had been allowed anywhere near the party was beyond Charming.
His outfit was tragic. The man wore a gaudy red doublet
that could barely contain his gut. Charming was about to
upbraid him for pulling him away from the revelry when
the grizzled fellow interjected, "Sorry to disturb you, Your
Highness, but you look like you could use a glass of wine."

Charming took the goblet but did not drink. He could
hear the ladies tittering and flirtatiously competing to
dance with Will. He, Prince Charming, had always been
the center of attention, yet now he was an afterthought. A
deep emptiness filled him. "I don't understand," he said.
"Why would they want to suffer injury and embarrassment with that village idiot when they could dazzle the
court with me?"

For once, his squire didn't have a sharp retort. "Perhaps you should sit out the first dance, Your Highness.
You did suffer a terrible fall a few days ago."

The man tugged at Charming's sleeve and gestured
to an antechamber. Charming looked at him and saw . . .
pity? That one of his servants might pity him made
Charming resent the squire even more, and he pulled his
arm away. "Nonsense! I will not run from Pickett. If the

court wishes to measure us, then let us be measured. I will show them the difference in our quality!"

He handed the untouched glass back, stretched his arms, and tested his jaw, opening and closing it to make certain that he was ready to achieve couplet. Now he was prepared to save the ladies of the king's court from a night spent in the company of William Pickett.

He had barely recomposed himself when the herald's voice once again rang out from the balcony above. "Lords and ladies, we have an announcement from His Royal Majesty, the King!"

The Prince blinked in shock. During his few moments of respite, the scene, which before had only been aggravating, had been transformed into something from a nightmare. Everyone had turned to look at the far end of the ballroom, where stood the high throne and, as if by some accursed conjuration, Will. He had been transported atop the throne dais and was standing to the right of the King, his father. To the left of his father, the King, stood Princess Gwendolyn with a strange, almost mournful, expression on her face.

The King cleared his royal throat and the room fell silent. "My lords and ladies, rejoice! The dragon is dead! Princess Gwendolyn is saved!" Exuberant cries of huzzah filled the ballroom. Charming ground his teeth in frustration. The King continued. "And here we have the man, the hero, responsible for delivering us from our oppressor, the Lord Protector of the Realm and Dragon Slayer, William Pickett!"

An even louder cheer echoed off the walls and ceiling

of the Great Hall. Charming noted that Will looked pale as a ghost, and seemed nervous to the point of being ill. At least he was suffering for his ill-deserved fame. The King raised his hands for silence, and the gathering was once again quieted.

"As reward for his valor, I hereby grant Lord William Pickett the land of his home, the Southern Valley, and all that lies therein as his and his progeny's in perpetuity."

There was a hushed murmur among the landed gentry; many of them would be dispossessed by this act. But if the King heard any of this disturbance, he showed no sign and pressed on.

"What is more, I have decided that the time has come to name an heir to my throne. So, in my wisdom, I decree that my throne shall go to either my son, Prince Charming, or to the Lord Protector, who has become like a son to me and is a hero to us all, whichever of these two fine men shall marry first!"

Cheers filled the air and squeals of delight came from the ladies who surged forward to be close to the now clearly terrified Lord William. Charming stood cold with shock. Is this what his father, the King, had been trying to warn him about? He looked toward the throne where the King, his father, stood. "But I am your son," the Prince whispered to himself. "How could you?"

The world he knew was gone. Pickett had stolen his quest, his glory, and now his father. Charming's breath came quickly. He grasped at the cool marble of the wall behind him for support. He found the wall but no stability.

The world had gone mad.

Chapter 6

Tripping the Glass Fantastic

LIZ STOOD IN the royal ballroom listening to the blood pound in her ears, the words of the King still reverberating through the hall. She needed time to think and air to breathe. *Damn this corset.* The King was considering giving his throne to *Will*? No, she corrected herself. He wasn't *considering*, he had *offered* the throne to Will. All her brother had to do was convince one of these foolish, simpering women to marry him. This had gone too far. Will hadn't killed the dragon; the stupid beast had landed on his pitchfork. If someone found out the truth . . .

She could imagine being thrown into the deepest dungeon in the castle. She would spend the rest of her days imprisoned with her brother, making friends with rats and being thankful for extra crumbs of stale bread.

Although, instead, they could be executed—for conspiring to steal the crown! As she weighed her chances of receiving the headsman's ax, being drawn and quartered, or burned at the stake, she swayed on her feet.

A firm hand gripped her elbow. It was the King. His kindly voice, soft in her ear, made her heart sink. "Dear Lady Elizabeth, you look unwell."

He guided her to a low settee positioned strategically in a quiet alcove to the right of the dais. A snap of his royal fingers summoned one of the servants with miraculous alacrity. "The lady needs attending. Bring her refreshment and repast at once." With the orders complete, he turned back to her. "Please forgive me for making you stand on that beastly stage for so long. I have a habit of being overly windy when I have an audience. Sadly, a trait my son has inherited."

His eyes laughed and his smile was contagious, but the deep lines of his face spoke of a man that had been burdened by a long sadness. She should tell him now, but her thoughts turned again to the dungeons. All she could muster was a weak, "Thank you, Your Royal Majesty, you are too kind. I—I am not used to balls. I'm afraid I am not quite up to the class of the ladies of your court."

The King's smile changed to something both more kindly and more serious. "My dear lady—because that is what you are, Lady Elizabeth—Princess Gwendolyn and the Lord Protector may well be the center of attention, but take it from someone who was once a young man at a ball much like this one, you are most certainly a lady and you are most certainly in the right place."

The servant returned with a chilled decanter of wine and matching crystal glass, and what looked to be a sampling of every delicacy the kingdom had to offer. He set them down next to her. The King had started to wave him away with the back of his hand when a cunning expression passed over his face. He stopped and gestured for the man to lean closer. Whispered words were exchanged, and the servant's eyebrows rose so high in surprise that they nearly disappeared beneath his powdered wig. The servant bowed before sprinting from the room. The King seemed to measure her with his eyes. "What you need, my dear, is a good-luck charm, and I have just the thing."

Liz protested. "Please, Your Majesty, you have been too kind already. What you have done for me and my brother is too generous. You see we didn't mean—"

"Nonsense! Your brother, the Lord Protector, saved me from a lifetime of humiliation and this kingdom from the dragon's terror. He has returned the woman who was my love to this court, where she can once again beguile a generation of men. There is nothing, *nothing*, that I can deny him." There may have been a quaver in his voice when he mentioned the Princess, but it never touched that gentle smile. Placing her hands in his, he carried on. "I have never spoken truer words than when I said that Lord William has become like a son to me. In turn, you have become like a daughter, if you would forgive the familiarity."

There was a movement behind them. The footman had returned. He carried before him a small silver chest, which he held with reverence.

"Excellent! Now, Lady Elizabeth, while the Royal Tailor has done us proud with the construction of your gown, the ensemble, if I may be so bold, is incomplete. You see, what makes a lady confident is not the dress, not even the jewelry, but the right pair of shoes."

He made a quick gesture, and the servant raised the lid of the chest to reveal a pair of dancing slippers so exquisite that they made Liz's breath catch in her throat. In fact, they were so beautiful that it took her a moment to realize what they were made of. "Your Majesty, are those made of—of—?"

"Yes, my dear, they are glass slippers!" He lifted each of the remarkable shoes from their velvet cradle and, bending, placed them on her feet. She expected the slippers not to fit, or to be hard and uncomfortable, but their cool smoothness fitted perfectly. "I knew they would fit you. I just knew it!"

The King's eyes were glassy—the man was on the verge of tears! Liz looked away to give him time to compose himself, and when she turned back, he had risen and was staring at her feet. "I hope you can forgive an old man the vice of sentimentality. You see these shoes were to be a wedding gift to my first love."

Terror gripped Elizabeth when she grasped the import of his words. These shoes, the shoes on her feet, had been originally made for his bride to be! "Your Highness, I cannot accept these! They belong to Princess Gwendolyn, not me!"

"I will hear nothing of the sort. I have always wanted to see these slippers worn at a grand ball by a beautiful young woman. We are at the grandest of balls, and you are young and undeniably beautiful. Just as you were meant to be here, the slippers are exactly where they were meant to be. Besides, I am quite certain that Princess Gwendolyn would not wish to wear them as she was not my *first* love."

There was that sadness in his voice again, and Liz recalled that it was Rosslyn, Gwendolyn's older sister, who had been the first lady pledged to the King's heart. But she had little time to think on this history as the King continued his speech. "If you will indulge me for just a moment, let me look at you in them."

She stood and carefully turned in place. The slippers drew and reflected the light from the hundreds of candles in the ballroom so that they appeared to glow with the light of a thousand fireflies. That remarkable, laughing smile returned to the King's face. "Beautiful, simply beautiful. I think that you are now ready for the ball. Please try not to break too many hearts this evening. Now, if you will excuse me." He gave her a shallow bow, and she watched as the old man ascended the stairs of the dais to sit once again on his throne.

Elizabeth Pickett had never felt smaller. This charade had gone too far. They hadn't been planning to deceive the entire kingdom; they had just hoped for enough gold to rebuild the farm. And they—she—certainly never intended to betray the trust of such a kindly old man. Now she was wearing the shoes he had meant for his *first* true love, because he considered her his daughter. She had to do something, but it had to make sense and not get her and Will killed. She felt the need to move, to take action, to find someone in this noble madhouse that could help. She tried to take a step and nearly lost her balance. The glass slippers may have been the most extraordinary shoes she'd ever seen, but walking in them on the polished marble floors of the ballroom was like trying to ice skate. She was also quietly terrified that she would break them.

As Liz struggled to relearn the art of walking, the music changed. She looked up to see the Princess gliding with an otherworldly grace down to the center of the ballroom, arm in arm with Will. Though he was paler than he'd been in years, Liz was amazed to see that he moved with little hesitation, and without slouching or chewing on his thumb. She bit her bottom lip and twisted her hands in the folds of her billowing dress. He was enjoying himself. He looked truly happy. He was living his fairy tale. He was gazing deeply into the eyes of the Princess. Her heart sank again. If he fell in love with *the Princess* . . .

She didn't dare complete the thought.

MOVING WITH A long-unused elegance, Princess Gwendolyn surveyed the nobility swirling about her as she twirled in time to the music. The men gazed appraisingly, and the courtly women cast critical gazes over their fans and whispered catty comments beneath them.

She sighed sadly.

She had hoped the courtly intrigue would fill her with

the same thrill it had in days past, but it seemed so mean-ingless. Nothing was right. Nothing was as she thought it would be. She had spent the weeks since her rescue not dressing in fine cloths and eating fine food, seeing and being seen by fine people, but locked in her room, terri-fied that the castle and the servants and the silks might dissolve around her, that this was just another dream planted by the fairy to torment her with what had been. Even now she was half convinced that she was still asleep in that tower—the dragon whispering confidences into her mute ear. And she had reason. It was not as though there had been a moment when she felt her curse finally and irrevocably lift. It was more as if she had been in deep water, drowning, and had now drifted closer to the surface, but the waters still swirled around, drag-ging and pulling her downward. The world itself seemed unreal; sometimes it blurred and stuttered. And then there were the visions. She felt them, right at the edge of her sight: leering faces half remembered from her long, dark dreams, which seemed to be peering from between the swirling dresses of the ladies at the edge of the floor; voices, in the air around her; distant tolling bells no one else could hear; and a rushing wind that did not touch the glowing candles.

She shuddered and clutched more tightly to the hand of her partner. Lord William was real. He felt solid, something she could trust, and he was nervous. He had been that way since she awoke in the back of his cart in Prosper. It made her smile to make a man nervous again. He was looking down at her now with that slightly stunned expression he always seemed to have when he touched her.

Is this my true love?

She rolled the question about in her mind as she led him through a complicated series of steps. It had taken quite a lot of persuading to get him to dance. He had been worried about making a fool of himself and, to his credit, her. He needn't have. Gwendolyn had been performing in the court since she was a little girl and could make anyone, even a pig farmer or whatever it was Lord William had been, look graceful. To his further credit, the boy made it easy. He was quite willing to follow her lead. She liked that about him also. In fact, despite everything, Gwendolyn found herself enjoying the dance. While she was moving, it was easier to imagine that things were just as they had been before. That they were all young again, she and Rupert and Rosslyn, and that events had turned out as they should have.

She frowned. Thinking about all those years of captivity brought a deep, slow anger back to her breast. She still could not bear to look at Rupert. Since her return, he had tried daily to seek an audience with her, but Gwendolyn had made a point not to speak to him. The truth was that she could not. Not yet. For one, she did not know if she could bear hearing his excuse for why she had been made to languish in that tower, imprisoned by the dragon, as the seasons changed and the decades passed. He had been her hero. The one she had believed would be her true love. She had been so sure that he would come to rescue her, but he never came.

Never.

Instead, he'd married another and ceded her to his son. The bitterness of it all galled her. And another thing—he was old, and seeing him made her feel her true age, and she did not like it. But more than all this, she feared the answer to one question.

Why?

She looked around as if she could find an answer somewhere in her surroundings. The dance spun them about and she saw the young prince standing at the edge of the floor, staring at Lord William with venom in his eyes. How long had the dragon whispered to her about him, about his beauty and strength, and how he must come for her one day soon? The dragon may have meant it as a cruelty, but it had been an unwitting kindness, because in her dreams he had been transformed into the man she had always wanted Rupert to be. For how many lifetimes had she imagined being with him: being rescued, having children, living happily ever after.

Now looking at this Prince Charming, a grown man of twenty summers, she felt none of that hope. He was flighty and insubstantial. From what she'd heard since her return, he'd spent his days dallying over clothes and verse and lancing the ladies. It was what she would expect of a spoiled courtly young man of twenty. It was the way the courtly young men had behaved in her day. But she was not a courtly young lady of twenty any longer, and she had no appetite for him. She sighed deeply. Everything was shadowy and gray. She knew she must try to forgive and move on, but a part of her, an undeniable and ugly part, wanted retribution more than forgiveness.

They had left her to rot, Rupert, Prince Charming, and the rest of the kingdom. They all deserved to suffer for their lies.

Gwen felt a sudden chill around her neck, like two cold hands at her throat, and once more she became aware of the thin gold chain and miniature lock resting like an icicle against her breast. It was a strange thing, that locket. Ever since the evening in Prosper when she finally clawed her way to consciousness, mostly out of irritation at the jar of pickled peas she'd been lying atop in the back of that peasant wagon, Gwendolyn had been on the verge of tearing the accursed thing off, but she could not. Not until everything had been made right. For a moment, she felt a rush of deadly ambition and purpose, saw herself on the throne, a queen at last. Then the pale face of her sister, Rosslyn, floated into her mind and all the energy left her. She felt so tired and so very old.

Lord William seemed to sense her mood. He leaned down a bit and whispered in her ear. "You seem tired, Princess Gwendolyn. Shall I take you back to the dais?"

"No, no. I am having a wonderful time, and . . . you are a wonderful dancer," she lied.

"No, I'm not a wonderful dancer, but you are, Your Highness."

He was young and naïve, but he was also solid—real. Someone trustworthy and true she could hold on to. Gwendolyn smiled at him, but the ghosts of the past were swirling close now and their cold touch would not let her feel the pleasure of the moment. The music reached a crescendo and the dance ended in stillness.

LIZ WATCHED THE end of the dance with rising fear. She knew her brother well enough to know that he was entranced. She needed to stop Will before he got too far out of hand. She needed to set things right while there was still a chance that they could keep their heads attached to their necks. She had to talk to her brother, but with the crowd surrounding him, it would not be easy. Carefully, Liz made her way onto the main floor of the ballroom and was pleasantly surprised that she didn't trip. Maybe she would make it through the night without landing on her bottom. As she moved through the masses gathered around the dance, she considered the problem. How could she stop Will from throwing himself into marriage with so many women willing to concede anything for a chance to be queen?

All Gretel had to do to nab him was show a little ankle, she thought. *Some of these women are offering a lot more than that. I should have thought of this before the ball. I had a week to do something. I'm supposed to be the responsible one.*

She looked around the room. There were so many ladies, showing so much bosom and sighing so sincerely. Any one of them might be too much for the foolish boy to resist, yet his eyes remained focused on Princess Gwendolyn. She considered that, perhaps, while that held true, there was still hope. Even if the Princess intended to marry Will as a reward for rescuing her, her station would demand that they spend some time courting. She had time. But how to stop what seemed inevitable?

Liz's eye fell on a fat balding man in a painfully bright tunic standing near the back of the room and looking very uncomfortable and out of place. Why did he seem familiar? The Prince . . . he was the Prince's squire. The solution came to her like a thunderbolt. There was one person in all the land who could stop Will from attaining the throne.

I need Prince Charming!

The Princess was always meant—no, destined—to marry Charming. If Charming married Princess Gwendolyn, she and Will could drift away from the castle and return safely to Prosper. Given enough quiet seclusion, they might even be forgotten completely, which would probably be for the best.

But where was Prince Charming? She had caught a glimpse of him at the edge of the ballroom earlier, but reflected that he had been noticeably absent for most of the night, which seemed odd given his reputation. She turned about, trying to spot him through the riot of swirling colors and movement of the dancers, but the sudden movement made the slick glass shoes slip from beneath her. A strong hand grasped her arm from behind and righted her.

Twice in one night. She hoped falling down was not going to become a new habit of hers. She smoothed her skirts and turned, more slowly this time, to thank her rescuer, and found herself inches from Charming. He rocked back on his heels and their eyes met, and she couldn't help staring. He had beautiful deep brown eyes. She read in those eyes a strange mixture of desire and confusion, and she found herself wishing that he would give voice to those feelings and confide in her. A long moment of oddly comfortable silence passed between them, then the Prince blinked as if waking from a dream. Hesitantly, perhaps reluctantly, he reached his hand out to her.

> "Fair Elizabeth, if you would wish
>   the chance,
> Then I bid you, take my hand so that we
>   may dance."

Surprising herself, she curtsied and placed her hand in his. A pleasant tingle ran through her body at the touch, but she managed a dignified, "I'd be honored, Your Highness."

He led her out to the dance floor. The Prince pulled Liz close to him. His grip was light, but strong, and he moved with a grace that should have made her feel clumsy, but instead made her body feel light as air. And then there were his eyes. She couldn't believe how handsome he was up close.

I could get lost in those eyes, she thought again. *Yes, you could, so remember why you are dancing with him. You need his help.*

The music swept them around the floor. The light

from the slippers danced about them, surrounding them with a flickering nimbus that drew eyes from around the great ballroom. For Liz, the room and the crowd had faded away; there was only the music and the Prince. She knew she should broach the topic of Will and the Princess, and somewhere the rational part of Elizabeth was shouting to get on with it, but she couldn't. Here she was, dancing in a royal ball with Prince Charming. This would probably be her last ball, and might well be her last night of freedom, so Liz ignored her own warnings and allowed herself to enjoy the music, the dance, and, yes, the skill and beauty of her partner. She sighed contentedly.

Her momentary joy was all too brief. As the dance swept them past the throne, she saw Will and the Princess seated side by side, engaged in some private conversation. Their bodies close. Her brother's expression of wonder and adoration was downright alarming. Enough was enough! She had to say something. When she looked back at Charming, his eyes, those wonderful eyes, were also on the dais with that same confused look of pain and desire. She admonished herself. *Of course he would rather be dancing with the Princess, you silly girl.*

She cleared her throat and his eyes flashed back to her. "I . . ." she began and stopped as her voice cracked. Liz knew what she had to say, but suddenly the idea of ceding the Prince to another was not so easy. *It must be so*, she urged silently to herself. *You are not a princess or a lady, and this is not a fairy tale.* She gathered her courage about her. "I'm sorry that our first meeting was—"

"A disaster?" he supplied, the hint of a smile passing over his face.

"Yes," she smiled back. "A disaster."

He closed his eyes briefly and then a deeper, satisfied smile creased his face, and he recited melodically:

> *"Do not concern yourself, lady dear,*
> *It is in the past and we are here."*

Liz began to laugh at his joke, but then stopped herself. The Prince seemed perfectly serious. He had an expectant, even triumphant, look on his face. She puzzled for a brief moment on the verse and how she should respond, and then said with care, "Yes, I agree. We should let bygones be bygones. In fact, I'm glad we had this chance to be alone, because I wanted to talk about Will . . . er . . . the Lord Protector."

Charming's whole body tensed and his beautiful smile vanished in a twinkling. He closed his eyes and there was another momentary delay before he responded, this time a little more stiffly than before.

> *"Dear Lady, let us not speak of such things,*
> *But to enjoy the dance as the music rings."*

The smile returned, but this time it was a little less certain. Unconsciously, she thinned her lips. Why was he speaking in nursery rhymes? Liz considered that she had never been with a prince and had no idea what was expected behavior. She tried once more to get to the heart of the matter. "Yes, that would be nice. It's just that I know you wish you could be dancing with someone else, with . . . with the Princess, in fact. I thought if I helped you woo her—"

He removed one of his hands from hers and silenced her with a gesture. There was another pause and then he responded with another verse, and this time he tilted his head in a peculiar manner and made sure to catch her eyes with his when he spoke.

> *"Lady Elizabeth, don't let yourself*
> *be alarmed,*
> *In the Prince's presence all the ladies*
> *are charmed."*

God, what an ass, she thought, and this time gave him the full weight of her glare before saying coldly, "Well, at the moment I would say the Princess is being charmed pretty thoroughly by my brother. And if he marries her, you won't be a prince anymore, so can we—"

Without warning, he stumbled slightly. He recovered and spun her expertly, if with a bit too much vigor, to reestablish the rhythm of their dance. Once they were back in step, he closed his eyes. Liz suspected more verse was coming, and she interrupted whatever it was he was trying to compose by asking the most obvious question.

"Why are you closing your eyes?"

He reopened them and was unable to hide his annoyance. "If you really must know, I was attempting to regain couplet. It's not as easy as I make it look. Now, ready yourself."

"Fair damsel—" he started.

"Please, no more poetry. We have things we need to discuss, and I don't think verse is going to help matters."

His smile reappeared, crooked and superior. "My dear Lady Elizabeth," he said in an annoyingly smug voice, "it's called couplet. As a true gentleman, I assure you that it is the finest, nay, the only way, to speak to a lady."

She looked at him in disbelief and spoke her thoughts without moderation. "Well, it seems ridiculous to me."

His smile faltered, and he spun her about in an obvious attempt to recover himself. "I forget your disadvantages. The customs of the cultured class are new to you. In time I'm sure you will learn the social mores of your new position."

Though it shouldn't have, the implied insult cut her deeply, and she felt her cheeks color. How dare the man treat her with such casual disrespect? She dropped her hand from his shoulder and pulled away. Their feet stuttered to stop and the other dancers swirled around them, casting curious glances at the suddenly motionless pair.

"You must think a great deal of yourself, Prince Charming," she seethed. "Just because I don't simper and coo at your every gesture does not mean that I am not a lady. And if being a proper lady of the court means that I must make the pretense of being as vapid and silly as you seem to want me to be, then I think I would prefer to decline the privilege."

The Prince flinched as though struck, and then his body stiffened and his expression hardened. "I am sorry that you find my company so displeasing, Lady Elizabeth," he said between lips that barely moved. "I'm sure a lady of your manifest courtesy and grace will find many other more suitable companions." He bowed sharply and turned on his heel.

Even before he turned away, Liz regretted her outburst and silently cursed her temper and tongue. He might have been thoughtlessly insulting, but she had been purposefully cruel. Besides, she needed Prince Charming's help. She took a step after him and called out plaintively, "I'm sorry, Your Highness. I did not mean—"

"Yes, you did," said a woman. "And because I fear the point of your statement might have been missed by your audience, I will be more blunt. Prince Charming is a joke and an ass."

Elizabeth looked past Charming and saw, advancing toward him, a woman wearing a scarlet dress and a bad wig. A murderous look gleamed in the woman's eyes. The trio formed a triangle in the middle of the dance.

Charming glared at the woman and said sharply, "This is none of your concern, Lady, um . . ."

"You can't even remember my name!" the strange woman shouted.

The dancers were stopping now to watch the unfolding drama. Liz moved forward and, gesturing toward one of the shadowed alcoves, said softly, "Perhaps we could conduct this conversation in private. I don't think any of us wants a scene here in the middle of the King's ball."

"Yes, milady—" began Charming, but he was interrupted.

"You're quite wrong, Lady Elizabeth," cried the woman, her voice ringing through the ballroom. "I want everyone to know what His Highness did to me." She gestured to the assembled nobles and shouted, "Look at me, Charming! LOOK AT ME! I am ruined, and it's YOUR fault!" She tore off the wig on her head, and Liz saw beneath it what might have once been incredibly long and beautiful hair, but for the patches here and there where it looked like chunks had been shorn or perhaps even torn out. She pointed an accusing finger straight at his chest. "And how dare you presume to lecture anyone, much less Lady Elizabeth, on social mores, when you, the supposed savior of the kingdom, were in my bedchamber when the dragon was killed!"

A shocked gasp erupted from the gathered nobles. Liz wanted to escape, but she was rooted in place, completely petrified by the scene unfolding before her.

Charming smiled his most condescending smile. "You are clearly deranged, Lady . . . Lady—"

Whatever Prince Charming might have said was interrupted as the woman punched him squarely on the nose. Screams of horror came from the impromptu audience. The Prince staggered back a few paces and fell on his backside, blood pouring down from his face onto his cream-colored silk shirt and green doublet.

The lady stood over him and screamed, "IT'S RAPUNZEL, YOU GREAT ASS!"

The Prince put a silk handkerchief to his nose with

one hand and pointed up at Rapunzel from his seated position with the other. "How dare you touch the Royal Person. I'll have you put in the dungeon for this, you wretched, ill-bred wench. If it was not against my nature to hurt ladies I would—"

Before he could finish, Rapunzel lunged at him with a shriek. Her long tapered nails reached toward Charming's face like talons. No one moved, except for Will. He was suddenly standing in the middle of the melee, lifting Lady Rapunzel off the floor. Struggling with the twisting woman, Will managed to grunt out, "Perhaps . . . if we . . . adjourned . . . to a private chamber . . . all the parties . . . could just—*please*, that was me—calm themselves . . ."

Prince Charming rose to his feet, the rapidly reddening handkerchief still at his nose, and advanced on Will and Rapunzel. His face white with anger, the Prince roared at the woman, "I AM PRINCE CHARMING! That you could ever have imagined that I would consider you as anything more than a trifle, given your family, is delusional."

This sent the lady into a frenzy of lashing fists and feet as she sought to break Will's grip on her. With an enormous effort, Will wrapped Rapunzel up with one arm and put his other hand against Charming's chest to keep him away. "This is not helping, Prince," he grunted. "Please, both of you, try and control yourselves. We are at the King's ball, let us have some—*ouch*—decorum. Perhaps, if you could leave while we calm the lady, Prince Charming, that would—*please*, Lady Rapunzel—be the best."

The Prince seemed to swell with anger at this suggestion. "You are dismissing me?" Then he knocked Will's arm aside and said in a dangerously low voice, "You dare to speak to me of decorum? You are barely off the farm and now would command me beneath my own roof? What right do you have to be here, and to lay claim to the crown? What is your lineage? You may have slain the dragon and returned the Princess, but you and your family are common, and low, and no matter the title, you will never be anything else!"

The room was alive with shocked murmurs. Lady Rapunzel gasped and stopped struggling. Will handed her to the Prince's squire, who had popped out of the crowd like a magician's trick. Will straightened himself to his true height, which was a half-head taller than the Prince. The only time Liz had seen her brother look this angry was when he'd faced down the townsfolk of Prosper. "Prince Charming," Will said in a voice that made Liz cringe, "I have shown restraint till now out of respect for the King, but you will not speak about me and my family in that manner. It is time that you leave. NOW!"

The two men stood less than an arm's length apart, each seething with anger. A ring of nobility had formed around them, but at the edge it began to part and, as Liz could see, the guards were clearing a path through the throng. Then the King's herald boomed, "MAKE WAY! MAKE WAY FOR THE KING!" Perhaps he could stop this madness.

At the announcement, Will turned and took a step

back, accidentally knocking into the Prince with the side of his shoulder.

Everything seemed to slow.

The Prince grabbed Will roughly and spun him back. Both men snarled in rage. Will lunged forward and the Prince reared back his fist to strike. With a loud scream of "NO!" Liz grabbed the Prince's arm, hoping to stop the fight before it could begin.

The Prince, who was focused entirely on evading Will, flung his arm back to shake Liz off. Her feet slipped out from under her. One of the glass slippers shot out along the polished stone floor and into the crowd. There was a terrific tearing noise, and she fell back onto the ground. The fall did not hurt, but weighted down by the awkward bulk of the dress, Elizabeth found it impossible to rise again. Worse still, the wide hoops that made up the foundation of the garment suspended her skirts in the air, exposing the layers upon layers of lacy undergarments beneath. A stunned silence fell like a shroud on the gathered nobles. Only a moment, a heartbeat, passed before she felt hands, gentle and practiced, help her back to her feet.

Liz tried to compose herself, but even as her breathing calmed, she felt a draft across her midsection, and looking down saw that there was a wide tear along the side of the dress from her shoulder nearly to her waist revealing the sheer shift and laced corset beneath. Everyone was staring. She was flush with embarrassment, and felt tears burning her cheeks. Everything was ruined. Among the nobles at the edge of the circle, she saw the King, ashen faced. She could not let him see her like this. She pulled off the other glass slipper and ran.

She ran out of the ballroom. She heard the King, Will, and even Prince Charming all shout her name as one, but she didn't care. Every eye in the ball was on her as she raced up the broad marble steps to the entry hall. Clutching the little shoe tightly against her breast, she ran through the castle halls. She ran and ran until she found her room. Locking the door behind her, Liz threw herself on the bed, and did the only thing she could do. Cry.

Chapter 7

Weaving a Tangled Web

THE MORNING AFTER the ball dawned gloriously. The sun rose above the distant mountains, sending waves of golden light spilling along the soft green folded hills that cascaded down from the eastern end of the castle. Birds nesting in the flowering vines that clung to the tower walls burst into song at first light.

On this beautiful morning, Will Pickett found himself sitting in bed, half awake and terribly hungover, his sister pacing back and forth across his room, doing what she did best, lecturing him about his behavior. That she had been crying all night was evident from her puffy eyes and the hoarseness of her voice; and given everything that had happened, Will couldn't blame her, which was also why he hadn't thrown her out . . . yet. Will wrapped his pillow around his aching head, hoping it would defend him against the constant hammering of his sister's voice, but she ripped the pillow out of his hands and shouted— *really* shouted.

"WILLIAM PICKETT! You may not mind being thrown into the dungeon, or having your head removed from your body, but I didn't spend the last ten years of my life keeping you alive to see you die because you were too much of a fool to listen."

A wave of pain and nausea rippled through his body. "Come off of it, Liz. No one's going to die. And, please, quit shouting! I'll listen. If you quit shouting, I'll listen. I promise."

She tapped her foot hard on the ground, and he turned his head to stare at it until she stopped. "Oh, for heaven's sake, all right, I won't shout, though I daresay you deserve it."

He opened his mouth to point out that it was the King, not he, that had insisted that the Lord Protector attend three separate after-ball fêtes; nor was it he that had initiated the dozens of toasts he had been forced to answer. But all that came out was a dry croak, so he cleared his throat and whispered.

"Okay, explain to me again why it is that we have to run away when the whole kingdom is celebrating us, and toasting us, and dancing with us." Despite his throbbing skull, Will smiled at the memory of his night with the Princess, that golden hair, those crystal blue eyes, her soft body.

Liz rolled her eyes. "You're thinking about the Princess again, aren't you? What would your girlfriend, Gretel, say? Didn't you promise her your undying affection not more than a month ago?"

He swallowed some life back into his voice. "Gretel? Gretel is really just a friend. Besides, she would understand that a fellow in my position—"

"Your position? Your position? You're as bad as the Prince."

Will didn't want a sermon on fidelity. "Is that what this is all about, Liz? The Prince? Is that why you want us to run?" Her lips thinned dangerously, but his head hurt too much to care anymore. "Look, I know what he said about me, about us. Last night was bad. You were embarrassed, and if I knew how to duel, I would."

Her voice, cold as a winter frost, cut him off, "No, you would not, William Jack Pickett." He winced at the use of his full name. That was never a good sign. "But let me answer your question. We have to leave because people have been *celebrating* YOU, and *toasting* YOU, and *dancing* with YOU, and offering YOU the CROWN, because they think YOU killed the dragon. What the Prince said to you at the ball was vile and hateful, but it was also true. We are nobodies, from a poor family, and we have done nothing to deserve our place in this castle."

Will could feel the heat rise in his face. He sat up a little straighter, which seemed to put more strength into his voice. "You're the one that is always reminding me that we are the descendants of lords and ladies. And what about the Princess? I did rescue the Princess. Does that count for nothing?"

Liz sat down on the edge of the bed, the pillow clutched tightly in her hands, and spoke softly. "Yes, we are, and, yes, you did, and you deserve something for that—but you didn't fight a dragon, you didn't *kill* the dragon. Will, don't you see, they think you're a great warrior, a hero."

"I never said I was. All I said was—"

"Don't play that game with me, William," she said sharply. "Don't think for a moment I haven't thought the same excuses a hundred times. 'We never said he killed the dragon, people only assumed it.' 'All I said was that his pitchfork killed the dragon, that's different.' 'We haven't lied, only not told the whole truth.'"

He felt a little sick as she counted off on her fingers each of the justifications he'd been clinging to for the last few weeks. He had to admit, spoken aloud they sounded pathetic.

Tears welled in Liz's eyes, though she held them back as she spoke. "The fact is that we've been lying. Your scarecrow killed the dragon, and he only managed that because you were too lazy to put your pitchfork away. We're the swindlers, Will. We've been the ones bending and twisting the truth to convince the King that we can spin gold from straw. He sees you as his son, Will, but even if he didn't, what we are doing isn't right."

Liz sighed and set the pillow back on the bed next to him. Standing, she walked slowly across the room to where he had hung the tapestry from the dragon's tower. Leaning close, she studied the stitched serpent and then turned back to him.

"Even if you care nothing for the King, think of the

people of this kingdom. In their eyes, you are the Lord Protector—their protector. What does either of us know about protecting anybody? Apart from the little wooden toys Father used to make you as a boy, you've never held a sword. What happens if the people really need you to defend them from some new terror? Will you abandon your post, or will you keep this precious lie even if it means dying?"

She moved to the door and put her hand on the latch. "Back in our field in Prosper, you told me that you could not and would not leave the Princess to rot away in her prison. You were right, Will. You were right to go after her, and I was wrong. I admire you for making me do the right thing. Let me return the favor. I'm not going to tell you what to do. You are a grown man, and you need to make your own decisions. But we are farmers, Will, and like it or not, that's all we know how to do. If you care at all for the people of this kingdom, if you care at all for the King, then you'll go to him and tell him what really happened in that field—that the dragon died and that we did the best we could. But more importantly, that you did everything you could to make sure the Princess was safe and returned to him. I think the King will understand."

He didn't move, didn't speak, as the door opened and then closed behind her. The sun rose higher in the sky, the sounds of horses and people joined and eventually drowned out the singing of the birds, and Will found himself still sitting in his bed, staring at the tapestry and thinking about the dragon and the lady stitched there.

Where was the Princess's knight in shining armor? Did

he exist, had he ever existed? Did she even care at this point?

PRINCESS GWENDOLYN WATCHED unseen from a deep alcove as Lady Elizabeth walked slowly down the hall away from her brother's chamber. She replayed the siblings' overheard conversation in her head again and again, the breakfast tray, originally meant for the Lord Protector, forgotten beside her. How long she stood in that dark corner she did not know, but the toast and tea were cold, and the eggs a congealed, inedible mass when finally she whispered, "It was all a lie, like everything else."

She felt the hope she had been trying to build around him crumble into dust. He wasn't true or trustworthy. No one in this accursed kingdom had even tried to save her. Absent a scarecrow, she would still be abandoned and forgotten, a discarded doll.

She sank to the stone floor and noticed in a detached way that her body was shaking and tears were rolling down her cheeks in little lines. She put out her tongue to taste the bitter saltiness. *Is this sorrow also a lie? No, it is real.* Even if her body still lay in the narrow stone bed atop the tower, and all the rest was illusion, the sorrow was with her as it always had been.

In times past, I ruled the courts. I bestowed favor with a glance and stripped status with a toss of my head. Now that I am a legend, the Princess rescued, I could use my beauty and my gifts to set things right. But I can't set everything to right.

"I wish things could be different," she whispered.

An answering whisper rode an icy current of air down the passage to her. *"Rosslyn."*

"NO!" She gripped the chain around her neck and twisted until the metal bit into the flesh of her neck. "Never again . . . no more wishes."

"Betrayed." She muttered the word to herself like a prayer. "Every time, I am betrayed."

The shadows lurking in the corners of the alcove, like children sensing a story, came away from the wall to crowd around her. Gwendolyn looked about at their half-formed faces and grimaced.

"My first wish was for true love," she whispered weakly. She felt the gold chain bite more deeply into her neck and vaguely wondered how long it would take her to faint. "Then I wished to be a real fairy-tale princess, one that everyone would remember." She could see that the shadows were enjoying her story, because laughing smiles in flickering patterns of light and dark kept appearing and disappearing on their faces. "And then I wished to be rescued, and to return to the world of the living. But ever am I betrayed. Rupert never loved me. My legend was purchased at the cost of my life. Even William Pickett was a lie, and he has brought me here but has left me alone and only half awake"—she paused and looked at her audience—"and surrounded by shadows."

A dull burning ache spread across her neck. With

a start, she remembered the necklace and released the pressure. A sensation like cold fingers raced across her scalp and she shivered at the feeling.

"Still, I suppose it is good to be awake," she said. The shadows looked at her doubtfully.

"Perhaps," she said looking past them and out into the sunlit hallway, "perhaps the problem is wishing. Wishes, like hope, are for the weak." She tilted her head to one side and ran a hand through her long hair, wondering where that phrase had come from. Two of the shadows slipped behind her and began weaving the strands into a filigree of braids. She shivered at their cold touch, but did not protest. When she next spoke, it was to them. "The dragon whispered that to me in my sleep."

While the shadows braided her hair and played at her feet, Gwendolyn reflected that, though cruel, at least the dragon had always been honest. "Oh yes, very honest. The dragon was always sure to tell me of important happenings. Rupert's marriage, the birth of the Prince, the death of my parents, the anniversary of my capture." She looked down at the necklace in her hands and a sudden inspiration struck her. "The dragon told me other things too, about history, magic, power . . . and fairy gold."

She could hear the beast's deep voice like the rumble of distant thunder in her memory. *The key is your lock, little princess. Fairies are not of this world, and their magics, though powerful, need a focus. They bind themselves to this world with their weaving. It is an ancient magic, but remember this, little princess, remember my words and you shall have the power to work your will on the world and make them pay for our imprisonment.*"

Gwendolyn sat there for a moment, staring at the chain in her hand while a plan spun itself in her mind like a web. Then her vision flickered. She shook her head and looked about at the empty alcove and the unused breakfast tray beside her. The shadows shrank away, leaving a half-dozen dark splotches on the floor.

Why am I sitting here alone in the dark? I don't need King Rupert, or Prince Charming or Lord William. I have my own power!

She was distantly aware of a deep sorrow lurking somewhere nearby, but that was the past. All she felt was a pleasant detached certainty, a certainty of action that made her stand and stride without a backward glance at the shadow-children returning now, watching her from the darkened alcove until she was out of sight.

As she made her way back toward her quarters, she considered the sudden change the morning had wrought. Last night she had made the decision to tie her fate to Lord William's, to offer herself to him as wife and lover, and trust, hope, and . . . *wish*, she spit like a curse—yes, *wish*—she repeated with a silent snarl—wish and hope that he could fulfill the happily-ever-after she and her sister had been deprived of: to be Queen of Castle White.

This time would be different. This time, Gwendolyn Mostfair would not wait patiently and contentedly accept what was given. This time she would not put her faith in another and feel the sting of betrayal. No, this time she would seize her happily-ever-after. It would take preparation, but the dragon had taught her all she needed to know. The only problem was time.

Weaving the magic would take time, and to be a queen she needed a king. With Prince Charming disgraced, that left Lord William, which meant he had to be the Lord Protector until she became queen. But if Lady Elizabeth got her way, the two would likely be dead, imprisoned, or on the run by the end of the day. The long and short of it was that Lord William could not be allowed to confess to the King. She could not stop him seeking an audience, so the King would have to be removed. She stopped at the entrance to her chamber and said slowly, "But how?"

With this question echoing in her mind, she entered her quarters. A waiting servant rushed forward to attend her. Waving the girl away and out, the Princess bolted the door. Alone, she wandered the chamber, seeking inspiration. Across the room stood a mirror. A strange woman looked back. It was her body twirling the necklace back and forth between her fingers, but her face was drawn, her eyes were red and swollen from weeping, and gray fingers of mist seemed to draw inward from the margins of the mirror to obscure and twist her features.

It was perfect.

The King was near mad with the desire to see her. She suspected that he wished to seek her forgiveness, forgiveness for a lifetime of neglect! She would give him that audience but would not forgive. She would tell him that seeing him at the ball, and remembering them together, had driven her to distraction—which was mostly true anyway. To relieve himself of even a measure of his guilt, he would go wherever she commanded for howsoever long she desired. After all, fleeing and hiding is what the King did best.

In the end, I was nothing to him but a poor substitute for Rosslyn.

Memories of Rosslyn came rushing unbidden out of the past. The visions played out on the surface of the mirror: a dark clearing in the forest, the fairy, her wish, and then finding her sister's lifeless body. The pain of her grief bent her double and threatened to sweep her into a deeper darkness. With an effort, Gwendolyn shook herself free from the memories. The gray mist and shadows departed, and her own reflection returned.

"I must hold myself together, to be this sad little princess for a time," she said to the reflection. "Let the King see my misery, and he will be gone from the castle within the hour."

She rose and strode from the room toward the King's chamber. As she walked, she turned the situation over again in her mind. *After the King, I must turn my attention to his son.* Though the Prince had certainly made an enemy of the Picketts with his performance last night, if sufficiently nagged by Elizabeth, William might choose to confess to the Prince instead. *I need time. Time to bind William to me.*

When she first met them, Gwendolyn had thought the Picketts were out of place in the castle, but on reflection, they were the perfect addition to the court: a pair of liars to bookend an old coward and a young fool.

AN INSISTENT POUNDING on the door of his bedchamber brought Charming awake with a groan. He blinked against the bright midday light streaming through the open balcony doors. The Prince had been having a dream that left him at once contented and melancholy. He grasped desperately at the fading visions, but the more he tried to remember, the more they slipped away.

He cradled a glass slipper against his chest, and it sparkled in the sunlight like a gem. It was her slipper, Lady Elizabeth's. She had been in his dream. How could he not dream of her? Last night they had danced, and it had been almost perfect. Then that damnable Lady Rapunzel interrupted. Well, Rapunzel could be sure of one thing—he'd never forget her name again. After his fight with Will, after his humiliation of Lady Elizabeth, he had been banished to his chambers by his father, the King, where he had drunk . . . *how much?* He looked around the room at the half-dozen discarded wine bottles and groaned.

The knocking returned and reminded him that he ached from head to toe, but mostly head. Though he intended to deliver a royal command, the words that escaped were a weak, "Go away. In the name of the King, go away!"

Princess Gwendolyn's voice came sweetly, but very firmly, through the door. "Prince Charming, are you there? If I may, I would like to have words with you."

Bloody hell! The Princess.

He sat up, and the sudden rise made his head spin and his vision grow dark. He looked at the mirror hung on the wall opposite his bed and barely suppressed a yelp of shock. Reflected in the glass was a horror. His eyes were shot with red and surrounded by heavy bags. His nose was mottled blue and purple, and looked two sizes larger than normal, and a brown-red trail of crusted blood twisted down the right side of his face. He blanched as he saw that even his perfectly coifed locks were matted and stiff. There was no one, apart from Lady Elizabeth, that he wished to see less right now than Princess Gwendolyn.

He attempted to answer her, but now his stomach had started to betray him. "Hmmm . . . hmm . . . Princess Gwendolyn, I am afraid I am indisposed at the moment. Perhaps I could call on you . . . hmmmm . . . later."

He closed his eyes. If she did not see him, and he regained couplet, he could save this from becoming another incident. Yet he found couplet was impossible when one was trying not to retch.

"I'm afraid that is impossible, Your Highness. This is a matter of urgency."

The handle to the door turned and, aghast, Charming realized that in last night's stupor, he had failed to bolt his door. He looked about the room for a place to hide, but it was impossible. He could barely move. If he tried to dash to his changing room, she would likely find him collapsed on the floor in a pool of his own sick. Still, he was Prince Charming, and if any man could find a way to salvage this, he would.

Thinking quickly, he pulled the cords holding back the curtains on his canopy bed. The door opened as the heavy velvet fabric fell into place on either side of him.

The side drapes threw dark shadows onto the head of the bed, partially obscuring him, and he settled himself as far back as he could into the darkness.

There was movement in the room. "Prince Charming? Are you still abed?"

Her voice sounded strange, like she was on the verge of laughing. He heard her graceful steps, and the curtain to his left rippled as though blown by a breeze. He gathered himself and then looked down at his hands. He was still holding the damned glass slipper, Lady Elizabeth's slipper. He shoved the incriminating footwear beneath his pillow just as Princess Gwendolyn appeared in the open square of light at the foot of his bed.

"Are you there, dear Prince?"

Couplet still escaped him. The mere thought of attempting verse made his head hammer with pain. He cleared his throat again, then said, "I am here, Princess Gwendolyn. I fear I find myself unwell this morning. I know that a man of my renowned constitution is rarely in such a condition, yet I fear that even I have had far better days. I was about to call the Royal Chirurgeon when you arrived, so perhaps it would be better if you called again later."

He could see her now, peering into the gloom. With a sharp intake of breath, she asked, "My dear Prince Charming, what has that deranged woman done to you?"

No sooner had the question slipped from her red lips, than she disappeared from view and the curtain to the right of him began undulating in and out as though she were searching for an opening. Charming grabbed the edge of the cloth, holding tight to prevent her from pulling it aside. A tug-of-war ensued that was as desperate as it was childish and pointless.

"My dear . . . Princess . . . Gwendolyn, please do not bother . . . yourself. I will be fine. I"—with a strength that was alarming, the Princess yanked the curtain from his hands. Bright sunlight flooded the bed, and he shielded his eyes from the stabbing pain that followed. Charming was winded from his struggle and could only gasp out a weak—"just need some rest."

Gwendolyn looked appalled when she gazed down on him. "My poor Prince Charming, let me tend your injuries." She looked first at his nose, and then pulled back his bangs uncovering the black-and-purple bruise there. "That awful woman. How many times did she strike you? To think that she would dare lay hands on you, and in front of the entire court."

From nowhere, she produced a cloth and a basin of cool water. With a surprisingly gentle hand, she began scrubbing off the dried blood.

"Please, Princess Gwendolyn, do not concern yourself with me. I assure you I have had worse," he lied. "Please, tell me what words we may exchange."

"Oh no, my prince," she protested, "I would not burden you, not now that I know your condition."

He overrode her. "Princess, I assure you, nothing would make me feel better than to put your mind at rest so that you may return to your leisure. After all, helping a lady in need is my highest aim."

"Oh, Prince Charming, you are so noble. I feel I cannot, not now."

Charming knew he was only barely holding himself together. This interview could not last much longer or he would either pass out or sick-up all over the lady. Barely stifling a belch, he began, "P-Please, Princess Gwendolyn, I will not rest easy until I know what has put you in such a state."

She did not look at him but rather turned her back and addressed the open window. "Prince, it is your father, the King, he—"

She turned, and her face was a mask of anguish. A sudden fear shot through Prince Charming. "My father, the King, is he unwell? Speak, tell me what is wrong?"

She paused a few agonizing heartbeats before answering, in which time all manner of terrible thoughts raced crossed the Prince's mind. Finally, when he thought he might have to shake her to get her to speak again, she said hurriedly, "No, he is well, it is just he —he—oh, how can I say this to you? The King has fled the castle, and no one is sure where he is."

He had imagined many things, but not this. His father, the King, had left? At this time? A sudden suspicion grew within him. "Did he say why he was leaving? And why do I receive the news from your lips, Princess?"

Gwendolyn moved to turn away again and he caught her arm. He continued, "Pray, tell me what you know of my father, and be quick!"

"Oh, Prince, my Prince, you must forgive him. He is not himself. He—"

The sickness in his stomach was returning. He felt

weak and tired and ill-mannered, so he cut her off mid-sentence. "Speak plainly, Princess. Pray speak plainly."

To her credit she did just as he asked, without emotion. "I have been told by advisors trusted to the King that he has abandoned the court out of shame. He fled early this morning and left word that he would not return until you have restored his good name, or the Lord Protector is crowned. Riders have been sent to all of the royal residences, but thus far there is no report of him." As an afterthought, she added a monotone, "I am sorry."

Charming was silent as the full weight of this revelation struck him. He knew the Princess was standing there, watching and measuring him, and for once he did not care. *My father, the King, would rather banish himself from the court he loves than stay another moment in my presence. Is this just a retreat or, even now, is my father, the King, being forced from the throne for my repeated failures?* He could feel the sting of tears in his eyes, and still he could not rise to fight them back.

Gwendolyn's voice cut through his thoughts. "My dear Prince, it gives me pain to see you like this. I just did not want you to hear the news from someone that did not care for you as I do."

Something in those last words made Charming look back at her. "Care for me? I thought Lord William, the Lord Protector—you danced with him the whole night." He stopped, realizing that the raw need in his voice was not for the Princess, but for another.

She was beside him in a flash, stroking the palm of his

hand with her fingertips. "Prince, don't you see that I was only doing my duty? I could barely keep the clod from breaking my toes, so often did he step on them during our dance. All night I looked for you, but you were engaged with Lady Rapunzel." She lifted his hand to her breast, clutching it tightly. "We were meant for each other, you and I, Prince. As for Lord William, I could no more be content with that dirt-farmer peasant than you could be with his sister." She laughed openly at the suggestion that he might feel something for Lady Elizabeth.

At Lady Elizabeth's name, his stomach became uneasy again. "Princess Gwendolyn, I don't think—"

"Shhh," she hushed him. "I know that it seems impossible now, but we can still be together."

"But what about my father, the King—?"

"Of course, you must do your best to seek his return," she interrupted again. He was already tired of her penchant for interrupting. A fortnight ago, no one would have dreamed of interrupting him. She continued. "But don't you see the solution to bringing us together and satisfying your father, the King, is one in the same?"

She dropped his hand and began speaking quickly. "You need a chance to rebuild your reputation in the court, but you'll never be able to do so while people are comparing your deeds with those of the Lord Protector. He killed a dragon, *the* dragon, and you have spent your days in more . . . romantic pursuits. No one can blame you for that, but you need to leave this castle, go out among the people, and prove your mettle. You have to show them the hero that you truly are and restore your name and honor."

He had to admit, it made sense. If his father, the King, was in trouble, it might give Charming a way to restore his name and position. He would venture forth and be the Lord Protector in deed, even if Will remained it in title. Just thinking about questing and fighting was making him feel like his old self again. He knew he was a better man than William Pickett, how could he not be? As far as he could tell, Will could not sing or recite poetry; and the way he slouched all the time, he would look a mess atop even the most noble of steeds. The Prince had spent his whole life being pampered and praised and told that he was destined to be the kingdom's hero and king. Now it was time to prove it.

At some point, the Princess had risen and was now standing at the foot of the bed, gazing into the mirror hung on the wall there. She turned and was highlighted perfectly by the sun. Gwendolyn was without a doubt beautiful, and honor demanded that a lady's beauty be recognized and remarked upon. He had to attempt couplet. He concentrated and felt a quiet confidence infuse his body. Prince Charming half rose in his bed, then turned so that only his less battered left side could be seen.

> "Gwendolyn, most fair, hear these words true,
> I shall venture forth and prove myself
> to you."

At long last, he had regained couplet.

The Princess sighed. "Oh, Prince Charming, you remind me of the King, when he was a younger man." She blew him a kiss and said, "Do not tarry a moment longer in your noble pursuit. Every day you delay is another day that our love is denied."

The Prince thought one more line of verse was in order, but by the time he had captured the proper turn of a phrase, the door was closing behind her. She was gone. He smiled. *She was clearly overwhelmed by my poetry and had to make her escape before she was overcome.*

He leaned back on his pillow, hands folded behind his head, and addressed the canopy above. "I know that duty demands that she be my queen, and I will do my duty in time, but I cannot say the thought fills me with joy. For now, it is best that she is gone."

Charming shook his head sadly. There was an inevitability to fulfilling the demands of honor that he had always avoided thinking about. He could not imagine being with the former love of his father, the King. The thought disgusted him. It would be like sleeping with his, well, mother in a way. In time he would learn to accept it, he supposed. He sighed softly to himself and then dismissed the issue as a problem for another day.

He considered the idea of a quest. There were certainly enough monstrosities roaming the lands. A manticore, a giant, possibly an ogre, or a troll or two would certainly remind the people, and maybe even Lady Elizabeth, who he was and, in turn, cover his father, the King, in reflected glory. The matter at hand now was how to make himself presentable enough to go out on a quest. Once he started receiving the cheers of the people, he would need to look the part of the hero. Perhaps with some subtle makeup and the right hat. Yes, there were certainly possibilities.

He swept the covers aside and jumped out of bed. He felt at once renewed as he imagined the songs of redemption and triumph that would be sung about him. He would be compared to the phoenix rising from the ashes.

Standing by the open window, he struck his most heroic pose and, taking a deep breath, declared, "I swear I will make my father, the King, proud—or die trying."

Then a wave of nausea struck and he fell to his knees retching.

WILL WAS WANDERING the castle halls, lost, both literally and metaphorically.

After giving himself what he thought was an appropriate amount of time to work up his courage and mourn what would certainly be his last day as Lord Protector and Dragon Slayer, he had packed a small satchel with his things, dressed in his farm clothes, and marched off to face the King. His plan was quite simple: confess to his lie and beg his sister's ignorance, not that she had to know that in advance. He hoped he would just be sent away in disgrace, but was prepared, as much as anyone could be, for the worst.

As usual, things didn't go to plan.

When he arrived at the throne room, he was informed that the King had left the castle and no one would tell him where His Royal Majesty had gone or when he would return. As confessing to the King was supposed to have removed future decision making from his hands, and maybe even his head from his body, he wasn't sure now what to do. On top of that, Will had a habit of wandering aimlessly when he needed to think. True to form, his feet had begun to roam, first down this hall and then through that great chamber and then up that stair, until he was adrift in the sea of stone that was the castle.

Thoroughly lost, he stopped at an intersection of five passages. Each corridor looked just like the other. They were each lined with armor, lit by candles, and decorated with the King's gaudy coat of arms. Will had just resigned himself to being lost when the Prince, dressed in what could only be described as fashionable adventuring garb, and wearing the largest, floppiest, featheriest hat Will had ever seen, rounded a corner and strode dramatically toward him.

The hat seemed to obscure most of the top half of the his face, down to his heavily powdered nose, and must have made it nearly impossible for the Prince to see any-thing that was not directly in front of him, which might explain why Charming didn't acknowledge or even react to Will's presence until he was a few paces from him. When their eyes did finally meet, there was a sharp intake of breath from the Prince and he stopped midstride.

The two men faced off across the five-sided space formed by the juncture of the passages. Will had no idea what to say, and feared a conversation with the Prince would lead to another fight. So he bit his lip and hoped the other man would pass, but the Prince just stood staring back through a curtain of brim and feathers. The silence stretched on uncomfortably.

"Prince Charming," he said gruffly with a short nod.

"Lord Protector," Charming said from behind the cover of his hat.

Another silence descended between them and Will began to feel guilty. In a way, the Prince had been right last night. Will suddenly realized he could solve at least one of his problems by confessing to the Prince. But how to begin?

"Um, nice hat," he said, remembering the Prince's fondness for fashion.

Prince Charming tilted his hat down as though examining the inside of its brim for something to say. "Thank you, Will. I do think it sets off my outfit rather well. I see you have chosen to wear something . . . comfortable. Perhaps the Royal Tailor has not had time to make you another suit, but never fear, the man is nothing if not industrious. Can you imagine that he put this remarkable chapeau together in just the last few hours?"

Will examined the mass of brims and feathers and peaks. The thing looked like what you'd get if you stitched four or five different hats together at random. Still, the Prince seemed proud of it, so he said the only thing he could think of. "That is hard to believe."

"I know! I know! Well, the man is a genius." Suddenly the Prince's eyes narrowed. At least, Will thought they narrowed. "Where are you off to, up here near the quarters of the Royal Family?"

So that's where I am. Now was the time; he had to confess. "To be honest, Prince Charming, I'm lost. You see I went to talk to the King about him making me the Lord Protector, but he was gone, and I don't know what to do. You see, there has been a terrible mistake. I'm just a farmer, and, well . . . I . . . I know you don't want me to talk about the dragon and all, but—"

In an instant, the Prince had closed the gap between them and wrapped his arm around Will's shoulder. For a moment, Will thought the Prince might put a hand over his mouth to stop him from talking. "Will, may I still call you Will?"

The Prince did not give him time to answer but continued, without pause. "I know what I did, what I said last night, was wrong, and I am sorry. And I am most dreadfully sorry for what happened to Lady Elizabeth, but, and I know one thing does not seem connected to the other—but they are. I must stress that you not talk about the dragon! It's . . . it's . . . unbecoming. So can we say bygones . . . ?"

This time the Prince did pause, but only for a second, and not really long enough for Will to do anything but say "Well"—before Charming rushed on—"Great. You know, a lesser man would not have been able to let that go. Now, back to your problem with the dragon. I think I know what you're going through."

The Prince gestured grandly at nothing and began to walk them down one of the corridors, "You see, William, all great heroes have a moment of crisis when they feel they do not really deserve the plaudits that have been bestowed upon them. These moments of doubt are only natural. I know you will be surprised to hear that I myself have recently had reason to question even myself."

The Prince took a hard left and led them onto a large open balcony that looked north across a dark wood to a marching line of snow-capped peaks beyond. It was amazing how he did that. Until a few seconds ago, Will was certain they were somewhere on the ground floor. The Prince pointed toward the mountain range. "What you need to do is get out there, where you can be a hero again."

The Prince stopped his oration and studied Will from beneath a particularly large peacock feather. Will regarded the Prince in return. Charming was being uncommonly decent, and it made the young Pickett suspicious. Up close and in the full light of day, Will could see that the Prince's nose had suffered mightily from Lady Rapunzel's anger, which probably explained the makeup and the hat, but there was something else, something in his eyes, something sly and cunning.

When the Prince spoke again he did so slowly, almost like he was picking his words with a very deliberate care. "Tell me, Will, have you thought about your duty to the kingdom? As Lord Protector, you know the people look to you to keep them safe. There are so many dangers out there beyond . . . the dragon."

"That is what I was trying to tell you earlier, Prince Charming. I haven't really *done* anything."

The Prince jumped on this comment, and now the calculation had been replaced by a manic enthusiasm.

"Exactly, Will, exactly. You really haven't. Trolls are still terrorizing innocent travelers, the woods are overrun with rabid boars, old hags cook children daily, and giants are dismembering knights at an alarming rate."

Will swallowed nervously. What the bloody hell was he supposed to do about giants! The Prince continued enthusiastically.

"I was about to venture forth to rid the kingdom of these threats once and for all." He gestured at his clothes and sword, which he seemed to think was final proof of his determination. "Come with me. Together we will be able to accomplish nearly twice as much. What is more, it will hearten the people to see us together, to be able to measure us . . . and celebrate our great deeds, of course."

Will was no fool. He could see that the Prince was thinking more about his own salvation than about confirming Will's position as Lord Protector, but it would give Will a chance to prove to his sister and the King and the people that he deserved his title. Maybe he could be more than a farmer after all, and what better person to show him how to be heroic than the man that had been training to be a hero since birth?

He was still thinking it all through when he heard himself say, "I would be honored to journey with you, Prince Charming."

"Excellent! Let us away to the stables." Charming turned to go and stopped. His eyes swept back over Will's clothes, "Well, perhaps first to the tailor. You need a proper questing outfit. We must be presentable."

Will wanted to ask who he needed to be "presentable" for if they were just going into the wilderness to fight trolls, but thought better of it. By now he knew there was no better way of annoying the Prince than questioning the value of fashion.

So it was, in the light of the setting sun, that Prince Charming and the Lord Protector, Dragon Slayer and Knight of the Realm, William Pickett, set forth on a pair of loyal and particularly noble-looking steeds. The Prince had determined that they should not advertise their leaving too broadly, so there was a sparse crowd of a few hundred of Charming's closest friends lining the road and waving banners from the battlements of the castle as they rode across the drawbridge and turned north into the dark woods, where rumor said there were many wicked creatures that needed slaying.

In a high balcony, far above the tumult of the well-wishers, Princess Gwendolyn scowled down at the two as they rode away. "The fool, the damned fool. The plan was so simple. Only a complete moron could mess it up, and yet he managed. All you had to do was leave, and LEAVE WILLIAM PICKETT TO ME!"

These last words were shouted, not that they could be heard over the roar of the mob below. She was not so worried about Will confessing to the Prince during their journey, not now that he was going off to prove himself. Surely, had he meant to admit his lie he would have done so, and even now be rotting in a cell beneath her feet. But how could she woo him while he was off on this idiotic quest. She was about to shout something else when she sensed movement behind her.

Lady Elizabeth rushed to the edge of the balcony and leaned over to peer at the shadowy figures in the distance. "William," she shouted pointlessly, "William Pickett! You come back here!"

Gwendolyn watched the woman out of the corner of her eye. A note was clutched in her hand. *So her brother hadn't the nerve to tell her that he was going in person.* He probably knew that would have been the end of his adventure. *Why are all the men in my life so useless?* The Princess sighed, then turned, fixing a look of alarm on her face.

"Dear Lady Elizabeth, please don't worry yourself. I'm sure the Lord Protector will keep the Prince safe."

The timing was perfect. She had caught the woman with her mouth open midshout. But the reaction was not what she had anticipated. Lady Elizabeth turned with flashing, stormy eyes, and an expression that almost made Gwendolyn flinch.

"Thank you, Princess Gwendolyn, I appreciate your reassurances. Unfortunately, I am not reassured. Those two boys can hardly be trusted to dress themselves, and now I'm supposed to believe they can go off and fight trolls or whatnot without getting their heads bashed open? Now, if you will excuse me, I must go see if I can find a rider to go after them, or a horse of my own if none are willing to try."

Before the Princess could respond, Lady Elizabeth

left the rail and withdrew into the castle. The Princess watched her as she left. *A formidable woman.* Perhaps, she thought, it would be best that the castle was empty of anyone of importance save she and Lady Elizabeth. It was clear that she would have to remove *the Lady* to have any chance of ensnaring her brother.

Chapter 8

Tolling the Troll

IN THE DAYS after the death of the dragon, a great many vile and noxious monsters came out of hiding, in part no longer afraid of becoming a treat for the dragon, and in part out of a desire to replace her in legend. For Gnarsh the Troll, it was the latter reason that brought him down out of a mountain cave where he had been lurking in semi-retirement for the better part of a decade.

Though he was a fearsome sight—fit to haunt night-mares—in the time of the dragon no one cared a whit about trolls generally, or about Gnarsh more particularly. Nothing seemed to impress the perpetually terrified and increasingly jaded peasants of the kingdom, not his long daggerlike talons, nor his great glowing googly eyes, nor his maw of bone-yellow pointed teeth dripping with fetid dark spittle that oozed and stank, nor his mottled green and black scaled flesh, nor even his imposing massive boulder-like size. There was just no way to compete with the dragon's flames, razor-sharp claws, and swordlike teeth.

It hadn't been right, not at all.

Now things would be different. The dragon was dead. The news had spread across the land and even reached his mountain refuge. It was his time, the time of Gnarsh. Of course, he well knew that he couldn't simply terrorize the nearest village and hope to replace the dragon as the most fearsome monster in the land. These things took time—it was all about location and marketing and of course who you ate.

Still, his comeback had started out pretty well, all things considered. He had found a bridge, a sturdy wide wooden bridge along an old road, over a deep rushing river, just at the edge of a dark forest. Though not a busy thoroughfare, it was the perfect place to build a reputation without putting himself at risk of being skewered. The fact is after so much time off, he wasn't in the best of shape. This quiet, secluded bridge would be exactly the sort of place where he could slowly grow his standing among the ranks of menacing beasties. Once his stature was assured, and paunch reduced, he could move to a more high-profile bridge and demand tolls of food or gold or virgins, depending on his mood, and spend the rest of his days lounging in the shadows, dangling his feet in the swift waters, and feeding his pet fish.

He liked fish. They were so elegantly slimy.

His great dream, of course, was to attack Castle White, to hear the screams of the men and women echoing through those stone corridors, to be the horror to the people that the dragon had been. A repulsive smile stretched across his face as he imagined the scene. The knights would flee in terror before him, then he would help himself to a light luncheon of any maidens that remained, and then Gnarsh the Troll, pleasantly satisfied, would retire to the moat to feed the goldfish there. In time, the castle would fall into a fashionably ruinous state of disrepair with lots of thick hanging vines, black-bodied spiders, and moss.

He also liked moss. It was such a miserable plant.

He looked down at the fish nibbling at the unidentifiable crud between his toes and worried that perhaps this bridge was too far off the beaten path. It had been two weeks since the dragon had died and no one had crossed, not even a single misplaced, lost, or abandoned child. It was getting so bad that he was tempted to eat the family of goats incessantly bleating in the nearby field. Thus far he had resisted. It would be terrible for his reputation if it got out that he had been reduced to eating common livestock. No, Gnarsh only ate people, lovely, juicy, crunchy people—he was a true humanitarian.

So, he waited—and reminded himself that he needed to be patient. *Patience.*

It wasn't right, not at all.

Today, though, something felt different. He could smell it in the damp air under his bridge. Beyond the intoxicating miasma of wood rot, body odor, and old bones that made this place home, there was something else, something wonderfully foul—to Gnarsh, it smelled like luck. Today would be his day.

"SO, WILL, ACCORDING to the venerable wise man we encountered at the wishing well, this should be the bridge where the evil troll lives," said the Prince, keeping the feathered hat down in front of his face. Will still had no idea how he managed to ride when he could barely see.

"Um, do you mean that old farmer back there?" asked Will. "I really wish you had let me or your squire, Tomas, stop and help him. He was having a hard time pulling up that bucket."

"William," said Charming in a tone that reminded Will ever so slightly of his sister, "We do not refer to our squires by name. They are perfectly happy being called squires, and then when the book is written things don't get mucked up with a lot of extra names." Will opened his mouth to say something about the fact that Tomas, the squire, could actually hear the words the Prince was saying, but Charming charged ahead. "I think I should take the lead in this battle. After all, we don't want a repeat of the incident with the witch, not to mention that debacle with the giant. As I've been trying to tell you these past days, when you are on an adventure, as we are, you must always consider the legend to be written. You must be constantly wary of being banal, or else you risk losing the true purpose of your quest—glory. Do you understand?"

"Yes," said Will out of habit, though like many things the Prince said, he really didn't find much wisdom in the words. Will thought their encounters with the witch and the giant had turned out well given that they hadn't been turned into frogs or eaten. The fact was, for all the man's reading and education, Charming didn't seem to have a lick of sense. For instance, the Prince had spent the better part of the previous morning trying to convince him that there existed in a nearby kingdom a pair of weavers that could spin cloth that only the most cultured and sophisticated of people could see. When Will had asked why in the world you would ever want clothes that were only visible to some people, the Prince had explained, without any apparent irony, that wearing such clothes would make it a simple matter to separate out those that were truly worthy of your company. All Will could think was that you would still be naked to everyone else. For not the first time since they had their talk, he shook away thoughts of the Princess in a gown of such fabric, and blushed.

"There is no need to be embarrassed Will, you'll learn these things," said Charming.

They were nearing the bridge when, without warning, Charming pulled hard on his reins with a, *"Ho, Champion!"*

The Prince's white charger reared back and pawed the air, and Charming leapt from the back of the horse in a cloud of dust. Behind them Will heard Tomas muttering darkly about young fools and the laming of horses. The Prince did not seem to notice, and stepping away from his horse, he spread his legs slightly, extended his arms out to each side, and shouted, "SQUIRE, PREPARE ME FOR BATTLE!" His words echoed across the bridge to the other side of the river, where a lush band of green grass grew, and then into the shadows of the dark wood beyond. A small herd of goats in the nearby field wandered down from the grassy hill where they'd been grazing to stand at the edge of the fence and bleat at them.

The Prince looked over in annoyance. "Will, you are"—he cleared his throat—"You were a farmer, could you deal with those wretched creatures? Their damnable braying is ruining this heroic moment."

Will was about to tell the Prince that goats don't bray, donkeys bray, but knew it was pointless, so he grabbed a loaf of hard bread from his pack and wandered over to the fence. He stuck his hand through the rails and began feeding pieces to the animals, which quieted as they chewed. Meanwhile, Tomas was busily tying and strapping and buckling armor onto Charming.

Will glanced down at the goats. There were three of them, and they were obviously a family. One was small, maybe a kid, one was of an average size, but the third was an enormous beast, rivaling a small pony in stature. The goats looked back at him.

He whispered, "I've got to tell you, this is not how I saw myself spending my first battle with a troll—no offense."

One of the goats bleated what almost sounded like a "Naaan Taaaken."

Will did a double-take, but the goats just stared at

him, their mouths still moving, chewing the hard bread. He turned his attention back to the Charming's preparations. Tomas had removed the large feathered hat from the Prince's head. Will cringed as he saw the bruises running across Charming's face and the swelling on his forehead.

Just as Will was wondering if it was a good idea for the Prince to even be standing, much less fighting, Tomas thrust a gleaming silver helmet down over Charming's head and onto his shoulders. The old man adjusted a few clasps and bolts, and then clapped the Prince on the back with a metallic bang. "You are ready for battle, Your Highness."

Gone was the fop with the enormous hat, and in his place was a powerful knight in full shining armor. Will caught his breath as he realized that the Prince did indeed look the part of a hero.

The Prince drew his sword and Tomas gave him a shield. He saluted Will. "I would advise preparing yourself, if not for combat, since I intend to slay the monster myself, then for observing, so that you may properly recount my victory." With this, he strode purposefully toward the wide wooden bridge. He raised the visor on his helmet with the edge of his sword hilt and shouted, "TROLL, SHOW YOURSELF. Your doom is at hand, but know this, your fall this day shall be recounted through the ages as one of the many triumphs for Prince Charming!"

"Niiice maaahnologue. You must aaadmit, he's gaaaht styyyle," said a voice from behind Will.

"Huh, I'm not iiimpressed. Diiid you see hiiis faaace?" asked a much deeper voice.

Will put his hand on his sword and turned, but all he saw were the goats. The trio looked at him with identically bored expressions. Then the littlest butted his head against Will's leg in an obvious request for more bread. Will absentmindedly fed the kid as he watched the unfolding drama on the bridge and quietly wondered if he was losing his mind.

"Troll, show yourself," commanded Charming as he beat on his shield with his sword and stepped onto the bridge.

GRABBING THE SIDE of the rail with one of his enormous taloned hands, Gnarsh vaulted from the riverbank beneath the bridge to land opposite the armored Charming. The wooden timbers of the structure creaked ominously beneath his massive bulk. The troll grinned, baring all of his bone-yellow pointed teeth dripping with fetid dark spittle that oozed and stank, and gave a terrifying roar, simultaneously extending his arms wide to demonstrate his massive size and give the Prince a full view of his long dagger-like talons and mottled green and black scales. Gnarsh smiled an evil smile as he saw the horses whinny and rear in panic and the squire and young man standing behind the knight flinch with obvious fear, but his smile turned to a frown as the knight . . . *laughed*? The troll blinked his great googly eyes in surprise.

Prince Charming chuckled merrily beneath his visor. "Aha! At last, you have chosen to show yourself, fearsome monster! I applaud your dramatic entrance. If you fight with as much flair, I promise you I shall place you foremost in my epic poem. Now let the battle BEGIN!" The Prince shouted enthusiastically as he charged to the attack, swinging his blade.

This isn't right, thought Gnarsh. *Not at all.*

WILL'S EYES GREW large as he watched Charming battle the massive creature. "That's one giant troll." He couldn't leave the Prince to face that monstrosity on his own. He had no idea what he could do, but he had to try. Will drew his sword, half raising it and taking a few halting paces forward.

The Prince must have sensed his movement, because even though locked in pitched battle with a creature three times his size, he paused, held the beast off with his shield, and pointed back at Will with his sword. "Hold, William! Your services will be best used in keeping those damnable goats quiet and witnessing my magnificence. I must face this creature alone! It is only as much as I—it— deserves."

Shamefaced, Will sheathed his sword and returned to the fence. "Smaaart move," one of the goats bleated, but Will did not hear. He felt suddenly very small. Liz was right. This is what the kingdom needed. How could he possibly protect the people? He was a farce, a lie. He began chewing on the side of his thumb.

On the bridge, the Prince was a blur of flashing metal as he whirled his sword about with expert skill and waded between the troll's talons with utter fearlessness, blocking the monster's strikes with his shield and slashing him here and there with his darting blade. Charming laughed again, as if he were truly enjoying the fight. Will shook his head in disbelief; the Prince seemed to have a death wish, why antagonize a creature that could pulverize you into jelly?

Charming's laughter did seem to be having an affect on the creature. If possible, the troll seemed to have swollen in size with his growing rage until he towered like a small mountain above the steel-clad Prince. "Laugh now, but you will learn fear, little man!" belched Gnarsh as he tried to catch the fast-moving Charming. "I'm Gnarsh the Nasty, foulest troll in the realm!"

The Prince stepped back and saluted the creature with his sword, "An excellent attempt to menace me, Gush. Will, pay close attention, a record must be kept of our dramatic exchange."

"My name is Gnarsh!" the troll bellowed sulfurously, smashing both of his fists on the spot the Prince had just vacated.

Will hoped the record would not include them all being eaten.

CHARMING WAS HAVING a spectacular time. Finally, he was doing what he was born to do—fighting monsters. That the creature had a name would make it all the better for the stories, if only he could trust Will and his brutish squire to bear accurate witness to his greatness. He was certain now that the Lord Protector, that Will, couldn't match him. The man was slack-jawed with shame, and this would be only the first of many humiliations for the buffoon on their adventure. This was how a hero's life should be, besting his rival and an evil creature at the same time.

Gnarsh reached out with his left arm and grabbed the Prince's shield, hoping to rip it away, but in doing so provided Charming with the opening he had been waiting for. Instead of backing away, as any other knight would have done, the Prince stepped forward so that he was inches from the beast. He inhaled the creature's foul rotting breath and smiled behind his steel visor—he *had* him. Charming planted his feet and slashed up violently at the beast as it grappled with his shield. The powerful stroke cut completely through the monster's shoulder, severing the troll's arm.

Gouts of black ichor spewed from the severed limb, coating the bridge like oil. The troll screamed in agony and collapsed, shaking the wooden timbers of the bridge in a single mighty shock.

Charming stepped away from the quivering body of the troll so that no more than an artistic spray of the foul blood stained his gleaming armor. His visor scarcely concealed his smile. He turned his back on the beast and walked back toward Will and the squire, tossing his shield aside and doffing his helmet.

"Did you see that, Will? That is how you defeat a monster!" The thought of his bruised face crossed the Prince's mind briefly, but Charming was too happy to care. He sheathed his sword emphatically and raised his arms above his head. *I'm back! My father, the King, will surely be impressed when I present him with the head of this horror.*

"Squire, retrieve the bottle of Chateau de Chateau, and the wine goblets," ordered the Prince as he sauntered back toward them across the bridge.

"My Prince! Behind you!" said the squire.

He looked up at the man. Something was wrong. Rather than the rapt admiration Charming had expected, both the squire and Will were staring past him in horror.

"Um, Prince Charming, I'm afraid he's not dead yet," said Will.

The goats next to Will bleated suddenly, and for all the world it sounded like they were laughing. Charming gave them a murderous look and they quieted. Surely, he thought, these men are overreacting. The blow had been a mortal wound, and the life would soon leave the troll even if the monster had not yet expired. He would just have to remove the head to make certain. He drew his sword and turned around.

The troll's green scales had turned a deep purple. Seething with fury, he shoved his severed arm back into his shoulder. With several audible cracks and pops, the sinews knitted back together. Gnarsh flexed his taloned hand. The little cocky Prince had laughed at him— AGAIN.

Gnarsh spun his googly eyes and gnashed his yellow teeth. "I'll crack your bones and suck the marrow!" he roared and loped across the bridge toward the knight.

Though he had tossed his shield aside and was unhelmed, Charming returned the creature's roar and ran to meet the beast's charge.

WILL HAD NEVER realized how truly insane Prince Charming was. Only half armored, Charming was certain to be crushed by the monster. Will chewed even harder on his finger as he realized that if the troll killed the Prince, he would be next.

"Whaaat an aaass!" the middle-sized goat seemed to say between bites of a prickly thistle plant that had grown up through the slats of the fence.

"You said it," a distracted Will murmured, and then shouted out, "PRINCE CHARMING, COME BACK! YOU ARE NOT FULLY ARMORED."

The Prince gave a jaunty wave in response, and then timing the troll's speed to perfection, he sidestepped the creature as it pounced and thrust his blade into the ribs of the beast as it landed. The sharp sword dug deep into the monster, sending black ichor spraying across the bridge. For once, Charming did not pause to admire his masterstroke. Instead, he spun behind the troll with the grace of a striking snake. The creature looked about for the Prince, it seemed to have no idea that he was standing directly behind him. Charming winked at Will and, smiling broadly, swung his blade in a wide arc and cut the monster off at the knees. Once again, the troll howled and collapsed to the ground.

The Prince, breathing a little heavier now, spun back to Will, who was wide-eyed in astonishment. After everything he had seen of Prince Charming at the castle, who knew that the man could actually fight, much less that he would be a true sword master. It made Will paled at the memory of their first meeting. *Absent the hand of fate, and a bloody great chunk of metal, he would have killed me without breaking a sweat.*

"Will, watch as I deliver the coup de grace. I will make it tasteful, as befits such a worthy opponent." Charming almost turned, then stopped and looked at him more closely. "Are you feeling okay? You look a little green."

As the Prince was talking, the troll was literally regathering himself. He lunged forward, grabbed his severed legs and, with a sickening wet sound and a painful grunt, shoved them back onto his kneecaps.

Finally, the Prince turned to address the creature, "Gash, prepare yourself . . ."

Charming blinked as the monster rose again and howled with rage, "My name is Gnarsh!" And the battle was rejoined.

The Prince's skill with arms was mesmerizing, but even Will's unsophisticated eyes could perceive that there was less flair with each assault. The Prince was beginning to tire.

"The fiiirst clump of thiiick green graaass iiin the

paaasture says the troll wiiins," said the medium-sized goat. "Aaany takers?"

"Heh, thaaat troll ain't aaall thaaat," said the big goat.

"Weeell, put your beeelly where your aaabsurd, gro-teeesquely laaarge mouth iiis."

Will was so engrossed in watching the desperate fight that, at first, he took no notice of the conversation between the two animals. But, as the bleating continued, little by little the words filtered through to the conscious part of his mind. Slowly he turned his head and, wide-eyed, looked down at the goats at his feet.

" . . . wait, aaare we betting thaaat the troll driiives hiiim off or eeeats hiiim?" the large goat was saying.

"Eeeats him," said the medium-sized goat, to Will's horror.

"IИ'll taaake it," said the big one.

Will knew that there were a great many things that he didn't know, but one thing he did know was goats, and these were not normal goats. Normal goats didn't talk, or at least no goat had ever spoken to him. There was the time a rather foppishly dressed house cat had given him advice on how to court Gretel, but admittedly that was in the alley behind the Toad & Donkey, and he had been pretty far into his cups. Still, he could say with confidence that no animal had ever spoken to him while he was stone-cold sober.

His silent, mouth-open stare finally caught the attention of the kid. "Guys, you haaave aaan aaaudience," it said in a high voice.

The arguing goats both turned and stared up at him

defiantly. The large one said, "Biiit of aaadvice friend, don't staaare. IIIt's rude."

"Aaand close your mouth, you look liiike a slaaack-jawed haaalf-wiiit," added the middle-sized beast.

Will closed his mouth with a snap and shook his head, trying to clear it. He had never spoken to a goat before, so he said the only thing that came to mind. "You talk?"

The small one giggled, the medium one snorted, and the large one said in a deep but quiet voice, "Weeell, we don't alwaaays saaay *baaah*, iiif thaaat's what you mean."

"Maaaybe he iiis a haaalf-wiiit," the middle one interjected.

"Cooome on, guys, giiive hiiim a breaaak," said the smallest one.

"A breaaak," bleated the big goat. "Heee's staaanding over here taaalking to us while hiiis friend gets offed by thaaat tosser of a troll."

"So, you aaadmit the troll wiiill wiiin," interrupted the middle-sized goat.

"III diiidn't saaay thaaat . . ."

The two goats started arguing with each other again and the smallest one rolled its eyes at them. "Don't worry aaabout theeem, theeey're just brothers."

Will held up his hands, "Please, please, normally I would be thrilled to talk to you. Trust me, I live for this kind of thing, but could you be quiet? I need to think. If that troll eats the Prince, I have to fight it. I don't know how to fight trolls. What am I going to do?"

He looked into the eyes of the three goats. They stared back silently. "And now I'm talking to goats. I'm going mad, that's it, isn't it? I'm going mad from the pressure."

Will ran a sweaty palm through his tousled hair and looked past the squire to where Charming was performing his deadly dance with the monster. Despite Charming's remarkable ability to avoid being hit, the troll didn't seem to be suffering much from all the abuse the Prince had delivered. All it would take would be one slip. If one of those talons struck him, it would be over.

Behind him the largest goat was talking again, "He's got skiiill, you haave to giiive hiiim thaaat. The problem is thaaat heee's using a sword—beginner's mistaaake. Now, whaaat III would do . . ." The words washed over Will, unacknowledged if not unheard. There was no solution; the Prince just had to beat the beast.

CHARMING WAS GROWING tired. Despite all the blows he had landed, all the seemingly fatal wounds he had inflicted, this troll (*Grush was it?*) would not die. The Prince almost felt sorry for the creature. It had waged its struggle valiantly, but the duel could only have one outcome. Still, he needed to end it soon. If only he could get the beast to bend down . . .

"Squire, I have need of my shield. Quickly!" He signaled with his hand, and the old man slid the shield over the wooden planks toward him. The troll did exactly what he had expected.

Gnarsh saw the movement and heard the sound of the shield sliding on the planks of the bridge. He lunged down and grabbed its edge with his dagger-like claws and, in a massive show of strength, bent the thing in half. The troll chortled menacingly. "Your precious shield won't save you this time, little man."

"Fortunate that I won't need it, then, don't you think?" asked Charming, and he launched his attack. The troll, distracted by the shield, had allowed the Prince too close. If Prince Charming had anything to do with it, that would be the beast's last mistake. Gripping the hilt of his sword with both hands, he swung the heavy blade upward and through the monster's neck. A fountain of ichor exploded skyward, raining Charming with black goo.

The Prince, breathing heavily and blinking away the sweat from his stinging eyes, moved back from the troll. They all watched as the headless body fell heavily onto the bridge. The severed head rolled over to the rail, where it came to a rest, its great googly eyes still staring angrily, if unmovingly, out at an unfriendly world. It had truly been a worthy battle.

Prince Charming raised his sword once in a wearied salute, and walked back toward Will and the squire. "Let it be known throughout the kingdom that, on this day, Prince Charming vanquished the mightiest of trolls, Gharsh, in single combat. Now, Squire, clean my armor. And Will, why don't you stop playing goatherd and retrieve the head?"

"IIIs HEEE ALWAAAYS this insufferaaable?" asked a deep voice.

"Always," Will answered quietly. He watched Charming strike a pose, and then in rising disbelief he saw the troll's arms twitch and reach out as though searching for something. At last the talons clutched the head and pulled it back onto the severed neck.

"Charming!" said Will, "Charming!" He waved his arms wildly, hoping to break the Prince's reverie.

"What is it? Can't you see I'm enjoying my moment of victory?" the Prince said in annoyance.

Pointing behind Charming, Will and Tomas both shouted, "He's not dead yet!"

"AND MY NAME is GNARSH!" roared the troll as he stood once more. Though its head was a little lopsided, the creature looked about the way it had when the battle began.

Charming's face became a scowl. He turned wearily back to the troll and walked slowly onto the bridge. "How dare you? I'm Prince Charming. I defeat monsters. You are a monster. You die. When I kill you, you should at least have the decency to stay dead."

The Prince raised his sword with a trembling arm, "Before I slay you—again—I want you to know that I was planning to put you in my epic poem. Now that you are being so childish about meeting your proper end, I doubt I will be inclined to mention you at all, you disgusting, filthy, ugly beast."

Gnarsh smiled his rotten smile. At least he was making the right impression. That was nice to hear. In high spirits, he bellowed, "I'm going to eat you! After today, no one will remember the Lord Protector and his dragon; they'll just remember that I, Gnarsh, ate Prince Charming! Then I will find this dragon slayer and eat him. How sweet would his meat taste? What a feeling, to devour the greatest hero in all the land."

Charming had been in the middle of a charge, but on hearing the troll's declaration that Will was the greatest hero in the land, he visibly paused as if the creature had finally landed a blow. His stride broken, the Prince stumbled in one of the many slick pools of black ichor that coated the bridge and fell to one knee. Seizing the opening, the troll brought one of its ham-sized fists down on Charming's unprotected head. He crumpled to the ground like a child's doll.

The Prince lay unconscious at the feet of the troll. Gnarsh laughed wickedly, a deep resonating laugh.

"LORD PROTECTOR, DO something!" Tomas shouted, pleading.

Will drew his sword clumsily and looked at the troll with wide eyes. All he could do with the useless piece of metal in his hand was die. It was hopeless. Then something the goats had been saying floated into his head. He spun on the animals, which all took a step back when they saw his wild eyes.

"You," he said pointing at the largest of the three, "you said you knew how to beat the troll?"

"Maaaybe, what's in iiit for us?" the goat replied.

"Anything on heaven or earth, just tell me you can do it," Will pleaded.

"Then prooomise to seeet us freee."

"Done!" Will said a little too quickly.

The goats all eyed him suspiciously and in a simultaneous three-part harmony, bleated, "Prooomise."

"I swear on my honor," he said with as much seriousness as he could muster, given that he was talking to a trio of farm animals.

The goats put their heads together in consultation.

Behind him, Tomas shouted, "Lord Protector, quickly, the troll is going to eat him!"

Turning to face him again, the biggest goat said, "Agreeed, just geeet meee ooout."

Will reared back on one foot and brought his hard-soled boot crashing against the rails of the fence. They split in the middle and clattered to the ground.

The big goat grinned a goaty grin and said, "Thiiis wiiill beee sweet revenge for aaall the tiiimes III haaaad to listen to that foul freaaak belch hiiis love for those bloody fiiish. Heee's a very disturbed troooll." With that, it pawed the ground with one of its massive hooves and charged straight for the bridge.

"Waaait," said the medium-sized goat, "III stiiill won the beeet, iiit doesn't count iiif you beeeat the troll."

The big goat's hooves tore massive clods of dirt out of the ground as he lowered his head. Gnarsh had just begun peeling back the Prince's armor to get at the soft flesh within. He looked up right into the horns of the charging ram. His eyes grew wide.

"It's not right. Not at all," the troll said, releasing Charming's armor.

The colossal goat slammed into the monster with a blow that resounded like thunder. The troll slid across the ichor-coated bridge, hit the rail, and went flying over the edge. With a massive splash, he plunged into the deep, fast rushing river and in an instant was swept away.

The big goat stood at the rail and stared for a moment, then looked back at the other goats who had made it through the broken fence and come to join him. The three nodded to each other and then at Will, and proceeded across to the sweet grass on the far bank.

Tomas rushed over to Will and knelt before him.

"Lord Protector William Pickett, you have saved the life of Prince Charming and rid the kingdom of the foul troll, Gnarsh. Thank you, you truly are a hero."

Will looked down at the Prince in his mangled, ichor-stained armor. He could see Charming was still breathing, but a second knot was growing on the other side of his head. He paled with shame and pointed at the unconscious man. "Tomas, that is your hero. I am just an ignorant farmer that got lucky again."

If Tomas heard, he made no signal as he had already turned his attention to Prince Charming and was busy stripping off the battered armor and tending to his beaten head.

Will left the squire to his ministrations and returned

to the broken fence and the now-empty field. He threw his sword to the ground in disgust. Liz had been right. As soon as Charming awoke, he would bring this charade to an end and take whatever punishment the Prince and the King meted out. William Pickett's days as Lord Protector were over.

Chapter 9

Lightning in a Bottle

LIZ SAT ON the deep ledge of her window and stared unseeing out at the wet gray-cloaked countryside below. The rain had started a few hours before dawn, and the rhythmic clamor as it beat down was only broken by the now-and-then plink-plunk of a drop as it found its way through the holes in the roof and fell into one of the many cups, pots, and tins she had set about her room. She pulled her knees in against her chest, looked over her new accommodations, and laughed bitterly.

Ever since the King had abandoned the castle to go who knows where, and the Prince and her brother had left on their idiotic quest to compare manhoods, the Princess, as the highest ranking noble, had held sway over the court, and it had not taken that woman long to teach Liz that she was out of her depth when it came to intrigue. Liz still couldn't believe how quickly her downfall had come. Sitting in her dripping room, she once again recalled the scene.

Princess Gwendolyn Mostfair had taken to hosting a wonderfully decadent tea every afternoon in one of the castle's numberless drawing rooms. There she would sit amid her coterie of sycophants-in-waiting, like a fat, awful—*oh, bloody hell*—a thin, radiant, terribly beautiful spider holding court. Liz did not particularly like the teas, but the cakes were almost irresistible, and so found herself, on one day, sitting in a corner near the back of the room munching an indescribably delicious apricot tart when the conversation turned to the ball. The Princess had said something particularly biting about Lady Rapunzel, and Liz had carelessly and rather acidly replied that the only shame was that more of the ladies of the court weren't as honest as Rapunzel. Then Gwendolyn had looked across the room at her and smiled a terrible, icy smile. Liz closed her eyes and replayed the words for the hundredth time since their confrontation.

"What a fascinating observation, Lady Elizabeth, I have been meaning to explore the subject of honesty with you for some time."

Gwendolyn had paused then to give her next words added effect.

"Your brother's defeat of the Great Wyrm of the South is a topic of much speculation in the court. As you know, I myself spent quite a bit of time with the dragon. She was an enormous creature, her blood boiled with the infernal

fires, her teeth were like swords, her claws like scythes, yet your brother, the Lord Protector and Dragon Slayer, was able to defeat her with a single thrust of a pitchfork? He must have gotten very close to the beast to make such a fatal strike, and yet he emerged unscathed, not a burn or serious wound to tell of the struggle. Impressive. Many have tried to get the Lord Protector and Dragon Slayer to tell his tale, but for some reason he is reticent to do so, almost as though he is ashamed. I ask, what could he possibly be ashamed of? I know we would all love to hear the REAL story."

Then she laughed, a terrible, malicious sound completely devoid of any humor or warmth.

Princess Gwendolyn knew. Somehow she knew that they were lying, knew that Will had not slain the dragon, and now she held their lives in her hand. Liz still did not know how she'd managed to laugh off the question, but she had. She had sat there in silence through the rest of the tea, with her heart in her throat and her hands clutched together to prevent them shaking.

When she tried to return to her room, the Royal Steward met her at the door, and, with many nasally apologies, explained that a dowager duchess was arriving and the suite had been given over to her. With many more bows and some seemingly genuine hand-wringing, he showed her to this room. A cold, stone circle exactly six paces across, stuck high atop a forlorn and neglected tower located at the furthest end of the servant's wing. For her comfort, there was a narrow straw bed, a worn vanity with a cloudy cracked glass, an equally rickety chair, and an empty lopsided wardrobe. To keep her company, the steward and his men had been kind enough to leave her with the many books she had borrowed from the royal library. Three times a day food was delivered: cold gruel in the morning, stale bread and cheese for luncheon, and a lukewarm soup for dinner. The poor quarters and bland meals suited Liz's mood.

Indeed, the irony was that it was all so unnecessary. Gwendolyn could have left her in her plush rooms and fed her chilled jellies and rich meats, and Liz still would have isolated herself from rest of the court. That icy smile had, in an instant, extinguished any hope Liz might have had that the Princess would feel an obligation to show them mercy in exchange for her rescue. The fact was, Liz was scared to death that the Princess would find a way to get rid of her before she was able to remove her brother from the castle and the woman's influence. So she kept to her little room in the vague hope that her absence would make the Princess forget about her.

A flash of lightning left the vastness of the castle momentarily silhouetted in brilliant white. Liz sighed through the rumbling thunder as she thought about how happy she and Will had been when they first rode through those grand gates. *Nothing to be done about it now, but keep out of the way till Will gets back and you both can make your escape.*

A knock at the door brought her head up with a start. Her heart hammered in her chest, but she still managed a steady, if not strong, "Yes?"

"Lady . . . Elizabeth," came a call that was at once out

of breath and angry. "Is that . . . you in there? It is Lady Rapunzel."

Rapunzel? Liz recognized her voice now. "Yes, just a moment, let me get the door."

She crossed the room, taking a moment to regard her thinning reflection in the cloudy mirror. Liz clucked at her own vanity and unbolted the thick wooden door.

It was Lady Rapunzel, or at least she thought it was. The woman, whose most notable feature when last she saw her had been a bizarre wig of absurd length, had removed the hairpiece to reveal a head of gold cut in a style for which Liz had no name. It was short like that of a man's, but for the drape of the bangs and the subtle curl around the ears and neck. The understated, yet complicated coiffure, perfectly framed her delicate face. The transformation from ridiculous to beautiful was stunning.

Liz gave a curtsy. "Lady Rapunzel, to what do I owe this unexpected honor?"

Lady Rapunzel gave a quick bob in return and looked about the room in shock, her jaw clenched and her eyes narrowed in anger. "My reason for visiting, Lady Elizabeth, is this . . . this . . . outrage!" She threw her arms wide, one laden with clothes and the other carrying a large picnic basket, to indicate the sad little room.

Liz blushed. "Well, Lady Rapunzel, I appreciate your concern, but there is no outrage, it is simply that the dowager duchess—"

If it was possible, Rapunzel's eyes grew even angrier and she spit out, "Dowager duchess, dowager duchess, a drunken fool of no consequence. This is the work of that vindictive tart Gwendolyn, and it can not be borne."

"Lady Rapunzel—"

"We do not know each other well, Lady Elizabeth, and I fear that my introduction to you was rude, but can we drop the titles for a time? My friends call me Elle."

For the first time in a week, Liz laughed. "How right you are, Elle, please call me Liz. And what a poor host I am. Please, may I take your burdens? You have carried them a long way up those stairs and must be weary."

Liz relieved Elle of the heavy basket. As she placed it on the little wooden vanity table, the scent of roast pheasant and buttered potatoes rose to meet her nose. Her mouth watered and her stomach rumbled at the heavenly aroma. From behind her, Elle said, "That is for you, Liz, as are these."

Liz turned to see Elle hanging the most beautiful of her courtly clothes in the battered armoire. "They should never have been taken away," Elle said without turning.

Seeing the clothes brought all the feelings to the surface Liz had been suppressing since her banishment. Tears spilled down her cheeks. "Thank you, Elle. You cannot know how much this kindness means to me."

"I am only returning what belongs to you. Those clothes are yours by right, Liz, just as by right you belong in the royal quarters and at the royal dining table."

Liz stood, looking at the clothes while anger and shame warred within her. "Elle, I don't know what to say. I thought I had been shunned by everyone in the court. I am, after all, a farmer, and absent my brother's newfound title, could look forward to little more in life than being a farmer's wife."

Elle snorted. "Absent your brother's title? I could just as well say that absent the King's royalty, Prince Charming would be the village idiot." Liz giggled, but Elle was not amused. "Your brother's title, your brother's deeds, give you as much right, if not more, to lead the court of this kingdom as Gwendolyn. She and all those pretentious, hollow, vacuous biddies should be kissing your feet."

Elle paced back and forth across the room. "Why is the Princess even doing it? It seems like the height of madness. Surely, she must know that when the King and your brother return she will have to answer for her actions. What is happening?"

Liz sat heavily on the tottery chair and looked at this strong woman through ashen eyes. The pallor of her face and the set of her eyes made Elle stop midstride.

"Liz, tell me what is wrong. I know that all you know of me is my embarrassing performance at the ball, but I am not a fool. I may be a shorn, ruined woman, but I can assure you that whatever has happened, whatever that woman has done to you, can be undone. But I must know why you have made of yourself a prisoner. I did not take you for someone that would turn from a fight."

Liz was crying now. Her body too exhausted to sob was still as silent tears rolled down her checks. She knew she must trust this woman. The lie was a poisonous boil, and it had to be lanced. Wiping her eyes with the edge of her skirt, she said without inflection, "Do you know the Dragon Slayer's Song, Elle?"

"Of course, it is on the lips of the whole of the king-dom. Why?"

Liz's voice lost its courage, so she whispered, "It is all a lie."

ON THE FAR side of the castle, in a bare and windowless antechamber, at the bottom of a dark and twisting stair, Princess Gwendolyn Mostfair sat cross-legged in her thin satin shift in the middle of an ever-growing circle of runes. Around her, shadows from the alcove danced naked in the flickering candlelight, making the light beat and pulse against the walls in uncertain and obscene patterns. Gwen ignored them and bent lower over the circle. Her hand was a blur of motion as she scratched the elaborate symbols into the cold stones with a piece of burnt ash-wood.

Gwen had been two days in this bare chamber transcribing the dragon's memories into the floor, breaking only occasionally when her body demanded. Her back ached, her knees and legs were bruised from squatting on the hard floor, and her hands and fingers were stiff from gripping the char pencil. Gone was the princess of fairy tale, and in its place had stepped something from darker legend—the hag. For Gwendolyn looked like nothing so much as a witch. Beneath the streaks and smudges of ash and soot, her face was gray and sick from lack of food, and the skin around her eyes was sunken and bruised from lack of sleep. Her hair had long escaped its intricate braids and now hung lank and knotted around her face in an untidy mass of greasy yellow. The delicate cloth of her white satin shift, now stained a dull gray from ash and dust, had frayed by the constant wear against the rough stone of the floor. What remained of the sheer garment clung to her dirty, sweaty body in a manner that, had she not looked so piteous, would have been obscene.

In her current state, such concerns were mere distraction, and Gwen had tried hard the last few days to prevent every possible distraction. The King and the Prince were gone, Elizabeth was isolated, the court had been dismissed. Her servants had been instructed to leave her in this chamber unmolested until she called them, and the door to the room had been bolted against unwanted intrusion. She was alone, and nothing but the growing pain in her writing arm would stop her in her task.

Finally, her hand cramped around the stick and she could not continue. Stretching her arms above her head to work out the muscles, Gwen took a moment to look about the wider room. Many of the candles surrounding her circle had gone out, and those that were still lit were down to stubs, small islands of light in a sea of melted wax. Beyond the dwindled candles and the thickening haze of smoke, it was impossible to tell how much, or even if any, time had passed. Everything looked the same.

On one side of the room the King's war table and a dozen stately chairs sat in a jumbled heap where she had pushed them to clear a space for the circle. A few paces away, by the bolted wooden door, lay the tray of bread, meat, and cheese she had brought to eat, but never found the time to touch. Beside that was her fine dress—a pile

of brilliant blue velvet, satin and lace, which she had discarded shortly after starting her transcription, partly
because the tight corset made it impossible to bend, and
partly out of fear that the flowing skirts would smudge
the precious runes.

Still, the tremors in her hands and legs, and the pain
in her stomach, told Gwen that she had been at her task
too long and should take a break, perhaps even sleep. Despite knowing this, she also knew she would go on. The
pattern was almost finished. The shadows, which had
paused with her, rejoined their dance.

It was not so much that Gwen knew the pattern was
almost finished, but it was more that she felt it. She felt it
in the whispered words of the dragon, words that were
coming to an end, like the last chapter of a story long
known but only half remembered.

It was strange that the dragon's voice, so long a terror
from which she had hoped to awaken, was now like an
old friend. It had been the dragon that had told her of her
lover's cowardice, while she still dreamed of his rescue. It
had been the dragon that had warned her that the fairy
would not release her, even if she did one day find a way
out of the labyrinth of dreams into which she'd been cast.
And now, it was the dragon that was showing her the way
to both redemption and revenge.

She made the last mark. Gwen blinked down at the
ash-wood stick in her hand, at her palm and fingers
stained black with char. It was done.

The shadows stopped their dance and drew near, curious and fearful. Gwen stood shakily and examined the

delicate tracings with a smile of satisfaction. It was incomprehensible, but felt right. Each symbol copied perfectly from the dragon's memory.

Gwen took hold of the hem of her shift and picked her way through the circle of runes, being careful not to smudge the complex drawing. Stepping into the shadows at the edge of the circle, she felt their hands grasp at her, their fingers twine in her hair and pull at the folds of the shift, trying to restrain her. She heard their voices whispering, pleading. "LEAVE ME BE," she screamed, brushing them aside and striding toward her discarded dress. "You are creatures of the fairy, and I am sick of you."

The shadow creatures drew away, but still she felt their hands brushing her body as she walked. She frowned at their growing boldness, but used the brief pause in their attentions to stoop down and draw from the folds of her dress an elegant round-bottom flask, almost a perfect sphere, topped by a very delicate ground-glass stopper. She examined it in the dying light. A light dusting of herbs, a sprig of holly, some mint and lavender dust coated the inside.

Satisfied that she had overlooked nothing, Gwen clutched the glass ball to her breast, retrieved one of the still burning candles from the floor, and, stepping carefully out of the reach of the shadows, which were now wrapping themselves around her ankles and legs in supplication, she reentered the circle. As she did, she felt power enter her body like a warm draught. It was not magic—that would come later—it was instead the power of action. For once, she was not waiting or hoping or wishing or dreaming. The power of her own resolve was intoxicating.

Reaching the center of the circle, she carefully placed the candle on the ground at her feet, and then holding the glass ball in one hand, she pulled the golden fairy chain from around her neck. She held the two objects before her, and in a voice high with emotion, she shouted, "FAIRY!"

And thus began the ritual formula the dragon had taught her in so many whispered words through so many dreams.

"Spirit of the Firmament and of the Ether," she cried, thrusting the ball and necklace high above her head.

"Upon the Earth and under the Earth." She made a sweeping gesture about her body like a circle within a circle.

"On dry Land, or in the Water." Another motion—her body moved as if in dance—like rain falling.

"Of whirling Air or of rushing Fire." And, here she twisted about in a pirouette of movement. The candle fluttered and almost failed.

"I call thee to . . ." She paused and clutched the golden chain tighter in her grip, and then shouted in a ringing voice, "JUDGMENT!"

At the word, the candle flared and the shadows at the edge of the circle drew back, slinking into the cracks and crevices of the walls and floors like beetles exposed to the sun. A choking smell of nutmeg—the smell of fairy magic—filled the room. Above her, the air shuddered and convulsed as though fighting against itself, and then all at once the light from the room splintered into a thousand little sparks. The sparks were drawn in a great swirling spiral down and into the golden chain, until it seemed a star had come to rest in her hand. Slowly, she lowered the chain into the vial and stoppered it. She retrieved the candle, now nothing more than a glowing ember, and began to seal the stopper with its wax.

As she did, she intoned these words in a ragged whisper of emotion:

> "Betrayed has been my desire by
> promises unfulfilled.
> Broken is our contract by magic and
> by deed.
> Bound are you with this gold, the price for
> my wish.
> Promise for promise; Deed for deed; Price
> for price.
> Till the breaking of this oath, thy servitude
> shall be my recompense."

Gwendolyn held the orb at arm's length and watched as the light within danced furiously around the golden lock, then moved from wall to wall trying to escape the delicate prison. At last, the glowing body slowed and then stopped.

The Princess cackled hysterically. "Trapped by your own fairy gold. It is ironic that, absent your cursed amulet, I could not have managed, and yet how many times since I was released did I yearn to throw the thing away, to rid myself of your reminder?"

An angry, disembodied voice echoed about the room. *"My powers cannot grant thee what thou wantest, Gwendolyn Mostfair. Free me now and all shall be forgotten."*

Gwendolyn barked a single sharp laugh, "All shall be forgotten?" she mocked. "But I will not forget, Fairy. I will not forget or forgive my stolen life or all those wasted years. I had determined to move on, but now that I have tasted the bitterness of the freedom so long dreamt of, now that I have you in my grasp, I will have my revenge. You may have been a pitiless jailer, but I shall be an even crueler mistress."

The voice returned, but the anger had been replaced by a deep sadness. *"I see that thy captivity has not diminished thy conceit. I had hoped with time thy willingness to sacrifice others for thine own ends would have diminished."*

Gwendolyn's rage returned with double force. "You accuse me of conceit, you that would twist my words and rob me of both my beloved sister and my rightful place in the world? And why? Was it your idea of a joke, a—a lesson? Without your bloody curse, I would have been queen years ago, and my sister would have . . . found another, and become a great lady in her own stead."

The fairy made its reply in a voice that rippled with laughter, *"The dragon did not teach thee well enough, Gwendolyn Mostfair. For thy sister's death were thou accursed to never see the throne until thy heart was melted by true love's warmth. Thy heart is still as cold and hard and unmoved by love as it was the day I lay the curse upon thee, and so it remains."*

"How dare you?" she hissed, feeling a rage so primal that she thought she might burst into flame. "How DARE you? I no more wished my sister's death than I wished myself into your waking nightmare. Only you made both so."

Gwendolyn's mind flew back through the years, through the dreams that had haunted her for decades, to the moment when it had all gone wrong. She had been so young and desperate, hoping for a magical godmother to grant her heart's desire. She remembered running back to the castle through the forest, but before the memory could take hold, the fairy spoke once again, drawing her back to the present, to the time after dreams and wishes had both died.

"Rosslyn's death may not have been thy first goal, Gwendolyn Mostfair, but it was in thy envious heart to steal thy sister's place in life and love and claim them for thine own. To have the one required the other, and so one wish is much the same as the other."

When next Gwendolyn spoke, her voice was low and menacing. "Do not think you can twist the truth with me, small one. I remember. I was there. From now on, it is my command that you shall not use my name, nor ever mention my sister again! As for the throne, we shall see which is more powerful, a fairy's curse or a fairy's magic."

The glass orb vibrated, and the flickering light within seemed to swell and deepen. *"I shall give one more warn-*

ing, mortal. You meddle in powers far beyond thy under-standing. This crystalline cage thou hast devised is a clever bit of magic, but it will not endure, and thy previous fate will seem as paradise itself to compare with the horrors I shall descend upon thee when next I am free."

Threats, Gwendolyn understood. She was calm now, and her voice came out emotionless. "Do you think me someone you can bully and threaten, Fairy? I have lived through your half-sleeping hell, aware, unmoving as day followed day in an endless unwaking cycle, interrupted only on that rare occasion when the dragon, bored by her own torment, deigned to speak to me. I am still here, Fairy. I survived. Let us see if you can say the same when I have finished with you." She raised the glass ball until it was inches from her face, "Now, acknowledge me as your mistress."

A palpable, expectant hush fell on the room, the shadows slipped from their hiding places to listen and bear witness, but the silence lingered, and, a red-faced Gwendolyn shook the flickering ember within the ball and screamed, "ACKNOWLEDGE ME, YOU WORTHLESS LITTLE BUG!"

Quietly the answer came. *"Yes, Mistress."*

The Princess smiled her most wicked smile. "Good. Now, let us turn our attentions to what can be done about Lady Elizabeth Pickett."

BY THE TIME Liz finished her tale, Elle had thrown caution aside and was sitting on the edge of the dubious straw bed.

"So you see, there is real danger for us," Liz concluded. "My only hope so far has been that Gwendolyn stays her hand until Will returns and we can make our escape."

There was a long pause, and in her guilt, Liz read disapproval in Elle's silent scrutiny. She had hoped Elle would understand, maybe even forgive, but perhaps it was asking too much. "It is okay, Lady Rapunzel, I understand."

"It is Elle to you, Liz, and let me tell you what I understand. Your brother, the *Lord Protector*, ran into an open field to face a dragon, *the* dragon, unarmed, in the hopes that he might draw its attention away from you and the house you were hiding in. Then, you ran after him because you thought your own presence would be the only way to keep him from jumping straight into the creature's belly. Then, after the two of you survived the fire-storm that accompanied the dragon's death, your brother rode up into the Cursed Mountains, along the Black Road, armed only with his pitchfork, and managed to recover the Princess without putting so much as a hair on her demented little head out of place. Do I have all that right, *Lady* Elizabeth Pickett?"

"Well, when you say it like that . . ." Liz started hesitantly.

"You mean, when I recount it as it actually happened, the two of you still sound like the most heroic figures in the history of this kingdom? Yes, I agree." Elle started pacing again. "In fact, it seems to me the only thing your brother did wrong was to bring that lunatic Princess back. Maybe the dragon had the right idea, locking her away all those years. It is too bad your brother is too thick to see how truly loathsome the crazy wench is."

Liz found herself defending Will. "You must not think Will stupid, Elle. He is actually quite clever but, in affairs of the heart, is at a disadvantage. Will is a terrible romantic. To be honest, I'm afraid we both are, otherwise how can I explain my continued fascination with the Prince?" She blushed at Elle's stern gaze, and added quickly, "I think Will is in love with the idea of the Princess far more than he is with the reality of Gwendolyn. I think, given time, he will realize that she will not make him happy, if not that she is a madwoman. But he needs time to overcome his infatuation and, frankly, his maleness."

Both women laughed and then Liz said, "I do not know why you risked Gwendolyn's wrath to come to me, Elle, but I am so glad you did."

Elle rose and embraced her. "It was not just for you, it was for me also. I told you, I am a ruined woman, and I was not exaggerating. My only quality of note was my hair and that is gone, so I cannot expect a marriage of advantage. And, after the scene I made at the ball, I am an outcast in society. You may regret having gone to Gwendolyn's tea, Liz, but at least you had an invitation. Now that I have nothing more to lose, the Gwendolyns of the world do not frighten me the way they once did. My whole life has been spent on the edge of the court, currying favor, slowly building my position and hoping that someone of higher birth would take notice. I was willing to throw my virtue away on a man that had no interest in me, beyond an afternoon's dalliance—well, that *and* those eyes of his," It was Elle's turn to blush. "When I heard what the Princess had done, especially after you defended me to her, I knew I had to help. "

Liz studied the younger woman behind pursed lips. Liz realized that she had accepted her imprisonment partly out of guilt, but also partly because she thought she deserved it. She recognized the same thing in Elle, and it was not acceptable. "I am thankful for your help and friendship, Elle, but that is the last time I want to hear you say that you are ruined. You are smart, courageous, and, though you won't admit it, beautiful."

Elle sat quietly staring at her shoes.

"Elle?" Liz said gently.

She looked up and tears were spilling down her face. In a rush, she sprang from her feet and wrapped her arms around Liz. "Thank you for saying that," she whispered.

"I only spoke you the truth, Elle."

"Maybe, but thank you anyway," Elle said, wiping her eyes. Then she took Liz's hand and led her to the window, where they sat side by side. "Now, about your plan, Liz. I'm afraid it isn't safe for you to hide out in this tower until your brother returns. You have no idea what Princess Gwendolyn is capable of. My mother was in the court when the King was young. You probably know that Gwendolyn was not his first choice?" Elle paused long enough to allow Liz to nod. "What most people don't know is that there was a rumor at the time that Rosslyn was poisoned." Liz gasped and put a hand to her mouth. Elle nodded and whispered, "Gwendolyn was there to comfort Rupert, and in time, a few months time I would add, his affections for the elder sister passed to the younger. The rest, as they say, is fairy tale."

"I never imagined," whispered Liz. "But your story only makes me more certain that I cannot abandon my brother, Elle. He wouldn't survive a night with the woman."

"I'm not suggesting that you do." Elle rose and began pacing again, clenching and unclenching her hands as she did. Elizabeth watched her crossing back and forth across the room and smiled—*so certain and full of energy.* "You can make your escape with my valet. I will prepare it for tomorrow night. We can disguise you as a servant and he can lead you to one of my family's country houses. We are of no great significance, so no one will think to look for you there. Meanwhile, I will take my own leave of the court and find your brother. I will bring him to you, and you both can go into hiding until the King returns. After that, we can deal with the Princess."

Liz laughed. "Let's not get ahead of ourselves, Elle. I will agree to your scheme on one condition: Do not put yourself in danger."

Elle snorted. "The only person that will be in any danger is the Prince. If he places so much as a foot out of line, I'll give him a black eye to match that broken nose."

They laughed again, and as the night deepened and

storm raged outside, Elle brought out her splendid picnic and the new friends ate in the light of the sputtering little oil lamp. Elle made Liz tell her all about Will, and they exchanged tales about their lives growing up. The scent of the spiced pheasant filled the room, so the two women never noticed a strange aroma of nutmeg in the air.

IN HER HIDDEN chamber, Gwendolyn gazed into the flickering glass orb on the table before her and watched a shadowy image of the laughing women. She closed her hand around the ball, covering it. Almost at once, the scene began to dissolve. The crystalline surface of the sphere cleared until only the incandescent glow of the fairy within remained.

"So, the court was spreading false rumors behind my back. I knew there was a reason I never liked that girl's mother." She shook her head. "No matter, in time I will devise a punishment for the poisonous old harpy. Right now, we must think on what to do about Lady Elizabeth and Lady Rapunzel."

Gwendolyn took the orb in her hands and rolled it between her palms as she thought. *They would make their escape from me would they? I think not.* She chortled and patted the little sphere. "We won't let that happen, will we?"

She unfolded her hands from around the orb and placed it back onto her lap. In a laughing voice, she chanted, "Fairy, fairy, tell no lies, bring the one I seek unto my eyes."

The light shimmered and faded, and the image of a large dark man took its place. He was tending a horse. "So, this is Lady Rapunzel's footman," she cackled. "We shall do her the favor of testing his loyalty, won't we, little one?

Chapter 10

Something Foul at the Cooked Goose

THERE ARE MANY quaint and distinguished taverns scattered about the kingdom, and almost all of them profess to be "renowned" for one reason or another. Some of these claims cannot be confirmed objectively. Does the Meddlesome Crow in Two Trees really have the "best meat pies in all the land?" Can the proprietors of the Four Dogs actually support the assertion that they have the "most buxom serving wenches?" Is it even a good idea for the bartender of the Gasping Fish in Timsley to declare that he has "the most potent farts west of the Southern Mountains?" And shouldn't he, as a public service, provide the identity of the individual east of those peaks to whom he dares not compare himself?

Others, however, are distinguished by right, and the

Cooked Goose is renowned and reviled throughout the land for having the worst-tasting ale in several kingdoms. In fact, over the years the debate has raged regarding exactly what the taste of the brew resembles: turpentine, lantern oil, raw sewage, but most agree with S. Tagger, author of *S. Tagger's Beers of the Realm*, who describes it as "virtually indistinguishable from mule piss."

Despite its reputation, Will and the squire, out of a total lack of other options, retreated to that disreputable inn following their fight with the troll. Mostly what Will remembered about the first couple of drinks at the Cooked Goose was how depressing the place was. The Cooked Goose was a place to get drunk. Frivolity was not encouraged. Fortunately, the gloom of the tavern perfectly matched his own foul mood.

Will cradled his head in his palms and, leaning his elbows heavily on the table, stared at the residue floating at the bottom of his third mug of beer. "You know, Tomas, I'll never be a hero."

"What are you talking about, Lord Protector?" said the squire, suppressing a belch. "You have now defeated a dragon and a troll, and saved the lives of Princess Gwendolyn and Prince Charming. That's a career for most, and I should know. The Prince is my third knight," he remarked, holding up two fingers.

"Huh," said Will, snapping out of his trance. How had the man gotten the idea that he had defeated the troll? Hadn't he been watching? Maybe he was drunk or distracted by sickness. The beer was really bad; it seemed to be numbing his tongue. He worried that his sense of taste was being permanently damaged.

With an effort he brought his thoughts back to the squire. "You know, I hardly had anything to do with defeating the troll. Charming did all the fighting, except for the end, and it was the goat that knocked the troll off the bridge. And as for the dragon . . ."

He looked the squire in the eye and chewed on the side of one finger. It was time to stop hiding from the truth. A saying from back home in Prosper popped into his head: *The man who turns his back on his problems, will find them kicking him in the ass.*

"The dragon, well— Ah, hell! The dragon impaled herself on my pitchfork by accident. I was hiding in a cornfield when she died."

There, he had done it. He had finally told someone the whole truth, and now the entire kingdom would know what he already knew, what Liz had tried to tell him. He wasn't a hero. He downed the dregs of his ale and, plunking the mug down heavily on the table, braced for the other man's response.

The squire laughed. The heat of Will's shame flushed over his neck and cheeks. He was being mocked, and rightly so. To be sure it was no more than he deserved. The man slapped his knee at the joke and then, noticing Will's crestfallen expression, suppressed his sniggers and, in a lowered voice, said, "You're serious?"

Will nodded. "Tomas, I had nothing to do with killing the dragon."

The man shook his head. "No, no, I mean you seriously don't believe you're a hero?"

Will didn't know what to say, so he stared mutely at the surface of the table and wished, despite all good sense, that he had another tankard of ale.

Tomas reached across the table and grasped Will's shoulder, forcing him to make eye contact. "Lord Protector William Pickett, what does it matter how the dragon died, or whose hand, or horn for that matter, defeated the troll? The fact is you rid the land of the dragon, whether by skill or luck, and Gnarsh the Troll, again either directly or indirectly, and in between you also rescued the Princess and saved the life of Prince Charming himself." He dropped his hand from Will's shoulder and put it to his breast. "On my honor, Your Lordship, I would trade a hundred swordsmen like the Prince for one man, like you, who can get things done."

Without another word, the squire hopped up on his chair and, wobbling slightly, looked about the smoke-filled tavern. He shouted, "WHO HERE BELIEVES THAT THE LORD PROTECTOR WILLIAM PICKETT IS THE TRUE HERO OF THE REALM?" There was an uncomfortable silence as the half-stoned assembly looked blearily up at him. Will tried to pull him down by the cuff of his pants, but Tomas would not be dissuaded. "I said, WHO HERE WOULD RAISE THEIR GLASS WITH ME TO THE LORD PROTECTOR AND DRAGON SLAYER, WILLIAM PICKETT?" With that, he grabbed Will's wrist and pulled him to his feet with a strength that belied the man's size and paunch.

There was but a moment's pause and then an overgrown-looking man at the bar blinked and his eyes went wide, then he sprang from his stool, pointing with a shaking hand, "Holy hell! It—it—it's the Lord Protector! I saw him wiff me own eyes when 'e firs' come to the castle wiff the dragon's blinkin' head!" He grabbed a tankard at random from the bar and raised it in matching salute. "You're one of us, Your Lordship, and I'll stand by you any day!"

"Das right, das right," slurred a fat, balding man with a dubious mustache further down the bar. "I seen him too. I will never forget dat face, ever," he continued without apparent irony. "Proudest moment o' my whole life." He stood and raised his cup unsteadily in the direction of Will.

A burly fellow with a jet-black beard sitting at one of the long benches rose ponderously and, pounding his fist on the table, thundered, "WHO SAYS THEY WON'T DRINK TO WILLIAM PICKETT? That bloody dragon et my Da', and it's 'cause of him that my family can sleep safe at night. I'd give my life to you, Your Lordship."

One of the older serving wenches screeched across the room, "AN 'E'S SO MUCH MORE A MAN THAN THAT FRAUD CHARMING EVER WAS."

"Too right! Pickett's a true hero!" echoed a thin man whose deep baritone voice was ill-matched to his body. "Charming's a fop. Only thing he ever conquered was the kingdom's virgins."

There was a wave of laughter at this and more voices joined in the raucous chorus. Chairs were pushed back and men stood in uneven salute to the young man. The proprietor, who had eyed Will suspiciously at first, saw a chance for commerce and seized the moment, shouting, "FILL YOUR TANKARDS AND RAISE 'EM TO RAFTERS, FELLOWS. Three cheers for our honored guest, the Lord Protector and Dragon Slayer, William Pickett!"

There was an enormous roar at the suggestion, and then the rough voices of the drunken mob sounded, "Huzzah, Huzzah, Huzzah!!" in a rising crescendo.

Will was struck dumb at the crowd's display of affection. Every face in the room was turned in his direction when someone yelled, "SPEECH!" Another wave of cheers washed over the Cooked Goose.

Maybe the squire was right. Maybe he was a hero. A buxom, if not entirely comely, barmaid pressed her bosom against his chest and refilled his mug with warm beer from a pitcher. His heart raced and his face flushed; and encouraged by her smiles, and the not insubstantial amount of drink he had imbibed, he raised his hands and a sudden hush descended.

"To you . . . my people . . . the people of the realm! Thank you all! I, William Pickett, Lord Protector of the Realm, swear that I will defend you all to my last breath, no matter what is asked of me!"

There were more cheers and jubilation and someone started to play a flute. Soon a tambour joined in, the tables were cleared away, and a merry dance was begun. Will felt a tide of euphoria rush through his body. He knew now what it must have been like for Charming. This adoration was intoxicating in a way that the beer in his hand could never be. Several of the increasingly attractive serving maids pressed around his table and someone started singing a bawdy tune about the dragon and flagons and tarts and farts, and the from there Will's memory became increasingly hazy.

On the balcony overlooking the common room of the Cooked Goose, Prince Charming stood, gripping the rail, his ears burning. The people thought he was a fop and a fool who preyed on innocent girls. They believed that Pickett had saved them and would keep them safe. *Were they wrong?*

Will had saved them. The dragon was dead, the Princess restored. Gnarsh the Troll was gone, and he owed Will his life for saving him from the beast. Somehow, despite all his planning, it had all gone terribly wrong again. Before Will, everything had been right. After Will . . . well, after Will nothing had been right.

At just this moment, a man with a long crooked nose and a distinct hunch came sliding up beside him. "Good evening to you," he said in a breathy voice that reeked of badly brewed ale. Charming recoiled from the smell. The man, undaunted, moved a little closer so he could be heard above the celebration below. "My name is Oliver, Ollie to my friends. Didn' the Lord Protector bring you in?"

"Yes, he did," croaked Charming.

The man looked at him from behind shifting eyes. "What a great honor it must be for you to ride and fight with 'is Lordship."

The Prince looked at the floor, unwilling to meet the

stranger's eyes. He didn't want to talk about William Pickett. Still, he owed Will his life, and that meant acknowledging his debt publicly. "Yes, a great honor," he said flatly.

The man, Ollie, must have heard something in Charming's response because he cocked his head to one side and then ran a finger down along the side of his long nose and tapped the end. "I get your meanin', friend, say no more. You and 'is Lordship, maybe you had a fallin' out, but maybe it's not your place to bad-mouth 'im, eh? Maybe he's the reason your face looks like a couple a miles of bad road?"

"You could say that," he spit out, and then wished he hadn't. It wasn't entirely true. Could he really blame the man for everything that had happened: being brained by a tree, the suit of falling armor, Rapunzel, the troll? Besides, this man was obviously a blackguard of the lowest order.

"Come with me, my friend. Let's go out back and get some air. It'll be easier to talk without these drunkards about," said Ollie, placing a hand on Charming's shoulder and directing him somewhat forcefully toward a dubious-looking plank door hanging crookedly over an opening in the back inn's wall.

There was enough of the Royal Prince left in Charming that he was instinctively offended that this peasant would dare touch his person, and he shook the hand off.

Ollie took a step back and squinted at him. "Is there a problem, friend?

"I'm Pr—" he started to say and then stopped. No one

on earth would recognize him as Prince Charming; and given his current condition, he was ashamed to reveal his true identity. He mumbled, "No, nothing."

"Good, because I think I may have just the way to take 'is High and Mightiness down a couple of pegs. Now, I ask you, that wouldn't be so bad, would it?" asked Ollie as he started down the creaking wooden stair behind the door.

Charming didn't answer. He wanted to be left alone. Ollie, however, must have taken his silence as assent because he kept up a steady chatter until they reached the mud that lay at the bottom of the stair. An old mule stood tied to a post in a fetid pool of foul-smelling water near the back wall, his nose buried in a trough filled with a fragrant mixture of hops and barley. A barmaid was standing near the rear of the mule, holding a large wooden bucket. She glanced at them nervously, then scuttled through a door and into what looked like the kitchen. A roar of noise filtered out into the still alley as the door opened, and muted again as it slammed to a close.

"Tell me, friend, do you think 'is Lordship is lookin' for more . . . adventure, more . . . glory to heap on 'imself?"

"I suppose," said Charming uncertainly. At this point, all he wanted was for this Ollie to leave him alone. His face hurt, his body ached, and his head was swimming.

"You jus' tell 'im that the local count, a man of great importance, will be travelin' up the road into the wood near midday tomorrow. Also tell 'im that the Masked Rascal and his, um . . . happy highwaymen—no, no his boisterous bandits—yeah, that's better . . . Anyway, um, well, tell 'im that the Scarlet Scoundrel and his men are planning to ambush the count at the firs' bridge."

Anyone else might have bought Ollie's story, but if Charming knew one thing it was the identity of every noble that resided in his father's kingdom and another two-dozen neighboring kingdoms besides; and he knew for a fact that there was no count within a week's ride of this forsaken place. There was not even so much as a penniless baroness that would bother to claim these lands as her own. This scum was asking Charming to betray Will—to knowingly send him into the clutches of some sort of desperate band of cutthroats.

Charming stepped away from his new "friend's" embrace and looked, really looked, at him. A cruel yellow, crooked smile appeared under Ollie's long hooked nose. "I think he'd be quite pleased with the news, friend," the man said in a mocking singsong voice. Then he handed the Prince a single silver coin. "For your trouble, my misshapen friend."

To think that anyone would suggest such a plot? To imagine that any man would attempt to bribe him, Prince Charming, with a single piece of silver? It was monstrous!

Charming felt his hands clench into fists. He advanced on Ollie, who drew back, confused but sensing the menace in the air. Perhaps the story would have ended with Charming thrashing the villain, but just then the kitchen door to the Cooked Goose was once more thrown wide by a barmaid, this time carrying an empty wooden bucket. The hearty sound of drunken mirth came rolling out the door into the alley, and a clearly drunk Will bellowed out, "And, you should have seen the look on Charming's face when Lady Rapunzel punched him in the nose—"

The door slammed shut, cutting off the rest of Will's story, but it could not mute the roar of laughter that followed. Charming's body slumped. He had become a joke, to be ridiculed in the same public houses in which he had once been toasted. Anger at the unfairness of his situation and his turn in fortune returned. Will had stripped him of everything. In the mind of his subjects was he really any better than Ollie? He twisted the silver coin between his fingers. He knew he could not do this, but when he opened his mouth he said, "I will tell him."

Ollie cackled and, pulling the hood of his cloak up, stalked away into the night.

The Prince closed his eyes and collapsed back against the wall of the tavern. After a time spent staring into the deeper black of the night sky, wondering whether he would go through with this betrayal, he shuffled back to his room and sat on the straw cot, tired but unable to sleep. In his palm lay the silver coin. He stared at it in the smoky light of the room's lone candle and saw a vague hint of his reflection, a purple and blue stain on the face of the shining circle.

Chapter 11

Through the Woods Darkly

IN EVERY FAIRY tale there is a point in the telling when the fire dies low and the dark of the night grows deeper and the children gather closer together and the storyteller lowers her voice and whispers, "Now, dear ones, this is the scary part." And then, inevitably, into the story steps the villain, and whether an evil queen or twisted stepmother or foul beast, the listener begins to doubt, maybe the hero doesn't make it, maybe there is no happily-ever-after.

Two days after her confession to Elle, as Elizabeth Pickett fled from Castle White, she assumed that the scary part of her story was at an end. That nothing could match the constant terror she'd felt at living under the power of Princess Gwendolyn. Sheltered in her deep cloak, she was content to watch from atop the back of a pretty gray mare as Elle's surprisingly stoic valet, Collins, led them slowly toward a darkly shadowed gap in the eastern horizon where the road left the open meadows of the cultivated countryside and entered the forested wilderness beyond.

While she was glad to be leaving, she wished they were doing it a bit quicker. Liz did not like the almost reluctant pace the man was setting. She felt naked out here in the open within sight of the castle walls, and kept expecting to hear the cry of the guard and the sound of pursuing horses.

Suddenly, a deep tolling gong rang out across the blue twilit fields. Liz started at the sound, and fought the urge to spur her horse forward into the gathering dusk, before recognizing that it was only the chapel bell striking the evening hour. She turned in her saddle to look back. The distant white stones of the palace shone under the silver moonlight like bleached bone. In the quiet of the coming night, it seemed otherworldly and dreadful.

For the love of light, Liz, get hold of your imagination.

Deliberately, she forced her eyes back to the road ahead. Despite her guide's apparent lack of urgency, they had come upon the forest with an eerie swiftness, and an unexpected shiver of dread passed through her body as the silent, brooding man led them under the first trees and into the dark of the wood. The reaching boughs closed in above their heads, obscuring the silver moon and the glittering stars. Between one breath and another, all was dark.

Collins stopped just within cover of the wood. There

was the sharp sound of stone on stone and a series of bright firefly sparks, then a flash of yellow-orange as the man lit his lantern. He turned about and regarded her behind the flickering light. The man's cloak was deeply hooded so that the light from the lantern concealed his face in a ghoulish mask of flickering shadows. The effect was disturbing and Liz recoiled involuntarily. He did not seem to notice her reaction, or at least did not comment on it. Nodding at nothing, he turned back around and spurred his horse forward, jerking the string of horses behind him into a reluctant walk.

What is wrong with you? she lectured herself. *Here you are escaping, and instead of being relieved, you're jumping about like a child on All Hallows' Eve. Now, calm down or Mr. Collins will think you're a madwoman.*

Still, she was unnerved. Liz had been so relieved that she was finally leaving the castle and the Princess behind that she had not really considered the nature of her guide, other than to note that he smelled a little like freshly baked pie. Now she studied him. Elle had warned her that he was not a proper valet, but more of a huntsman that her father had forced on her as a chaperon. Still, Elle had marked him as quite an affable fellow. But either he was changed, or Elle had very low standards, because Liz doubted he had spoken two words to her since their meeting in the stables. For the sake of her own nerves, she decided to try and strike up a conversation.

"Collins—" The sudden sound of her own voice in the stillness of the wood made Liz jump, and her horse pranced nervously in response. She breathed in deeply. "I say, Mr. Collins, I wanted to thank you for your help."

"My-pleasure-Your-Ladyship." His answer came in an unpleasant, broken monotone that belied his words.

She frowned in the darkness. "How long have you been in the Lady Rapunzel's service, Mr. Collins?"

There was an inordinately long pause, and at first Liz was afraid he might not answer at all, but in time he rasped out, "Long-enough-Your-Ladyship."

Interesting, thought Liz, *perhaps he is not the happy servant Elle made him out to be.* She would try something else to break his maddening formality. "Please, Mr. Collins, you do not have to be so proper with me, call me Elizabeth or Liz."

She waited for him to extend the same courtesy, but instead he looked back and regarded her silently from beneath his hooded cloak, his face a formless void. Without comment, he turned his gaze back to the road ahead. Liz clucked her tongue against her teeth. The man was a boor. Any thought of further conversation vanished, and Liz fell into a petulant silence. She would have words with Elle when next she saw her.

The horses plodded on in the quiet air, and, after a time, Liz found her eyes drooping. Yawning, she spoke up again, hoping for a better result. "Mr. Collins, it is getting late. How much further do you intend us to go tonight?"

The man moved implacably forward for a few breaths until Liz thought she might have to repeat herself, but as she opened her mouth, he responded, "Not-far-Your-Ladyship-we-turn-off-just-ahead."

Liz sat up at this. "Then we are leaving the road, Mr. Collins?"

If she had expected a treatise on his plan, she was sorely disappointed, because he responded in that same terse and stilted manner. "Yes-Your-Ladyship."

"Is there an inn ahead, then?"

"No-Your-Ladyship."

"Then we will be camping in—in the woods tonight?"

"Yes-Your-Ladyship."

This was a change of plans, and normally she would have questioned him further, but she was growing tired, and besides she had no desire to talk to the man anymore. She thought she might scream if he said Yes-Your-Ladyship or No-Your-Ladyship one more time.

The riders settled back into an uneasy silence and then the horse in front of her stopped. Collins abruptly thrust his lantern toward the left side of the road and pointed into a shadowy gap in the trees. "Here-Your-Ladyship."

Liz stared into the wooded maw, and saw . . . nothing. The path, if it could be called that, was barely wide enough for a single horse and dark as pitch. It took her eyes a full minute to discern anything beyond the opening, and then all she could make out were the shadowy outlines of the trees that marked the edges of the trail and the reflecting eyes of invisible night-creatures blinking on and off as they stared back from the darkness beyond. Collins began moving into the gap. Liz watched the forest swallow him and shuddered.

"Is this really necessary, Mr. Collins?" Liz called after him weakly. "Can't we just press on along the road a bit further?" She knew her voice sounded small and scared, and she cursed her fear but could not master it.

His muted voice reached back to her from inside the forest tunnel. "Yes-Your-Ladyship. No-Your-Ladyship. We-must-not-be-found-on-the-road-Your-Ladyship."

Liz supposed there was sense in that, but a seed of fear had set root in her mind. This had not been part of the plan, and it did not feel like something Elle would have her do.

As she hesitated on the brink of the dark trail, Collins continued forward; and as he did, the glow of the lantern also moved into the dense woods, leaving Liz in growing shadow. She took a last, longing look at the broad paved road and spurred her horse after the rapidly fading light, cursing, as she did, this man *and* Elle, who had lent him to her, *and* the Princess, who had made her flight necessary, *and* her brother, who had been so sure that being in a fairy tale would be easy, *and* the dragon, and her father, and her father's father, and so on, until the path twisted and she was well and truly in the arms of the night.

The trees crowded in around her, their branches reaching greedily out from the edge of the trail to pull at her cloak. Liz focused her whole being on the comforting will-o'-the-wisp glow of the lantern as it bobbed and weaved its way along the path. At times the trail would make a sharp turn and the comforting little light would momentarily disappear. It was at these times that Liz's curses turned to prayers, and she regretted her regular blasphemies.

What seemed like an eternity later, the trail emerged into a circular glade about forty paces across. Overhead, a dome of dark green branches let a little glow of moonlight slip through to the grassy floor of the clearing. For Liz, it seemed like the dawn. She let out the breath she had not known she was holding, and relaxed. Perhaps the night would not be as unpleasant as she had feared. Liz had always enjoyed the woods, and in the daylight she imagined that this was quite a pleasant spot.

Collins was at the far end of the clearing, the lantern set on the ground behind him as he hobbled the last of the pack animals for the night. Liz took off her riding gloves and laid them across the top of her saddle. "Will you attend to my horse also, Mr. Collins?"

"As-you-wish-Your-Ladyship," he said in a hissing exhale, and turned stiffly to look at her.

Liz gasped and felt her heart take flight. Collins had lowered his hood as he worked with the animals, and now the flickering light of the lantern revealed his face, and across his face was etched a smile. It was a cunning smile, a dead, cold smile, and Liz had seen its twin only once before . . . over tea at Castle White. It was an expression she would never forget. She knew not how, but she was certain that she was not looking into the eyes of Elle's valet, Collins, but those of Princess Gwendolyn Mostfair.

While Liz battled to calm her nerves, Collins bent stiffly to retrieve the lantern and then began advancing erratically toward her, the light thrust forward in one hand and something bright and sharply tapered poorly concealed in the other. This was madness. It was Collins, it must be, and yet just as clearly it was not. Indeed, now that her suspicions had a focus, the strangeness of his mannerism was clearly revealed. It was as though the man's body was at war with itself. Every movement was a battle, some won, some lost. But whatever the character of his struggle, its will seemed the stronger. She had to accept that whatever this thing was standing across from her, it was not Elle's Collins, or at least it was not Mr. Collins in mind even if it was his body.

A hundred thoughts struck her at once. She should turn the horse about and run. But she had no light to flee by, no weapon to fight with, nowhere to run that he could not follow. And then there he was at the head of her horse, grabbing at the reins.

"You-will-need-to-dismount-Your-Ladyship."

Fearing her voice would crack if she attempted speech, Liz nodded mutely. Collins's body smiled that ghastly, wicked smile again. A renewed surge of terror rushed through her body. Her hands began to shake. Despite everything, Liz had been holding out hope that her fear was just the mad invention of her imagination, but that depraved smirk was all the confirmation she needed. She took a deep breath and tried to replace the fear with cold resolve.

I may be without hope, but I will not yield without a fight.

Liz handed him the reins and at the same moment gave the horse a subtle nudge in the sides with her heeled boots. The animal tried to surge forward, forcing Collins to wrestle with the beast to calm it. Liz used the time to study her would-be assassin. Collins stood a head taller, and outweighed her by five stone, all of which seemed to be muscle. A straight fight would be pointless, but maybe guile would win where strength could not. Her mind raced.

Perhaps if I can get him to bend down a bit. . .

She started to rise from the saddle to dismount, but then paused in midmovement and pretended to struggle with her riding skirts. She put as much helplessness as she could into her voice—for once it was not difficult. "I am sorry, Mr. Collins, but my skirt seems to be stuck beneath the cinch, could you help me with it?"

"Of-course-Your-Ladyship," he said heavily and then began moving along the side of the horse toward her, one hand still holding the reins awkwardly behind him.

Liz could feel the heat of his body against her dangling leg as he searched through the flowing fabric of the riding skirt for the tangle. And his smell, an overpowering smell of nutmeg clung to him so intense that she thought she would choke. She pointed vaguely below the stirrup, and in a breathy voice said, "There, Mr. Collins . . . I think . . . perhaps . . . a bit lower."

He dropped the reins, grabbed the cinch strap in one hand, and began tracing it along the horse's underside. As soon as he bent down Liz turned and fumbled in her pack for anything she might use as a weapon. Her hand fell on a copy of the "Dragon's Tale" she had appropriated from the castle. It was a heavy thing, beautifully bound with a thick wood cover front and back. Grabbing it with both hands, she stood in the stirrups and, lifting the book high above her, brought it down violently on the man's unprotected head. There was a sickening crack, and Collins collapsed in a heap on the ground. His unconscious body rolled beneath the horse, and the nervy animal, already spooked, reared up and leapt forward.

Liz fell from the saddle. She put out her left hand to catch her fall. A terrible blinding pain raced from her wrist to her shoulder, and she cried out. The horse whinnied and danced away to join the tethered herd. She looked over to where Collins lay.

The lantern had shattered on impact with the ground, and she watched as the exposed flame guttered in the breeze. In the dim light that remained, she could see the man's eyes flutter. *At least I didn't kill him*, she thought with relief. Then he groaned and his hands moved haltingly to his head. In an instant, her relief turned to a curse. *Bloody hell, how thick is that man's skull*? She looked over at the book that had fallen beside him and got her answer—thick enough to snap the solid wooden cover in half. She needed to find a way to restrain him.

Looking about, she saw that her leather satchel had fallen with her. She picked up the bag with her good hand and slung it over her shoulder. Cradling her aching arm gingerly against her body, Liz rose and stumbled in the direction of the lantern. She had just reached it when Collins's eyes snapped open. The wind rose and swirled. The flame winked out, and the deep, darkness of the woods returned, and with it so did Liz's terror.

She ran. She ran into the dark wall of trees that encircled them, and she kept running directionless. Even had she known where to go, in the dense woods there were no stars to guide her, only the dim shadows of tree and bush. At one point she thought she heard the man's rough voice calling from the clearing, but there was no sound of pursuit, and in time his shouts were lost. Still, she ran on.

Mostly blind, she ran without caution. Roots caught at her ankles, sending her more than once to the ground. Limbs slashed at her arms and face. Vines and thorn-bushes tore at her dress and skirt. If she fell, she rose again. If she was caught, she pulled herself free with brute force. Speed and distance were all she cared about now—to put enough forest between her and Gwendolyn's marionette that he could not hope to find her. And then, between one stride and the next, she stepped into empty space and fell. She landed on her back. Her head snapped back violently and struck something hard, and the world went black.

IN HER HIDDEN chamber in the castle, Princess Gwendolyn Mostfair stared hard into the swirling black mist of the ball. "What is the meaning of this, Fairy? Why can I not see what is happening?"

A smug, self-satisfied voice seemed to drift down from somewhere near the ceiling. *"I canst only show what is, not what thou wishest to see."*

With a violent curse, she covered the sphere and the

mist dissolved, leaving only the tiny otherworldly light burning within. "Do not play word games with me, little one. I demand to know what has happened."

There was a short pause, and then the voice returned. *"There has been a struggle in the woods, Mistress, and Lady Elizabeth Pickett is lost."*

Gwendolyn held the ball in one hand, and tapped at its glass surface with the long painted nail of her forefinger. "This is a true account? Rapunzel's man . . . he—she—is gone?"

"I can tell no lie, Mistress. The Lady Pickett struggled with your man, and now she is gone."

The Princess put the glass sphere in its holder and leaned back in her chair. A sudden chill had entered the room. She looked over at the fire that blazed in the grate and shivered. The shadows had taken up residence around it, and they seemed to suck all the heat from the flames.

"I did not mean for it to happen." Gwendolyn looked over at the fairy, expecting a reply. "I only asked him to hold her in the woods until I could ascend the throne. That was all he was instructed to do, not"—she fluttered her hands in the air in frustration—"not this."

The fairy flickered dimly and without comment. Gwen willed herself to look away. *I will not seek absolution.* She closed her eyes and a wave of fatigue washed over her body. She rubbed her eyelids to try and relieve the pressure in her head. The man's resolve had been stronger than she had expected. His loyalty to Lady Rapunzel was commendable. He had fought her every moment, but she was stronger. Unconsciously, her mind began to review the last few minutes in the clearing. How had everything gone so wrong?

It is done. I will not waste time on regret.

Still, she could not get the girl's face out of her mind. The fairy light pulsed on without changing, and the silent judgment of the creature was too much. Her anger boiled to a fine rage, and she stood so that she towered above the delicate little sphere. "I DID NOT MEAN TO KILL HER!" she shouted.

The fairy's bone-dry answer came straightaway. *"For someone that does not mean to kill, it would seem that you manage it with some regularity, Mistress."*

Gwendolyn's hands shook with fury. She wanted to smash the smug little sprite. She wanted it to die, to—

The shadows sprung from their place to crowd around her, whispering and giggling. Briefly, from among the voices, she thought she could hear Rosslyn screaming in terror. She swung her arms up to ward them off; the room spun dangerously, and Gwendolyn fell back into her chair. She put a hand to her throbbing temple. It was no use spending her energy fighting with the winged demon or these visions. There was still so much to do. She had to find some way of dealing with Rapunzel, and there was the matter of working up a good charm to ensnare Will when he returned. Yes, there was much to do, but now she needed rest. She would be clearheaded in the morning, and the shadows and Liz and her guilt would be forgotten.

JAMES COLLINS, VALET of Lady Rapunzel and former mindless puppet of Princess Gwendolyn Mostfair, was gasping for air on the ground, listening to the receding clamor of Lady Elizabeth as she fled. Through sheer will, he rose to his feet and tried, once more, to follow. This time he made it three full steps before the world tilted violently and he dropped to the ground retching. There was no use. He didn't even have the strength or breath to try calling out again, not that he had any reason to believe she would listen to his pleas. He would have to wait until morning to begin his pursuit.

James rolled onto his back and stared up through the opening in the forest canopy at the twinkling night. A terrible, helpless fatigue fell over him. Marshaling his remaining wits, he tried to recall everything that had happened over the last two days. The last thing he could remember clearly was an audience with the Princess, kneeling before her, an orb of swirling light in her hand, and then a blinding pain as Lady Elizabeth smashed that bloody book over his head.

What happened? What have I done? His eyes drifted closed. *What has been done to me?* His breathing evened and grew steady. *Is Lady Rapunzel safe, or does the Princess have a plot for her as well?* It was with this last troubled thought swirling in his battered skull that he slipped gratefully into the oblivion of sleep.

Chapter 12

Goodbye, Couplet

CHARMING SPENT THE night lying awake on his bed, twisting the silver coin, standing and pacing, lying down again, waiting, and all the time indulging and rejecting all the excuses he had for betraying Will, Elizabeth, and himself. In time, dawn worked its way through the spaces in the wooden wall. He watched the dirty light crawl across the floor and then a ray fell across his eyes and he blinked, as though waking from a dream. He whispered the one inescapable thought that had echoed in his mind the whole night: "I may have never been a hero, but I am not yet a villain."

He glanced over at the other cots. Will and the squire hadn't made it back to the room last night. He sighed deeply. It was time to wake the hero and withdraw to the castle. Charming put the silver coin into his pouch, grunted and stood. His head felt wrong where the troll had smashed it, and the world kept trying to roll over. He blinked his vision clear and staggered through the hall and down the steps.

Reaching the common room of the inn, he was overwhelmed by a terrible stench. Men and women were passed out on, and in some cases, under almost every table; and the plank floor was coated in a terrifying mixture of spilled ale and sick. The only person upright and conscious in the whole place was a lazy-eyed crone who was halfheartedly wiping a filthy cloth across the surface of the bar. Charming had a whole new appreciation for the term "unwashed masses." He gagged and, vainly trying to filter the smell with his sleeve, began his search for the two men.

In due course, he found them both. The squire sat slumped in a chair, while Will was laid out on one of the tables. Charming leaned close, cleared his throat, and said, "Lord Protector."

After an extended groan Will's eyes fluttered open. "Char—Charming, what are you doing up?"

"It's actually rather late in the morning," Charming replied dryly.

"Is it?" Will burped and a terrible noxious odor issued forth. He smacked his lips and gave Charming an appraising glance. "You . . . my friend . . . are a complete mess. I'm sure no one would believe that I had been the one drinking all night and you had been the one to take to your bed early."

The wench at the bar cackled, "No indeed, Your Lordship, but then you are the very model of manliness."

Charming watched a pleased little smile flicker over Will's face. The Prince raised an eyebrow. This was not the William Pickett he had left on the bridge. Whether it had been born from the night's revels, or his defeat of the troll, Charming knew that Will finally believed himself to be a hero. From personal experience, he also knew how dangerous and heady a feeling it was. Perhaps the odious little man from last night had been right—perhaps it was time to take "His Lordship" down a few rungs. Charming would, however, make sure he was there to save the day!

WILL CRADLED HIS head in his hands as the room spun about him. He tried listen to Charming going on about whatever he was going on about, but the Prince's long-winded prattling was beginning to wear.

" . . . so, my point being, Will, that the Red Renegade, or the Scarlet Scoundrel, or whatever it is, is planning an ambush on the forest road bridge. Anyway, someone has to stop them, and—"

Will cut him off. "Fine. I'll take care of it." He smacked a hand on the table and bellowed, "Tomas!"

The squire awoke with a start and fell back off his chair. With a colorful curse, he began to gather himself from the ground.

Charming looked at Will with wide eyes. The fool was actually planning on riding out, unaccompanied, against a band of brigands? The Will he knew would never— But then, this was not the Will he knew. He had to stop this, now, before his betrayal was made real.

"Wait! No, you don't understand! I thought we would both go. We don't know how many of them are out there. More importantly, the Count isn't . . . are you listening? It's a mistake to go alone."

The Prince waved a pleading hand at Tomas for support, but the squire seemed unsure of even where he was and just kept repeating, "Wassat? Wassat?"

Charming's words were barely discernable over the buzz in Will's head, and his stomach was a roiling knot. Will needed to end this conversation now. Besides, Will suspected the "mistake" was that he would, once again, get all the glory. So Will decided to preempt any lengthy discussion the only way he knew how, by talking about the dragon and the Prince's battered face. "Look, I defeated the dragon and the troll. I can handle a bandit. Besides, you need your rest. You look terrible."

With that, Will lifted Tomas to his feet and strode away, half dragging the wobbly squire to the door. As he reached the threshold, though, he realized he had no idea where he was going. He looked back at Charming for a moment. "Um"—he bit his lip—"where is the . . . ?"

The Prince was strangely silent. He looked up at Will, eyes wide and mouth open. The serving wench answered instead. "The bridge? Further along the forest road, Your Lordship. A few leagues short of the King's hunting lodge."

Something the woman said seemed to shake Charming out of his momentary silence, because he sprang to his feet and called out, "No! Stop! Will . . . Lord Protector, please, you don't understand—"

But Will never heard whatever it was Charming wanted him to understand, because the Prince grabbed at his head, swayed violently on his feet, and toppled forward. He was unconscious before he hit the floor.

Will leaned Tomas against the doorway, ran to Charming and knelt down beside him. "Damned fool! Doesn't he know you can't jump about like that when you have as many knocks on the head as he has?"

"Probably not," Tomas rasped from the doorway. "I don't know that he's ever *been* knocked on the head before. Well, except the tree and the armor . . . still . . ."

Will gestured to the barmaid, who fluffed her hair, pulled the neck of her dress down to expose as much bosom as possible, and swayed her way over to him. "Yes, Your Lordship?"

He gave her a winning smile and asked, "Can you get some of the men to carry my friend up to his room?" She looked at Charming dubiously and Will shoved a couple of silver coins into her hand. "It would mean a lot to me."

She winked and gave him a black-toothed smile. "Anything for you, Lord Protector."

Outside Tomas handed Will a water skin and a pouch full of sunflower seeds. He choked out, "The salt should . . . hmmm . . . help with the sickness."

They both chewed on the salty seeds and emptied their water skins, trying to clear their heads and settle their stomachs. It was while spitting out shells and some other unidentifiable things from deeper in his gut that Will explained their task. The squire's reaction was not particularly encouraging.

"You're bloody kidding, right?"

"No, Tomas, I am not."

"Are ye still drunk?"

"No." At least Will did not think so. "No! We must save Count . . . um . . . well the count." Will tried to remember what Charming had said, but on reflection it all seemed muddled. "It does not matter who the man is, Tomas, the important point is that he needs my help."

"But, we don't know squat about these woods, Will. We could be walking into a hundred men for all we know."

Will considered the point, but felt that he had to live up to the title he had so proudly claimed the night before. He stood, putting his hands to his hips, and assumed a commanding tone that he hoped sounded like the Prince. "I am committed, Tomas. There is no point arguing. Now, let us away to our—" It was at this point that Will noticed their horses were nowhere to be seen. "Tomas . . ." he croaked, then swallowed hard in a vain attempt to clear his throat. "Hmmmm . . . where are our horses?"

The squire looked blearily about and spat, "Probably still in the stable, *Yarrr* Lardship. Unless they got smart and took a runner."

"Well, would you, I mean could you . . . ?" Will pleaded lamely.

The squire muttered to himself as he stomped off toward the stables. "He has about as much sense as the damned Prince."

When Tomas returned, he was not leading Will's much-beloved horse, Jasper, from the stables, but the Prince's dramatic and ill-tempered white charger. Will massaged his temples, "Um . . . Tomas, I think you have the wrong horse there."

"No, *Yarr* Lardship," he replied as he led the champing stallion toward him.

"But that is the Prince's horse."

"Yes, *Yarr* Lardship," Tomas said as he helped Will up into the high stirrup of the creature.

"But I am not the Prince," he said with a grunt as he struggled to control the horse.

"I had thought not," said the squire flatly as he mounted his own brown gelding. "But you're making a good go of it this morning." With that, the squire spurred his horse forward, leaving Will to stare openmouthed at his retreating back.

The two men rode in silence through the thickening woods. He wanted to explain, but each time he tried to strike up a conversation, the squire would mutter darkly about "young fools" and "swelled heads," so he gave up. Perhaps it was the dark nature of the forest, or the squire's attitude, but as each mile passed, Will's uneasiness grew. This was madness! What was he doing? Tomas was right. He should turn back now. But then what? What was the point of being Lord Protector if he could not protect the people?

While his mind was spinning on these thoughts he half heard the sound of wood echoing beneath the hooves of his horse. He looked up. They had reached the bridge. It was a narrow thing constructed of planks laid over enormous logs. He signaled to Tomas to hold up and, dismounting, led his horse onto the middle of the span.

It was a pleasant spot. Beneath marching lines of vaulting gray-green trees, a shallow sun-dappled stream laughed its way over a pebbly bed of smooth rocks. A light breeze swirled now and then through the leaves, bringing with it a coolness that hinted at the just-departed winter. The only disturbances to the tranquility were the harsh calls of a flock of crows roosting in the high branches of a dark-trunked tree that loomed over the far bank. Seeing no threat, he motioned for the squire to join him.

"No sign of the count or the bandits," he said with a casualness he did not feel. "Maybe this whole quest will turn out to be nothing after—"

"AHA!" came a shout, which made him flinch and spooked the crows into a noisy, panicked flight.

Will saw a figure flying through the air at the end of a long rope. The man let go and gracefully landed at the other end of the bridge. He was tall and thin and elegantly dressed in a forest green tunic and matching tights, all topped off with a large feathered cap. He had a sword at his hip, a bow around his chest, and a quiver of arrows at his back. A gleam of confidence shone in his eye and he smiled as he looked at Will and the squire.

With a flourish of his feathered cap, he bowed to them. Then, putting his cap back on his head, he twisted the end of an elaborate mustache and shouted. "Aha! I am the Scarlet Scoundrel, Champion of the Poor, Hero of the People, Terror to Tyrants and these"—he made another elaborate flourish with both hands, and from the trees on either side of the bridge dozens of green-, black-, and brown-clad figures sprang out of hiding, surrounding them— "are my Horrible Hooligans."

There was a stir among the men surrounding the bridge and one of them, a short fat fellow, sprinted forward till he was standing just behind the Scoundrel. For a half-beat, the green-clad bandit tried to ignore the man's presence, though he was clearly straining to maintain his brilliant smile.

"Ahem . . ." The henchman cleared his throat and tugged at the Scoundrel's sleeve.

The Scoundrel's smile vanished, and, sighing deeply, he held up a finger. "I am sorry, Lord Protector, if you will but give me a moment to confer with my henchman here."

He turned his back on Will and a soft, if heated, discussion ensued. They could only make out bits and pieces, but it seemed to have something to do with the name he'd used for his henchmen.

" . . . *ruining everything* . . ." the Scoundrel hissed.

" . . . *we agreed . . . Hoodlums . . .*" his henchman shot back.

"*Are you sure? . . . Heinous . . . better alliteration . . . intimidating . . .*" The bandit captain ticked off points on his fingers.

" . . . *voted Merry Men!*" the fat man hissed.

Suddenly, the Scoundrel raised his voice, "Merry Men? Bah! We shall deal with this later." He spun back toward Will and the squire. "Sorry about that Lord Protector. We are still working out our *noms de guerre*. Anyone in our line of business will tell you the right name can make all the difference, but please do not let this trouble you, I assure you both, we are professionals. The point is, these are my men, and I am the Heinous Highwayman—no, no, dammit, they've got me all confused now, the Scarlet Scoundrel . . ."

His voice trailed off.

Will and the squire both watched quizzically as he twisted his mustache and looked up into the trees. After a few deep breaths, he reconstructed his smile, lowered his gaze again, and shouting, "AHA!" once more, drew his sword.

Will fumbled with the sword at his side, but only managed to pinch his finger in the scabbard before yelping out, "Aha what?"

The Highwayman or Scoundrel smiled and laughed. "Aha, Lord Protector, you are my prisoner! I'm holding you for ransom."

Will wasn't exactly sure what to do, but this was not going the way he thought it would. He looked around. There were at least two dozen of them, if not more, and every one had an arrow nocked and aimed in their general direction. Oddly enough, though, they looked as nervous as he felt. This gave him an idea. A mad idea to be sure, but still it was something to work with.

Will puffed up his chest in his best imitation of

Charming, and announced, "Well, I am the Lord Protector and Dragon Slayer, and as far as I am concerned, you are my prisoner, as are all of your men. I shall give you one chance to surrender, and I will remind you all that when I killed the dragon, I didn't have my sword with me, and when I defeated the troll I didn't even bother to draw it. So, you may wish to try me, but I wouldn't." He punctuated this last by placing his hand very deliberately on the pommel of his sword.

"And," one of the men, who looked vaguely familiar, shouted from the leafy border, "he drank a dozen mugs of ale at the Cooked Goose."

At this, a collective gasp came from the men, and even the bandit captain quailed.

"My God, man, what sort of stuff are you made of?" asked the Scoundrel. He waved a hand and his men lowered their bows. "I see we are at an impasse—you, with your legendary skill at arms and epic constitution, and I, with my overwhelming odds and ever-growing reputation, but I have something up my sleeve, a hidden ace."

The Scoundrel clapped twice. Two of his men disappeared behind a dense screen of undergrowth. When they emerged a few moments later, one was holding His Royal Majesty, the King. The other was holding a fair-haired man in royal livery. One of the henchmen prodded the liveried man with a dirk and the prisoner announced in a booming, yet nervous voice, "Presenting His Royal Majesty, the King in captivity, prisoner of the Red Renegade and his Bleeding Brigands."

"AHA!" the Scoundrel shouted at Will, then he spun

on the captives, "No, wait, weren't you at the meeting this morning? I am now the Scarlet Scoundrel, and my men are the . . . the, *ahem*—at least I'm the Scarlet Scoundrel, that is without dispute." He put his hands to his hips and glared. "You call yourself the Royal Herald. I have to say I am very disappointed."

The Scoundrel looked back to Will. "Where was I? Oh yes . . . Aha! As you can see, I have His Royal Majesty, the King. So surrender, or else."

"Or else what?" Will asked with honest curiosity.

"I'll have to . . . you know." The Scoundrel drug one finger across his throat.

"Why, you bloody fiend," hissed the squire, "I'll . . ."

Will raised his hand to silence the squire. All he needed now was for the man to try something heroic and get them both killed. "Now, Tomas, don't worry. I'm sure the Scarlet Scoundrel has no intention of harming His Royal Majesty.

"I wouldn't count on that, Lord Protector. We are desperate men . . . the Terrors of the Trees, the Fiends of the Forest, the Wastrels of the Woods . . . the . . ." The Scoundrel stopped and gave Will an embarrassed smile. "Sorry, that last one didn't work very well."

Will lowered his voice again. "Just an observation, but I think you're using alliteration a little too much. I mean it's nice on occasion, but if you overuse it, well . . . it can sound silly."

The bandit nodded his head in agreement and said quietly, "I know. I guess you could call it my fatal flaw." Then his features hardened "But don't think I will allow you to exploit my weakness. I will give the order to execute the King if you force my hand."

Will almost asked the man how he could possibly exploit his penchant for first-syllable rhyming schemes to defeat him, but decided that they really needed to get back to the matter at hand. So Will put as much concern as he could into his voice and said, "What? You would kill the King?" Will shook his head sadly. "I guess you are the expert in banditry, but I can't say that would be my plan. If you hurt the King, he won't be worth much ransom, and then, of course, every knight in the land, including me, will have to come after you." Will made a low whistling sound in his teeth. "I don't like your odds. Killing him will make you the most hated man in all the kingdom. How can you be a people's hero if the people hate you?"

"Well, I hadn't . . . Why are you making this so difficult?"

Will shrugged. "Sorry."

They stood in a shifting uneasy silence for a time, and, though he didn't want to break the impasse, Will had to admit this was getting awkward. Looking about for some inspiration, he noticed that the crows were returning to their tree in a fluttering cloud of black. The crows and the little pouch of seeds Tomas had given him earlier brought an idea to his mind. Despite the dire situation, he smiled. It probably wouldn't work, but it was a better plan than waiting for the bandits to tire of his bluffs and fill him full of arrows.

"Perhaps," said Will, "I have a resolution to our standoff."

The Scoundrel's smile broadened, "Really? Because I have to tell you I am at a loss. For my part, I have to apologize. I really think this would have gone better had I had gotten the name right at the beginning."

The man was obsessed. Will closed his eyes in aggravation, but said softly, "Don't beat yourself up about that, Scoundrel. As far as I'm concerned, it never happened."

"That's very big of you, Lord Protector." He laughed aloud again, "Now, what's your resolution?"

Steadying his face, Will said, "If you have a sling among your men, then you and I can settle this conflict ourselves in a contest of skill. If you win, I surrender peacefully. If I win, you let me have the King. Either way, it will make a great story and will expand our legends greatly." Lowering his voice, he added, "Plus, it has the distinct advantage of not requiring one of us to die."

The Scarlet Scoundrel winked at Will. "I get your meaning . . . it's genius," he said softly. Then, in a much louder voice, he proclaimed, "That is an excellent idea. What sort of contest did you have in mind, Lord Protector?"

This was the craziest idea Will had ever had. He tried not to think about the fact that he was surrounded by a group of armed, and possibly dangerously deranged, men. He gestured at the Scoundrel and projected his voice so that all could hear. "I suspect that you consider yourself a great archer, Scarlet Scoundrel. So I propose a contest of shooting skill." He pointed dramatically at the crow-laden tree. "Do you see that tree full of birds? I wager that I can bring down more birds with one loose of a sling than you can with three shots from your bow. The man who *brings down* the most birds wins."

The Scarlet Scoundrel's face brightened. "Let me understand this, Lord Protector. You will have but one throw with a sling, and I may shoot my bow thrice? Victory will be determined by the number of birds we bring down from the tree? And you will swear to abide by the result of this contest?"

"You have my word as Lord Protector of this realm."

Behind him Tomas hissed, "*This is madness, Will, you'll never be able to . . .*"

The Scarlet Scoundrel did not allow the squire any more time to talk, "I agree! Let's shake on it."

Will offered his hand warily, but there were no tricks. The Scoundrel had a firm and warm handshake. As soon as he withdrew his hand, the bandit laughed, "Aha! You have just cost yourself your freedom, as well as the freedom of the King and your squire."

The Scoundrel stepped forward and, in a single fluid motion, drew his bow and fitted an arrow to the string. "Everyone bear witness. I, the most skilled archer in all the land, shall now provide you with a display of shooting fit for legend."

He aimed but briefly and then loosed an arrow. The first shaft struck a bird high in the tree. It exploded in a spray of black feathers. Before it had even hit the ground, a second arrow was on its way. It neatly impaled another bird, sending it plummeting to the ground. The first two shots had happened so quickly, and so quietly, that the remaining birds had not stirred a feather. This time the Scoundrel took a moment to aim, then, exhaling deeply, he loosed his last bolt. The arrow flew straight into the densest grouping of birds. A black mass dropped from the tree to the ground below, and the remaining birds took to the air in a cacophony of shrieking caws.

Will whistled, "Very impressive shooting Scarlet. One for each arrow, so that would be three . . ."

"I think you will find it is four, Lord Protector," the Scoundrel countered with a rather poor attempt at humility.

Sure enough, one of the Scoundrel's men came forward carrying the carcasses of four large crows, the last shot having impaled two.

Will bowed to the man. "I stand corrected. You are surely an archer beyond compare. Now, if you will supply me a sling and allow a few moments for the birds to return, I shall prepare myself."

The Scarlet Scoundrel doffed his cap with a flourish and made a deep bow. "As you wish, Lord Protector." A man came forward and offered Will a much-worn slingshot. He gave it a few practice twirls to get a feel for it. The men chuckled and jeered, but the Scoundrel raised his hand and glowered at his band. "Quiet. Show some respect."

Slowly, the birds returned to their perches in the tree. Will stepped forward and poured out a measure of Tomas's seeds into the sling's cradle. He took a deep breath and, taking careful aim at the tree, spun the sling rapidly over his head and loosed his shot. The little projectiles flew straight and true, but landed harmlessly at the base of the tree.

The Scarlet Scoundrel stretched his hands out in puzzlement. "Lord Protector, you . . . you missed entirely. I can't believe it. I have to say I'm more than a little dis—"

Suddenly, there was a rustling movement in the tree and, en masse, the remaining birds descended from their perches and began scrabbling at the ground where the seed had fallen.

"—appointed?"

Will squinted toward the milling throng and mouthed silently as he counted. "I am not sure how many birds I just *brought down*, Scarlet Scoundrel, but I would ask that you agree as a gentleman that it is more than four."

Silence fell over the bandits, and even the Scoundrel was speechless, well, nearly speechless. "H—How . . ."

Will tossed the Scoundrel the little bag in answer. The bandit stared at it in confusion, and then, at Will's prompting, emptied the contents into his palm. The bandit's eyes grew wide, and there was a moment when Will feared the man might kill him anyway, but then he threw back his head and laughed loudly, "Seeds! Sunflower seeds!" He bowed to Will with a sweep of his feathered cap. "Well done, Sir! You have defeated me fairly, the King is yours." He turned to the men holding the elderly monarch. "Release His Royal Majesty, immediately!"

With a gesture from their leader, the Scarlet Scoundrel's men melted into the trees, leaving the King and the herald standing in openmouthed disbelief. Alone on the bridge, the bandit leader clasped Will's hand once more. "It has been an honor to match wits with you, Lord Protector. You truly are a formidable foe, and I can see now why you are considered the greatest hero in all the realm. I hope that one day the name of . . . the Green Phantom and his Boisterous Band . . . will be as well known."

The Scoundrel arched an eyebrow and looked hopefully at him. Will rubbed his temples, and said flatly, "Better, Scar . . . Phantom. Better. While we're on other topics, though, can I ask you a question that has been puzzling me?

"Anything, Lord Protector."

"You seem to be a man of honor, Phantom, so why have you turned bandit?"

To his credit, the man blushed bright red. "To be honest, Lord Protector, it was little more than pique that started it, an insult by the King that could not be borne. But now I rather enjoy the life. Ah, speak of the devil . . ."

Will turned to see the King making his way slowly onto the bridge with the help of his herald. The Scoundrel gave a jaunty little salute. "Farewell, Lord Protector, William Pickett. As for you, Your Majesty, we have unfinished business."

And, with a shouted, "AHA!" he made a running grab for the rope that still dangled above the bridge and swung himself back into the safety of the trees.

Will shook his head at the retreating man and then

turned his attention to the King. He and Tomas each dropped to a knee. "Your Majesty, it is good to see that you are well."

The King placed a hand on Will's shoulder. "Rise, Lord Protector, William Pickett, you should bow to no one. You have now twice saved me. First from my shame, and now from capture. When this story is told, and I will make sure that it is, your legend as the hero of the realm will be ensured for all time. For what you have done for me, I would give you anything. If you asked of me the throne, I swear I would make it yours."

Will stayed on his knee and stared at the planks of the bridge. "Please, Your Majesty, don't say that, there is too much that I need to tell you . . ." Will's heart was hammering in his chest.

Behind him, Tomas groaned audibly. "Perhaps this can wait for another time, Your Lordship."

"No, Tomas. The time has come for me to give the King the truth about how the dragon died."

And so he did. When he finished, the King stroked his chin and intoned ponderously, "Well, well, that explains quite a lot."

"Yes, Your Majesty. But please, Sire, my sister, Elizabeth, she is innocent. I forced her to undertake this deception. "

The King laughed aloud at this. "You are at a disadvantage, Lord William. You forget that I have met your most formidable sister. Forced? I think not. Now, let me ask you a question. Why have you told me this?"

"Because it is the truth, Your Majesty. I am not a

hero, and I should not be the kingdom's Lord Protector. I—I don't even know how to hold a sword, much less swing one."

The King laughed again, but this time it had a hard bitter sound to it. "Will, you are talking to a man who has lived a life of cowardice. If I am the measure of what it takes to be a king, then you have proven yourself many times over. Now, I shall hear no more about this. The kingdom needs a hero, and I charge you with fulfilling that role, understood?"

Will sighed in relief. "Yes, Your Majesty. Thank you, Your Majesty. But, please, Sire, could we not discuss the throne just yet? It scares me senseless."

"Agreed," the King declared with a laugh. "Now, let us away. The Scarlet Scoundrel was a most welcoming host, but his bathing facilities were not exactly up to my standards."

Will helped the King onto the waiting charger. "So the bandits were not too rough with you, Your Majesty?"

"Rough? What? Daniel, I mean the Scarlet Phantom, or whatever he has decided to call himself, would never hurt me."

"Wait! Daniel? You know him? The Green Scoun— I mean, the Scarlet Phant— Well, *him*, Your Majesty?"

"Yes, yes." The King waved dismissively. "His father has been one of my good friends and hunting companions for years. I have known Daniel since he was a young boy."

"But why, then, did he kidnap you, Sire?"

"Oh, he's gotten the crazy idea in his head that I

snubbed his family. He says it's about unfair income distribution or something equally ridiculous, but there you go."

The King prattled on as they rode, and all Will could think was that nobles really were mad as snakes. It was while he was trying to puzzle out the why of it that he heard the King ask him a question in a tone that seemed to indicate it was not his first attempt.

"Sorry, Your Majesty. What was that?"

"I said, how did you know where I was?"

"We did not, Your Majesty. It was purest chance. The Prince found out that some bandits were planning to abduct the local count and . . ."

"Local count? Are you sure my son told you this?"

"Yes, Your Majesty," said Will, turning as best he could to answer the King.

The King's face was drawn and pale, almost like a cloud had descended over it. "But there is no local count here."

"Well, I'm sure he just got it wrong," Will said, adding in an offhand way, "Everyone makes mistakes now and then."

The King reined his horse to a stop, forcing Will to follow suit. The monarch fixed him with a gaze that was hard and regal, and reminded Will that he was in the presence of a man used to commanding men and demanding absolute obedience. "No, Will," he said gravely, "just as not all mistakes are allowable, not everyone is allowed to make mistakes."

The rest of the journey back to the Cooked Goose was made in silence.

PRINCE CHARMING AWOKE to the sound of hoofbeats. A late afternoon sun was streaming through the window. "My father, the King!" he shouted. "He must have retired to his hunting cottage. That is where he has been hiding all this time. The bandits! I must warn Will." He fought his swimming head and forced himself to his feet.

Just then a well-trained voice boomed and echoed from outside. "HEAR YE, HEAR YE, MAKE WAY FOR HIS ROYAL MAJESTY, THE KING, WHO HAS BEEN RESCUED THIS VERY DAY BY THE LORD PROTECTOR FROM THE CLUTCHES OF THE VILE VILLAIN, THE SCARLET PHANTOM."

Charming's heart dropped and he shambled to the window. Will was helping his father, the King, dismount from the back of his charger. The Prince stumbled out the front of the tavern in a rush. "Father, Father, have you been harmed?"

At first, the King recoiled at the beaten figure stumbling toward him. Then there was a flash of recognition, and the monarch's features hardened. "Edward."

As soon as Charming heard his father's tone, he stopped. Somehow his treachery had been discovered. Charming fell to his knees in supplication, and did the bravest thing he had ever done—he looked into the eyes of his father, the King.

"I will give you one chance to explain, Edward."

"I . . ." He ran through his list of excuses, and rejected them all. "I have betrayed the Lord Protector, Your Majesty. There can be no explanation, and I will offer no excuse."

The King looked down at his son somberly. "You know what I must do, what I have vowed I will do."

Charming nodded mutely and turned his eyes to the ground.

"Why?" It was as close to a plea as Charming had ever heard from his father, the King.

"I don't know."

The King's voice took on its most commanding tone. "Edward Michael Charming, for your base cowardice and treachery, I hereby strip you of all titles and banish you from the court."

A sob choked from Charming's throat and he looked up at his father, the King, with his eyes stinging. "I am sorry, Father, I—"

The King's eyes flashed with anger. "How dare you address me so? From this day, I have no son."

"Your Majesty," Will pleaded. "I don't under—"

The King held up a hand, silencing his entreaties. "This is not a matter open for discussion, Lord Protector." He turned his attention back to Charming, on his knees at the King's feet. "You are not welcome here, Edward. You must find your accommodations somewhere else."

"Y-Yes, Your Majesty," Charming stuttered.

The former Prince watched his father sweep nobly into the tavern without a backward glance. The Royal

Herald gave him a downward sneer, and then followed in the King's wake. As soon as the two men were out of sight, Tomas and Will were at Charming's side, helping him to his feet.

"Prince Charming," Tomas said softly, "I'm sure I don't know what is going on, but whatever you've done, your father's temper will cool."

Charming brushed the squire's hands away. "No, Tomas. I have betrayed everything he taught me to represent. I am lost."

Will patted him on the back, "Come now, things aren't so black as they seem. I can explain how you didn't betray me. I mean all you did . . ."

Charming cut his attempted consolation off. "I betrayed you, Will. I told you to go to that bridge knowing that it was a trap." He bowed very low. "I do not expect your forgiveness, but I wish to offer my deepest apologies, Your Lordship."

Blushing, Will said, "Please, Prince Charming, don't call me that."

"I am not Prince Charming any longer," he snapped. "You may call me what you wish, if you wish to consider me at all, but I no longer have a title. Now, by order of the King, I must go." He pulled himself upright and began marching along the road toward the dark woods.

"What about your things, your horse?" Tomas called out after him.

He walked on without turning, "Those belong to Prince Charming, Tomas. They are not mine."

Had any of the three turned at that moment to look

back at the Cooked Goose, they would have seen in the window of the upper floor chamber, the pale face of the King staring down through the gray glass as his beloved only child disappeared along the road. There he would remain through the night, long after the dark, and the forest, had utterly consumed his son.

EVENING FOUND EDWARD Charming stumbling through the deep forest. As darkness descended, rain began to fall. He staggered on until he fell exhausted to the ground. He looked up into the sky, rain pelting his face.

"I am no longer Prince Charming. I . . ."

He did not know what else to say. His mind was a fog, and his thoughts wandered from his father and Will to the dragon, at last finding their way to Elizabeth and the night at the ball. He remembered their dance and their fight, and then his heart sank as a cold truth struck him.

"I shall never use couplet again."

Epilogue

Hi-ho!

MORNING FOUND JAMES Collins deep in the woods tracking Liz. He was an expert woodsman and had spent nearly his whole life in the wild, hunting for game. He had followed Lady Elizabeth's trail to the edge of a deep, dry creek bed, where her prints just stopped. Naturally, he thought she must have fallen, but at the bottom there was no Lady Elizabeth, nor any sign of her having left. Instead, there was a confused jumble that could only have been made by dozens and dozens of tiny booted feet. They marched in a double-file line along the rocky creek bed. James followed them thinking, *Children? What would children be doing in the middle of this godforsaken wood?*

After about a hundred paces, the trace entered a hard stone cavern and vanished. He peered into the darkness of the cave's mouth. It smelled of rock and damp. The man grimaced and spat. "Not children, dwarves. Of all the beastly luck, they'll have her doing their laundry and cooking their meals in no time. Lazy little blighters—dwarves."

He took a few steps into the cave. The cool wet air closed in around him and almost immediately the light began to fail. He stopped again and cursed. He would not follow a march of dwarves into an unknown cavern without a light. There was just no use in it, he would either get lost or fall down one of their damned mines, and then Princess Gwendolyn would be free to move against his mistress. He would have to return to Lady Rapunzel, ensure her safety, and then come back with a proper hunting party to track down the filthy little ruffians.

He began to turn back but paused, and put both hands around his mouth, he shouted, "LADY ELIZABETH, DO NOT DESPAIR. I WILL RETURN. AND, DWARVES, IF YOU HARM HER, OR FORCE HER TO DO EVEN A SINGLE DISH, YOU WILL ANSWER TO ME!"

His voiced echoed back for a time in an endless loop and then faded. He frowned again at the dark hole. Perhaps he had imagined it, but he could have sworn he heard a tiny little voice echo back, "Hi-Ho!"

Volume II:
Happily Never After

A winged shadow of starkest black,
A darkened glade where the weak and
wishful tarry.
A curse screamed from dream's dark depths,
A thousand guises and a single name.
Fairy.
—Untitled Verse by Princess
Gwendolyn Mostfair

Prologue

Couplet Revisited

MIDNIGHT'S QUIET HAD wrapped itself about Castle White as a twelve-year-old Charming padded down the long hall in his slippered feet. He was on his way back from the kitchens, having liberated another of the lovely apricot tarts the baker so jealously guarded. He savored his victory with a bite, reveling in the perfection of the pastry.

Such raids were strictly forbidden, of course, and indeed all of the servants were abuzz with the question of who could be stealing the King's favorite desserts, but Charming was no novice at such intrigues. He knew the castle well enough to evade the traps the head cook had set, to slip past the alcoves in the hall where the night footmen stood guard, and to avoid the curtains in the music salon where a maid sat waiting. He even knew about the broom closet where, tonight, the baker himself had tried to keep vigil.

What a laugh, thought Charming. *All my father's horses and all of his men couldn't keep me from those tarts. They are like blind cats sitting before a blank wall thinking it's a mouse hole.*

They would never catch him. The castle with its twisting halls and endless rooms was his domain. He took another bite and chuckled.

He was just passing the Royal Library when he heard the voice of his father from within. It was not unusual for him to be up this late, consulting with this lord or that, on that problem or this, but whomever his father was talking with, and whatever the topic, it was serious. Charming knew his father's moods well, and, though muffled, Charming could tell from the tone of his voice that his father was being even grimmer than usual.

Charming was about to continue on, feeling lucky that it was not he who was on the other side of whatever lecture was being given, when a single word, rising above the general murmur, stopped him dead in his tracks.

"... *dragon!*"

Holding the tart away from his body, he pressed his ear against the keyhole. At once, he recognized that there were three people in the room besides his father, and not just any three people but the three most highly ranked members of the court: Duke Northingham of North Northingham, the richest noble in the kingdom; Lord

Jocksley, his father's closest friend and hunting companion; and Lady Greenleaf, without a doubt the sharpest mind and tongue of the court.

"But, Your Majesty," Northingham was saying, "the monster is destroying trade in the kingdom, and killing people beside."

"Some are beginning to grumble a bit, Rupert," Jocksley added in his customary drawl.

"Grumble?" Lady Greenleaf said acidly. "I see that your powers of understatement remain without peer, Jocksley. The fact is, Your Majesty, the dragon has terrorized Royaume for years, and the people are fed up. What's more, the creature is growing bolder, each year going further and further afield."

"Lady Greenleaf is right," Northingham verbally pounced. "The beasty used to be satisfied with attacking towns of no consequence, like Prosper and Two Trees, but now it dares go after places that actually matter!"

"I think you are taking gross liberties with *my* argument, Northingham," said Lady Greenleaf archly. "However, Your Majesty, he is correct that if something is not done soon, the people will demand *action*."

There was a pause, and Charming could picture his father puckering his brow and fixing the three nobles with the commanding gaze he gave when he was challenged.

"What would you have me do? Would you have me send more knights, more troops after it? We've lost nearly four-score men trying to hunt the creature down. How many more would you have me sacrifice? And why? The prophecy is quite clear that it is my son who will defeat the dragon."

"Frankly," Northingham said, "it's the Prince we are interested in talking to you about."

"Is there a problem with the Prince?"

"Look, Rupert," Jocksley said with forced cheerfulness, "it isn't that anyone questions the Prince, or you—"

"As well they shouldn't."

"But—" Jocksley tried to continue.

"But?"

"Let us cut to the chase," Lady Greenleaf interceded. "The Prince is twelve, soon to be thirteen. I don't think I need to tell Your Majesty that, for many peasants, thirteen marks the age of majority. Farmer's sons on my estate are getting married at thirteen, and many more are beginning to keep their own fields at that age."

"And what exactly is your point?"

"The point, Your Majesty," she said, "is that the people are beginning to question when the Prince will be ready for his quest, or, indeed, if he will ever be ready."

From behind the door, Charming felt blood rush to his face and an emptiness fill his chest. *Are the people really beginning to question me?*

There was a spluttering noise that Charming took to be his father trying to compose himself, and then Jocksley stepped into the fray. "Look, Rupert, all we are asking is how realistic is it to imagine that a boy of thirteen, or fifteen, or even seventeen, is going to be able to slay a dragon. Take my son, Daniel. I love the boy to death, but he's sixteen now and has taken to running about in the woods with a bunch of his friends, doing who knows what. Boys like Daniel and Charming are just . . ."

"There is no 'boy' like Charming," his father said. "Look, Jocksley, Lady Greenleaf, Duke Northingham, I know that this delegation represents the leading nobility of the kingdom, and you have been charged to deliver this message to me. I appreciate your candor, but you can send this response to the nobles, and be at peace in your own hearts: All is in hand. The Prince will be ready—and soon. I have spared no expense or effort in his education. He trains daily at combat and arms, and at building his body to the peak of physical readiness. He studies under the finest tutors to sharpen his mind and to develop his strategies and tactics. In short, he is growing into the very model of honor and chivalry, an example to hold up to the rest of the kingdom."

Charming's heart swelled as he listened to his father defend him. He felt, almost, that he could ride out tonight to fight the dragon. Nothing could stop him.

Suddenly, a sharp pain raced through his left ear.

"I caught you, you little thief—and red-handed, no less!"

The baker had his ear. The beefy man pulled him away from the door and ripped the tart out of his hand. Charming had no time to plead as the baker knocked loudly at the door.

"Come!" said the King.

As the door was thrown open, Charming saw his father standing behind his enormous gold-gilt desk. He was holding a scroll in one of his many-ringed hands, and gesturing broadly about the room. On the opposite side of the desk, the three nobles turned to look.

"What is the meaning of this?" his father asked. "Charming, what are you doing up at this time? And, Baker Crumplet, what gives you the right to handle my son, the Prince, in this unseemly manner?"

The baker released Charming and then bowed low. Charming rubbed his stinging ear.

"You may rise. Now, Crumplet, I expect an answer to my question."

"Y-Your Royal Majesty," the baker said with a slight stutter of nerves, "I beg your forgiveness for this intrusion, but I have caught the tart thief." The odious man held the apricot tart high in the air, beaming.

The King's gaze settled on the apricot tart and his face clouded with anger. There was a stifled chuckle from Jocksley, and Duke Northingham cleared his throat uncomfortably. Lady Greenleaf was disdainfully silent.

"Edward?" his father said coldly.

Charming felt his heart thump violently in his chest, and a sudden queasiness rose in his throat. His father may never have been warm to him, but Charming had also never been the target of his father's full wrath.

"Explain."

"I—I cannot," Charming said, his voice catching.

"I see. So this is how you choose to repay me for all your years of privilege, education, and training? To steal the bread from my own table, LIKE A COMMON THIEF?" his father roared. "Shall I deal with you as I would deal with any other thief? Shall I put you in irons, or perhaps parade you through the village for the people to throw rocks at and to spit on? Is this what you want?"

Charming could not speak.

"Answer me!"

"N-N-No, Father," Charming finally choked out.

"What punishment would you have me mete out, if I am denied my customary due?"

Charming had no answer, and so remained silent, and the silence stretched on and became oppressive.

Jocksley's voice cut through the tension. "Come now, Rupert. What boy doesn't sneak a treat from the kitchens now and then? We never caught whoever was stealing from our kitchens. All we ever found were arrows. Strange, but as in this case, no harm done."

"Jocksley, did I not just assure you—no, did I not just *demand*—that you deliver a message to the entire court that, upon *my* honor the Prince was like 'no other boy,' and that they could place their faith in his character? Does my honor and name mean that little that my words should be thus proved false before they have even left the ears of those that hear them?"

Jocksley said nothing at this and the King addressed Charming again. "I am waiting for an answer, Edward. By what means can this wrong be righted?"

Charming had never felt so empty and low. Death would be preferable to this. And then, with the clarity of youth, he knew what he had to do. Taking a few deep breaths, he raised his blurry eyes. "You must send me against the dragon, Father. It is the only way that I can redeem myself—and if I fail, then it will be of no great loss if I am gone."

There was a long silence at this pronouncement, during which the nobles and his father, whose face had grown suddenly white, did not move or speak. Beside him the baker stared, dumbfounded.

Finally, his father cleared his throat. "Well, we have said enough on the subject for now. I have important matters to discuss with the, um, delegation from the court. Return to your chambers and we will talk tomorrow."

"Please, Father," Charming pleaded. "I can go tonight. I have dishonored you, and I do not feel right staying here in the castle.

"You are a child, Edward! You do not know what you are saying! You are not ready! I forbid you to speak of this again! Now leave us."

Anger burned through Charming's breast. He was not a child, and he was prophesied to be the dragon slayer. His hands clenched into fists. "What about the people who died, who are dying? Shouldn't I go help them? Isn't it my duty? The people think I should go." He stabbed a finger at the three nobles. "Father, even they say so."

A gasp escaped from Lady Greenleaf, and Charming thought that the baker swayed on his feet. His father's face flushed red with fury. "Edward Michael Charming! You will always remember that I am not only your father but also your King. You are not just my son, but also my subject, and you will follow my commands without dissent! I will tell you when it is time for you to ride against the dragon, and this is not that time. Now, go!"

Charming dropped to a knee and, struggling to keep his voice from cracking, said, "Yes, Fath—" His father, the King, looked at him sharply and Charming quickly amended with, "Your Majesty."

His body shook as he rose. He bowed stiffly to his father, the King, and marched from the room. Once out of sight, he took to his heels, running as tears splashed across his face in confusion, shame, and anguish.

Chapter 1

Once Upon, Once Again

"ONCE UPON A TIME," everyone can agree, is a fairly inaccurate way of marking time. "Once upon a time when?" one might well ask. Of course, most fairy tales live in their own blurry and disconnected time, neither now nor exactly then, and so the relative "when" of the story doesn't matter. But in Charming's tale, where you inconveniently have more than one "Once Upon a Time," it can be important to know whether any particular "Once Upon a Time" came before or after any other "Once Upon a Time" that had been or is to come.

And so . . .

Once upon a time, at about the same time that the recently disowned Charming wandered lost in his own melancholy, Elizabeth Pickett awoke from a muddled dream about the Prince, little men, and fairies as a badly metered couplet was running through her head. She lay in bed staring at a short man perched atop a tall stool. His back was to her, and all she could see of him, apart from a waistcoat of garish purple, was a thin head of wild white hair. He had his arm cocked back and seemed on the verge of throwing a small leather book he was holding through the open window where a rainbow flock of songbirds chirruped loudly.

She had no idea where she was.

Liz sat up. As she did, the birds fell silent and stared at her. For his part, the strange little man spun about quickly, nearly unseating himself. As he struggled to regain his balance, she studied him. Putting aside his size, he was most singular. He had a white beard that matched the disorder of the hair on his head, and he wore a tiny pair of wire-frame glasses that perched unsteadily on his long thin nose.

Finally reseated, he smiling and said, "The poet speaks, the lady stirs . . ."

She started to say that poetry could be deadly in the wrong hands when *another* pair of eyes, sitting just above a short fat nose and topped by a head of curly black hair, appeared above the foot of the bed. The eyes of this second little man narrowed, and then a deep voice boomed, "HEY, EVERYONE! . . . THE BROAD'S AWAKE!"

This announcement provoked an alarming racket from the room beyond. There was an explosive sneeze, something heavy crashed to the floor, then crockery shattered and someone with a high, wheezy voice let loose a remarkably colorful curse, all followed by the sound of booted feet thundering unseen through the door. Then, like gophers in a field, four more heads popped up over the edge of the bed's footboard. Red hair and yellow, hatted and bare, thin nosed and broad, and each with the same sharp beetle-black eyes. Liz mouthed silently as she counted out the number: . . . *four . . . five . . . six. Six little men. No! Not little men . . . dwarves!*

Her head felt strangely foggy, so when she spoke, it was without thought. "Wait a minute, I've heard of you. You're dwarfs! Or is it *dwarves*?" Both words sounded wrong to her.

"Actually," said the white-haired dwarf on the stool in a pedantic tone, "the etymology of the plural of *dwarf* has been the subject of debate for some time. Of course, a morphologist would tell you that words ending in a fricative should be pluralized by the simple addition of an *s*. Therefore, *dwarf* would be *dwarfs*." He concluded by nodding his head sharply as though that brought the matter to a close.

"I disagree," smiled a very happily disagreeable fellow to his left. "There are plenty of examples of irregular fricative pluralizations, like loaves and thieves."

From atop his stool, the bespectacled dwarf frowned down at him. "I'm not saying it's a universal rule. There are no universal rules in morphophonemics. There is only quasi-regularity, and you know it."

The grim-looking dwarf that had earlier called her a broad frowned. "Well, I think the problem is that you are using the term *fricative* too loosely. Are we talking about spirant or strident fricatives?"

"Don't be an idiot," snapped the white-haired dwarf gesturing violently at his fellow debaters with the book. "How could *dwarf* be a strident fricative; there's no tongue involved." He demonstrated by over-enunciating the word *dwarf.* "It's spirant fricatives we're talking about, so stop trying to complicate the matter."

"Oh," said the angry dwarf. "So I'm an idiot now, am I? Is that it?" He took a menacing step toward the seated fellow.

The white-haired dwarf held up his hands. "Now, now, you know that's not what I meant—"

A dwarf with a violently red nose interrupted. "Actually, *dwarf* is a voiceless labiodental fricative, and a word like *staff* can be pluralized *staffs* or *staves*, depending on whether you are talking about a group of people or a walking stick . . . so . . ."

This was too much for the white-haired fellow, who chucked his book across the room. It hit red-nose square on his red nose, eliciting a loud sneeze from the victim and a roar of laughter from the other dwarves.

The white-haired dwarf straightened his glasses unnecessarily. "Now that that is settled, we can have a civilized discussion about the issue . . ."

Liz was finding it very hard to concentrate and, besides, felt they were getting slightly off topic, so she simply cut to the point she'd been going to make. "The point is, if you *are* the dwarfs . . . dwarves—whatever— if you are the fellows from the story, you know the one, aren't there supposed to be seven of you? Wait—wait, let me guess your names . . ." She studied the arc of faces. There was one with a bright red nose, and one that seemed to be continuously flushing and who, at her glance, slipped behind a nearby curtain to hide. Another was snoring soundly and softly at her feet. She laughed. "Well, he's obvious," she said, pointing at the sleeping figure. "He fell asleep right in the middle of our introductions, so he must be Slee—"

The bespectacled, white-haired dwarf interrupted her before she could finish. "Now, wait. You see . . ." Clearly uncertain how to continue, he stopped.

The smiling dwarf took up the thread in a high-pitched squeak. "We don't—"

"—that's right," said the bright-nosed fellow in a nasally voice, "we don't . . ."

The angry-looking fellow glared at the other dwarves in disgust. "Don't hurt yourselves." He climbed up onto the foot of the bed, straddling the sleeping dwarf, put his hands on his hips, and growled, "Listen, lady, we don't appreciate being reduced to one-dimensional caricatures. How would you like it if I decided to call you Clumsy for falling down a perfectly obvious ravine and breaking your arm, or Trampy because you are apparently perfectly comfortable receiving six men into your bedroom dressed in next to nothing?"

Liz looked down. The odious little man was right. There she was, covers around her waist, wearing nothing but a sheer shift that, in the morning light, was, at the least, immodest. She pulled the blanket up to her chin. The angry dwarf kept haranguing her about the evils of stereotyping, but she didn't hear any of it. Her mind was fully engaged, trying in vain to remember how she had gotten into this bed, why her arm was covered from elbow to wrist in plaster, and what had happened to her dress. Liz blushed when the inevitable answer to the last question came to her.

" . . . I mean, now for instance, I could just as well call you Blotchy—"

The white-haired dwarf interrupted the lecture with a frown. "Steady on, Grady, steady on."

Grady returned the frown. "Well, *Dorian*," he said with a one-eyed sneer at Liz, "I expect more manners from someone we saved from certain death, carried a good five miles over rocks and through caves, all the while enduring the threats and slanderous insults of her lunatic boyfriend. But, maybe, I'm old-fashioned." He ended by shrugging dramatically and bristling his prodigious brows at Liz.

The sleepy dwarf half opened his eyes at this and yawned. "Besides, narcolepsy is nothing to laugh at."

"Exactly, Sloane," Grady spit, "that's right—"

"Allergies aren't either." The red-nosed fellow sniffed. "I'm normally not this bad, by the way," he said in an aside apparently meant for Liz. "Only . . . Only . . . Only—ACHOO! I'm terribly allergic to lavender."

"Precisely, Sneedon," Grady exclaimed "You see—"

"Or maybe it's the pollen in the air," Sneedon continued. "You know, people don't know how deadly springtime can be. Spring, and nuts of course. Oh. And berries, not to mention shellfish. And then, there's gluten and—"

Grady reached over and tweaked Sneedon's nose roughly.

"Youch!"

"Dammit," Grady complained. "We don't have time to run through a list of your allergies. We'll be here until next week. The point I'm trying to make is—"

"Actually, I think narcolepsy is pretty funny," giggled the cheerful fellow.

"Me too," said a whisper of a voice from behind the curtain that must have come from the now-hidden dwarf.

"Hayden and Baldwin have a point," Dorian said. "We have used Sloane as a pretty regular punch line in our plays."

"Yeah," sniffed Sneedon, who still looked a little hurt that the topic of his allergies had been dropped so quickly. "Like our humorous adaption of *Rumpelstilt . . .*" He sneezed again. " . . . *skin*. Come to think of it, didn't you script it so I was to sneeze every time I said Rumpelstilt . . ." Achoo! " . . . skin?"

With rising irritation, Grady said, "That's entirely different Sneedon . . ."

"Or, the send-up we gave him in *The Dwarf and the Pea*," suggested the hidden dwarf.

"All right, Baldwin, you've made your—"

"Or *Sleeping Ugly*," Sloane murmured with another wide yawn.

"Well, that was just—HEY, WAIT A MINUTE!"

shouted Grady. "We've never done a play called *Sleeping Ugly.*"

The hidden dwarf, whose name Liz thought was Baldwin, giggled. "No, but it is a really good idea."

Grady raised a finger to the sky and opened his mouth to argue, but stopped short and, lowering his hand, said, "Granted, but we're getting off topic. The point is . . ."

Liz was finally awake, at least partially from having to shift her gaze this way and that to keep up with the six-way debate, and had come to the conclusion that enough was enough. "The point is, I have been a terribly ungracious guest. For this I apologize. I am clearly deeply in your debt. But, could you indulge me a few questions?"

She paused a moment to see if the talkative Grady would continue his sermon. He did not, but looked none too pleased at having his monologue interrupted—again. Liz nodded and raised her forefinger. "Where am I?" She raised her middle finger: "If you are not the Seven Dwarfs, then who are you?" She raised her ring finger: "How did I get here?" She let those questions linger for a heartbeat, and then raised her pinkie emphatically: "And where are my clothes?"

The five visible dwarves blushed from neck to forehead. Even Sloane woke up long enough to turn a bright cherry red before falling asleep again. They all looked at Dorian, who was sweating so profusely, Liz was afraid for his health. He put a finger under his collar and pulled. Then gulping air like a landed fish, stuttered, "W-Well, you see . . . now then . . . that is . . . what I mean to say . . . well, we . . . ahhhh . . . er, that is, I had to, um, examine you."

"Examine me?" Liz said, her voice raising several octaves.

"I am a doctor," he said gravely.

"Of literature . . ." the voice of Baldwin whispered from his hiding place.

Dorian glared in the direction of the curtain. "Yes, well, regardless, I did bandage your head and fix your arm."

"I still . . . still say her arm didn't look all that bad," Sloane said between yawns.

"How would you know?" Dorian asked. "You slept through the whole thing."

"I did not," Sloane said with a lazy blink. "I was . . ." He yawned violently, and Liz found that she couldn't help but follow suit. After a sleepy smack of his lips, Sloane began again, " . . . watching and—"

But that was as far as he got. A gentle snore erupted from the dwarf and a visibly relieved Dorian continued. "The point is, your arm was broken. A fracture of the humorous, if you must know." He wiggled his glasses at her in what could only be described as a professorial manner.

Liz had broken her arm as a child. The way she could wiggle her fingers without pain made her think the little man was exaggerating. "I think it is pronounced *humerus*, Dorian," she said. "And, it doesn't feel broken."

"That's because it wasn't broken," Sloane said with eyes so heavily lidded that it was impossible to know if he was awake or talking in his sleep.

"Right," Dorian said, ignoring Sloane's comments. "So, with your arm broken and your head bashed in, I—"

"Removed my dress!?"

Dorian blushed again and Grady decided to answer. "Some gratitude. I told you we shouldn't have helped her, Dorian." He shook a finger at Liz. "Look, lady, we find you at the bottom of a ravine, your arm bent all wrong, and your head bleeding, and all you can do is complain about your modesty?"

"It's not so much my modesty," Liz lied, "and more a question of whether any of you are qualified to *examine* young women? I mean, you're— "

"What? Miners?" Grady reddened around the neck and squinted at her. "There you go making assumptions again. We're dwarves so we must be miners, eh? I'll have you know we are artists, and you, Miss, are not that young."

Liz glared back at him for the remark about her age, and said, "I was going to say writers."

"We're actually actors," Hayden said with a smile and a wink.

"We are not actors," Grady countered with a snarl.

"But we act."

"Perhaps I should say that we are not merely actors," Grady said. "We are artists that on occasion author, produce, and perform dramatic works."

"But we do act," Hayden said in happy, but relentless, repetition.

"I won't have this argument again," Grady said. "We are a bloody artist collective, and you know it!" He turned back to Liz and said in honest, if aggressive, confusion, "Now, where were we?"

Liz fought her growing desire to laugh. Maybe her arm wasn't broken, but they had done what they thought was best, and no real harm had come of it. Still, she decided they should squirm a little more. She cleared her throat. "You were telling me how being an actor—I mean, an artist—qualifies you to examine me?"

"I thought that would have been obvious!" he replied matter-of-factly, "We are used to dealing with the exposed form—in all its shapes—no matter the flaws."

Liz could not help blushing, and to his credit, so did Grady.

"Yes, well, perhaps we could move on," Dorian pleaded, wiping his forehead with the end of his beard.

Apart from a twittering of birds, there was a general silence that he took for consensus. Dorian poked at his glasses with his thumb, until they were listing badly to the left, and nodded. He raised his forefinger. "Let's see, your first question was where are you? You are in the Cottage of the Seven Players, deep in the White Wood. You have been with us something a little short of a week."

"And, you were right," Baldwin said, briefly poking his head out from behind the curtain and eyeing Grady, "we are the Seven Dwarfs . . . at least we are *six* of the Seven Dwarfs. You-know-who is in rehab."

"We are *not* the *Seven Dwarfs*, Baldwin," Grady barked, emphasizing the *"Seven Dwarfs"* with imaginary quotation marks. "We, each of us, played *one* of the seven dwarves in that awful play."*

"Awful play?" Liz protested. "It was fantastic. My mother took us to see it when we were children. I loved it, especially the singing numbers." She hummed a few bars of one of the songs.

"Thank you," five of the dwarves said in unison.

"Crass commercial fluff," rasped Grady.

"Wait," Liz said firmly, "you called the seventh dwarf 'You-know-who.' Who? Do you mean Dop—?"

"Shhh . . ." hissed the dwarves.

"Don't," Grady said with real urgency. "The rights to that name, in particular, were sold, and well, in fact, we sold the rights to the whole play to pay off some um, ill-advised, well . . . I guess you could call them investments."

"He means, we lost big on the horses," Hayden translated with a smile.

Grady glared at him and continued. "The point is, if you don't want to wind up in the poorhouse with us, you'll not mention That Play again. The new owner lives in another magical kingdom, but he has some bloody good lawyers. They could be anywhere."

The dwarves looked about uncomfortably as though

---

* The Seven Players have asked, or rather legally compelled us, to point out that, despite the fact that the first two letters of each of their names *might* correspond to the first two letters of the names of the dwarves in "That Play," such correspondence or resemblance to such fictitious characters or persons is purely coincidental, and that all persons (or at least dwarves) appearing in this work are not fictitious, but are entirely real, alive and taking bookings.

these lawyers might actually be hiding somewhere in the room.

Grady's muffled growl broke the tension. "Anyway, if you must know, his name is really Dominic. He went solo. Made a mockery of his art by going around *entertaining* the masses in a one-man comedy show called *Big Ears and All*."

"Quite successful too," Dorian said softly. "It was after he made it big that we got the offer for the rights to . . . *That* Play."

"Yeah, and we sold it," said Grady.

"Poor Dominic," Hayden said in a happily mournful voice.

"What happened to him?" Liz asked.

Baldwin piped up from his hiding place. "After the lawyers from that other kingdom gave him the cease and desist, he got hooked on snuff. Put all his money up his nose. Sad, really."

"I'm allergic to snuff." Sneedon sniffed seriously. "Did you know I'm also allergic to—"

Grady slapped Sneedon's nose, eliciting a violent sneeze and a round of chuckles from the other dwarves. "I warned you, I won't tolerate any more talk about your allergies." Sneedon rubbed his nose sadly while Grady concluded. "Point is, Dominic was a sellout and deserved everything he got."

"Oh, ignore Grady," Dorian said, "he's just grump—uh, angry because he has writer's block."

"Speaking of which," Grady harrumphed loudly. "I don't have time for idle chatter and neither do you,

Sneedon." He jumped from the foot of the bed and stomped toward the door. "Coming, Sneedon?"

Sneedon shook his head, which made the tasseled cap perched atop it wiggle. "Uh-uh. I want to hear the answer to her last question."

The dwarves all turned back to Liz. Baldwin's face appeared from behind the curtain. Sloane's eyes opened and, for once, stayed that way.

"That's right," Dorian said. "You asked us how you got here. We want to know the same thing. How does a lady appear at the bottom of a ravine, in the middle of the woods, with a broken arm and shattered head?"

"I'm warning you, it has all the hallmarks of something a crazed stalker-groupie would do," Grady muttered under his breath.

Suddenly, Liz's mind cleared—and the events since her escape from the tower came flooding back. Her eyes widened in alarm. "My God, the Princess has some evil power! Elle! Will! I—I must warn them."

She was moving before the words were out of her mouth, but with the movement came a flood of pain that radiated simultaneously from her bandaged head and plastered arm. Gasping, she fell back into bed.

Dorian sprang to her side, "Lady . . ."

"Liz," she grunted. "My name is Liz."

"Liz," he said. "You shouldn't move. The boys were right before. You were in terrible shape when we found you." He scratched his head. "Doctor or not, the fact is you shouldn't be up and moving about."

Liz sighed and lay back against the pillow. She felt so

weak. "I have to. My brother, he may return to the castle at any time. I must get a message to Elle. Do you have a horse? Is there anyone nearby? An inn perhaps?" She wanted to say more, but her head was swimming and she felt nauseous.

Dorian scratched his tangled beard. "We're pretty far out in the woods, Liz, and we don't own any horses ourselves on account of, well—"

"On account of horses being great untrustworthy beasts," Grady spit before concluding with a muttered, "Samson to win. I mean, really, what kind of tip is that? Didn't I say that Samson had only shown any real speed on turf courses . . ."

While Grady spluttered on, in a soft, almost whisper of a voice, Hayden said, "There is our patron . . ."

At this suggestion, Baldwin disappeared, once more, behind his curtain, and the remaining dwarves exchanged uneasy glances.

"Patron?" Liz murmured weakly.

"Well," Dorian replied, rubbing a hand along the back of his neck, "I suppose technically he is not our patron."

"Yet . . ." Sloane added vaguely.

"He's more of a patron . . . in waiting." Sneedon sneezed.

"All we need to do is get an audience with him and we're sure we'll be able to win him over," chirped Hayden merrily.

"What? You've never seen the fellow?" Liz asked.

"No, not yet," Dorian admitted.

"It's his damnable butler," Grady groused, seemingly having exhausted himself on the topic of horses.

"He has no artistic soul," Sneedon agreed.

"Last time, he set the dogs on us," Sloane said between snores.

"But this time will be different," Dorian said, trying to rally the other dwarves. "You'll see. This time, we'll give the man a performance that will knock him out."

Grady grunted, "How? This time we've got nothing. Neither Sneedon nor I have had a decent idea for months. We don't even have enough material for a one-act, much less a proper play."

A deep silence fell on the room.

"I have a story," Elizabeth interjected. "A story that might melt even the butler's heart of stone." She looked about the room, "Did you find a bag with me?"

Dorian nodded and brought it to her. She rummaged through it, and then, with a flourish, she pulled out the crystal slipper and held it in the air for a moment, so that it flashed in the sun. It was an act of unconscious stage-craft that worked magic on her audience. The dwarves sat staring dumbly at the little sparkling shoe.

"How did I get here?" she said in a faraway voice. Liz cradled the shoe in her lap, remembering the only night she had worn it and the man with whom she had danced. Tears rose in her eyes. The shining image swam and wavered, and she whispered, "I suppose you could say I am here because my family has, for generations, believed in Happily Ever Afters . . ."

The dwarves exchanged collective glances. Grady opened his mouth to say something and the other dwarves silenced him with a simultaneous hiss.

Liz shook away the sadness and smiled. "Well, my own little fairy story started the night the dragon attacked our farm. We had doused all the lights when we heard, on the night air, its first cry, and then saw the sky light up with its fires." She was staring out the window at the trees beyond. "Well, we were sitting there, in the dark, and Will grabbed my hand, put a book in it, and said, 'Liz, you sit tight. I've got to go do something.' And off he went, just like that."

Liz blinked, and the gathered tears streamed two-by-two down her cheeks. "By the moonlight, I could see that the book he'd given me was the *Dragon's Tale*, and I knew he had no intention of coming back. He was going to try and do something heroic. All he ever really wanted was a chance to do something noble."

"Holy hell!" yelled Grady. "You're the dragon slayer's sister?"

The other dwarves whistled in unison.

"I suppose," she responded, "but that night we were just William and Elizabeth Pickett."

"Mmmhmmm," the dwarves hummed together. "And?"

And so, Liz told her story, and the sun rose high as the dragon died and Will journeyed to the dark tower. Lunch was served, and, over bowls of steaming soup, they listened, enraptured, as she danced with Prince Charming at the ball. And, as the sun began to dip again toward the horizon, she was finally riding her horse into the dark wood with the bewitched valet. When at last she stopped, dark shadows had crept across the room. At some point in her telling, a fire had been laid in the deep stone hearth, and the dwarves were sitting in its orange glow, staring at her with rapt attention.

She blinked at them and wet her lips. "Well, what do you think? Is it a good story?"

"Good?" Grady crowed. "Sister, with a few rewrites it could be a sensation!"

"Rewrites?" she asked.

"Sure, sure," he said smoothly, and nodded over to Sneedon, who pulled a pencil and pad of paper from the open cuff of his sleeve. "A little tweak here or there for drama, you understand, and to smooth out the rough spots in the narrative."

"Rough spots, but—but all that was the truth. What really happened."

Grady waved her to silence. "Now, now, the Seven Players have no use for pride of authorship, Liz. It's about creating the best theater possible. That means writing rich characters, providing those characters with the right dramatic arcs, putting them in appropriate settings, and so forth." He ran a hand through his hair and snapped, "I've *got it*! Squash . . . no, pumpkins! A metamorphosis of mice and pumpkins. I mean the symbolism . . ." He turned to the door, spun on his heel, and called out, "Well, come on, Sneedon. We've got work to do."

Liz looked at Dorian in confusion, "Pumpkins? There were no pumpkins in my story."

He reached across and patted her hand. "My dear, that is what we call artistic license. Let them work. Perhaps a little poetry would help you fall asleep."

Dorian retrieved his book from where it had landed after thumping Sneedon as the remaining dwarves slipped quietly out behind him. Even the birds on the window dispersed in a sudden blur of fluttering colors. Alone with her poetic tormentor, she groaned in defeat.

"I see the pain is growing worse," he consoled. "Don't worry, Liz, you're in good hands." Dorian positioned his glasses on the very tip of his nose and opened his book. "Couplet will take your mind off your body's agonies."

THE NEXT MORNING the sun rose, and with it so did the curtain on what Grady had entitled, *Ash and Cinders: The Elizabeth Pickett Story.* He and Sneedon, his co-author, had worked on the play all night and were anxious for an audience. So, with the hearth as a backdrop and the foot of the bed as a stage, Liz watched as the dwarves ran through a marionette production that resembled her and Will's story in almost no respect. There was a wicked stepmother instead of the Princess, the dragon seemed to have fallen by the wayside (apparently the puppet proved too challenging to construct); there was a kindly fairy (mostly because they had a fairy puppet on hand from an earlier production), a pumpkin carriage, and a disappearing gown. It was all wrong and she might have said so, except that somehow they had managed to capture her emotions, with such perfection, particularly during the ball scene: her terror at the beginning, rising elation as she danced with the Prince, and then despair as she fled up that long stair. When the curtain fell (quite literally, as it had been strung between the bedposts with a particularly dubious length of string), she found herself in tears.

"Well, what do you think?" Grady asked with none of his usual growls. All the dwarves poked their heads above the foot of the bed and waited eagerly for her review.

Liz wiped her eyes dry and smiled at the little group. "I think the butler would have to be a fool not to let you see his master."

The dwarves gave a huzzah, broke out a large crockery jug of ale, and after a few rounds began dancing about the room. Elizabeth clapped along with them until Grady stopped the frivolity with a shout—"HEY! What are we doing? We need to get this stuff packed up, you guys. It's off to the Beast's we go! On foot, it'll take us a day or two at least to get there, so we have to get started." There was another shouted cheer and the little group danced out the door in a clatter of boots and caterwaul of off-key singing.

Liz beckoned Dorian to stop, and the elderly dwarf, still red in the face from the dance, puffed over. She put a hand on his head. "Thank you, Dorian, for doing me this favor. You cannot know what it means to me."

He blushed. "Don't think anything of it. To be truthful, we haven't had a good story to tell for years. Our last few have been . . . well, awful. We've needed some inspiration, and"—he paused and winked at her—"it doesn't hurt that our new muse is easy on the eyes."

She smiled sweetly. "Oh, how you flatter, Dorian, but thank you." Then she straightened her face. "Now, remember, if you manage to see your Patron, you must ask him to take my warning to Lady Rapunzel." The dwarf nodded seriously and she continued. "And if he is in any doubt as to the truth of my existence and need, you should give him this." She handed him the slipper.

"I—We can't . . . No!" the dwarf spluttered.

"Please take it, and use it to the best effect. I shall always have the memory, and trust me when I say that the memory is all that will ever come of my time with the Prince. If this silly glass shoe can help my brother and the King and my friend escape the Princess, then I will be happy."

Dorian raised himself up to his full height, all two feet and nine inches, put a hand over his heart, and bowed deeply. "I swear to you, Lady Elizabeth, we will return, and we will bring help."

She bent down and kissed the top of his head. "Thank you. Oh, and Dorian, the humerus is up here." She pointed to the unplastered part of her arm above the elbow.

Dorian blushed from the top of his ears to the tip of his nose and scurried to the door.

"One last thing," she called to him. "What did Grady mean, 'It's off to the Beast's we go'?"

The smile on the dwarf's face faltered momentarily, and then he said with affected lightness, "Don't you worry yourself about that, it's just a little inside joke. You know Grady." Before Liz had a chance to say anything further, he slipped out the door.

Chapter 2

At the Crossroads

THE KING'S PARTY slept one miserable night at the Cooked Goose, which should have been a great boon to the inn's reputation, except that a fierce attack of bed bugs roused the monarch in the wee hours of pre-dawn, and put him in a terrible rage, which he directed entirely at the proprietor of the Cooked Goose. The result of which is that, despite the truth of the matter, the Cooked Goose is the only public house in the kingdom that does not profess to have hosted the King.

The King's early morning meant that His Royal Majesty, Will, Tomas, and the Royal Herald were already on the road south to Castle White by the time the sun had risen. It was a silent and mournful ride. The King, wrapped heavily in his grief, said not a word, and the others did their best to match his mood. Even the weather fell into line, alternating between driving rain and drizzle.

Midday found them eating, if not enjoying, a damp luncheon at an overgrown crossroads. They had taken shelter under a dripping hawthorn tree, which was terribly uncomfortable. The low branches forced them to constantly hunch and offered dubious defense against the rain. And so, when Lady Rapunzel's carriage arrived with a shout and whistle from her driver and a clatter of ironclad wheels, it was welcome relief from what had become a rather moist and depressing journey.

A pale, delicate face framed by the hood of a red riding cloak emerged from a paneled window. "Your Royal Highness?"

All of the men looked up, and the Royal Herald, seizing the opportunity to practice his craft, called out, "Presenting the Lady Rapunzel!"

The King sighed. He began to rise slowly and stiffly. Beside him, Will stood to attention with a start, smacking his head hard on one of the low branches. A shower of raindrops and a muffled curse followed. Will's squire, Tomas, muttered in a low voice, "Watch your language, Lord Protector, there's a lady present."

Will flushed, and the King lowered his head and grinned. The squire had been the perfect companion for his son.

The thought of Edward wiped the smile from the King's face, and his black despair descended again. He rose, shaking, and felt Will's strong hand on his arm.

The lad was a comfort, but the King wanted to suffer. He shook the hand off and moved unsteadily to meet the lady. Will stepped forward beside him, and he felt Tomas and the Royal Herald fall in behind them.

Lady Rapunzel watched their approach behind a handkerchief, which the King suspected was there to hide the smile he saw in her eyes. The King reflected that, as wet as they were, they probably looked a bit ridiculous—pathetic—but also ridiculous. Still, when she spoke, her voice held the proper note of respect. "Your Majesty and Lord Protector, well met."

The King bowed in return. Will started to wave awkwardly before stumbling to perform his own bow. Rapunzel's eyes lingered on Will a moment longer than strict propriety would have deemed appropriate. The King noticed and sadly recalled the competition to marry he had started between Will and Edward. It hardly mattered anymore, but he couldn't help wondering if it—if *he*—had played a role in his son's fall. The King cleared the lump that had formed in his throat and spoke. "Lady Rapunzel, well met. If you wouldn't mind, might we conduct the remainder of our conversation inside your coach?"

Rapunzel pulled her gaze away from Will, blinked, and lurched into speech. "Of course, Your Majesty. Please, come in and accept whatever small comfort I may offer. I also have urgent news to convey."

The King stepped into the carriage and said in a firmer, more commanding tone, "Urgent news from Castle White? Is all well there, Lady Rapunzel?"

He took a seat across from her in the plush coach

as she hesitantly lowered her scarlet hood. She reached a hand up and tucked the ends of her short blond hair behind her ears before she answered. "I fear not, Your Majesty. I bring dark tidings from the court."

The King held up his hand to stop her. Will was backing away to join the squire and the herald in the rain. The King silently cursed Will's unwillingness to take the role history demanded, but aloud he said, "Lord Protector, Lady Rapunzel has urgent news from the castle. Please join us. I require your counsel."

Will hesitated, but then bent his massive frame through the door of the coach and into the tiny compartment. He stood, awkwardly bent over and looked between the two benches. Lady Rapunzel gracefully resolved the point of protocol by sliding to one side and gesturing to the bench next to her.

"Please, Lord Protector, be seated and be welcome," she said.

Will mumbled a thanks and sat. The quarters were close, and Will had to cram himself against the wall to avoid having his legs brush against Lady Rapunzel's skirts. She smiled at him in that knowing way only a woman can when she knows a man's discomfort. The smile broke as she reached up to touch the ends of her hair again.

Normally, the King would have found diversion in the scene, but he was in no mood today. "Lady Rapunzel, you mentioned urgent news from Castle White?"

"Yes, Your Majesty. It began the day after you and the Lord Protector left."

Rapunzel told them about Princess Gwendolyn seizing control of the court, her humiliation of Lady Elizabeth, their flight from the castle, and her suspicions concerning the Princess's designs on the throne. The King listened silently behind steepled hands.

Will blurted out, "What? You can't be serious."

Rapunzel turned to face Will and, between pursed lips, said, "I am perfectly serious, Lord Protector."

Will mirrored her movement, turning in his seat to face her. "Princess Gwendolyn? What could she possibly have against us . . . against Liz, Lady Rapunzel?"

"You can't be that naïve. She wants the throne."

"That's absurd. She's the princess and a princess wouldn't engage in such schemes, Lady Rapunzel."

"That's your argument?" she said in a voice rich with sarcasm. "That she's too much a lady?"

"Kind of," he said lamely, but with conviction.

"Like any other lady, Princess Gwendolyn is perfectly capable of being a conniving, backstabbing schemer."

"Now you're just being mean, you have no evidence that Princess Gwendolyn is any of those things. Apart from a couple of slights against my sister, it doesn't seem to me she has done anything wrong."

The King barely heard a word of their back and forth. His mind was filled with black thoughts, and it took all of his courtly skill not to show his grief, but to instead keep his face frozen in an expression of mild disinterest. Fortunately, he had many long years of practice at this so he wore the look quite naturally. "I am inclined to agree with the Lord Protector in conclusion, if not reasoning," he finally opined. "With all due respect to you, Lady Rapunzel, and to your fair sister, Lord Protector, it sounds like the Princess is guilty of little more than being a poor hostess and badly overstepping her station. I think jealousy—yes, Lord Protector," he said, forestalling Will's nascent protest—"jealousy rather than ambition is the likely culprit behind Princess Gwendolyn's behavior."

Rapunzel tried to keep her face respectful, but the King could see that she did not agree with his conclusion. Visibly gathering herself, she said, "Your Majesty, I hate to be contrary, but . . ."

"But you're going to be anyway," he replied, and admired the lady's resolve on the subject.

"Yes, Your Majesty, I am," she said with a hint of rebellion in her tone.

The King held up his hand, cutting her off. "Lady Rapunzel, I understand that Princess Gwendolyn can be cold and haughty, and I know better than most that her temper can be downright nasty, particularly when she feels she has been slighted, but it is my opinion that you and Lady Elizabeth have overreacted."

Will, who had been listening to the debate in silence, now dropped the finger he had been chewing—a nasty habit he needed to be broken of—and leaned forward. "Sire, are you absolutely sure there is no danger? I do not worry about myself, but I do not want Liz placed in any harm."

The King paused, surprised to hear Will speak at all. He saw the color rush to the lad's cheeks as he realized that he was, in effect, contradicting his monarch.

Lady Rapunzel used the moment to renew her assault. "Indeed, Your Majesty, Will should be with his sister. Besides, you and Prince Charming should be able to handle the Princess."

The King felt the warmth drain from his face, and Rapunzel's voice trailed off as she recognized that she had said something very wrong. An awkward silence followed, and no one seemed to wish to be the first to break it.

Finally, Lady Rapunzel spoke, but in a much softer tone. "Where is your son, the Prince, Your Majesty? I should have thought he would be at your side."

Where was Edward? He felt old and tired, and responded in a voice that seemed to come to him from very far away. "Prince Charming is no more."

Lady Rapunzel gasped in shock, and tears welled in her eyes. "The Prince? No! Forgive me, had I known . . . I am terribly sorry . . ."

She reached out for him, and the King watched himself first clasp and then pat her hand before releasing it, but he could not feel the touch. Some courtly reflex made him respond. "You could not know, as it was only a day hence that I . . . I . . ." *killed him*, he finished silently. Only a deep sigh marked the thought. "It doesn't matter. The fact is that the Prince will not return. Yet another reason I need the Lord Protector with me at the castle. You will take the news of his safe return to Lady Elizabeth at your family's country estate and bring her back to Castle White. Now, if you will allow me, I am tired and need to rest."

Lady Rapunzel took the dismissal with remarkable grace. Without hesitation, she lifted the red hood back over her hair and replied, "Of course, you must be exhausted, Your Majesty. If, however, I may beg your indulgence, Your Grace. I have been trapped in this beastly carriage for two days, and would dearly like to ride a while in the fresh air. May I be excused?"

In a single stroke, Lady Rapunzel had not only accepted her dispossession with aplomb, but also relieved him of the responsibility of evicting her. The King nodded his approval. She rose, and, despite the tight confines of the carriage, managed a respectful curtsy. Will stood with her, but too quickly, and slammed his head into the roof of the coach. This time he managed not to curse. Rapunzel covered his fumble by putting out her hand to him. "Lord Protector, would you help me down?"

The squire, who must have been standing just outside, opened the door of the carriage and dazzling sunlight flooded the little compartment. While they had debated and discussed, the skies had cleared, and outside the afternoon sky was a crisp blue traced through with linen-sharp streaks of white. That the rains were gone assuaged the King's guilt a little. When the door shut behind Will and Rapunzel, the King fell back into the lonely twilight of his grief and wept for his lost son.

WILL BLINKED AT the brilliant sky and stepped onto the wet road. As he helped Lady Rapunzel descend, Will suddenly became very aware of her hand in his. A hint of flowers floated in the air around her, not roses like Princess Gwendolyn but something else . . . jasmine. The perfume reminded him of home, where a vine of jasmine had climbed the wall outside his bedroom window. He found himself holding her hand for a moment even after she had stepped onto the road. She favored him with a smile of surprise and a blush of color, so swift, that he wondered after she turned away if he had imagined it.

She walked toward the head of the coach, and he had a chance to admire the waist of her traveling dress and the long flow of swishing skirt that followed. Perhaps she felt his eyes on her, because she glanced back, and when she saw him looking, she adjusted the hood of her traveling cloak, pulling it further down over her face. Will pretended to be in deep contemplation of his mud-crusted boot.

Alone for the moment, he considered Rapunzel. What a change from the ball. She was still overly opinionated and quick to anger, but there was something about her that made his throat catch every time he tried to talk to her. Sadly, he reminded himself, she was unlikely to be favorably disposed toward him, given their argument. He replayed the conversation in the coach and winced.

By the time he had reviewed and regretted all the stupid things he'd said, the carriage was moving away, and the Royal Herald was scrambling to mount up and follow. "I must hurry," the man exclaimed dramatically. "The King cannot possibly travel without being properly announced."

Meanwhile, Tomas had taken a small cloth pavilion

out of one of Rapunzel's many trunks, and was assembling it on the glittering green grass of a nearby field. Will wandered over to the squire and watched as he drove the last peg into the ground. "What is that for?"

"Haven't you ever traveled with a Lady, Will? She's going to need to change into her riding clothes, and she's not about to do that out in the open so you can ogle her in her all-natural. Not that you'd mind, I'd reckon, given how you've been staring after her."

Will's cheeks flamed. Tomas gave a low, knowing chuckle, and then stalked off toward Rapunzel. "Now I know why Charming always called him a gnarled hobgoblin," Will muttered to himself.

Will was still mumbling to himself when Lady Rapunzel arrived. He tried to transform—midword—his unintelligible mutterings into a song so she would not think him mad. The curled smile that followed told him that it hadn't worked. Still smiling, she stepped into the small enclosure to begin changing. Will turned to leave.

"Lord William, would you stay?"

He turned back and saw the cloth wall of the tent flutter. The opening gaped for a moment and Will glimpsed the outline of her body silhouetted within. He turned away and managed a throaty, "Yes . . . yes . . . of course."

Will looked about for Tomas, but the man had vanished entirely, so he gazed up at the clouds, then down at the wet grass, and wondered how pretty girls always made him feel so uncomfortable. And then he realized . . . Lady Rapunzel was pretty—very pretty, and funny, and—

"Are you listening to me?" She sounded as if she had been repeating herself.

Will dared to glance over. Her face was visible in the flap of the pavilion and she had that same annoyed look that Liz always had when he had been thinking too much. "What?" he asked, feeling awkward.

"I said, I want to know what happened to Prince Charming—and this may be our only chance to talk without the King being present. So, tell me how he died. Our last meeting may not have gone well, but I always felt that the prince was . . . well, invulnerable."

"Oh, he didn't really die."

"What?" she asked and stuck her head out even farther. Will caught a glimpse of a bare shoulder and shut his eyes for a moment, then opened them again. Lady Rapunzel stared at him like he had sprouted a second head. "What is *wrong* with you?"

He spluttered incoherently and pointed at her and the tent. She looked down at the slight opening and smiled a cunning smile. "Am I making you uncomfortable?"

Will blushed yet again and nodded mutely.

"How sweet." Her eyes danced with pleasure as she looked at him appraisingly. "You and your sister both have the most marvelous color when you blush. She might have mentioned it when we were talking about you. It's really quite becoming."

This comment only made him blush deeper. It was completely unfair for Liz to talk to other women about him, especially now that he was Lord Protector. He had a reputation, or something like that, to maintain.

Lady Rapunzel's lilting voice interrupted his thoughts again. "If I must be dressed for you to talk to me, then I will finish."

She disappeared back inside the tent. Several moments passed, the tent flap open, and out stepped Lady Rapunzel, mercifully dressed in her riding skirts. It was an elegant costume only ruined by the addition of a bulky cloak that did not seem to match. Adjusting the hood over her head, she said, "I think it will be safe for you to talk now."

He stammered something idiotic and she giggled, a delightful sound. Their eyes met. Had her eyes always been such a brilliant green? She was a woman, and beautiful, but there was also something different about her. She was more familiar, more real than the Princess. She had a little of the tavern girl in her. It reminded him of the best parts of Gretel, how she would pull him into the storeroom for a quick kiss, or slap him when he was too forward.

"Now, I mean no disrespect, Lord Protector, but Liz told me you could be, well, vague, so please tell me what happened to the Prince?"

He hesitated, not sure exactly what to say. *Was he betraying the King's confidence somehow to speak of it?* As he paused, her expression grew harder, and he realized with horror that he was, in fact, being vague. But it was so hard to concentrate when she was pursing her very red lips like that.

She tilted her head. "Did you hear me? I asked you

what happened. Why does the King say the Prince is dead, and yet you say he is not? And, if he's not dead, why is the King acting like a man that has lost his child? And, what in heaven's name is he not telling me?"

Will opened his mouth to answer the first question, and then closed it again when he decided it made more sense to answer the second first, and then repeated the performance when he realized he had no idea how to answer the third question at all. She stamped her foot on the ground, which was really adorable, and the hood slipped off her head. As she said something else, he found himself admiring the way her short hair curled about her ears and framed her face.

She reached up to adjust her hood again, "Please, Lord Protector."

The earnestness of her plea brought him up short and made him realize what an ass he was being. "I apologize, Lady Rapunzel. Let me begin by swearing that, as far as I know, the Prince still lives. He and the King had a falling out and the King has disowned him."

If possible, this seemed to shock her even more. She let the hood fall back again and instead started absent-mindedly tucking the stray ends of her hair behind her ears.

"I never imagined. Charming was conceited and a fool, but I never thought the King would do such a thing." She stroked her chin thoughtfully. "There is more to this than the story you've told, probably more than you or I know. Perhaps the court has been putting pressure on King Rupert."

Elle stood, lost in quiet contemplation of some intrigue, which Will didn't quite follow. It was clear that Lady Rapunzel was a thoughtful woman, like his sister. But she was also pretty, much prettier than Gretel, and he realized in an instant—even prettier than the Princess. He found himself, again, distracted by her and furtively admiring more than just her intelligence.

"I know you're not listening to me anymore, so what are you thinking about?" she asked. It was an accusation.

Will paused and swallowed. He had been caught ogling her, and he knew there was nothing to be done because, if he took the time to think of something clever to say, she would know. But even the time he'd taken to consider whether to consider what to say, seemed to have taken too long, because she stepped toward him, hands on hips.

"I confess that I was just thinking that you are smart like my sister, but prettier than any girl I've ever known," he blurted. His hand twitched, demanding that he bite it, and Will felt the blush hit his face and burn incredibly hot. He closed his eyes, awaiting the brutal tongue-lashing that he would surely receive. *Why am I so bad at this?*

After a pause, Will opened his eyes to see Rapunzel's emerald eyes staring into his. They glistened with unshed tears, making them even more beautiful, and there was a pale confusion on her face.

ELLE'S HEAD WAS a muddle of half-formed thoughts. *He thinks I'm smart? That's a first—for a man. And he thinks I'm pretty, even though he's seen my hair? Could he ac-*

tually be interested in me? She had been having such a good time with Lord William, but she had also thought him far out of her league and certain to think her a lunatic after her behavior at the ball. *But he hasn't mentioned the ball once, and he doesn't even seem to be aware that I ever had long hair or to be concerned that I threw my virtue at Prince Charming. And, when you come to it, he's not bad-looking.* Granted, he was impossibly vague and obnoxiously stubborn, but he was also honest and kindhearted—two qualities that were hard to find in courtly men. Indeed, she had been taught from an early age that at court romance and intrigue were always intertwined, and that every encounter with a man was a contest of wits, with disgrace and ruin the punishment for losing—at least if you were a woman. This felt different, just a boy and a girl talking to each other.

Still, standing there with him looking at her like that, she didn't know what to say. She'd had a lifetime of being told that she should set her expectations low, and praised, on those rare occasions when she was praised, only for her looks, and, truth be told, mostly for her hair. In the moment, words couldn't find their way past her lips. She stood and gaped. Tears fell across her cheeks, and she reached up to brush them aside.

Will's face went white. He murmured, "I . . . I am sorry I upset you. I will fetch Tomas to see to your needs while I ride ahead."

She watched helplessly as he turned and nearly ran from the field, not knowing what to say, and unsure that she would be able to speak if she did know what to say.

Eventually, Tomas sauntered over and found her still standing as Will had left her. With a tip of his cap he began readying her horse. "Lord William's ridden ahead to make sure the King is alright. Won't be a moment, Lady Rapunzel, and we'll have you on your way also."

When the horse was ready, she mounted, still trying to figure out how she was going to explain things to Lord William. She knew it was silly, but she'd spent so many years trading on her legendary hair, and the reputation for beauty it lent her, that she simply couldn't believe that he—no, that anyone—but particularly someone in his position, might take the time to see that there was more to her. She hadn't come up with anything approaching a reasonable plan when she turned a bend in the road and found the procession mired to the axles in mud.

She pulled the horse to a halt and surveyed the scene. The carriage was well and truly stuck. Her driver and her footman were gathered about the back end trying to the pry the thing onto solid ground. And there, standing knee deep in the muck, was Lord William.

Although Elle admired the way the muscles of Lord William's broad back moved beneath the thin cloth of his undershirt, it was the unlikely nature of his presence there in the mud that held her gaze. She knew that for anyone from the court it would be unthinkable that a lord of the realm, much less the Lord Protector and likely the next King, would place himself in such an undignified position. Yet Elle was sure that Lord William had not thought a moment before trying to help.

And, in a sudden rush, Elle knew she wanted to be

just as thoughtless. She dismounted and strode over to where he was pushing against a tree branch to lever the carriage up. She lifted her skirt and stepped into the mud beside him.

"Lady Rapunzel? But . . ." Will said, eyes wide.

"But nothing. Let's move this carriage!" She put her shoulder against the wheel and pushed. She wasn't sure whether her efforts made any difference, but her attempt seemed to inspire Will. The veins rose beneath his flesh, his muscles flexed, he flushed a deep purple, and the carriage rolled free.

Unfortunately, as it moved, Elle felt her feet slip in the mud and her legs go out from under her. But instead of ending up face-first in the muck, she found herself in Will's strong arms.

"Thank you," she whispered.

"My pleasure," he said, and set her effortlessly onto the road.

The King's voice reached out from within the carriage. "Well done, Lord Protector."

Will stepped out of the mire, wiped his hands on his breeches, and moved toward the door of the carriage. He paused to look at Elle. She favored him with her best smile, and he gave her a broad muddy grin in return.

OVER THE NEXT two days, Will and Elle never found a single moment to be alone. There was always something in the way—usually the Royal Herald. After the third time the Royal Herald boomed out, "Lord Protector and

Dragon Slayer William Pickett approaches Lady Rapunzel for a private tête-à-tête!" or "Lady Rapunzel wishes a personal interview with his Lordship William Pickett— alone!" Will and Elle gave up. So, when they reached the fork in the road that would take Elle to her family's estate and Will to the castle and his destiny, they had not had a chance to exchange anything much more personal or significant than "Good day, Lady Rapunzel" or "Good morning, Lord Protector."

As Rapunzel was bidding goodbye to the King, and Will was helping to move Elle's luggage from the carriage to one of the packhorses, they both realized that their moment was slipping away.

Something had to be done.

After mounting her horse, Elle screwed up her courage, favored Will with a glance, and dropped her lace handkerchief in such a way that he was bound to see it fluttering to the ground. Unfortunately, Will took this moment to look down at the dirt between his feet and chew on his thumb. Elle cursed under her breath, but anything else she might do would be wanton and make her appear desperate. In defeat, she pulled her hood into position over her head, turned her horse toward home and spurred it to a slow walk.

By the time Will had figured out the words he wanted to say to her, Rapunzel and her servants were turning around a bend in the road. He felt his heart sink into his stomach. She hadn't even said goodbye. He had a sure feeling that he had missed his opportunity.

The King leaned out of the carriage and pointed to a

speck of delicate white cloth. "Lord Protector, I believe Lady Rapunzel dropped her handkerchief. Would you return it to her?"

Before Will could say yes, the King signaled the driver and the borrowed carriage continued its journey to Castle White. As it rolled away, Will could clearly hear the King inside muttering something about "young idiots." Silently agreeing, he sprinted across the road, plucked the handkerchief from the ground, and jumped on his horse.

"Lady Rapunzel! Lady Rapunzel!"

A thrill of relief rushed through Elle as she heard Will's voice. She reined her horse to a stop. Will brought his mount beside hers. She briefly bowed her head and then looked up into his eyes. She let her gaze linger.

They both waited for the other to speak.

"Lord Protector . . ."

"Lady Rapunzel . . ."

They both said together, "Please you go first."

Another silence followed.

Will wanted to tell her that being in her company the last few days had been like a fairy tale—even if it had been a fairy tale with an insufferably overbearing Royal Herald as the narrator—and that he hoped the fairy tale would go on and on to its inevitable happily ever after. When he finally spoke all he managed was, "I . . . I . . ."

Elle wanted to tell him that she liked his company, was worried about him, and wanted to go on worrying about him if he would let her. Instead, she said, "I am sorry that we didn't have a chance to talk alone. Perhaps we can when I return to Castle White with your sister."

"Yes," he said. "I suppose." She waited a moment to see if he would say more, but his eyes seemed to be frozen on the reins in his hands. She moved as if to turn her horse away, but as she did Will put out his hand. "Lady Rapunzel . . . Elle, wait."

In the past Will might have let the moment pass, or he would not have even noticed it passing. But this time, a sudden strength of resolve surged through him, and he took her hand in his and placed the tips of her fingers gently to his lips. She thrilled at his touch and felt her breath catch, this time in pleasure, as he kissed her hand.

His eyes locked on hers and he murmured into her palm, "What I mean to say, what I want to say, is that you have captured my heart, Lady Rapunzel. And though, given my recent infatuation with Princess Gwendolyn, I might be exposing myself as inconstant and fickle—if you allow, I shall do all in my power to prove myself to you."

Rapunzel's face flushed as she was stunned to silence. Then her color cleared and a smile, a beautiful radiant smile, rose in her face. She bent forward, closed her eyes, and rested her lips on his fingers in return. "I will allow, Lord William."

"You will?"

"Of course," she said and her eyes opened on his. "I have wished for it ever since the night we met and I tried to claw you to death."

They both laughed in a mutual sigh of relief, and then they found themselves engulfed in another silence, only this one felt so comfortable neither wanted to break it. They sat there a while in the middle of the road, hands entwined, the horses beneath them occasionally shifting impatiently on their feet.

Finally, Elle said, "I have to go."

"I know," Will replied slowly, but did not release her hand.

She leaned forward in her saddle, her face a pale flower within the folds of her hooded cloak, and kissed him softly on the check. He breathed in her heady jasmine scent and then, reaching up, slowly lowered her hood, and ran his fingers through her hair, tucking a loose strand behind her ear. Her eyes, wide with shock, were two brilliant emeralds shining in the afternoon sun. Kissing her hand again he said, "Fair travels, Lady Rapunzel."

"Fair travels, Lord William," she replied softly.

She began to turn her horse. The moment of mastery past, he stuttered, "Oh, I . . . I was supposed to give you this." He held out the dripping mess of her soiled handkerchief.

"Keep it as a token of my devotion until our next meeting," she said and pressed it back into his hand.

Long after she had gone, Will sat on his horse holding the handkerchief and staring after her. Finally, he turned his horse and trotted after the King. For the first time since the dragon died, he found himself thinking about the future. He did not know what life held in store for him. Perhaps one day he would be king. Perhaps the Prince would return in triumph and he would find himself back on the farm in Prosper. But none of that mattered anymore, because one thing was certain. He was in love.

Chapter 3

Dark Days in Castle White

PRINCESS GWENDOLYN DROVE her fingernails into her palms, her face twisting with anger, as she watched the unfolding of Elle and Will's affair from her darkened sanctuary in Castle White. "That little harlot," she snarled as she hunched lower over the glass ball and stared at the flickering images.

"Just look at her!" she urged the dead faces. The shadows twisted and stretched from their corners to peer over her shoulder. "Fluttering her eyes like a common street-walker. '*Fair travels*,'" she mocked, and there were whispers of cold gaiety from her bodiless companions.

The shades were ever-present now. Even when she was in the middle of court, she could see them mingling with the other nobles, whispering secrets and staring boldly down the dresses of the ladies. She knew that she should be afraid of them, but she was not. They were familiar, and even if she did not trust them, she would have felt alone without them.

"He will be mine," she said with a conviction that was belied by the worried frown that came unbidden as she watched Will stare after Elle. "He must be mine. There has to be someone for me," she pleaded in a voice that belonged to a young woman from decades ago, a scared young woman who believed that love could be found in a wish. For a brief moment, the shadows withdrew, but, within a heartbeat, they were back in numbers drawing Gwendolyn's attention away from the scene and her mind back to the present.

With a forced serenity, she said, "Of course, the boy will want me. I am Princess Gwendolyn Mostfair. I am the most beautiful woman in the world. I am his desire, and he will get his fill and more." By the time the last word escaped her lips, calm confidence colored her tone.

She thought over her plans, and a sly smile replaced the worried frown as she tapped her crimson nails against the glowing ball. All was in readiness. The charms for Will and the King were finished. For the power of the fairy to work, all she needed was their presence, and they were coming.

They were coming. But the waiting was driving her mad. Her face contorted again, and the shadows, sensing one of her rages, swirled about in anticipation. A large one seemed to flap enormous bat-like wings. She shrieked, "*Fairy, do something!*"

"*What wouldst thou have me do, Mistress?*" came the tired voice.

"Seize control of the Royal Herald or the squire. No, one of Rapunzel's servants."

Her shadow court liked all these plans and howled its approval with shrieks that made the hair stand on the back of Gwendolyn's neck.

"*Such is beyond my powers, Mistress. To seize a person's mind, they must be in mine presence,*" the voice said flatly, as though it was something it had often repeated.

Perhaps Gwendolyn had asked it before, she really couldn't say. The last week had mostly been a blur of dark enchantments, evil incantations, and planning the wedding. Now, with her plots in order, she spent more and more of her time in this dank little room, consulting with the shadows and waiting.

"It is nice to hear that you have your limits, little one," Gwendolyn smirked.

"*Yes, Mistress, we do seem to have more in common than I had originally thought,*" came the dour reply.

If Gwendolyn heard, she did not honor the fairy with a sign, but fell back into her chair, exhausted. There was danger in fatigue. The shades always seemed to grow more daring and malicious. Even now, they were transforming. They swirled and boiled into wispy apparitions—ghosts stolen from her past: a young King Rupert, her mother and father, her sister. She wondered, not for the first time, if these visions were the lingering dreams from her long sleep or the result of trying to harness fairy magic. If it was the former, it would fade in time, she tried to reassure herself; and if the latter, it was a price that had to be paid. The fairy was no help. All she would say is that they were dangerous, but danger or no, Gwendolyn had promises to keep. She turned her head and tried to catch the image of Rosslyn, her sister, but it flickered away again to hover just out of sight. She stood and began to pace. She had found the only way to keep the ghosts at bay was to keep moving. *I must not allow the madness to consume me*, she thought. *Not yet*. But, after only a few turns about the room, her weariness forced her back to her chair. She shielded her eyes from the fairy's glow with her intertwined hands. "I wish you were not quite so bright."

"*Sorry, Mistress, we cannot all be dull,*" the fairy replied, adding an unnecessary twinkle out of spite.

The fairy congratulated itself on the insult, but glimmered in annoyance that it had been wasted—Gwendolyn had fallen asleep. Spent from magic and madness, her breath slowed, and the shadows encircled her, bending inward, already making designs on her dreams.

THE NEXT EVENING, the King's procession came over a small rise—and there stood Castle White, painted in reds and purples by the setting sun. The carriage came to a reluctant stop, and His Majesty opened the window and waved Will over. "You lead us into the castle, Lord Protector," the King said brightly. "The people must see their hero returning in glory."

"Yes, Your Majesty," Will responded. He gripped his

reins but hesitated, looking over to the King. "Your Majesty, what do you think about Princess Gwendolyn?"

The King raised an eyebrow. "Do I think she is plotting our demise?"

"Yes, Your Majesty."

The King did not answer for several heartbeats. Then he spoke slowly and deliberately. "No, Will. That is to say, she could, but I don't believe the woman I remember would, if you understand."

"I suppose so, Your Majesty," Will replied with a sense that he knew far less of the Princess than he had imagined. He reached into his pouch and fingered Elle's handkerchief for comfort. The King tapped the roof of the carriage with his ringed fist. The driver whistled and Will, along with the coach, began a slow ride up the rolling hills to the main gate of the great keep.

By the time they reached the bridge across the moat, news of the Lord Protector and the King's return had spread throughout the castle, and they made their entrance to a roaring crowd of well-wishers. Gwendolyn, however, was not present to greet them, rather, the Royal Steward stepped forward as the Royal Herald announced, "Presenting, the Lord Protector and His Royal Majesty, the King!"

A purple carpet was unrolled between the carriage and the door of the castle, and as the servants opened the carriage door, the assembled masses bowed as one. The King took a deep breath as he set both feet on the carpet and surveyed the castle. Then he walked over to the Royal Steward. "You may rise," the King said.

The Royal Steward rose, stretched out his hands, and, with many apologies, told the King that the Princess had taken ill just the night before, and that she had been secluded in her rooms ever since. The King nodded and gestured for Will, the Royal Herald, and Tomas to follow him as he entered the castle proper. Will tried to fall back, but Tomas gently nudged him into position alongside the King.

"Bit of luck there, Will," the King remarked as he strode through the halls toward Gwendolyn's rooms.

"What do you mean, Your Majesty?"

"I mean that I will be able to confront her in private. There will be no risk of a scene. God, how I hate scenes."

After too short a walk, they reached her door. Somewhere along the way, Tomas and the Royal Herald had vanished. The King put an arm around Will's shoulder and whispered, "I will go in first, Will, and then once I've set her in her place, I shall bid you enter. I think it will give her a lift to see you, but let's not mention Lady Rapunzel." He frowned at this. "No need to broach that subject just yet."

Will started to say that he didn't feel comfortable deceiving the Princess, but the King was already knocking imperiously on her chamber door. The King was admitted, and Will found himself leaning against the wall of the corridor, waiting for a summons and thinking about Elle. *How* are *you going to tell the princess about Elle?* he asked himself. *Last time we were together, you were dancing with her and telling her how magical she was.*

It was with this last thought, and his guilt over it still

rattling around in his head, that the door opened and the King stood in the doorway with a broad, almost slack-jawed smile on his face. He looked as if all the stress and sadness of the last few days had been utterly wiped away. He spread his arms wide, and in a strange stilted monotone said, "William-good-to-see-you."

Will pushed himself off the wall, "Your Majesty? Are you okay? I take it there was no scene?"

"Scene? No. She-explained-everything. It-was-a-misunderstanding." The King took a step forward and gripped Will firmly, very firmly, by the arm. "Come-my-boy-she-is-anxious-to-see-you."

Boy? When has the King ever called me 'boy'? But his retrospection was cut short as the King pushed him into Gwendolyn's chamber.

Will coughed. The smell of burnt nutmeg was overpowering. He opened his mouth to say something about it to the King when his eyes fell on the Princess. She was arrayed on a low settee in a splendorous dressing gown of white and blue surrounded by the warm light of dozens of candles. Yet, despite the perfection of the setting, there was something wrong. She looked ill. Her face was pale, her hair dull and disheveled, and her eyes were sunken and dark.

"Dear Lord Protector William, it is so nice to see you," she was saying. "I am sorry about what happened with your sister, but I have something here that will explain everything."

He heard the bolt being thrown on the door behind him. Some part of his mind found that odd, but at the same time he was distracted by a glowing ball of light the Princess drew from the folds of her clothing. The shadows in the corners of the room seemed to spring from their places and close in around him. Before he could react, she thrust the flickering sphere under his nose. "Now, my dear, for the wedding I think you shall wear blue or maybe green . . ."

My dear? he thought, followed quickly by, *wedding?* The light in the orb began to dance, and he stopped thinking altogether.

A FEW DAYS later, while the King was announcing the upcoming nuptials of the Lord Protector and Princess Gwendolyn Mostfair to the court, Lady Rapunzel arrived home to discover that things had not gone as she had intended.

She had barely dismounted before beginning an interrogation of her footman, Collins. His answers made Elle increasingly concerned and confused. "I just don't understand it, Collins. How did you lose Lady Pickett, and what do you mean you can't 'remember' anything after meeting with the Princess?"

"That's just it, Your Ladyship. I remember kneeling down to pay my respects, then she pulled out a sort of ball of light or some such, and then . . . nothing."

Elle tapped a finger against her lips. "I don't know, but it sounds like sorcery, Collins." She shrugged emphatically. "Well, I've called her a witch before, but I never thought there might be truth to it." She turned her attention back to the man. "I suppose you can't be blamed for being enchanted."

"Thank you, Your Ladyship."

"But," she said sharply, and Collins winced, "Liz is in the woods all alone. When the spell was broken, why didn't you go after her?"

"Well, there was this cave, and . . . dwarves!"

"And dwarves!" she snapped, and began pacing back and forth across the floor of the stables, gesturing wildly, her face flashing between a pale white and a bright red. "Well, we simply must go back and collect her."

"We? Your Ladyship, but you shouldn't . . ."

"Of course I'm going, Collins. This is the Lord Protector's sister we are speaking of. We can't afford to have any more foul-ups."

"But, Your Ladyship—"

"Be still, Collins. There is nothing further to discuss. You and I will go and save Lady Pickett, and then the three of us will continue onto the castle, where we will almost certainly have to save the Lord Protector and His Royal Highness from Gwendolyn's sorcery." She swiveled on her toe and began marching back to the main house. "Saddle the horses. We leave at once! . . . Oh. And, Collins. Tell the stable hands to clean the stalls. There's an odd smell in here."

Collins sniffed intently at the air. Perhaps the air did smell heavily of spice. He checked his armpit suspiciously and flinched at the odor, but shrugged and went back to his work. After all it was a stable.

For the servants' sake, Elle maintained her composure

until she got back to her rooms, and then she collapsed on her bed with a sob. "Oh, William, Liz, please be safe."

"YOU LIED TO ME!" Gwendolyn screamed into the transparent little ball as the flickering spark hovered and danced and the scene from Rapunzel's home dissolved. Around her the shadows spun like a whirlwind.

"*Nay, Mistress, I cannot lie,*" the fairy said smugly.

"You told me Elizabeth Pickett was dead!"

"*Nay, Mistress, I merely said she was gone. It was thou that concluded that she was 'dead.'*"

"You deceptive little insect!" the Princess hissed. "Well, it won't matter. I already have Will and the King. Nothing more is needed. The wedding is scheduled for a week from today, and after that I shall be queen."

"*Thy plotting will not work to bringeth thy desires to thee, Mistress. Thou art still under the curse of thy own wish.*"

Princess Gwendolyn held the ball before her face and laughed hysterically. "You still believe in the power of your impotent curse? Did your curse keep me trapped in that tower, or prevent me from capturing William Pickett or the King? Your curse is broken, it has no power over me anymore."

"*If thou sayst so, Mistress.*"

"I do." Then quietly she said, "But how to ensure that there are no complications . . ." Putting the ball in her pocket, Gwendolyn rose from her seat and ascended to the great hall above. She took her place on one of the high seats there, arranged her garments, and rang the bell. A footman appeared and made a low bow. "Fetch me the Captain of the Royal Guard."

"At once, Princess Gwendolyn," he said, and bowed his way backward out of the room.

As soon as the door closed, she pulled the ball once more from its hiding place. "Now, little firefly, let us set your 'half-truth' to the right."

The shadows at her side stared down at the ball and whispered dark secrets, full of black magic and malice. Gwendolyn shuddered. For a moment she wavered, and then the shadows parted and she saw Rosslyn—sculpted from patterns of light and dark. Gwendolyn felt her heart turn to ice, and she reached out for her sister. "Rosslyn?"

The vision held out its hands; in them was a golden circlet. Tears of flickering light fell from blank eyes. "Return what is mine," it moaned, and then dissolved as though smoke dispersed by a strong wind. Gwendolyn scrambled backward off the chair to cower against the wall—shaking in fear—tears stinging her eyes. "What is happening to me, fairy? What are these visions?"

The light in the globe shrank to a glowing ember. "*It is a warning, Mistress. This power is beyond thee. In the end thou willst not be able to control the visions, and they will drive thee mad. Free me now, and I can still put things to right. I swear it can be done.*"

Gwendolyn raised her hand as though to dash the orb to the ground, but one of the shadows reminded her about another of the fairy's promises made long ago.

Hatred burned fresh inside her, and fear transformed back to resolve.

"No." She rose to her feet. "I have heard your promises before. You promised to make my wishes come true. You promised me true love. You promised the dragon a life of glory. Your promises are empty and cruel." She resumed her seat on the high chair, the ball resting in her lap.

"Then thou art doomed, Mistress."

"Perhaps, but this time the doom will be of my own making."

Chapter 4

Beastly Luck

CHARMING WAS LOST. The last few days he had wandered aimlessly—until now, when he found himself staggering along an overgrown cart path through the dark forest in the Northern Waste. The branches of ancient black-trunked trees formed a dense roof that kept out most, but not all, of the steady, driving rain that he could hear pelting the canopy. At his feet, a spider web of roots reached like grasping hands across the road, making his footing slippery and treacherous. He hadn't slept nor eaten more than a few handfuls of nuts and some wild berries since he'd left the Cooked Goose. He was tired and hungry but did not care—he couldn't escape that last look of loathing on the face of his father, the King.

With a deep sigh, he left the path and rested against

a hard tree trunk. He leaned his head back and tried to see something of the sky through the dense branches. "Is it day or night?" he wondered aloud. "How long have I wandered in these wretched woods? Does it matter? Is this where I will find my end?"

Don't be absurd, his mind rebuked. *It has only been a few days since your former father, the King, cast you away like a common piece of refuse.*

Charming reflected that, though this might be true, in his heart (and legs) it felt like weeks had passed since he had known the comforts of companionship and camaraderie (and saddle) that had marked his previous life.

"Perhaps my body has been slain by heartbreak and fatigue, and has fallen somewhere in this dark forest . . . and I am naught but a specter, an accursed wraith, left behind to struggle on through this hell for all eternity."

Let's think about that for a moment, he suggested to himself. *If your body has fallen, then death has not been the cure for mortal pains that the priests always claimed it would be.*

True, he ached all over with weariness. And, based on the throbbing of his feet, he could only imagine the blisters that must be forming. Wraiths don't get blisters. "This is the worst," he groused. "I was intended for jousting, fighting, leaping. But endless walking over and over . . . no. Now walking is my fate, my doom, to walk and walk and walk in never-ending . . ." As he realized that he had stopped walking, he pursed his lips and reconsidered his words: "hardly ever-ending . . . *penance*. Why am I so cursed?"

Then his mind's eye conjured up the face of his father, the King, and again that last look of loathing. A deep melancholy drove him and his inner monologue to silence. He stood and shuffled away from his tree.

This is why we keep moving, his thoughts ventured after a time.

They were right. Every time he had tried resting since beginning this pointless pilgrimage, his mind eventually wandered to some dark place and he would force himself to stagger on.

"But to what end?" he asked. "I have fallen. I am doomed to live this miserable existence—wandering aimlessly, an unknown, dirty vagabond, suffering righteously, as a moral lesson for all who would let pride lead them down the path of wickedness and deceit."

Say, there's a good couplet in there, he suggested to himself.

The monstrous nature of the thought caught Charming off guard. He paused midstride and, clenching his fist, shouted, "No!" The now-dark forest echoed the word back at him. Suddenly, aware of the stillness of the trees, he muttered quietly, "I am unworthy of couplet . . ."

"Perhaps I should take a vow of silence," he considered aloud. "Then there would be no temptation to break into verse." He paused and raised both arms to the sky. "I swear by the moon above that if I am redeemed, I will put things to right—"

That's a stupid oath, he interrupted himself silently. *Am I really this ridiculous? Why do I need to keep turning everything into melodrama?*

Of course, he had only ever been Prince Charming, and Prince Charming only existed for drama's sake. Everybody he'd ever known had turned even the most commonplace moments of his life into epic events, such as the weeklong festival that had been declared to commemorate his first steps. He sighed again and looked up at the heavens to try to find the moon upon which he had been about to swear.

I don't even think there is a moon tonight. Is it even night? It seems awfully dark. How can I swear on something that isn't there?

He shook his head to clear his thoughts and wondered if he was growing delirious from hunger. Out loud, he said, "That's just semantics—"

His silent thoughts cut him off again. *Am I resorting to semantics? If there is no moon, then I can't possibly have sworn on the 'moon above.' And, beyond that, what does it even mean to say 'if I'm redeemed I'll put things right?' That's like saying, 'if I'm redeemed, I'll be redeemed.' The problem is that I never think before speaking, or acting for that matter. Ask anyone. It has been an issue for a while. Now, if I had thought for a moment, I would have told myself to swear on the Morning Star, or the Northern Mountain, or my name . . .*

Okay, never mind that one—

"Enough!" Charming said sharply to the night air (as he was sure now that it was night), and then more quietly to himself, "I am being silly." He rocked back on his heels and sat in the crook of two massive roots, tired and ashamed. "Here I am, arguing with myself about oaths and meaning. This *has* been my problem for years; I would rather swear a meaningless oath and make an empty promise than actually *do* the right thing. The people in the tavern were right: I am a fool and have always been a fool."

It was growing colder, and he shivered beneath his thin shirt. Nothing seemed real anymore, not even the growing numbness in his fingers and toes. He knew he should keep moving but could not muster the energy or the will to stand again. "I'm tired of running. Let me stay here and be done."

Charming sat and waited. After a time, he wondered how long it would take. Having decided to give up, he was strangely impatient for the end, and this perch was not particularly comfortable. Something was poking into his side. He shifted slightly and adjusted a small leather pouch on his belt, only to realize with a sudden disorientation that that's where he'd put Elizabeth's glass slipper before leaving the castle.

He drew it out and stared at its smooth sparkling surface and thought of her. He remembered the smell of her hair, the touch of her hand as they danced. He remembered her smile and the fire in her eyes.

"Why did you take this from the ballroom?" he asked aloud. And then, after only a moment's reflection, answered softly, "Love of course, but it doesn't seem possible."

He closed his eyes and clasped the slipper to his breast. Time passed and Charming slipped in and out of sleep, all the while trying to ponder this last mystery. At some point he heard a voice, distantly . . .

"As I thought, milord," came an irritated voice, "it's just another drunk. He must have wandered up from the Cooked Goose. I'm told by the groundskeeper that there was a large revel there a few nights ago. Perhaps it would be best to leave him here to sleep it off."

Another voice, a deep voice, responded from further off. "Giles, he is on my estate. It is the duty of a host to care for all in need; and, surely, if anyone is in need, this man is. But do remind me to speak to the groundskeeper about his choice of taverns."

"Yes, milord."

Charming saw a lantern and felt hands lifting him from the ground, and then he slipped back out of consciousness.

CHARMING WOKE FROM a dark sleep into the soft caress of silk and the subtle airs of fine oil and incense. He sat up slowly, the vague memories of his dreams flying at his remembrances like a flock of frightened birds. For a warm, peaceful moment, he imagined that he was home and that, for the past few weeks, the death of the dragon, the glories of William Pickett and his own dishonor had all been a terrible nightmare. But as he looked around, he realized that this was not his own bed, and that he was not in Castle White.

He stretched and studied his surroundings. He was

resting in a large four-poster bed surrounded by drifts of snow-white bedding. The room itself was handsomely appointed. A warming fire had been laid in the stone hearth set in the far wall, and he had been bathed. For the first time since he had left home, he felt clean. The question was, who had bathed him and put him to bed? Then a sudden panic seized him, and he sat up with a start. "The slipper! Where's the slipper?"

Charming looked about frantically, but his clothes were nowhere to be seen. He threw back the covers and pawed at the linen nightclothes he was wearing. The slipper was gone. There was no trace of it. A sense of dread came over him, gnawing softly at his insides.

Where am I? There are no noblemen in this forest, so who is this lordly host? Is he friend or foe, honorable man or thief?

As if in response to his unvoiced thoughts, the door opened and a tall scarecrow of a man dressed in subdued finery stepped inside. He put a hand to his chest, cleared his throat, looked down at Charming along his long nose, and sniffed disdainfully. "Good, you are awake. If you have recovered sufficiently to return to whatever passes for your life, then my lord has instructed me to provide you with some clothing so that you may go."

"I . . ." Charming started hesitantly, but then realized that this man must have taken the slipper or knew who did. He rose from the bed and, squaring his shoulders, put all the command of his former self in his voice. "You, whatever your name is . . . where are my possessions?"

The man took a step back, momentarily stunned by

his outburst, but recovering said, "You will not use that tone in this residence, and certainly not with me, or I shall send you packing with the dogs on your heels."

"Are you my host? If so, then either return my possessions, or, despite this fine manor, I deem you nothing but a common thief!" Charming snapped, making his way around the bed and toward the man.

The thin man reddened at the accusation and then seemed to swell with indignation. "How dare you question me? My name is Giles, and I am my lord's butler. As for the slipper, my lord wishes to question you about that. Specifically, he wishes to know who you stole it from."

"What?" Charming stuttered, "I—I would never steal . . ."

Despite this denial, the memory of his recent treachery drained him. He lost the anger that had given him strength and sat back down on the edge of the bed. *What manner of man am I? Have not my actions been the definition of villainy?*

Giles grunted derisively. "I warn you, the dogs will be ready."

At that moment, there was the sound of movement beyond the door. Giles looked into the hall at something Charming could not see. A deep resonant voice that was somehow familiar came from outside the room. "Giles, help our guest find suitable clothing. I wish to have an audience with him."

"But, my lord," said Giles, not turning his eyes from Charming, "I must say this fellow seems mad, and his denial rings of insincerity."

Charming wanted to shout, "I am Prince Charming!" But, he wasn't anymore. The whole world had gone mad. He put his hands to his head and mumbled something indistinct and incoherent.

There was a long silence, and it was perhaps for the best that Charming never saw the look of disdain on Giles's face. "You see what I mean, my lord? Are you certain about the audience? The dogs could see to him without trouble."

"I am, Giles. Now, help this poor man, and I will consider another matter while I wait. I think I should revisit the incident involving the hounds'—how did you call it? . . . 'fortuitous escape' when the dwarves last visited?"

Giles fiddled with his collar, keeping his eyes on Charming. "I'll help him straightaway, my lord."

The door shut gently.

Deaf to the exchange between master and servant, Charming muttered on. " . . . never had the courage to reach the unreachable . . ."

Giles rolled his eyes as he crossed the room to a large wardrobe. He rummaged in it for a few seconds and emerged with a drab and hideously out-of-date outfit. A deep and bottomless despair gripped Charming. He knew it was shallow, but to be robbed of fashion seemed the last insult.

Laying out the clothes on the bed, Giles clucked his tongue in irritation. "I will warn you only once not to waste my lord's time. He is too generous and good-hearted, and a great many try to presume upon his nature. We have a troupe of insufferable dwarves that are constantly . . . well, let's just say, answer his questions and be on your way."

Charming nodded stiffly in response. Once he was dressed and had been approved by Giles, he was led through the stone halls of the castle to a set of gilt doors. Giles rested a bony hand on the handle and smiled thinly at Charming. There was something about his eyes, a mischievous glee, that made Charming uneasy. The butler leaned forward, coming uncomfortably close, and whispered, "I hope you don't scare easily. My lord can be . . . disconcerting."

Before Charming could respond, or even decide how he would respond, Giles pulled open the door and gestured Charming inside. The door closed behind him. The hall itself was dimly lit by a few candles burning in high sconces set into the walls, and appeared to be more of a dining room than a proper audience chamber. High-backed chairs surrounded a great wooden table that dominated the center of the space. A cloaked figure, which Charming could only assume was Giles's master, sat at the far end of the table, obscured by shadows.

"Come forward," resounded that now-familiar deep voice.

He moved closer. As he approached, he noted first the man's breathing. It was deep and powerful, almost like panting. Beyond that there was a general impression of size. Whoever he was, he was massive. In fact, his shoulders resembled Gnarsh the Troll's more than those of an ordinary man. But even standing next to him, his host's face was indistinct, a mask of shadows beneath a deeply hooded cloak. Perhaps he should have been scared, but he didn't have enough energy left for fear.

Once upon a time, I was Prince Charming.

He drew a chair to the lord's right. "May I take this seat?"

"Be my guest," came the low response.

Remembering the butler's request, Charming decided to come right to the point. "Thank you for your kindness, Your Lordship. I am truly in your debt and do not wish to impose on your hospitality, but before I take my leave I would ask . . . no, beg you, please return to me the glass slipper." Charming stared down at the table as he spoke and felt a burning in his eyes. He blinked away the half-formed tears.

"I will ask you simply and request only your honesty. Did you steal it?"

Charming thought hard about the night at the ball, about Elizabeth running up the stairs, about retrieving the slipper from where it lay beneath a curtain at the edge of the ballroom. He raised his eyes and stared into the shadowy void of his questioner's face. "No. I am not proud of how I came to hold the slipper, but I did not steal it. It was lost. I wish only to return it to its rightful owner."

There was a long pause from his faceless host before he replied, "I am satisfied, but let us speak more about this remarkable shoe as we dine. I apologize in advance if my appearance disturbs you."

He pulled back the hood of his cloak.

Charming had not known what he expected to see,

perhaps that his host was badly disfigured or scarred, but what sat across from him was more monster than man. Seemingly a cross between a boar and a wolf, this lord, his host, resembled a taxidermist's nightmare come to life. His face was twisted into an elongated snout with sharp white teeth and short tusks jutting upward from his lower jaw. Thick coarse fur covered his head and poked out from beneath a fashionably high lace collar, and sharp ears flicked back and forth as he gazed at Charming with yellow animal eyes.

Instinctively, Charming gasped and his hand reached down for the sword that was not there. A few days, even hours, before, he would have leapt to his feet, ready to slay such a monster, to battle it like a hero. But he was not a hero any longer. He took in a deep breath, but otherwise did not move from his chair.

The man—beast—cocked his head, studying his reaction. Charming knew he was being measured, but did not care. He had already been judged and found wanting. With nothing to lose, he asked, or tried to ask, the obvious question, the only question: "How did you . . . I mean . . . I'm sorry, are you cursed?"

The yellow eyes softened, and, to his surprise, Charming realized that there was something distinctly human behind those eyes, and, what was more, something manifestly good. Gray streaks ran through the creature's fur, and Charming determined that the monster before him must be well past its prime. The creature spoke: "Do you wish to know why I appear the way I do?"

"I apologize, good sir, but yes, I do."

The beast gave a deep, gentle rumbling chuckle and began playing with a small golden charm he had on a chain around his neck. The yellow eyes smiled. "First, let us dispense with the titles. My name is Adam. In the tales, I am simply the Beast. As to how I came to look like this, I suppose I could say that I was the victim of a magical curse, but that would be to deny my own part in what happened." Adam paused, considering how to start, and after a measured moment said, "How do these stories begin? Ah, yes . . .

"Once upon a time, this part of the kingdom was a thriving land, and this forest and much beyond even that was part of my family's estate. My father was a good man, and a wise lord, but he and my mother died of fever while I was still young." The Beast's voice broke here and he paused to collect himself. "I was a man, but I was immature. Perhaps in time I might have grown into my new position, but I was impatient and lazy. Rather than apply myself, I summoned a fairy spirit and asked it to make me a great lord, strong in battle and feared by all. The fairy, as I have since learned, is quite literal in granting wishes, and turned me into the creature you see before you. Perhaps she thought that it would teach me a lesson." He held up his hands in a half-shrug.

While he spoke, servants slipped quietly into the room and placed covered trays in front of the two men and poured two goblets of wine. The Beast gestured at the dishes. "I would guess that you have not had a good meal in days. Come, let's eat!" He reached forward, and removed the lid of a large tray to reveal a turkey, cooked a perfect golden brown. Charming swallowed in anticipation. "Ah, the kitchen is trying to impress you. They do tire of cooking for one. If you would be so kind as to do the honor?" The Beast indicated with one of his clawed hands an elegant silvered carving knife and matching serving fork set beside the tray. "I signaled the servants to give us some time before they check on us again. I suspect we both have stories to tell that would be best told with fewer ears listening."

Charming regarded his host, who was still playing with the end of the little gold necklace he was wearing. It was remarkable. The creature, Adam, was so well-mannered that Charming was finding it necessary to remind himself that his host was a monster and not some aged lord.

As Charming carved and served the turkey, the Beast picked up the thread of his story. "As I said, I was transformed by a fairy who had a remarkably strong sense of right and wrong. But if the fairy's goal was to teach me a lesson, then I learned nothing. I was bitter and angry, and I used my new form to become a true tyrant. One day, several years after I became what I am, a merchant trespassed on my land. I was enraged, and was near to killing him. The man pleaded for his life, offering me anything, even his own daughter in exchange for his freedom."

"But surely you didn't accept," Charming said, not able to hide the disgust in his voice.

The Beast smiled, but it was a humorless smile, a grim, self-mocking smile. Then he raised his goblet and took a sip of wine, and the smile was gone. "But I did. I think that act alone—that I could join in such a cruelty—justified the fairy's punishment. I know that I have never been more deserving of this form than I was at that moment. However, then she arrived." His voice softened. "When first I saw her, I lost my heart."

Despite his hunger, Charming had forgotten the food, and he asked the question that had been burning in his mind for weeks, "So, you believe in love at first sight?

The question broke the Beast's grim mood, and he smiled and winked at Charming with real affection. "My boy, every person's life is a fairy tale. And, if you live in a fairy tale and don't believe in love at first sight, then you are missing half the story. Yes, I believe in love at first sight, because I have felt its keen sting."

"What did she think of you?" Charming asked.

"Oh, she was terrified. She hated me. How could she not? I had imprisoned her father and now held her hostage. I can only imagine what she thought my intentions were. Was she to die or suffer some other violation?" His eyes grew hard and his jaw clenched in anger at the memory of himself. "I can say now that there is nothing in this life I will ever do that can make up for the fear and pain I put her through in those early days." The Beast paused, his face alive with a swirl of competing emotions, and then that same little self-mocking smile flickered out and the moment passed. He tucked the necklace back into his shirt and began tearing at his meat with massive clawed hands. In between bites, he continued. "Nevertheless, I tried to court her."

"Did it work?" Charming asked as he cut another slice of meat.

The Beast wiped his snout and chuckled, "Not a bit."

Charming served himself and, after a few ravenous bites, leaned closer to the Beast, intrigued. "Then how did you win her?"

"I didn't *win* her," he answered with another of his knowing winks. "As improbable as it sounds, she and I became friends; and in time, she decided that she could love me, and I, for my part, learned to trust that I was worthy of her love." He raised his goblet. "I have found that love isn't about conquest, but having the strength to surrender."

They ate in silence for a time before the Beast came back to his story. "We married and, apart from a few squabbles that she always won, lived happily thereafter. My anger was gone and I dedicated myself to being the man my beloved deserved. We lived and loved well and long, and then, two winters ago, she . . . she left this world."

"I am sorry."

He waved away the concern. "I am old. Death is not as frightening a specter as it was in my youth. My love passed peacefully, without pain, and I was with her at the end. There were no words left unsaid between us. I mourn her absence, but she is always with me in my heart." Having finished eating, and telling his story, the Beast leaned back in his chair. "I have done all the talking, and all about my own ancient history. What about you? I am most interested in how you ended up in the mud outside my unfashionable manor, and bearing such an unusual trophy."

With that, he produced the glass slipper from beneath his cloak and placed it on the table between them. It drew in the candlelight and threw a halo of sparks into the air. "If you would like to tell me your story, I am willing to listen—and I promise, young man, that your words shall not travel beyond this table."

Charming looked up from his plate to the slipper, and, reaching out, he plucked it from the table and cradled it in his hands. The old man leaned forward and poured them both another glass of wine. Charming took no notice, his gaze completely held by the glowing slipper. Then, without noticing, he began to speak. "I'm not sure where to begin. I suppose that I was Prince Charming. Maybe you've heard of me?" He looked up with hopeful eyes.

The Beast pulled out an elegant pipe and packed it with tobacco. Then he lit it and, after his first few puffs of blue smoke, gave one of his kind, toothy smiles and nodded. "Everyone's heard of Prince Charming."

"Then you know all about me."

The Beast shrugged and pointed the stem of the pipe at his guest. "People called me 'the Beast,' but it is only a title. It is who people think I should be, not who I am. Is 'Prince Charming' who you are?"

The question caught Charming off guard. All of his life he had been Prince Charming, and he had heard nothing but praise for what he *would* do.

Voices from his past sang in his head:

We await our savior's coming in glory with the same certainty that we await the day that Prince Charming shall free us from the Dragon!

Oh, when you speak in couplet, I'm so moved that I nearly swoon. . .

There is no 'boy' like Charming.

As Royal Tailor I can say without hesitation, no one else can carry off purple hose with such aplomb.

They had all been wrong. He wasn't the slayer of the dragon. He wasn't the Princess's savior. Now he was not even Prince Charming, although perhaps he could still carry off purple hose. Nonetheless, he was just Edward, and he wasn't sure who that was. He had never been just Edward before.

His head was swimming again, and his hands were shaking. To calm his nerves, Charming took a sip of his wine, and then another; and when he placed his goblet back on the table, he was surprised to see that it was nearly empty.

That deep kindly voice broke the silence. "I am sorry if my question was too personal. You do not have to answer."

Charming gazed once more at Elizabeth's slipper. *Why am I so afraid? I have nothing to lose more valuable than what is already gone. I have nowhere left to fall that is worse than where I am.* He looked back at the Beast, drawn to those kind yellow eyes, and the words came spilling out. "I don't think I know who I am." He downed the rest of the wine in his goblet. "All I really ever wanted was . . ." Charming fell silent. He felt warm. *The wine must be getting to me.*

"What did you want?" said the Beast quietly, as though afraid to break the spell of his speech.

The answer echoed in Charming's heart, but his voice resisted saying it aloud. When he spoke it was with a reluctant slowness. "I wanted the King—no—I wanted my father to be proud of me, and now it is the one thing I can never have." Charming slammed the table with his fist. "You ask who I am? How should I know? I am disowned. I have no family, no friends, no title, nothing. I was supposed to kill the dragon, and someone else did. I was supposed to rescue the Princess, and someone else did. I was supposed to be a great hero, and had to be rescued time and again. I have no place, no purpose . . ." He slumped in his chair. "The world doesn't need Prince Charming."

A brief silence greeted this pronouncement, and Charming wondered if he had shared too much. Then the Beast laughed, a short, sharp explosion of sound. Charming looked up, startled at the outburst. The other man was leaning forward in his chair, a look of surprised amusement on his face. His pipe lay forgotten in his left hand, still trailing a thin tendril of blue-gray smoke. Charming blushed. He was being laughed at. It was not an unreasonable response, but he had not expected it from his kindly host.

Charming shrugged. "You are right, it is rather pathetic, ridiculous really."

"What—"

"I was just saying that I understand why you would laugh at me, I'm pathetic."

The Beast shook his impressive mane as though clearing his head. "No! No! You don't understand. I'm laughing at myself. Here I was thinking that I would listen to your story and dispense some sage advice on life, and then pat you on the head and send you back off into the world. Instead, I find myself discovering truths that, even at my age, I didn't realize I didn't know."

"You are . . . you're mocking me."

The strange smile on the Beast's face vanished in a twinkling. He dropped his pipe on the table and leaned forward, encircling the younger man's forearm in his massive claw. "Charming, I am abjectly sorry for my reaction. I can only beg you to understand that I was overcome." He let go of Charming's wrist and used the free hand to paw at his neck until he managed to free the little golden necklace from his elaborate lace collar. Charming leaned back so he could focus on the tiny golden charm—it was a wolf's head.

"When I was cursed, the fairy gave me this blasted wolf's head necklace. Its symbolism cannot be mistaken, but I've spent my life wondering when I would earn the right to be a man again. Despite the undeserved good fortune of finding my true love, I always held a kernel of bitterness in my heart that things were not different. Only now, because of your words, do I understand. This charm will never vanish, because I will never be the man that I was. That man is dead—slain—for better or worse by my life as the Beast. In your words, the world does not need who I was."

"I don't understand."

His host leaned back in his chair, a mysterious smile on his face as he twirled the little golden wolf on its chain. "If you did, I would feel myself an even greater fool. Perhaps in time understanding will come to you as it did me. For now, I would merely say that perhaps the world never did need you."

Charming chuckled bitterly. "I know you are trying to help me, Adam, but I honestly cannot say that being told I am useless, and likely always have been, is particularly encouraging."

The Beast waved an admonishing finger in the air at his guest. "I did not say that you are useless. What I am trying to suggest is that you stop trying to be Prince Charming, if you can, and just be Charming. Find your own meaning."

Charming pulled the glass slipper protectively against his chest.

The Beast smiled. "I don't know the whole story of that slipper, young man, but if the foot matches the shoe, then I would say you are definitely on the right track."

Charming laughed, this time a little less bitterly than before. "I know you're right, but whereas when I was Prince Charming I was fool enough to think she was beneath me, now that I am only 'Charming,' she is so far above me that I doubt I shall ever be given the chance to speak to her again."

"Ah, but that is a problem that can be met, not a crisis

of the soul. I think if you give your lady fair the chance to love the real you, you may find an almost limitless reservoir of forgiveness."

Without another word, he pulled the golden chain with the little wolf from his neck. "May I give this to you? I have no more need of it, and for some reason I think it might be of help to you."

Charming took the chain and put it on. "It would be my honor."

The Beast drew back and breathed deeply. He seemed less weary. "Thank you. Now, please enjoy my hospitality and stay as long as you need. Charming, my home is yours."

So IT CAME to pass that Charming stayed in the manor of Adam, the Beast, much to the irritation of his butler, Giles. After a time, his smile returned and he found it increasingly easy to laugh. It was as though a burden had been lifted from his mind. He thought that he might enjoy being simply Edward Charming. It had also become more and more apparent to him how deeply he had fallen for Elizabeth Pickett. She was in his thoughts constantly, and he spent most of his time staring at her glass slipper and wondering how he might win her back.

It was toward the end of a pleasant afternoon tea, during which Charming and the Beast had spent their time discussing ways in which an audience might be gained with Lady Elizabeth, that Giles made an announcement. "My lord, the dwarves are here again with another play, begging for patronage. Normally, I would have sent them away, my lord, but after your instructions the other night, I thought I should ask."

"Now, now, Giles," said the Beast. "They deserve the opportunity to perform, and we are at our leisure." The Beast spoke to Charming. "Apparently they are the troupe behind that *Snow White* play that was all the rage a number of years ago. Would you be interested?"

"Lord Adam, if you are at your leisure, then I am at yours."

Giles sighed deeply and bowed. "As you wish, milords."

The butler left to make arrangements. Adam directed Charming to a small reviewing balcony that looked out over a plaza on which a group of dwarves were busy at work putting the finishing touches on a makeshift marionette stage that they seemed to have constructed out of the bits and pieces of a cart. While he did enjoy theater, Charming was not truly in the mood for diversion. Were it not for Adam's interest, he would have preferred they continue their discussion of Elizabeth. The bumps and bruises he had suffered were mostly healed, and he had a growing sense that it was time for him to depart. He needed to return to Castle White and find her.

The Beast cleared his throat and gestured to a pair of chairs on the balcony. "I think the players are ready to begin."

Charming nodded absent-mindedly and took his seat. The preparations were complete, and two dwarves, one with an almost comically bright red nose and one with a perpetual frown, stood next to each other on one side of the stage arguing. A third, who looked to be asleep, sat slumped on the other side of the stage, a curtain rope in his hand. The Beast and Charming shared a chuckle as the grim fellow reached out and tweaked red-nose's red nose. The frowning dwarf then stepped forward, glared up at the balcony, and announced, "Grand patron and esteemed guest, I am proud to present the premiere showing of *Ash and Cinders*, based on the true account of a dear maiden who we rescued, and . . ."

The sleeping dwarf awoke with a start, shouted, "Act One!," and then jerked on the rope. The curtain opened on three very surprised dwarves who were still wrestling with an armload of tangled puppets. The two dwarves who had been introducing the play jumped at this premature start to the production and dove behind the stage, colliding with the other three and sending the whole group tumbling out of sight with a loud crash. The curtain closed.

While the Beast and Charming laughed aloud, Giles exhaled harshly and tapped his foot. After many muffled curses, the play began—again. The curtain rose on a castle and a beautiful servant girl and her brother, enslaved in the house of a cruel mistress. The play then followed the two through a series of misadventures that eventually led them to receiving an invitation to a royal ball. While the marionettes were beautifully crafted and skillfully operated, the dwarves' constant bickering spoiled the performance. Every scene change was met by a very audible debate over the merits of the previous scene and how one performer or the other was "ruining the artistic integrity of the play." This in turn, would lead to an incredibly technical, if still voluble, debate about the meaning of integrity in a modern theatrical context. Which in turn would lead to what sounded like an all-out brawl. It was not long before Charming began to regret Adam's benevolence.

He had long lost interest and was really only half paying attention when the servant girl made her appearance at the royal ball. At the festivities, there was a mad woman with absurdly long hair and a prince that made an utter fool of himself.

Charming sat straight in his chair. *Could this possibly be about William and Elizabeth? I suppose it's possible that the story of my disgrace at the ball could have made it this far into the wilderness.* But then the story wandered away from reality as an agent of an evil queen chased the servant girl into a deep wood. Charming's attention slipped away again as he daydreamed about dancing with Elizabeth. He became vaguely aware that the stage had gone dark as pitch. A single light illuminated the little servant-girl puppet. Then a glittering star flashed on the stage. The puppet was holding a slipper—Lady Elizabeth's other crystal slipper.

Charming, eyes wide and mouth open, rose in his chair and shouted, "Stop! How can this be?"

From behind him, Giles said, "He is right, my lord. I should never have let it go this long. I will get the dogs and put an end to this debacle."

"What? No!" said Charming. He turned to the Beast,

his eyes pleading. "It's about Elizabeth. They have the other slipper. I must know what happened."

The Beast looked between Charming and the dwarves, who, after a moment's peace, had all begun to speak at once, offering a variety of admonitions about breaking the fourth wall and interfering with the artistic process. Giles added to the chaos by heaping criticism and contempt at the dwarves. The Beast put a claw to his temple and roared, "SILENCE!"

A blessed quiet descended. The Beast addressed the players below. "My guest has some questions for you. You will answer them honestly, and without arguing, or you will answer to me." He then turned to Giles. "And, you . . . oh, go get us some tea or something."

The Beast turned back to the dwarves as the butler scurried out the door. The older dwarf stepped forward, ran a hand through his hair, which had the effect of making it even more unruly, adjusted the spectacles on his nose, which resulted in them listing badly, and said, "On my honor, Your Lordship, we will speak honestly, but I can't promise we won't argue."

The Beast sighed. "Do your best."

The dwarf bowed gracefully.

Charming leaned forward over the rail. "The story in the play, is it true?"

The elderly dwarf scratched at his chin. "Well, now that depends on what you mean by truth. I mean, who can say what happened here this evening? Each of us might have had a different experience."

The glowering fellow interrupted him from behind. "Dorian, don't try to obscure the point with that relativistic nonsense."

"It isn't nonsense, Grady. You have had a very different experience than have I. The shiner I gave you in Act Two is proof enough of that."

"Oh yeah? Well, I can give you a matching one if you'd like to experience my reality." Grady advanced menacingly.

Charming rolled his eyes. "Stop it, both of you. I don't mean, is the whole story the truth. I was there, and I can see you've taken a great deal of 'artistic license' with the facts."

The angry dwarf bristled at this, but Charming did not give him a chance to argue. "What I want to know is, did the lady flee the castle, and was she chased into the woods by this ensorcelled huntsman?"

Both the dwarves started to speak, and Charming stopped them with a brisk motion. "I don't want any philosophy, just a yes or no."

"Yes," said Dorian, the gray-haired dwarf.

"No," said Grady. "It was not a huntsman. I think Liz said it was Rapunzel's valet."

Charming felt his knees buckle under him. He grasped the rail to keep himself upright. They had seen Elizabeth. "Is she safe? Is she well? Tell me where she is!"

Grady, the angry dwarf, started to speak, but the elderly fellow grabbed at his sleeve and stopped him. He gathered the group of performers together in a huddle, and they conferenced for a minute in low whispers. Finally, Dorian emerged, narrowing his eyes at Charming. "And who is it that's asking?"

"What?" said Charming.

"Well, we know His Lordship here, at least by reputation, but we don't know you. Who exactly are you? How do we know your intentions?"

"I am Prince—" he started to say, and then bit his tongue.

The elderly dwarf responded with a stuttered, "You are a prince?"

"No," Charming said with a shake of his head, "Prince Charming is no more, I am . . ." He hesitated and then straightened himself. "I am just a man that loves Lady Elizabeth, and I swear on my life that I shall allow no harm to come to her." With that, he pulled the glittering shoe from its hiding place and placed it on the railing before him.

The dwarves looked between the two shoes with wide-eyed disbelief. "Well, we'll be," they all said in unison.

"Now, where is she? Is she safe?"

Dorian answered, "She's perfectly safe. She's at our cottage in the woods—recuperating."

"Recuperating?" Charming said sharply. "Was she hurt?"

Dorian blinked. "Oh, yes. But she's fine now. Nothing more than a busted head and, um, a broken arm?"

Charming paled. "Broken arm? Busted head?"

"Yes, at least that was my preliminary diagnosis," the dwarf said in a suddenly nervous voice. "Others may disagree, but you've got to understand the circumstances. A great deal of latitude must be given for the rather crude medical tools I had at my disposal. Anyway, not knowing her medical history, any reasonable practitioner would choose to be a bit overcautious in their treatment."

The dwarf rambled on, but Charming had already stopped listening. He paced along the balcony, deep in thought. As if concluding some internal debate, he stopped and asked, "How long has it taken you to journey here?"

Dorian shrugged. "Not too long, a few days. But, then, we walked."

"You can't trust horses!" Grady interjected.

The others nodded their mute agreement.

Charming turned to his host. "Your Lordship, Adam, I need . . ."

"You need to go to her, young man," Adam answered. He snapped at the butler, who had returned with a massive silver tea tray. "Giles, give Charming anything he needs."

"All I need is a sword and Your Lord's fastest horse."

I am coming, Elizabeth.

Chapter 5

On Bended Knee

LIKE THE FORESTS of most fairy tale kingdoms, the woods of Royaume are littered with cottages, which is odd, given that these same forests are also filled with giant boars, gruesome trolls, and a host of deranged woodland creatures. Nevertheless, whether you are a red-hooded girl frolicking carefree along a woodland path or a raven-haired beauty fleeing for her life into the trackless depths, it seems that no matter where you go, some little house will pop up like a toadstool in the night. If you're lucky it might be the home of a family of benevolently domestic, if overly trusting, bears, or of a kindly old grandmother with a protective, ax-wielding son-in-law. However, if you are unlucky, you could end up at the front door of an impoverished and morally bankrupt woodcutter or a witch with a sweet tooth and cannibalistic tendencies.

Of course, Elizabeth Pickett had gotten very lucky. She found the dwarves' home unexpectedly cozy. It was filled with an incredibly eccentric collection of books, plenty of nooks to read them in, and a fantastic quantity of fine ale to drink while reading. For rest and recuperation, it was nearly ideal. Every day she grew stronger, and soon she was able to abandon her sickbed. She also smashed her obviously unnecessary cast with a hammer she found under Grady's bed. The arm was tender but otherwise fine, and she reminded herself to make sure Dorian got a full measure of her tongue when he returned.

But, for all of the appeal of the cottage, the surrounding wood was infested with the most obnoxiously endearing wildlife. First, there was the flock of songbirds. The twittering freaks had decided to make it their business to wake her every morning at the first sign of dawn with their incoherent chirps and tweets. Then there were the deer, big, brown-eyed, and adorable, but also thieving scum. Twice, they had raided her laundry line and tried to carry her undergarments off into the woods. Only a strong arm, another indication that Dorian's doctoring left a lot to be desired, and good aim had prevented them from leaving her in a state of forced indecency. But the last straw was the afternoon she had caught two inordinately cute bunnies and a rather seedy squirrel peering with disturbing intensity at her through an open window while she took her bath. Of course, she did the only thing she could—scream, then lob her bar of soap at the Peeping Toms. She spent the rest of the day fashioning a sling and collecting stones.

Despite these annoyances, Liz enjoyed her time in the wood. She soon settled into a routine of cleaning, reading, setting snares for bunnies, gardening, reading, taking potshots at birds, cooking, reading, and planning dishes that required large amounts of venison. Then one afternoon, as she was setting a particularly cunning squirrel trap by the stream near her wash line, Liz noticed that a sudden calm had come over the woods around the cottage. After days of near-constant chirrups, tweets, peeps, and twitters, the silence was eerie. She peeked around the smooth trunk of an ash tree and across the small flower-covered meadow to the cottage. Everything appeared normal, but the quiet made her suspicious. Where were the deer, the hopping bunnies, and the damnable frolicking squirrels?

Liz hoisted the clothes basket onto her hip and headed toward the house. Halfway across the meadow, the unmistakable feeling of being watched crawled its way along her spine. She hurried her steps to the cottage, wondering when she'd become such a hysterical woman. *A cup of tea should calm my nerves.*

She pulled open the door and the same strange odor of nutmeg that had clung to Collins when they fought in the clearing came rolling out. She froze as four men dressed in the livery of the Royal Guard stepped forward. She knew that she should run, scream, or simply faint in a properly ladylike manner, but that wasn't her. She advanced into the threshold.

"What are you doing in my house?" she shouted, pointing her finger at them. "How dare you?"

Her scolding had clearly left them uncertain as to how they should respond.

"Um . . ." one of them started. "I . . ." said another. "Uh . . . Captain?" said a third, while the fourth took a few steps back as though trying to shrink back into the shadows.

"She-is-to-be-apprehended-and-taken-back-to-the-castle," said a fifth man who entered from the back bedroom.

She didn't know the voice, but she would never forget that awful inhuman tone. She looked into the man's face and saw the now-familiar dead expression. He might have been wearing the insignia of the Captain of the Royal Guard, but there could be no doubt, it was Gwendolyn.

"You witch!" she shouted, and reaching into her basket, picked a garment out and flung it at the captain, "Leave me alone!"

The captain clawed Liz's underclothes from his face. "She-is-mad. Get-her."

The guards looked at each other, then charged. She threw the basket at them and, turning, ran toward the waiting arms of the trees. She had always been a fast runner, and she knew that she had a good chance of being able to outrun the men, weighted down as they were by their heavy swords and chain shirts. But halfway to the tree line, her foot caught on something. She tripped, tumbling hard down the hill, twisting her already injured arm beneath her. Spots flickered before her eyes. The soldiers surrounded her where she lay.

She swallowed her fear. "Would one of you be willing to help me up, or do you only like to frighten women?"

The men looked guiltily at each other, and one gently helped her to her feet.

"Well-done-men. Tie-her-up," came the captain's dead voice. He walked stiffly over to her.

Just then, a thundering sound of hooves came through the forest. All of the soldiers turned. There was a resounding crash in the underbrush surrounding the glade, and a voice rang out, "UNHAND HER!"

The rider charged up the hill into the clearing, a sword in hand. He wore no armor, and his clothes were gray and drab and lacked any sort of heraldry. When he got near, the horse reared dramatically, and the man brandished the blade so that the sunlight caught and spun off its edge.

"Who? . . ." whispered Liz, and tried to blink away the flickering spots that were still swirling in her eyes. Then, blade still unsheathed, her savior leapt effortlessly from the back of his horse to land in a perfect dueling crouch on the uneven ground before the four guardsmen. Despite herself, Liz clucked her tongue. She knew who it was now. Only one man was reckless and arrogant enough to try something that dangerous.

"Who-are-you?" demanded the captain.

"It doesn't matter who I am." He stopped to pose dramatically and point his sword at the men, moving it from one to the other as he continued. "What matters is that you unhand that lady, or you will answer to me." He swept his hair out of his face, and his chiseled features left no doubt . . . Prince Charming had arrived.

"Prince Charming!" the guards gasped and released Liz so suddenly that she reeled backward and fell once again.

"WHAT-ARE-YOU-DOING?" the captain shouted. "Get-him. The-King-has-disowned-him. He-is-not-our-Prince-anymore-and-he-is-interfering-with-my-plans-I-mean-orders."

The guards still hesitated.

"By-order-of-the-King-stop-him-or-I-swear-you-will-all-be-in-the-stocks-by-the-end-of-the-day."

The men drew their blades as one and advanced toward Charming. The former prince twisted his blade in his hand and sneered at them. "Come, if you will, but I warn you, I will offer no quarter."

Liz clambered slowly to her knees, still dazed from her fall and the shooting pains in her arm. She blinked the swimming black spots from her vision. "Don't hurt them. It's Gwendolyn. She's controlling them."

Charming's confidently suave demeanor broke for a moment and he took a step back. "Wait? You don't want me to hurt them? That will make this rescue more than a touch difficult, milady."

A yellow songbird alighted on Liz's shoulder and began a frenzied chirp. Liz slapped it away with her good hand. "That is hardly my fault. You are the one that decided to try and rescue me. Why don't you take it up with your princess when you get back to the castle?" Just then, a stag came bolting out the front door of the cottage with her laundry wrapped around its antlers. "Damned deer, those are my clothes!"

"I suppose I should rescue those as well, milady?"

"Don't be ridiculous," she said as he clashed with two of the guards at once.

"No, no, my pleasure," he said with a confident grin as he parried the men's blades, both of which had been aimed at his midsection. "And by the way, you are being rather unfair. Gwendolyn is hardly 'my princess.'"

His attackers rushed him again, but Charming pushed them back toward the cottage with the strength of his sword arm. He continued. "I never really had any interest in her myself."

With a quick parry, and a flick of his wrist, he disarmed one opponent and dropped the second with a kick to the ribs.

"What-do-you-mean-you-had-no-interest?" asked the captain, who was standing motionless watching the fight. "Princess-Gwendolyn-is-the-most-beautiful-woman-in-all-the-world."

"And . . ." Liz gasped as she flexed her hand and again felt shooting pains in her arm. "You couldn't take your eyes off of her at the ball, even while we were dancing."

Charming dodged another sword thrust. "Maybe we could talk about this later. I hardly think"—he leapt over the body of the guard who had fallen—"this is the time to discuss my"—and ran after the deer—"love life."

"No! You-must-explain. Why-you-are-risking-yourself-for-her? She-is-nothing," spit the captain as he began to slowly lurch toward Liz.

"I agree with Princess Gwendolyn's mindless thrall," Liz said as she levered herself to her feet and stumbled away from the advancing man. "What better time to discuss why you would come for me?"

"I admit, I was confused at the ball, but I do know that while Gwendolyn might have been my duty, she was never my love. Elizabeth Pickett, I fell in love with you the first moment I saw you. Besides"—he paused as he caught up to the stag, then grasped it from behind—"do you have any idea how old the princess is?"

"WHAT?" cried the captain and Liz in unison.

"You love me?" Elizabeth gasped, this time not only from pain.

Charming, trying to wrestle Liz's laundry from the antlers of the deer, opened his mouth to answer but was cut short by the red-faced captain, who stamped his foot in a very uncaptain-like way and shouted, "I-AM-NOT-OLD! I-am-still-young-and-beautiful. Look-at-me-and-weep-with-desire-you-fool."

Everyone—a still-flushed Liz, the guards who had recovered and nearly reached Charming, the former prince, who was in a desperate tug of war with the deer over a particularly frilly shift, and even the deer—all turned to stare at the captain.

The captain stared back and hissed, "What?"

"Sir? Are you all right?" one of the guards asked.

Seeming to come back to himself, the captain barked in a deep, if emotionless, baritone, "DON'T-question-me-you-fool! You-have-your-orders. Now-get-him!"

"Yes, sir!" said the guards with a collective flinch.

Charming took advantage of the exchange to lock an arm around the neck of the deer and untangle Liz's clothes from the beast's head. "Of course, I love you," he said as he freed the last dress, "why else do you think I was trying to impress you at the ball with my"—he gasped as the deer kicked back at him and connected— "my couplets?"

"Was that what you were trying to do?" Liz asked in disbelief. "I thought maybe that you were drunk or possessed by a poetic, but meter-challenged, pixie."

Charming, who was still trying to recover from the deer's kick, opened his mouth to respond when all four guards came at him in a rush. He realized that he wasn't going to be able to bring his sword to bear in time, and so spun the stag about instead and parried the four blows on the creature's antlers. Charming waved the shift about in victory and grinned at Liz, who rolled her eyes. "What?" he said, noticing her reaction. "You have to admit, that was pretty impressive."

The deer, now mad with fear, began snorting and rearing at the men surrounding it. The guards shuffled from side to side, trying, somehow, to avoid the stag and get at Charming, who was holding on more out of self-preservation than for any tactical advantage.

"This is your problem," Liz complained as she edged

away from the captain, whose whole body seemed to be fighting against itself. "You don't think about the consequences of your actions, and you are insufferable when you succeed at even the simplest of things."

Charming gestured at the deer. "You can't possibly think that that was simple."

"Focus!" Liz shouted.

"What?" Charming said.

The four guards had regrouped and arranged themselves in a rough semicircle around Charming and the struggling deer.

"Look out!" she yelled.

Charming turned his attention back to the men just in time to duck beneath one blade and dodge another thrust. He gave Liz a wink and a smile and, in a sudden movement, released the stag.

The beast leapt forward, slamming into two of the guards and knocking them flat before running off into the woods. Charming tried to turn to engage the remaining guards, but the deer's flight had sent him spinning off balance. The men took full advantage, springing forward in a concerted strike. Charming brought his sword up in a desperate defensive move that only just prevented the first stroke from piercing his heart. Even he could not avoid the second blade, which sliced deeply into his sword arm. He dropped to the ground and rolled backward to create space between himself and the pair of advancing foes.

Liz screamed, "NO!"

Blood flowed freely from the wound, and his fingers

began to go numb. Charming dropped the hard-won clothes and switched the sword to his left hand. He smiled over at Liz and, affecting his smoothest voice, said, "Dear Lady, it is but a scratch. No more. I have been meaning to practice with my off hand for weeks now."

The two guards still standing spread out along his flanks. Charming stepped carefully around the pile of Liz's clothes and gazed into the eyes of the one whose blade was bloodied. He remembered the man from the practice grounds. *He had always been good. Too bad I never paid attention to their names, but I was once their commander. I wonder. . .*

Charming allowed the guard to advance a few paces, and then putting all the command he could muster into his voice, he barked, "GUARDSMAN! BE careful not to trod the lady's dress, you're going to ruin it."

Instinctively, the guard glanced down. Charming used the distraction to clout him with the flat of his blade. The man fell to the ground unconscious.

Charming was breathing hard now, but there was to be no respite. The other guard was still up, and, blade at the ready, he came forward with a scowl. He was a large fellow, half a head taller than the others. Charming lifted his weapon and tucked his injured right arm against his body as a bloodstain spread down the sleeve toward his hand.

Over his shoulder, Charming heard Liz grunt in pain. He risked a quick glance. Gwendolyn had clearly gained some deeper level of control over the captain's body, because he was walking steadily toward Liz now. She was cornered against the side of the cottage but somehow had gotten hold of a broom that she was swinging at the captain as if trying to beat a rug. "Keep away from me, you witch."

This has to end before someone, before Elizabeth, gets killed, he thought.

Ignoring the pain, Charming switched his sword back to his right hand, and gripped and regripped the hilt in an attempt to draw a little strength back into his weakening arm. Then, with a sudden violent movement, he feinted left and dropped his guard in apparent fatigue, so that his right side was momentarily exposed. The guard fell for the deception, attacking aggressively.

Charming parried and, using all of his strength, beat violently at the man's blade. It fell to the ground with a clatter. The guard dove for the sword, but Charming was too fast. His boot came down on top of the blade as the man's hand grasped its hilt. Charming put the tip of his sword to his opponent's throat and, gesturing for him to rise, kicked the fallen weapon away. Behind him, he heard the two men who had taken the impact of the stag's charge rise and begin to close in.

"I could have gone for a riposte instead of trying to disarm you. Now, tell them to back off, or I swear I will cut your throat."

"Never," the man grunted. "It would be treason."

Across the clearing, Charming saw that Liz had lost her broom and was trying to dodge around the captain and into the cottage.

"You-are-pathetic," crowed the captain to Liz. "Just-look-at-you. Your-hair-is-that-awful-bark-brown-you-wear-dishrags-for-clothes-and-you've-got-no-bust-to-speak-of."

Charming looked down his sword at the guard he had just disarmed, and swiveled his head to take in the others as well. "That is not your captain speaking. It's Princess Gwendolyn. I don't know how, but she is controlling him."

The guards looked between Charming and the captain in obvious disbelief, and, for a heartbeat, they seemed on the edge of renewing their attack when their captain shouted, "I'M-TEN-TIMES-THE-WOMAN-YOU-ARE!"

The men stared at their leader, mouths open, and then dropped their blades.

"Good." Charming sighed with relief. "Now, take your friend and go home."

The guards picked up their fallen comrade, and Charming turned toward the cottage. He tried to take a step forward, but his knees buckled and his vision swam. Only through sheer force of will did he manage to keep his feet.

Shaking his head to clear it, he called out, "Stay away from the lady, Captain, or you will answer to me."

The captain turned toward Charming, eyelashes fluttering and smirking. "Oh-has-little-Eddie-come-to-save-his-peasant-girl? My-dear-no-one-cares-about-you-anymore. You-are-finished."

Charming smiled his most infuriating smile. "I don't care what you or anyone else thinks of me." He dropped the smile and fixed his eyes on Liz. "There is only one person in this world that I care about."

The captain swung his sword away from Liz to point at Charming instead. "You-can't-love-this-nobody. She-is-so-common."

"My God, you really are insufferable, aren't you, Princess?"

Face contorted in rage, the captain swung wildly at Charming. He sidestepped the attack and countered with a slash across his opponent's midsection that cut a fine gash in his chain shirt.

Concern flashed across Liz's face. "It's not his fault, Prince," she pleaded. "Please don't hurt him."

"Anything you wish, milady," Charming said with more confidence than he felt. He parried the captain's second thrust, then turned his sword to the side and struck with the flat of his blade, which the captain parried in turn. They exchanged a series of attacks and counterattacks.

Charming felt his reactions slow. His sword was growing heavier, and the edges of his vision kept blurring. The captain pressed his advantage, driving Charming back, away from the cottage and toward the edge of the wood.

They disengaged for a moment as the captain couldn't quite keep up with Charming's retreat. Charming planted the tip of his blade into the ground, leaned against it, and laughed aloud.

The outburst was so unexpected that the captain paused and looked quizzically at him. "Why-are-you-laughing?"

"Because of the absurdity of all of this."

"What-do-you-mean?"

"Well, you are mad at me because I love her," he said pointing over at Elizabeth. "But, if my guess is right, you are intending to marry her brother, Lord William. That means that if I can convince Lady Elizabeth to marry me, which I have every intention of doing, then we will be family and you would be killing your brother for not being interested in his sister." He shook his head and then spit out, "And you call me mad, you gnarled old hag."

The captain flushed red in anger, but then the color drained away and the rage was replaced with a devious grin. "Is-that-your-way-of-asking-Lady-Elizabeth-to-marry-you-Eddie? It-is-not-up-to-your-usual-poetic-standards. Why-don't-you-ask-her-properly? Drop-to-one-knee-and-make-it-official. I-will-even-be-chivalrous-and-step-back." With that, the possessed captain lowered his blade and backed away.

With an evil laugh, Gwendolyn's minion retreated to the other end of the meadow. Charming knew some plot lay behind this gesture from the Princess, but he could not figure out what it might be, and frankly didn't care. This was his chance. He took a few paces toward Elizabeth, but then his legs gave out. Using his sword as support, he dropped to one knee. He lowered his eyes to gather his thoughts and saw a small pool of his blood on the ground beneath him.

It doesn't matter, he thought.

Charming looked at Liz, and for the first time since the battle began, their eyes met. Nothing had ever mattered as much as this moment. Liz stood motionless, waiting, her whole body tense like a delicate vase balanced on a knife's edge. Confusion and doubt were etched on her face. Given his reputation and their last encounter at the ball, how could she not doubt him? He doubted himself. Not that he loved her, but that he was worthy of her.

At last he understood what Adam had been trying to tell him. From almost the first instant, she had captured his heart; and despite his attempts to resist her, his path from then to now had been set. The only difference between now and then was his willingness to accept that it was his fate to love her, and his fate to surrender to her.

So Charming surrendered. He did not use flowery speech or couplet; instead, he cast his heart on the wind and spoke the truth, and in the magic of the moment, his soft words carried on the air of the silent meadow so that she heard them like a whisper in her ear. "Elizabeth Pickett, I love you. And, if you would do me the honor of granting me your hand, I promise that I shall spend the remainder of my days striving to make myself worthy of you."

All was quiet. Liz and the captain stared at him with similar expressions of wonderment. Liz opened her mouth to say something, but the captain, shaking his head clear, spoke first. "Before-you-answer-Lady-Elizabeth-ask-Eddie-why-he-is-no-longer-a-prince. Ask-him-why-his-father-disowned-him. Ask-him-why-he-sold-your-brother-to-murderous-bandits-for-a-single-silver-coin. Ask-him-how-a-man-that-could-love-you-so-deeply-could-also-betray-your-beloved-brother-so-villainously."

Liz stared at Charming with glassy eyes. He paled and dropped his gaze back to the growing pool of blood.

"ASK-HIM!" the captain said with a shout so loud that the forest echoed the command back at them.

Liz flinched as though struck. "Is . . . Is this true?"

He met her beautiful hazel eyes again. She was crying. "It is."

All the color had drained from her face. "You betrayed my brother? Why? Was it because of the dragon? Were you angry about what we did?"

"No, it had nothing to do with the dragon," he said, shaking his head. At least he knew that much was true. The dragon, oddly, meant nothing to him now.

"Then why?" she asked again, her voice shaking.

Charming did not know how to answer. What had he wanted to happen that day? What had he expected the bandits to do? "I do not know."

"You don't know? That can only mean that you were indifferent to his fate, to whether he lived or not. I knew you were selfish, Edward Charming, but I did not know that you could be that unfeeling."

He had no answer to this, and so kept silent. Her face was a mask of grief, but she was master of her voice, and her words were cold and resolute. "If this is your final word, then know that I could never love you and that I match your indifference with my own."

Charming had known it must be so, but still the blow of her judgment fell heavily. He felt the strength leave his body. Distantly, Charming heard a scream of emotionless laughter from the captain. He looked up as the man began to charge across the field. "THANK-YOU-LADY-ELIZABETH-I-COULD-NOT-HAVE-SAID-IT-BETTER," the captain shouted as he ran.

Charming tried to move, but realized he could not rise. Beyond feeling empty with grief, his body was suddenly so weak. The pool of blood now surrounded him. It would be so easy to let the captain's blow fall. But he had to make sure Elizabeth was safe.

I cannot win this fight, but I can make sure that Gwendolyn loses.

There would be no happy ending for him, but there still might be at least some measure of redemption. He closed his eyes against what was to come and breathed deeply.

LIZ STOOD PARALYZED. She watched the captain's charge. He was already halfway to Charming and still the Prince had not moved to defend himself. He knelt, body slack, his sword untouched at his side. A rush of fear shot through Liz's body like a firestorm.

He is not moving. Why is he not moving?

She looked at his face, still unable to believe that Prince Charming would give up. What she saw there sent an icy shiver along her spine. His face, his eyes, were dead.

Oh, God, he is going to let the man kill him.

Whatever power, whatever maddening, infuriating, beautiful essence it was that made the Prince, Prince Charming, was gone.

He does not kneel there because he wishes to die. He is already dead. He has given up because of me.

Still her mind refused to believe.

I cannot mean that much to him.

Her thoughts raced and collided in a disordered tangle.

How can I trust him? He says he loves me, yet admits that he betrayed Will. How can I trust a man that would send my brother to his death? What kind of sister would that make me? Who is he? Is he the man from the ball or is he this man . . . a man who would risk everything to save me?

She didn't know what had happened between the prince and her brother, but something about Charming was different, something had changed in him, and, between one breath and the next, she knew that she could not bear the thought that she might never see him again.

Liz rose to her feet and began to rush forward, but it was too late. The captain slowed a stride before he reached Charming and swung his sword in a wide arc at the kneeling man's neck.

"NO!" Liz screamed, reaching her hands out helplessly.

In a nearly inhuman burst of speed, and with a grace that was his alone, Charming rose and pivoted on the balls of his feet. The captain's sword cut into his side, opening a long gash in his body below the ribs even as Charming brought his fist into the man's jaw in a vicious uppercut. The blow had in it all the strength left to Charming's body. There was an audible crack, and the captain was lifted upward and then thrown backward. He was unconscious before he hit the ground.

For a moment, Charming stood swaying on his feet. He looked down at his tunic, now drenched in scarlet, and at the pool of his blood spreading outward onto the delicate snowy white shift he had fought so hard to save. He looked across the meadow, toward the house and Liz. She was running toward him. Their eyes met again. He gasped something inaudible and then collapsed.

Liz reached Charming's side as he fell. She had never seen so much blood. Her heart was cold with fear as she clutched him to her and heard the rattle of his ragged breathing. Gathering up the bloodied shift, she ripped it in two and started dressing Charming's wounds, her own pains forgotten.

His eyes flickered open at her touch. "Elizabeth . . ." he sighed. His eyes shut and then opened again in slowing movements. He took a few labored breaths and then said, "I'm so sorry, Elizabeth, I never meant to hurt you . . . I was such a coward." He reached his one good hand up toward her face "You are safe. Everything will be all right . . . now." She felt his cold touch on her cheek, then his hand dropped and his eyes fluttered closed again.

"No, you don't," she said as she tightened a tourniquet around his arm and pressed a second silken bandage against his side. "I won't let you go that easy. I won't let you die, not now."

His breaths were coming in shallow gasps. She tied off the bindings and rested his head in her lap. She stroked her hand across his brow—it was hot and clammy. Her fingers traced the outline of a pale shadow that was all that remained of the injury he'd had when she first met him. It may have only been weeks, but it seemed like such an impossibly long time ago. Now it was likely that he would die in her arms. She began to hum an old lullaby she used to sing to Will when he was a child and afraid of the coming night. The song seemed to calm Charming, but it might also have been that he was slipping away. A tear fell from her cheek onto his forehead. She had not even known she was crying. Liz wiped away the moisture with her finger, then leaned close and whispered the words she knew he longed to hear: "I do not know why, but I know that I do love you, Edward Charming. You are and will ever be my prince. You are going to marry me, and you are going to love me, and we will live happily ever after." It was only after speaking them that Liz realized that they were true—every word.

Charming exhaled deeply, almost sighing, and, for a moment, Liz thought he was gone. But then he inhaled again, his breathing steadied, and his head seemed to cool. Liz looked around. The clearing was strangely empty. The guards had gathered themselves up and slipped away. The captain lay sprawled and unconscious on the ground. And, with the exception of Charming's horse, which was grazing quietly at the far edge of the meadow, there was not a single creature to be seen.

"Now what?" she asked.

Chapter 6

Something Borrowed

WHILE MANY A little girl dreams of a fairy tale wedding, actual fairy tales give the occasion rather short shrift. Typically, a fairy tale wedding, whether it be between prince and princess, commoner and king, or lady and beast, amounts to a few brief words shoehorned between a villain "never being seen or heard from again" and the "happily ever after." A fairy tale wedding might be boiled down to, "And the prince carried the fair maiden off to his castle in the clouds, they were married, and lived happily . . ." and so on. If Princess Gwendolyn Mostfair had determined one thing, it was that this would not be her fate. Everyone would remember her wedding.

"The wedding is everything," Princess Gwendolyn announced to no one in particular, or possibly to no one at all, as she paraded through the halls of Castle White surrounded by a halo of shadows that fluttered behind her like a tattered cloak.

She had tried to make everything perfect. The wedding dinner was planned down to the garnish on the dessert. She had hand selected the mythical beasts—matching unicorns—that would be used for her processional menagerie. She had threatened the gardeners to ensure that the flowers would bloom on schedule. She had even, despite her better inclinations, descended into the kitchens to explain what type of cake she wanted—monumental. Of course, there was the moat, with its foul waters. She had to think of some way to fix that.

Her sister came once again to mind. "For Rosslyn's sake, it must be perfect," she muttered.

As if she had spoken the final incantation of a spell, the shadows melted into the floor. What had Rosslyn wanted for her wedding to Rupert? Was this wedding for her sister, or was it the one she had wished for herself so long ago? Was this still part of her curse? She touched her face, running her fingertips over her cheeks. Was she awake or asleep?

Before her thoughts could travel any further, a question swept them away and the shadows rose again to take their positions.

"Your Royal Highness, Princess Gwendolyn Mostfair, if I may. I am in dire need of your opinion. Do you have a moment?"

Gwendolyn frowned at the Royal Tailor's interruption, but the man was in the middle of a deep bow and did not notice her displeasure. She reminded herself that he would be making her dress, and promptly bent her frown into a fluttering smile. "Of course, how may I be of assistance? As you know, I am keenly interested in every aspect of the wedding clothes."

The man rose with a high laugh. "Most amusing, Your Royal Highness, but my question has nothing to do with the wedding. No, no, you must come and help me. This is in regards to the coronation!" He punctuated the declaration by thrusting a pair of tailoring shears skyward. Then, with an audacity that she could scarcely believe, he turned on his heel and marched toward an open door in the hall, as if he had no doubts that she would follow. A sudden unwarranted anger rose up in her breast; the candles in the hallway flickered, and she watched the dark black shadows crawl from around her feet and reach toward the man's retreating back. She almost let them go, but then with an enormous effort willed them back to roil at her feet.

Breathing hard, she fell into step behind the diminutive but forceful man. "Of course, the coronation is just a prelude to my wedding, when I will become queen!" He seemed not to hear so she quickened her step and, catching the tailor at the door, turned him with a firm hand on his shoulder and gave him her best smile.

He blinked at her and, pointing with the tips of his pinkie fingers to the skin beneath his own eyes, said, "You need to get some rest, Princess Gwendolyn. You have terrible dark circles around your eyes." Gwendolyn's smile evaporated, replaced by an icy glare, but he was completely unmoved by either her charms or her anger. He fluttered his hands around his head and clucked, "Now, where was I?" He snapped his fingers after two taps of his chin. "Oh, yes! As I was saying, we must make sure that this great moment in history is not lost."

They reached the doorway, and the tailor pirouetted and made a flourished gesture that drew her eyes to the contents of the chamber. The room was a chambermaid's nightmare. Bolts of cloth and satin, yards of dyed leather, boxes of beads and feathers, and hundreds of spools of ribbon and lace and thread were scattered about with no apparent design. It was such a blinding riot of color and texture that it took Gwendolyn a moment to realize that, in the middle of the chaos, standing as still and quiet as a tailor's mannequin, was her future husband, William Pickett. She gasped.

"Behold, the form of man in all its glory, the Lord Protector, William Pickett, who on this day will be our true King. Stunning." The tailor snapped his fingers with one hand while pointing with the shears. "See how straight and unmoving the Lord Protector stands. He understands the magnitude of this event. It is truly the greatest moment any of us will experience, and we must have perfection."

"You mean, the greatest moment, until the Royal Wedding," the Princess said sternly, folding her arms across her bosom.

"Look at the fit of these clothes," said the Royal Tailor, ignoring her and tapping Will's rear as his assistants moved aside for him. "To have the honor of framing this solid masculine bu—*um*, these calves for all to see, why they are magnificent! But, have we done enough? I ask you."

Gwendolyn had to admit that Will did look impressive standing on a stool in the center of the room, his back ramrod straight and his arms outstretched. The Royal Tailor prattled on about the coronation, picking up different colored silks and velvets to hold against Will's body for her consideration, but Gwendolyn did not hear a word. Across Will's face was a mask of shadows; where the warm brown of his eyes once lay were empty black pits, like raven's eyes. Something in her heart caught, and Gwendolyn felt real doubt, both as to what she was doing and as to whether she could still control the forces she had unleashed.

The Royal Tailor's voice sliced through her thoughts like a knife. "You don't like it, Your Royal Highness?" the man said with an edge of desolation.

The Princess shook her head clear of this new and troubling attack of conscience, but Will's mask remained and she turned away, unable to look. Will would be fine. In time, he would learn to love her and she him. The focus at the moment had to be on the wedding and clarifying—in no uncertain terms—the Royal Tailor's priorities.

"He looks fine," she said, addressing the opposite side of the room so that she was in no danger of catching sight of Will. "I like that shade of blue on him, and the gold accent will work as well. Besides, it's only for the coronation. It's just a formality, and other than the King and the

Archbishop, hardly anyone will be—be . . . will be there," she stuttered as she watched one of the tailor's mannequins draped itself in ragged black. Then it turned and stared at her—with Rosslyn's eyes.

The Royal Tailor gasped. For a second, Gwendolyn thought he had seen her vision, and fear and hope battled with each other for her heart, but the tailor stepped around so that he stood in front of her and said, "But *why*? How can we deny the people the glory and spectacle of this man, our beautiful, powerful, majestic Lord Protector becoming King?" As the question left his lips, a tremor went through the Royal Tailor, shaking the shears in his hand. *"Why?"*

Gwendolyn dug her nails into the palm of her hand to keep from screaming, then said in a voice tight with fear, "Now, now, you have done well, and there will be time enough for everyone to see him *at the wedding*. Do you understand?"

The Royal Tailor swallowed and nodded slowly, but she saw that he was not convinced. She had to get out of this room—now—but he also had to be made to understand. So as Rosslyn mouthed at her wordlessly over his shoulder, Gwendolyn reached out with her thoughts and pulled at the magical strand connecting her mind to Will's and said in a voice that rose and rose until it was a shrill screech, "WILL! TELL HIM."

"It is-all-about-her. It-is-her-wedding"—he said dully, but then ended with a whispered, "her plot."

She paused. She hadn't intended him to say "her plot." For a flickered second, the shadow mask had slipped. She glanced around to see if the tailor had noticed the odd wording of his response. To her relief, he merely bowed with a frown.

Her eyes were drawn back, against her will, to the dress form. Rosslyn was now robed in a shadowy wedding gown. She was beautiful and sad, and her condemning glare cut to the quick. Panic gripped Gwendolyn.

"I must go," she said, waving her hands at the Royal Tailor, who blinked at her sudden change of mood. "Carry on. Finish quickly."

With that, she fled the room, heading for the secret chamber and the fairy. As she walked, she considered Will's momentary rebellion. Her emotions were causing problems again. It had happened before with the Captain of the Guard at the cottage. In that case, though, she had gotten so angry at Prince Charming that she had lost control of the magic entirely; it had been like watching a pantomime of her worst impulses played out to a tragedy. The fairy said it was because violent, uncontrolled emotions were anathema to her race. Of course, the fairy liked nothing more than to make her crazy. Still, Gwendolyn found it increasingly difficult to control her own emotions and sometimes to know what was real and unreal.

There would be time for weakness, but this was not it. There was too much at stake, too many promises to keep. She could not afford to lose control of Will—not yet. The shadows skipped along beside her, extinguishing the torches and candles along the way so that the hall behind her was thrown into darkness.

WILL WATCHED HER leave, and, for the hundredth time, he wished that he could lower his arms or utter even a single plea for help. He felt as if he were acting a role in a play. The Princess's every suggestion was an inviolable law, a command from the heavens, which he was unable to resist. He had tried to twist her words, to find some crack in the wall of dominion she had built around him, but they were ironclad in their simplicity—*Obey me.*

He had never felt so helpless. The sickening part was that she controlled the King also, and who knew how many others in the palace. He should have listened to Elle, but he had been so sure that Gwendolyn posed no danger. *She's a princess,* he mocked to himself. This was his fault. He had freed her, unleashed her on the world. He felt his body turn in slavish obedience to one of the tailor's requests.

"RUN YOU, FOOLS! SHE'S MAD! SHE'S EVIL! CAN'T YOU SEE THE MAGIC SWIRLING ABOUT HER!" he screamed.

Except, he didn't scream. No sound was allowed to escape his lips. He was standing stoically while the man measured his waist and then pinned a gaudy pink silk to his chest. He found himself wishing for someone to save him, but who could imagine that the Lord Protector would need protecting? Besides, the only man in the kingdom with the nerve and skill to make the attempt was gone—banished. Even his borrowed squire, Tomas, was gone, imprisoned by the Princess after he had suggested, in an admittedly undiplomatic way, that the green dress she was wearing was unflattering. *Face it, the man said she looked like a toad.* He giggled in his head, but it died away as he remembered the pained look on Tomas's face as he was hauled away, and that he had been helplessness to stop it.

No one was coming to save the day. If Liz had been here, she would have thought of something, but she was gone too.

And what of Lady Rapunzel . . . Elle?

Always, his thoughts turned back to Elle. Those eyes. That face . . . her smell—Gwendolyn may have taken control of his mind, but apparently she could not remove his memory of her. Still, he *had* done something—he'd shown a glimmer of free will. He had forced the words "*her plot*" out of his mouth, though barely. They weren't the words he had wanted to say, but still, this act was the first sliver of hope he'd had since his enslavement.

His body turned again, so that the Royal Tailor could measure him for another suit. Inside his head, he considered his rebellious moment. She was mad, angry with the tailor. Could it be that simple? If it was true, there was an opportunity, a chance. But how could he use these fleeting moments of freedom? If he could speak no more than a single word, what warning could he give? If he could take no more than a single step, how could he escape?

Turned once again by the tailor, Will's eyes fell on the tapestry he had taken from the dragon's tower. Beneath it, half covered by a virulent pink silk, was the golden key. His mind traveled back to the beginning. He remembered how beautiful the Princess had looked when he first found her, bound by that strange lock. Now he was the one whose mind was locked in a nightmare. Was this what it had been like for her all those years? His heart shuddered. Then a strange and disturbing thought came to him. *What if I have only woken her body, but not her mind? What if this is some dark spirit and not Gwendolyn at all?*

Then his daydreams shattered and he became viscerally aware of his surroundings as the tailor adjusted his codpiece a bit too tightly.

ON REACHING HER sanctuary, Princess Gwendolyn snatched up the fairy orb, ignoring the clawing shadow hands as they also encircled the globe. "Tell me what is happening. Why am I having these visions? How was Will able to resist my control? I only need a few more days. I can't chance anything." She shook the globe holding the fairy violently enough that pixie dust filled it with a small blizzard. "The wedding is coming! The wedding!"

In the swirling tempest within the globe, she saw another reflection of Rosslyn. This time Rosslyn pointed at her, shouting silent accusations. Gwendolyn couldn't hear the words, but she desperately tried to read her dead sister's lips. The Princess pressed her face nearer the orb. "I didn't mean for you to die, Rosslyn. It was just a foolish girl's wish for . . ."

The confession caught in her throat, and in the next moment the dust cleared. Through the glass she saw the hated fairy. "You," Gwendolyn hissed. "You think you can manipulate me with these visions?"

The infuriating slow drawl of the fairy whispered out of the air around her. "I assurest thee, Mistress, whatever thou saw in thy globe was a vision of thy own creation. I can do nothing now without thy command."

Gwendolyn grunted derisively. "It doesn't matter. My control over your powers is increasing. When I possessed the Captain of the Guard, it was almost as though it were my arm swinging his sword. I . . ." Her voice faltered as she recalled the sickening feeling of the blade as it entered Charming's body.

The Princess sank into her chair, letting the orb drop to her lap. She felt tears on her cheeks and wiped them away with a shaking hand. "I don't understand. I never meant for things to get so out of hand. I never meant for anyone to die. It was unreal, like a dream." She sat up, scattering the shadows to dark corners under the furniture. She took up the orb and shook it again until it clouded over, and the little light inside bounced from wall to wall. "If you are trying to control me, to control my actions . . ."

"'Tis not me, Mistress," said the fairy with a mocking laugh. "I have never been able to control thee. Thou didst release my magick, and now it has brought out thy true self. Thou art the one responsible. Thou art responsible for everything. Thou art guilty, just as thou were guilty when thou killed thy own sister. Ever has it been *thy* will giving form to my magick."

Gwendolyn opened her mouth to speak, but her head was so muddled with plans and stratagems and flower arrangements that it was hard to focus. The fairy was playing with her, or at least the fairy magic was. It was those wishes, wishes of years past, wishes of a jealous scared girl, wishes that had been twisted and mangled and tortured beyond her wildest imagination. A sudden violent wellspring of rage rose up in her and she shook the ball again. "Insolent insect! Whatever you are trying, it won't work. I AM STRONGER THAN YOU!"

Around her, the shadows howled their agreement, and somewhere in another part of her mind she felt Will flex his fingers. She calmed her breathing and rebuilt her walls about him. She trembled, the fairy snickered, and Gwendolyn realized how close she had just come to losing control for the second time that morning.

"I must keep my eyes on you, little bug. I think I shall keep you close to me from now on. No one will get in the way of THIS WEDDING, and that includes you."

She took a breath, ignoring the wretched sprite's echoing laughter and the shadow creatures' howls of delight, and, tucking the fairy ball away in the folds of her dress, marched out of the room and up the stairs. It was time for the coronation.

With a snap of her fingers and a few thoughts, she had both the King and the Lord Protector leave their rooms, much to the disdain of the Royal Tailor, and knew that the Archbishop would be more than ready to do his part. She had taken control of him earlier that morning. After all, she could leave nothing about her wedding to chance, and the coronation was part of preparing her groom.

Without a king to marry, she could not be queen, and that was the point. That was part of her promise.

A passing mirror showed her an old woman—wan and disheveled. She frowned at her reflection, and after a disconcerting hesitation, her reflection frowned back. With a second thought, Gwendolyn pushed back the time of the coronation: The three men would stand in silence in the coronation chamber—until her grand entrance. In the meantime, she would summon her handmaidens and let them make certain that she was at her finest before heading to the chapel. Even if the coronation was nothing more than a formality, it was still important to look her best. After all, Will deserved a beautiful woman at his side. If things went to plan, and she was sure they would, eventually he would be her husband and come to love her of his free will. Then she would be able to release him, and they would live happily ever after, on her terms.

A FEW HOURS later, it came to pass that in the chapel of Castle White, in a tiny cramped room in front of a small handful of courtiers, King William I was given the crown to the Kingdom of Royaume. For those few witnesses in attendance, the ceremony was noteworthy for its brevity and for the impassiveness of all the participants. The crown was placed on King William's head, and he immediately ordered everyone away to prepare for the wedding in that strange stilted monotone he had affected ever since his return to the castle.

As SHE STRODE back to her room afterward, surrounded again by the shades that would no longer leave her side, Gwendolyn was pleased that at least one unnecessary distraction had been dispensed with. She turned her attention back to more important matters, like devising a solution to the "moat issue."

She was so deeply engaged in these thoughts that she failed to consult the glowing crystal ball in her pocket, and so never saw the swirling images formed within of Rapunzel and her huntsman as they moved through a deep forest toward a small cottage in a clearing. Nor would she have much time in the coming days to turn her attention to the fairy's visions, though they had been her life these last few weeks. The wedding was her only focus. She had to make sure that she became queen. Nothing else mattered.

Chapter 7

Second Chances

THOUGH WE REMEMBER fairy tales most for their happily-ever-afters, death is everywhere within them. Death stalks openly through the resplendent halls of the grandest of castles to claim king and queen, prince and princess alike. It knocks at the door of the homeliest of huts to embrace peasant and hag and urchin. It takes the old and infirm and wicked, and, far too often, the young and virile and innocent, because every evil stepmother requires a dead mother, and every brave orphan two dead parents. There is always a moment when the candle burns low, spectral hands reach from the shadows, and a curtain falls.

Prince Charming wondered if this was that time in his story. He had no idea of where he was, or even when he was. He felt himself floating in a river beneath soft green and brown trees, whispers of sunlight caressing him as he drifted. At another time, it would have been odd that sunlight could whisper and caress, but here, in this place, it seemed right. A sense of deep peace had settled over him. The thought that repeated itself through his head was: *Elizabeth is safe. Nothing else matters.*

A smile warmed him from the inside. Something warm and soft pressed against his lips, and then pulled away.

It was a kiss.

The soft bubbling of the stream became a roar in his ears. He opened his eyes . . . and experienced the rapture of love at first sight for the second time as he gazed upon the loveliest woman he had ever seen. Her skin was alabaster, gently kissed with the blush of the sunrise, and her auburn tresses, though disheveled, fell lightly on her shoulders. This time he knew her name.

"Elizabeth."

"Charming. You woke up." She took his hand in hers. He was lying in a small bed in a small room before a roaring fire. Elizabeth sat on a little wooden stool beside him, a pitcher of water on a table beside her and a wet cloth forgotten in her lap.

He was exactly where he wanted to be. "You kissed me," he said.

She dropped his hand and raised an eyebrow. "No couplet."

"Never again," he said, shaking his head. "I realize now that couplet is shallow and inadequate. You, Elizabeth Pickett, have depths that I can scarcely imagine. I can feel myself drowning when I look into your eyes."

For reasons that Charming did not quite understand, she sighed and put a finger to his lips. "If you are well enough, we have a lot to talk about. But first, Captain Alain is outside. He will not leave until he has the chance to apologize to you. The man is . . ."

"Honorable?" Charming supplied.

"No, I was going to say a little maudlin." She turned her head to the door and said in a loud voice, "Charming's awake."

The door to the room flew open and the captain was there. "I'm so sorry," he said, and then dropped to a knee and began blathering on about shame and Gwendolyn and sorcery and the humiliation of it all.

"Alain, you have no reason to apologize. I do not hold you responsible for the actions of Princess Gwendolyn."

Alain released a clump of his hair, which he had started pulling during his long-winded apology, and swallowed. "Thank you, I just feel the need to explain. You see—"

He might have gone on again about his youth and his failings, but Elizabeth interrupted.

"Captain!" Her sharp tone silenced the man. More pleasantly, she said, "Please check the clearing. I need to speak with Charming—alone."

"As you wish," said Alain, rising with a bow. He backed out of the room and shut the door.

They sat there in silence, Elizabeth plucking at a cloth

in her lap. Despite the constant buzzing in his head and a biting pain in his side, Charming could see that she was troubled. He knew in his heart that it was about his betrayal of her brother. He also knew that he must tell her the whole story, and that once he had, she would likely never wish to speak to him again. His whole being begged him to delay that inevitability, but he would not stay silent any longer.

"I know what is troubling you, Elizabeth," he said in as smooth a voice as he could muster, given the fear in his heart and the difficulty he was having breathing. "You don't have to pretend to have feelings for me because of my condition. I understand that everything you've done for me, even . . . even the kiss, came from a place of compassion, not love."

"You know all that, do you?" she said with a frown, her eyes still focused on the cloth she was worrying in her hands. "You know a great deal more of my thoughts and feelings than I do, Edward Charming. What I am thinking and wondering, what I want to know, is whether you meant what you said?"

The time had come at last. Charming swallowed and nodded. "Yes. I betrayed your brother."

He told her everything, the entire story, even backtracking at one point to discuss the scheme he had dreamt up in the castle to discredit and humiliate her brother by leading him on a series of impossible quests. He talked about the Cooked Goose, and the deal he had made with the villain. He spent much of the time staring at the open window, not daring to meet Elizabeth's eyes. He paused only briefly to catch his breath, and then told her about sending Will off into the arms of the villain's gang.

She listened in silence, but when he finished she only shook her head at his words. "I'm not interested in all that. You may be a fool, Edward, but what I want to know is whether you meant what you said about *me*." She raised her eyes to meet his. "Do you love me?"

Shocked by the question, he spluttered into speech: "I—I did, I mean, I do, I . . ." He stopped himself and took a deep breath. "I love you, Elizabeth Pickett."

"Why? How?" she asked. Tears were forming in her eyes. "And why do you have my other shoe?"

She plucked the glass slippers from under the cloth in her lap and set them, with a high ringing noise, on a little table at his side. Charming's vision blurred and two sets of brown eyes were staring at the sparkling slippers as they recalled the memory of the night at the ball. He looked up at Elizabeth and his heart raced. "I . . . I found it after you fled and took it—to remember you."

"No!" she said angrily, dashing the tears from her cheeks in a quick motion with the back of her hand. "At the ball, your eyes were always on the Princess. I saw you watching her while we were dancing. And then you said . . ." She turned her back on him, and her shoulders started shaking.

Charming quailed at the memory of the dance and their fight. Sitting, helplessly watching her cry, he hated himself as he never had before. In a voice thick with remorse and self-loathing, he spit, "*I was . . .* NO, I *am* a coward, Elizabeth. I—I—" Despite his best effort, his voice caught. "I do not expect you to believe me, but it is only a measure of my own weakness that I could not admit, even to myself, my true feelings. Instead, I lashed out, and I am sorry I hurt you. "

She sat beside him, stiff and rigid and pale. "But, you are supposed to hate me."

"I could never hate you, Elizabeth."

"How can you not hate me?" She stood and began to pace the room, her voice rising with every word. "My brother and I have lied to you about everything. We are frauds, and we have cheated you out of everything. Because of us, you have lost your rightful place as the kingdom's hero, and now I find you have even lost your place at your father's side. We—I—have ruined your life."

"What are you talking about?" Charming asked, his head swimming in confusion. "You and the Lord Protector have been nothing but kind and generous, despite my unforgiveable behavior."

Elizabeth's step faltered, and Charming watched as the blood drained from her face and she swayed on her feet. Fearing she would fall, he tried to rise, but the pain in his side tore at him and he dropped back.

"You . . . You don't know." With a shaking hand, she reached out for the post of the bed to steady herself.

"Elizabeth, come and sit before you fall."

"Please, give me a moment, Charming," she said, breathing deeply, her hand gripped about the bedpost like her very life depended on its solidity. "I had thought . . . I assumed my brother had told you. You two have been traveling together for weeks now, and we had agreed that he would tell you."

Releasing the bedpost, she lowered her arms and held them rigidly at her side. Her face was still pale, but determination had replaced her earlier shock. "I need to confess, Edward. I need to give you the chance to hate me."

"That's not possible."

"I'm not sure," she said. "Just know that I will understand if you do."

He nodded as a sliver of fear and doubt crept into his heart.

"Will did not kill the dragon."

She told him everything. Charming stared at Elizabeth in disbelief. The whole story was so improbable, so ridiculous that if she had not been so serious and obviously distressed, he would have believed it all an elaborate joke. And then, he realized that he was not mad at her in the least, and that it was all a joke, the whole thing: the dragon, the Princess, himself. He understood at last what Adam had meant, and he laughed.

He laughed because his whole living memory had been leading to this one moment, this one act, and it had been accomplished at long last by a scarecrow. He laughed at himself and there was joy in the laughter. And then he felt a pull in his side and gasped as a ripping pain radiated through his body.

Elizabeth rushed to his side as he tried to catch his breath through gritted teeth. She put a cool cloth to his head and repositioned the pillow. "I am sorry, Charming. I am so sorry. I understand if you want to be alone . . ."

He reached out and grasped her hand. "Elizabeth, the only thing that matters to me is whether or not you will have me."

She took a seat beside him on the bed, and her gaze joined his, staring at their entwined hands. "How can this not matter to you? It was *your* dragon."

He took a moment to collect the threads of his splintered thoughts and bind them together. He attempted an explanation. "People have long wondered why I never went after the dragon. I'm sure, living as close to the beast as you did, you wondered the same thing." He looked and found confirmation in her eyes. "I think it's because the whole quest never made sense to me. The dragon came before I was born and stole away my father's love, and I was to go slay it and wake this woman I had never known with 'love's first kiss?' I wasn't sure that I could defeat the dragon, come to think of it neither was my father, the King, but I knew that I knew nothing about true love. Now, having met and fallen in love with you, I know that it was never possible. You and your brother didn't steal anything from me that was real. It was all a fabrication. Now, I ask again, can you forgive me for betraying Will?"

"He deserved it."

Charming blinked twice. "What . . . What do you mean? I betrayed him."

She rolled her eyes and then began lecturing. "You give yourself too much credit, as usual, and him too little—perhaps rightly. First, your betrayal was poorly planned and abortive. Second, you'd been brained by a troll. Why on earth he would believe anything you said at that point is beyond me. For the love of life, you tried to warn him almost as soon as the words were out of your mouth. Besides, even if you hadn't warned him, if he had just used the few wits he has, I'm sure he would have seen through the scheme. You were addled, exhausted, and pathetic."

Charming raised a hand and said softly, "Well, I'm not sure *pathetic* is the word I'd use."

If Liz heard him, she didn't bother acknowledging him. She stood, put her hands on her hips and looked up at the ceiling. "He just doesn't think. Going off in the woods with you was stupid enough, but by himself? What if he had run into some highwaymen?"

"Well, I don't think it was stupid, and, as for the highwaymen, he did, sort of . . ."

But she was not to be stopped. She began to pace around his bed. "Did you know that he doesn't even know how to use a sword? His only practice has been with toy sticks and pitchforks."

"I . . . I'm . . ."

Liz suddenly seemed to realize that Charming was in the room again. She stopped in midstride and looked down at him. "You *what*?"

"I'm sorry," he said softly. "That's all, I'm sorry."

She pursed her lips and opened her mouth to say something, but then paused. Her face softened and Charming thought that her eyes looked wet. "You are forgiven."

"Just like that? For everything? Even what I said to you at the ball?" he asked. "I didn't expect, well, I didn't think you could."

She sat next to him again and placed a warm hand

on his cheek. "You think little of me if you believe I cannot forgive a man for not knowing his heart, when it has taken me so long to know my own. I have been cruel and condescending to you at nearly every turn. And, in return, you have been as pompous an ass as ever I have met. My question is, how is it that we have fallen in love?"

He answered with a smile that was pure Charming. "That I can't answer, only maybe we stopped trying not to love each other long enough to fall in love." And then he realized what was implied in her question. "Wait, does that mean you do love me?"

"Yes," she whispered. Her face flushed and she dropped her eyes to her lap.

He tried to rise but could not, so she bent down to him and they kissed—a slow gentle exchange of breaths. Finally, she broke away, and they sat hand in hand staring at each other, both slightly surprised.

His heart swelled and a couplet sprung fully formed into his head. He looked up to the ceiling and opened his mouth to woo her, but something in his movement gave her warning, and she looked at him sternly.

"None of that, Edward. We don't have time for it, and besides, you promised." He closed his mouth. She nodded and spoke in a firm, matter-of-fact way. "We need to talk about Princess Gwendolyn and this new-found power she has. Alain told me everything while you were unconscious, and now we need to figure out how we might stop her."

"Yes, let's bring the captain in here. I have some questions for the man myself."

She shook her head at the suggestion. "I don't think so. For one thing, he's ashamed to face you after what she made him do. Secondly, you may not have noticed, but he has a tendency to run on, and time is of the essence. I'm afraid if I let the two of you share more stories of shame, you would *both* get maudlin—and I don't need two grown men weeping at each other when we are still in danger."

"Weepy . . . maudlin . . ." Charming started.

Liz pursed her lips and stared at him until he quieted. When he did, she smiled, plucked up her cloth, and began telling him Alain's story while mopping his brow. Charming found it nearly impossible to focus on anything but the curve of her lips, the sparkle in her eyes, and the way her hair fell around the nape of her neck. There was something about a ball of glass and a fairy and mind control . . . and his mind drifted and his eyes grew heavy under the spell cast by her lilting voice. She finished by saying, "Apparently, Alain was aware but powerless to do anything."

"Yes, yes, I see," said Charming with a sudden yawn.

Liz leaned closer to him. "You must be very tired. Get your rest. You need to regain your strength."

He nodded, feeling rather exhausted. She smoothed his hair back one last time, stood, and left, shutting the door behind her. A final question came to him before he closed his eyes. "So, about the proposal of marriage, what was your answer?" But she had already gone.

Through the remainder of the day, Liz spent her time checking on and caring for Charming, mostly by fussing over his bandages and trying to get him to eat. He wouldn't admit it, but her concern was warranted. He felt a terrible stabbing pain in his side every time he moved even a little, and he was as weak as an infant. Charming had resigned himself to life in bed, at least for a day or two, but, as twilight fell, he heard a shout from Alain, who was keeping watch in the outer room. "RIDERS AP-PROACH!"

With a sudden jolt of energy, Charming threw off the covers and rolled from the side of the bed to land with a thunk on the floor. "Sword!" he gasped, trying to pull himself to his feet. The door swung open as he made it to his knees. It was Liz. He shuffled toward her on his knees and choked out, "Sword! I must have a sword, the Princess has returned!"

A flutter of emotions passed over her face, but she settled on annoyance. "*What* are you doing? Get back in bed." She crossed the room and grabbed him but full strength hadn't returned to her injured arm, and she couldn't heft him back onto the bed.

Charming grabbed on to her, still vainly trying to stand. His face was contorted with pain, but he squeaked out, "Please, it could be Gwendolyn sending more men."

"No! I'm not letting you anywhere near a sword until you are well. Now, get into that bed."

He managed to drag himself up to his feet, but a deep horrible pain wracked him and he rocked forward into Elizabeth's body, knocking them both flat. "You're going to kill both of us thrashing about like this," she grunted from beneath him.

The door to the room opened, and both Charming

and Liz looked up from the ground to see Lady Rapunzel standing there. She tapped her foot and crossed her arms, but, despite herself, a smile broadened across her face. "I'll warn you, I've been in the same position, Liz, and you'll be lucky if you don't lose your hair."

"Elle!" shouted Liz with a smile of joy. She struggled out from under Charming, gathered herself, and went over to her friend, pulling her into a tight hug.

Charming grabbed hold of the bedcovers in another attempt to stand, but only managed to pull the blankets on top of himself. With a sigh, he managed a muffled but audible, "Good to see you again, Lady Rapunzel."

Eventually, with the help of Alain and Rapunzel's huntsman-cum-valet, Collins, Charming was returned to bed. Rapunzel took Liz by the shoulder and, along with the two men, left the room. The door swung shut. Charming lay his head back down against his pillow, exhausted. He had never felt so weak and helpless. He began to fall asleep, but then the door to his room swung open again. Liz stood there, eyes flashing with anger. "Didn't Gwendolyn say that she had Will and the King under her power?"

Charming blinked his eyes open, swallowed, and managed a quick, "Yes."

"She's controlling Will. She's going to marry him. We have to stop her," she said and then, turning abruptly, strode back through the door, closing it behind her with a bang. Almost immediately it opened again, slowly. Liz looked in with a gentle smile. "Sorry, are you going to sleep?"

"I think so," he answered.

"I'll tell you everything in the morning. Sleep well."

He nodded. "Elizabeth, if your brother is in danger, I will do everything I can to help him."

"Of course you will," she said kindly.

"However, I'll need a sword."

She chuckled, then with a serious look said, "No. Now, good night." The door shut for the last time.

Chapter 8

The Magnificent Seventh

WHEN MORNING CAME, a loud, incessant, and mindless chirping woke Charming. He blinked open his eyes and saw a half-dozen birds in a rainbow of colors perched on his windowsill, twittering at him. "Lady Elizabeth," he called.

At her name, the birds fell silent and flew away in a great flutter. Charming shrugged and, using the headboard for support, levered himself until he was sitting up. After catching his breath, he swung his legs off the bed and tried to stand. With great effort, he managed to pull himself to his feet. The room spun a few times and he braced himself against the wall to keep from falling. He was still leaning against the wall, breathing heavily, when Liz entered the room.

"What are you doing?" she asked in exasperation.

"I'm going to Castle White to save your brother and my father, the King, from the Princess. That is, as soon as you bring me a sword."

"Get into that bed."

He managed to sit down without collapsing, but only just.

Rapunzel made her way into the room, arms folded. "What is he doing?"

"Miladies, I need to go to Castle White. I owe it to Lady Elizabeth's brother, and, well, she has the King and his kingdom under her sway."

Liz and Elle shared a look. Rapunzel spoke first. "What would you propose to do? March up to the castle and bleed on everyone?"

Charming wasn't sure what to say. It was quite an odd feeling.

Liz forced him to lie back down, then arranged the pillows and blankets around him. "What we shouldn't do is rush. I am not entirely healed, and Edward shouldn't be moving at all."

Rapunzel rolled her eyes. "We don't need him, and Will's going to be married in a few days. We should leave immediately."

Liz glowered back at her friend. "That's just ridiculous . . ."

The two women began a very heated exchange about the best way and time to make their assault on the castle. It was apparently the continuation of a much longer argument they'd had for most of the previous night. Finally,

Charming interjected, "If there is to be a wedding, then all we need is an invitation."

The two women looked at him like he was mad.

"And how are we going to get an invitation to Princess Gwendolyn's wedding?" Elle asked sardonically. "I would imagine that people she's trying to kill would be left off the guest list."

Charming smiled his most obnoxious smile. "If the King left every nobleman he hated off his guest lists, we would never have parties at all. Besides, royals never actually spend time looking at the guest list. It is usually left to some minor official, like the Royal Steward. I'm sure he will have invited me and, likely, also Lady Rapunzel."

Liz looked thoughtful, but Rapunzel said sharply, "You've been disowned and I am a court outcast."

"That doesn't necessarily mean that someone wouldn't let us in, after all—"

"WALKERS APPROACH!" shouted Alain.

Charming tensed, but then Collins yelled right after, "BLOODY HELL, IT'S A MARCH OF DWARVES!" Then, in a lower voice, they heard Collins tell Alain, "Watch yourself, friend, or they'll have you chopping wood and weeding their garden. Lazy little blighters, dwarves."

The faint sound of voices raised in argument reached the cottage.

"The dwarves are back!" exclaimed Liz.

A loud, angry voice, which Charming recognized from the performance at the Beast's, shouted, "WHO

ARE YOU? WHAT HAVE YOU DONE WITH ELIZA-
BETH? IF YOU'VE TOUCHED HER . . ."

"Uh-oh," Liz said as something shattered in the front
room of the house and a man bellowed in pain. Both
women raced for the door. Charming heard a muffled
shout and someone, maybe Alain, cursing, followed by
what could only be a china cupboard crashing to the
floor. He strained to see what was happening, but the
angle was all wrong.

"Stop this instant," he heard Liz shout among the clatter of falling crockery.

"Collins," came Elle's voice, "put that dwarf down."
There was a loud thud and then someone grunted in pain.

"I saw that, Sloane," Liz chastised, "it is not very
gentlem—*dwarfly* to kick Mr. Collins there. Now, if you
will all calm down, I can explain everything."

Charming called out as loud as he could, "MILADY, IF
I COULD BUT HAVE A SWORD, I'M SURE I COULD
CALM THE SITUATION."

He heard an audible groan in response and then Liz
mutter loudly, "Pig-headed fool . . . Okay, everyone, into
the bedroom before Edward decides to try and get out of
bed again."

They all marched in. Seven little dwarves, Liz, Rapunzel, a limping Collins, and Alain, who was rubbing at a
spot on the back of his head and glaring at Grady. Liz
spun on the group, shaking her index finger. "I'll have no
more of this fighting and biting—"

"And bloody kicking people in the bloody—" Collins

began, only to have Liz cut him off with a stare. "Thank you, Collins."

"You'll get more than that next time, beanpole," Grady said under his breath.

"That will be quite enough, Grady," Liz said as she turned back to the dwarves. "And, what did you six . . . seven? Wait, where did you come from?" she asked a skinny, big-eared dwarf standing in the back of the room.

"What?" Grady challenged. "We can't bring a friend over to our own house now?" He turned to Dorian. "See, I warned you, you let a woman in, and suddenly she's telling you what to do and tidying up your underwear."

"Calm down, Grady," Dorian sighed. He bowed to Liz. "Lady Elizabeth . . ." He stopped himself and stared at her arm. "What happened to your cast?"

Her lips disappeared into that now telltale thin line. "It wasn't broken."

Sloane murmured, "Told you."

Dorian blushed, and seeking somehow to change the subject, turned back to the newcomer. "As I was saying, Lady Elizabeth, may I introduce our missing member, Dop—" He sighed. "I almost forgot, those lawyers. Our missing member, Dominic."

Elle and Liz gasped together. He was comically striking and absolutely singular in appearance. His hair was straw straight and cut in a perfect circle around his head so that his bangs hung down in front of his eyes in a curtain of brown. His freckled face was graced with a soft mouth and a small nose, which would have been fine and fitting but they were made ridiculous by his ears, which were enormous and stuck out from the sides of his head like the handles of a pitcher.

Dominic stepped forward and bowed low, which made his ears flap and wobble like the sails of a ship in a light breeze. "It is a pleasure to meet you, Lady Elizabeth." The others in the room stifled a collective giggle as Dominic rose and turned to Charming. "And, if I'm not mistaken, this is Prince Edward Charming."

He started to bow again, but Grady caught him by the back of the collar and kept him from bending. "Stop showing off and tell us why you're here."

"Gently now, Grady, gently," soothed Dorian.

"No!" Grady shouted. "We all deserve an answer as to why he was lurking on the path to our house. After all, *he* left *us*, and I think his exact words at the time were, 'I need to get away from you losers.'" Dominic opened his mouth to say something, but Grady cut him off. "Well, isn't that what you said?"

But it wasn't Dominic that answered, instead Hayden said cheerfully, "Actually, I don't think it was. You and he were arguing about something, and I think his exact words were, 'I need to be on my own. I'll never have the chance to do anything great working with a no-talent writer like you, Grady.'"

"No, he called Gr . . . Gr . . . Grady a talentless hack," sneezed Sneedon.

"I beg to differ, Sneedon. I distinctly remember that Dominic called Grady a 'no-talent hack,'" Dorian said authoritatively.

" 'Washed-up,' " yawned Sloane.

"What?" Dorian asked.

Sloane's eyes popped open just long enough for him to say, "He called Grady a 'washed-up, no-talent hack.'"

"Oh, yes. That was it," Dorian said with satisfaction. "I knew I was forgetting something."

"I'm confused." Baldwin's voice sounded from behind a curtain. "Is he a 'washed-up, talentless hack' or a 'no-talent, washed-up hack'?"

Grady, who had been gradually turning brighter and brighter shades of red, finally erupted, "IT DOESN'T MATTER! The point is he stabbed us all in the back!"

"Funny that," Hayden interrupted with a big smile.

"What's funny about him stabbing us in the back?" Grady demanded.

"No, not that," Hayden said with a rare frown. "I think it's funny that he would call you a washed-up, no-talent hack."

Grady grinded his teeth audibly. "I'm having trouble seeing the humor."

"Well," Hayden said cheerfully, "if you have 'no-talent' and are a 'hack,' then what got 'washed-up'?"

"Maybe he meant that Grady once had talent, but that he got 'washed-up,' and is now, as a result, a 'no-talent hack,'" Dorian suggested helpfully.

"Oh, that makes more sense," Hayden agreed.

"Thank you for clarifying, Dorian," Grady said between clenched teeth. "Now, if we can get back to the point." He turned on Dominic and growled, "Why are you here?"

"Is it to gloat over our lousy reviews?" asked Hayden.

"Or to th . . . th . . . threaten us, because we sold all the rights to *That* Play?" Sneedon sneezed violently.

"Or maybe to murder us all in our sleep in some demented vengeance ritual?" Grady asked, pantomiming in graphic detail someone getting simultaneously stabbed and strangled.

"No, no. And *what*?" Dominic answered. "It's nothing like that, it's . . ." He ground his foot into the ground and stared at the floor. "I came to ask if you'll have me back."

"Why would you want to come back here?" Grady asked suspiciously. "You had everything, if you go in for success and money and all that."

"Did you get tired of the fame?" asked Hayden.

"No . . ." Dominic said slowly.

"With rolling in dough?" suggested Sneedon, remarkably without sneezing.

"No, that was okay," Dominic said after some thought.

"With the women?" the invisible Baldwin asked.

"Definitely not," he replied quickly, which led to scowls from Liz and Elle.

"Well, what then? What was so awful about being rich, famous, and surrounded by loose women?" Grady snapped.

"I missed arguing with you, you daft twit," he bellowed. "You wouldn't believe how obnoxious it is to have people bowing and scraping to you all day." Dominic shook his head sadly. "No one to put a rise in. No one to disagree with. I'm telling you fellows, it's no way to live."

The others nodded along with him, and Dorian murmured, "That would be tough to take."

"Besides," he said brightly, "we have a gig!"

"What do you mean 'we'," asked Grady, emphasizing the *we* with air quotes.

"Yeah, I 'mean,' we haven't 'been' *we* for years," said Dorian, trying to mimic Grady's air quotes, but somehow getting his fingers badly out of sync.

"I think you meant to say, 'we,'" Hayden said and then added, "unless you meant to suggest an ambiguity in the meaning of the word *mean*."

"We all know that meaning is prone to ambiguity in postmodern society," Grady noted.

"Did you"—Sloane said, yawning widely—"Did you . . . know that ambiguity is by definition an inexactness in the meaning of . . ." He fell asleep midsentence.

"Language," Dorian finished. "Yes, everyone knows that. My question is, why would someone air quote *been*, the past perfect progressive tense of the verb *to be*. It just doesn't make sense."

"Wait, wasn't that you?" Baldwin asked, sticking his head out from the curtain he was hiding behind.

There was a moment of confusion, and Dominic took advantage. He held up a gilt scroll. "The 'we' I mean is 'we' the SEVEN players, because 'we' the SEVEN players have been invited to play Castle White."

The dwarves were so busy admiring Dominic's deft use of air quotes that it took them a moment to realize what he'd said. Then, "What? A royal invitation?" they all said in unison, ending with a long drawn out multi-tonal whistle that came out like the worst flute symphony ever.

"Why didn't you say so from the beginning?" asked Dorian.

"Well, I was afraid you'd think it was selling out."

"Which it is," spit Grady.

"Shut up," the others said, then Dorian added, "A royal invitation means big money."

The others nodded again in mutual agreement, but Grady frowned. "How can we be sure this invitation is legitimate?"

"Well, it is made of gold." Dominic waved the scroll in the air.

"Wow!" Hayden said in open admiration.

"Nice!" Sloane said between yawns.

"Classy!" Dorian added.

Grady produced a jeweler's lens from his sleeve and examined the invite. "I'll grant you, that is a nice touch. So, when is our performance?"

Dominic cleared his throat. "About that, it's in seven days."

"Seven days!" the dwarves said in unison.

"Th . . . that's no time at all," protested Sneedon between sniffles.

"What's the rush?" asked Dorian.

"Apparently, we are going to be the entertainment at some royal's wedding," Dominic said casually.

Liz, who had been as patient as she could be with the dwarves' interruption (this was after all their house) immediately recognized that this could be their key to getting into the castle. "Wait a minute," She snapped.

"Are you saying this is an invitation to the Princess's wedding?"

"I think so." Dominic opened the scroll and squinted at it. "Damned hard to read. Whoever wrote it used gold ink on gold paper."

Dorian pulled it from his hand. "Why, this is incomprehensible!"

Hayden peered over his right shoulder. "Illegible!"

Sneedon crowded in on Dorian's left, blew another trumpet sound into his handkerchief, and sniffed. "Unreadable!"

Grady snatched it away from Dorian. "And gaudy to boot. This is why you should never trust a woman to plan a wedding."

Liz grabbed the invitation from Grady mid-critique. She ignored his glare and studied it. "It is. This invites 'The Seven Players' to perform at 'the celebration of the wedding of Princess Gwendolyn Mostfair to King—'" She stopped in midsentence, her mouth open, and her face suddenly pale.

Instinctively, Charming tried to rise in aid of her. Elle, also sensing her sudden distress, moved closer. "Liz, what is it?"

Silently, Liz handed the invitation over to her friend and sat down next to Charming on the bed. He wrapped his hand around hers. "What is it, milady?"

Liz just shook her head in silence. After a moment's study of the scroll, Elle's face flushing bright red, she said, "That crazy woman has gone and made him King!"

"What?" Charming asked incredulously. "Who?"

"Gwendolyn. She's had Will crowned."

"My father, the . . . well, my father, he has been deposed?" Charming said in disbelief. "This is monstrous. We must put a stop to this immediately."

"Exactly my point," Rapunzel said in a forceful voice directed at Liz. "There is no time to lose."

Charming pulled Liz's hand into his body. "Give me a sword, milady, and I will ride to the castle tonight."

The color had finally returned to Liz's face, and Charming's request seemed to have restored her voice as well. "You'll do nothing of the sort."

"No, he's too weak," Elle agreed. "But Collins and I, we can."

"You'll do nothing of the sort either," Liz said firmly.

She snapped the paper out of Elle's hand and waved it at the group. "We are going to Castle White, and we are going to stop this wedding, and we are going to try very hard not to get killed."

There was a second of silence, and then Dorian said, "Well, you'll need some brains." He turned to the other dwarves. "I know we usually espouse a philosophy of nonviolence . . ." Liz couldn't help but snort at this. Dorian stared at her hard over the tops of his glasses, then he continued. "As I said, I know we typically do not believe in getting involved in conflict, but it seems to me that this Gwendolyn dame has to go. Agreed?"

For once, the dwarves were in unanimous agreement, and seven voices were raised as one—"AYE!"

Chapter 9

We Are Gathered Here

OF ALL THE legends that have been born from the lives, trials, and loves of the Pickett siblings, none has undergone more revision or suffered greater embellishment than the wedding of King William Pickett and Princess Gwendolyn Mostfair. It is simply not true that the bridal party was carried into the great chapel of Castle White on the backs of matching unicorns—the royal huntsman having been unable to capture a pair of satisfactory splendor. And it is disgraceful that some still spread the story that the princess commanded that the moat surrounding the castle be drained, refilled with spirits, and stocked with hundreds of white swans. Firstly, there were only ever eighty-eight swans, and, secondly, they had to be removed almost immediately because, thirdly, they kept drinking themselves into a stupor and drowning.

However, there are some stories that do have a basis in reality. For instance, while the Princess's dress was not spun by fairy magic, it was not for a lack of trying. In fact, Gwendolyn spent many days leading up to the ceremony demanding that the fairy do just that. And, as the fairy explained, repeatedly, and with increasing impatience, she could do just that if the princess would let her out of the glass ball so she could gather the proper color of morning dew. Needless to say, they reached an impasse.

Another true story is that the wedding was the very first time the actors—artists—of the Seven Players Company, known better by their stage name, the Seven Dwarfs, reunited with lead writer Dominic to perform their smash hit, "Ash and Cinders: The Elizabeth Pickett Story."** It would be the beginning of an incredibly lucrative reunion tour, the residuals for which would end up making Elizabeth, as a reluctant co-author, the wealthiest lady in the kingdom.†‡

** We are contractually obligated by the Seven Players attorneys to include the following disclaimer: "Ash and Cinders: The Elizabeth Pickett Story" is a registered trademark of the Seven Players and all text, graphics, artwork and other materials are copyrighted and may not be published, rewritten or redistributed without permission.

† Lady Elizabeth Pickett insists on pain of a broom against our backside that we include the following disclaimer: The use of Lady Eliabeth Pickett's name does not imply that "Ash and Cinders: The Elizabeth Pickett Story" is in any way endorsed by Lady Elizabeth Pickett, or reflects in even the vaguest way anything that actually happened to Lady Elizabeth..

‡ The Seven Players, who really do have a lot of attorneys, insisted that

However it happened, the morning of the wedding found Alain, the former captain of the Royal Guard, and Collins, Elle's valet-cum-huntsman or huntsman-cum-valet, dressed as stagehands, driving a covered tinker's wagon that had been hastily painted with a rather graphic mural of the dwarves "acting," under which a rather overdone and flowery hand had written "The Seven Players." Preceding the wagon and marching somewhat in unison, Dorian, Grady, and Dominic did their best to lead. In the back of the wagon, hidden amid the costumes and marionettes, backdrops and props, Charming, Liz, Elle, and the four remaining dwarves bounced uncomfortably.

After much debate, the party had agreed upon a plan that involved driving the wagon to the back gate, luring the guards there into the wagon and having the dwarves ambush them, then performing a quick "costume" change so that Collins and Alain could take their places.

So, as Collins cracked his whip and drove the wagon toward the castle, they were all relieved to see that only four men had been set to guard this lesser gate. As expected, the group of soldiers, all dressed in violent shades of pink, shouted a challenge as they approached.

---

if we included Lady Elizabeth's disclaimer that we also include the following disclaimer . . . disclaimer: "Ash and Cinders: The Elizabeth Pickett Story" is *inspired* by, not *based* on, the life and times of Lady Elizabeth Pickett, as we have repeatedly explained to her, and any inconsistencies between reality and the play represent artistic license taken by the authors to improve the dramatic arc of the story, and the natural uncertainty of truth in a post-modern world. (Italics added at the direction fo the Seven Players.).

"Halt, in the name of the King!"

Two of the four pink-clad soldiers stepped forward. They loosely held their pikes. One even leaned against his, as if it were holding him up and not the other way around. Unlike the other gates, this one seemed to have little traffic, and the men seemed much less alert, if not outright drunk, and in the air there was the overwhelming smell of drink.

In the lead position was Dorian, who smiled, cleared his throat, and, with a sweeping flourish, asked, "Is there a problem, Officers?"

"No problem," one in a particularly gaudy pink-plumed helmet answered, "We need to see your invitation and inspect the wagon."

Dorian produced the invitation with a twist of his wrist. "I think you will find everything is in order. We are *The* Seven Players, and have been ordered to perform for the Royal Couple by special request."

The man took the gilt invitation and squinted at it dubiously before handing it back. "I guess that's fine. Now, we need to examine the wagon."

Grady stomped forward. "Now, look here, Captain." Grady shook a meaty finger in the general direction of the man's stomach. "Do you know who we are?"

"I'm a lieutenant. And you are the seven players?"

"Not just 'seven players'—*The* Seven Players," Grady bristled. "Capitalize it when you say it. I won't be insulted by a common foot soldier."

"My apologies."

Grady had been expecting more fight from the man,

and opened and closed his mouth in obvious disappointment before starting again. "Yes, well, don't let it happen again. As I was saying, we are world-renowned artists. Our names are legend, and we will not submit to the indignity of a search."

"By Royal Command, we must examine every vehicle entering the castle—no exceptions," he said automatically.

"But we are ex*cept*ional," Grady said, adding a pronounced flourish to the last word.

"You may be exceptional, but we are allowed to make no exceptions."

Grady bristled his brows. "What is this really about? Do you have something against dwarves?"

"Sir," the man said, shuffling from side to side. "I love dwarfs."

"It's *dwarves*. Dwarfs is considered demeaning."

"Er, dwarf . . . ves. Anyway, as I said before, everyone is being searched today."

Dorian held up his hands in a gesture of peace. "Captain . . ."

"Lieutenant."

Dorian adjusted his glasses as he struggled to keep a smile fixed to his face. "Lieutenant, we can overlook your prejudice, but we can't risk our livelihood. We have spent the better part of two years preparing for this performance. We have a number of props and costumes that are exceedingly delicate in the wagon. Perhaps, if we could oversee the search . . . ?"

The lieutenant sighed and gestured to the other

guards. "All right. Bring them along. But keep an eye on them, especially bristly brows," he said, pointing at Grady. So all four guards surrounded the three dwarves in a wall of pink and cream crinoline, and marched in step to the side of the wagon. As the lieutenant stretched out his hand to open the door, he asked, "By the way, you said you were The *Seven* Players, but there are only three of you. Where are the others?"

The three dwarves smiled in unison. "Excellent question."

The door swung open and a swarm of miniature hands and diminutive bodies with ropes and sticks emerged from the darkened interior. The lieutenant managed one muffled cry of horror, and then the four guards were pulled into the maw of the caravan. Dorian, Grady, and Dominic followed behind, the door swung shut with a crack, the wagon rocked violently once, twice, three times, and then was still. As choreographed, Collins and Alain dismounted from their positions and opened the back of the wagon, then clambered inside, while Charming, wearing a deeply cowled hood, climbed out.

A few moments later, Alain and Collins, appearing to the world as two disheveled pink-clad guards, emerged back onto the bridge and waved the wagon across and through the gate.

Alain whispered to Collins, "Those poor bastards never knew what hit them. Remind me never to cross a dwarf." The other man, still wide-eyed from the horror, nodded in silent agreement and watched the wagon, a heavily cloaked Charming at the reins, slip out of sight into the inner courtyard of Castle White.

Inside the wagon, the seven dwarves sat in raucous satisfaction atop the bruised, bloodied, and bound soldiers, cheering their victory.

"What a fight!" Grady trumpeted as he put a finger to his tender eye.

"You said it." Hayden sniffed happily as he rubbed blood away from his battered nose. "That was a real donnybrook."

"I think I lost a tooth!" Dorian said proudly, and stuck his tongue through a blank space in his smile.

"Nice one," the others exclaimed.

"Well, if you ask me—" Elle started.

"And, we didn't," Grady grunted. The others nodded in agreement.

"I thought we agreed that there would be no unnecessary violence," Liz said with a disapproving glare.

Grady stood up on one of the bound soldiers and bounced on his toes, eliciting a grunt from the man beneath him. "I defy you to point to a single instance of 'unnecessary' violence."

Liz put her hands on her hips and shook her finger at the group of dwarves. "Dorian, what about when you bit that man's nose?"

"Essential to our plan of attack," he explained.

"And Grady," Elle asked, "poking that poor fellow in the eye?"

"Elementary tactics. You've got to blind the enemy," he lectured, and then demonstrated by poking his fingers into the air at an imaginary attacker.

"I see," Liz continued. "And kicking the lieutenant in the head after he was down, Sneedon?"

"He was . . . *ah*. He was . . . *aaah*. He was"—the dwarf sneezed—"resisting."

"Mmmhmm," the two women said together, then Elle turned to Hayden. "Should we even bother asking what you were doing to that poor man's . . . well, his . . . ?"

Hayden smiled. "Demoralizing my foe."

Liz and Elle exchanged a glance. Liz shook her head and sat down. "Now that they are properly 'demoralized,' can we trust you boys not to abuse them while we're gone?"

The seven dwarves looked up with matching expressions of unconvincing innocence and sang, "You have our word."

Liz looked at the four half-naked men and shrugged to Elle. "I'm not sure we have any choice."

Just then the lieutenant's eyes flickered open and his body immediately tensed against the ropes as he struggled to break free. Liz leaned in close to the man. "Of course, if they do try to escape . . ."

" . . . or call out for help . . ." Elle added, kneeling down next to him.

The two women looked at each other and smiled. "You would have to do whatever was necessary to subdue them."

All seven of the little men's faces stretched into evil grins, and as one they nodded. The lieutenant's face paled, his eyes rolled back into his head, and his body went slack. As the women rose to their feet, the wagon came to a stop with a jerk. From above, there was a grunt, and then Charming opened the door with a swirl of his cloak and an elegant half-bow that was only marred by an accompanying grimace of pain.

"Ladies and dwarves," he said with a heavy breath, "we have arrived."

Liz and Elle descended the wagon into the gloom of an otherwise empty livery stable. They took one last look at the dwarves, who were literally standing and sitting guard over the soldiers, and closed the door.

"Do you think they will be safe?" Charming asked with some concern.

The women looked at one another for a moment, then Liz said, "The dwarves can handle themselves."

"I was thinking about the soldiers."

Liz tucked her arm through Charming's. "We have enough to worry about ourselves, so let's—" Suddenly she drew away from him and threw aside his cloak. "What is that?" she asked, pointing an accusing finger. A long scabbard, festooned in pink and silver, hung at his side.

"It's my sword," he said with a sly smile, but his face faltered under her glare and he stammered, "Li-Liz, try to understand."

Elle smirked at him and clucked her tongue. She moved away in anticipation of an argument. "Here it comes."

Liz gave Elle a warning glance that backed her further away, then she turned her attention to Charming. "What should I understand? That you don't care a wit if you leave me a widow before I'm even married?"

Charming started to respond, but stopped with a sudden hush of expectation. "Is that a yes?"

Liz flushed and bit her lip. "Don't you go trying to change the subject, Edward Charming."

"I'm not," he said in a voice so earnest that it silenced her. "I am wearing this sword because of you." She started to interrupt, but he forestalled her rebuttal by grabbing her hands and locking his eyes onto hers. "I have no intention of making you a widow, Elizabeth Pickett, but I will not be a widower even if it means that I must stain every stone of this castle red with blood and tear the heavens from the sky to stop it. If you will promise to leave this place now and return to the cottage in the woods, then I will happily lay down this weapon and take my chances, but I will not walk into that chapel with you at my side and face the Princess unarmed, and you will have to kill me yourself to stop me."

A quiet smile stole over Elizabeth's face. She withdrew her hands from his and smoothed her skirt. She looked back into his eyes and said, "Well then, it's a shame about the color, I don't think pink suits you."

Charming frowned at the sword. "I know. It's a damned nuisance. I'm much more of an autumn than a spring."

Liz rolled her eyes and laughed aloud. "Elle, it is time to go. Edward will always be Charming, and all is well between us."

With that, the trio cracked open the stable door and peeked out onto the main courtyard and a scene of utter chaos. Servants, in a cacophonous rainbow of livery, but dominantly pink, raced here and there carrying silver this and gold-plated that, and every manner of silk, satin, and brocade this and that.

"Now what?" Liz asked, pulling the stable door closed again. "We can't possibly go out there without being spotted."

"You're right," Charming said. "Someone would be bound to recognize *me*. But fear not, I have a plan. Follow me."

With that, he led the ladies, who exchanged an unspoken "that's Charming" moment behind his back, through the livery and into a door half hidden behind some moldering crates. Elle muttered something dark about her confidence in his "plan" under her breath, which Charming chose to let pass without comment. He had to admit he had earned her distrust. His behavior at the tower and the ball had been disgraceful, not to mention the fact that he had pulled out most of her hair.

The passage gave way to a series of unused storerooms beneath the castle. Light flickered down through the dusty air from a row of barred windows set high in the walls above. Their footsteps echoed in the damp emptiness. Charming felt Liz shiver.

She leaned close and spoke softly so as not to disturb the eerie quiet of the chamber. "Are you sure this is right?"

He squeezed her hand and gave a reassuring smile. "As you know, in my former life as prince I was renowned for a number of skills—most I now realize absolutely useless—but one, which we are now benefiting from now, was my near preternatural ability to pop up anywhere in the castle at the most opportune or inopportune times, depending on the mischief I was interested in getting into, which most of the time involved procuring apricot tarts."

"Oh, I love those," said Liz. "But how did you do it?"

Charming smiled at her. "The truth is that every twist and turn, every stone of this place, is etched into the marrow of my bones. At the moment, we are walking through a series of vast storerooms that were used in dark times as a granary when siege was thought imminent. In another moment, there will be a turning, and then a rough stair . . . ahhh."

As if by magic, the way turned and a kind of hewn ramp appeared. The flickering light of torches reached them from above. "Now please, no more questions. I haven't used this route since I was a young boy, when my greatest desire in life was to steal a glance at the women's bath, so I need to concentrate."

Charming smiled to himself at the two exasperated clucks he received in response.

Their progress was slow, partly because of the need for stealth, but also because Charming found the walk, and especially the stairs, taxing. He was breathing harder and starting to limp. Still, he led the ladies steadily up into the heart of the castle. The hallways grew grander, and, at last, they found themselves crouched behind a suit of armor set in an alcove along a marbled passageway across from a pair of ornate double doors.

"Is that the entrance to the chapel? Is Will in there?" Elle whispered.

Charming, engrossed by a leather strap that ran from the back of the armor to a bolt that seemed newly driven into the wall, didn't answer. "Looks secure . . ." he muttered to himself.

Elle cleared her throat and hissed, "I asked if this is the way to the chapel," she repeated.

Charming gave one last suspicious glance at the armor and said, "The chapel? No, we are miles from there. You, my dear Lady Rapunzel, are looking at the door to none other than the Royal Tailor." He grinned.

"WHAT?" Elle shouted, and then slapped a hand over her own mouth. "I mean," she said in a violent whisper, "What? My God, are you mad? We're going to miss the ceremony."

"Nonsense," he said. "By my reckoning, we have fully three hours before the wedding begins." At this, there was a loud gong that reverberated through the castle. Charming frowned, "Hmmm, the noon chime. Okay, I stand corrected, two hours. Still plenty of time."

"For what?" Elle asked in dismay.

"Why, I thought that would be obvious. We are here so the tailor can make us proper clothes."

Liz shook her head.

Elle whispered, "Clothes! You have gone mad. Why in the world do we need clothes?"

Charming paused for an instant and the hint of a grin tugged at his mouth as he suppressed the obvious answer, but he composed himself. "If we are going to be servants to a queen, we must look the part. As I always say, clothes make the man. Of course, it goes without saying that the sentiment applies to the fairer sex as well. Now, quickly, the hall is empty."

With that, Charming grabbed Liz's hand and pulled her across the passage. Elle followed red-faced with anger and bewilderment. He paused for a single heartbeat to listen at the door and then, opening it, ushered both women in. He glanced up and down the corridor, shut the door softly behind them, and threw the bolt.

It was as though they had stepped inside a kaleidoscope. The room was a fractured riot of colors and textures. Bolts of cloth, rolls of ribbon and lace, boxes of beads, buttons, and bangles lay in heaps and drifts across a massive workspace that was divided into a series of rows by enormous worktables, that were themselves littered with bits of half-finished pieces and, of course, the tools of the trade. Liz and Elle were still looking around in wonder when they realized that there was a short man, impeccably dressed but having the disheveled appearance of someone that has just completed a footrace, standing in front of one of the tables, talking to Charming.

The two men looked up from their private conference. A man they assumed was the Royal Tailor swept the women with an appraising glance and shook his head. "It will never work."

"I'm sure it will. Dressed as servants no one will look at us twice. We can walk straight into the chapel."

"No, you don't understand," the Royal Tailor said with a dismissive flutter of his hands. "The Princess has forbidden any of the female servants from entering the chapel during the wedding. There will only be footmen.

She says that the men will present a more aesthetic backdrop for her wedding party, but everyone knows it is because she is terrified of being upstaged. I mean, look at the bridesmaids' dresses she dreamed up." He flicked a pointed finger at three puffs of pink standing in the corner.

"Those are the bridesmaids' dresses?" Charming choked. "But, they look . . . they look . . ."

"Like clown costumes for a group of flat-chested fat men?" the Royal Tailor said with disdain. "Yes, I know. Worse still, the Princess made me add a pink veil. The poor ladies will look like they've been encased in a virulent pink cocoon. It is—"

"PERFECT!" Charming said with a shout.

"What?" the Royal Tailor, Elle, and Liz all said together.

"They are hideous," the Royal Tailor protested.

"Revolting!" spit Elle.

"Disturbing," Liz added.

"All true, but they are perfect disguises," Charming persisted. "With the veil, it will be impossible for anyone to know who is beneath the dress."

The tailor cocked his head in thought.

Liz said, "You aren't suggesting that Elle and I join the wedding party. Don't you think the Princess will recognize that something is amiss when two extra bridesmaids show up to the chapel?"

The Royal Tailor shook his head. "No, not really. The number of bridesmaids in the wedding party has changed more often than Charming changes clothes."

Liz and Elle giggled as Charming spluttered; the tailor smiled at him and winked. "Don't take that as a criticism. I love you for it. Anyway, let me explain about the bridesmaids. At first all the ladies of the court wanted to be in the wedding, and, after a fierce competition, Gwendolyn selected the six ugliest. Then the bridesmaids saw the dresses and they began to fall ill, or break limbs, or simply disappear. Last time I checked, we were down to three ladies that were either too obsequious or too stupid to flee. I doubt even Gwendolyn knows how many are going to be there, so a couple extra won't raise one eyebrow on her demented, but perfectly formed, head."

"Then you'll do it?" Charming asked.

"I should refuse," the Royal Tailor said with a frown.

Charming's face fell. "Why would you deny me this? Is it because I have been renounced?"

The Royal Tailor said with sudden passion, "Of course not, I should refuse you because to put you in pink, and these beautiful ladies into the abominations dreamed up by that cow, Gwendolyn, is a sin against fashion and good taste."

Charming put a hand to his chest. "I understand. You know I would not request such a thing if it were not essential. But we have two hours to stop the Princess from marrying Will ... er ... King William, or she will define style for the next fifty years."

The Royal Tailor shuddered and put a fluttering hand to his head. For a moment, he seemed close to fainting, then he took a few deep breaths and fanned himself. "Please, no more. I will do what I must."

Charming put an arm around the man's shoulder. "Thank you. Now, if you have a little extra time, could you see to a few modifications on my outfit?"

"Extra time?" Elle erupted from across the room. "We now have less than two hours before Princess Gwendolyn will be Queen Gwendolyn for all time, and you are talking about extra time! There is no way he can make three outfits in two hours."

Both Charming and the tailor shared a chuckle together. "Is she always this emotional?" the tailor said with a snort of laughter.

"Always," Charming said, "but in this case, she has reason. She wants to marry King William herself."

"Ahhhh," the Royal Tailor exhaled. He crossed to Elle and bowed briefly. "My dear, I once made a hand-stitched couture gown for the Duchess of Dearly, who is a woman of formidable dimension, in a half hour. I can fit two bridesmaid dresses and put together a footmen's uniform in my sleep. In fact, over the last week I think I have. Now, please, place yourself in my hands, and all will be well."

The Royal Tailor was as good as his word. In less than an hour, and a little more than an hour after making several modifications to Charming's outfit—a demi-cape to hide his sword, a few tucks and pleats for better fit, and several other custom refinements—the three were dressed, hideously dressed, but dressed.

Elle and Liz helped each other adjust the veils that encased the top-third of their bodies with matching giggles. But the moment their costumes were complete, Elle turned to Charming, who was evaluating himself critically in the full-length mirror. "Now what?"

"Well, I think if we tried a slightly more subdued shade of pink, or something with more of a sheen, we might have something here."

"No!" said Elle.

"Actually, I think he has a point," the Royal Tailor said between pursed lips as he studied Charming's behind in the tight-fitting breeches.

"No," she said again. "I mean what do we do now to save Will? Remember him? Liz's brother, the man who is going to be married in less than an hour?"

Charming tore his gaze away from the mirror. "We walk down to the chapel and wait for the opportune moment to seize the day and rescue poor King William, and the Kingdom of Royaume itself, from the Princess."

"That's it?" she asked incredulously.

He nodded. "Yes. With those dresses and my uniform, no one will question us."

Elle spluttered about needing more of a plan, but Liz shrugged her shoulders. "It sounds reasonable, Elle. We won't know what the Princess has planned until we get down there and see for ourselves."

Charming embraced the Royal Tailor and smiled. "Thank you, I hope to see you again."

"And I you, Edward Charming, but next time in something blue."

"Agreed. Adieu, dear friend! You have my thanks!"

The three stepped out of the door and right into a

group of nobles. After untangling the ladies dresses, there was a beat of confusion in which the nobles stared uncomfortably at each other and Charming. Elle took a step forward so that Charming was beside her and kicked him surreptitiously in the shin. "Bow!" she whispered from beneath her veil.

Through teeth gritted in pain, Charming executed a shallow bow. Elle made a sweeping curtsy that was half-heartedly copied by Liz, and answered by bows and curt-sies from the other nobles. From beneath Elle's veil came an unrecognizably shrill voice. "Excuse us, Duchess and Duke Faircourt, Lady Greenleaf. We must make haste to the chapel. Footman, lead on."

Charming bowed again and walked quickly down the hall and away from the party of still-murmuring courtiers. Elle and Liz puffed to keep up. Finally, they turned a corner and Liz hissed, "Edward, slow down! People will find it highly suspicious if they see two bridesmaids and a footman sprinting through the halls of the castle."

"Right, sorry," he said, grabbing his wounded side and gasping for breath. "I guess I panicked a little. I've known Lady Greenleaf since I was five, and the Duchess of Fair-court and I, well, we're familiar."

Liz stroked his cheek. "Are you all right?"

"Fine, just fine," he said with a broad smile that was ruined only by the beads of sweet on his brow.

She tenderly wiped his forehead dry and then gave him a playful slap. "We shall talk about your 'familiarity' with the Duchess some other time. For now get us safely, and slowly, to the chapel."

He bowed as gracefully as his body would allow and smiled. "As the Lady commands." Then he turned on his heel and, at a stately pace, led the women through the castle and the growing crowds of nobles and courtiers to the sanctuary of the ancient chapel of Castle White.

Chapter 10

Or Forever Hold Your Peace

IN A SMALL, sunlit chamber behind the chapel, Princess Gwendolyn stood alone, frowning at the image in a large gilt-framed looking glass. The woman in the mirror was a vision. The dress she was wearing was not fairy made, but it could have been. It was a delicate affair of lace and silk layered like the petals of a flower. Her golden hair was arranged in an intricate coif of spirals and waves and curls that seemed lighter than air. From head to toe, jewels sparkled here and there, drawing in the light and casting it out like stars.

And yet, Gwendolyn was not happy.

Something wasn't right. Around her, the shadow handmaidens swirled, straightening her veil here, fixing a loose strand of hair there. Inside her head, other minds—Will's, Rupert's, the priest's and dozens of others, crowded for attention. They would give her no peace, no rest. At one time either or both would have driven her to distraction, but she was used to them by now: the feel of the cold shadow hands, the clamor of other people's thoughts. It was the woman in the mirror that disturbed her. She saw a sad woman with soulful eyes, and it was not her.

"Who are you? What do you want?" Gwendolyn asked the phantasm.

Don't you recognize me? came the answer in a voice that was as soft as the whispered wind.

Gwendolyn stared into the glass and gasped. "Rosslyn?"

She grasped for the glass ball partially hidden among the flowers of her wedding bouquet and shook it. "Fairy, if it is you conjuring this image . . ."

The orb swirled with a jumble of rapidly flickering and confused images, but the light of the pixie shone only dimly. A weak, bitter voice floated through the air to her: "*Thou thinkest much of me, if thou believes that I canst bend the wills of thy groom, thy King, thy priest, and a score more so that thee can control them and still defy thee. Thy vision is thine alone, Mistress. Live it thyself and leave me in peace.*"

Though hateful, the words rang true. In disgust, she dropped the bouquet on the vanity.

Gwenie? came the spectral voice from the mirror.

It was a nickname only her sister had called her. Gwendolyn felt her hair rise and her flesh crawl. She turned slowly back to the mirror. There stood Rosslyn, dressed for her wedding, the wedding that she never had a chance to celebrate. Gwendolyn's legs gave out and she fell to her knees. Behind the glass, Rosslyn mirrored the movement so that they knelt face-to-face.

Why did you do it?

Gwendolyn sobbed. "You can't think it was on purpose, I only meant . . ."

The image in the mirror was crying as well, tears of silvered water running down her face. *Meant what? To steal my love?*

"No! It is just that I—"

Yes, Gwenie?

Gwendolyn could not bring herself to look into her sister's eyes, so she stared down at her white-gloved hands. "I remember that day. I ran into the forest and called for the fairy. I thought she was my magical godmother. I thought she wanted to help me. You were going to marry Rupert, and you didn't love him, not like I did. When I traveled here with you, attending you, hovering in the background, I saw everything. You just wanted the kingdom. You wanted Castle White. I wanted Rupert to be my prince. I had dreams, Rosslyn, my dreams. All I did was wish. I wished that you would not marry Rupert, that I would be with my true love, and that I would be a princess remembered like no other." Gwendolyn looked up into her sister's eyes. "I swear, I did not mean for you to die."

I know you did not mean it, the voice said sadly, *but I did die. Your wishes killed me, Gwenie, and now you are wishing again to satisfy your desire for the Crown. You must put a stop to this madness.*

"But this time is different," she pleaded.

Why Gwenie? Why is this different?

"Before I relied on the fairy, and I was selfish and full of pride. But I have changed." She clasped her hands in front of her, begging. "While I was locked away with the dragon, I had time to think, to dream, about what I would do to make things right. I realized that the only way I could redress my wrongs would be to reclaim everything that I had lost with the force of my own will. I promised myself that I would marry the King, and I would claim the throne that was meant for you, and I would have the wedding and the love I . . . We lost to the fairy's curse. Rosslyn, I am doing this for us. I'm doing it for you."

You are doing this for me, Gwenie?

"For you, Rosslyn. I swear it."

Her sister's piercing green eyes bore into her. *Then stop, Gwenie. Stop before it is too late. You have lost yourself in hatred and insanity. It will not bring me back, and it will destroy you.*

Gwendolyn shook her head throughout her sister's speech—"No, no, no, no, no. This one last thing and all the wrongs we have suffered will be avenged."

Gwenie, I can understand and forgive your anger toward the fairy and the King, and even the Prince, but these things that you have done, they aren't you. You never wanted to hurt anyone. She gave a tender, sad smile. *Even me, dear sister. Can't you see what this magic is doing to you? It is driving you mad. You don't even look yourself. You look like a wraith—so tired and haunted. Stop this now.*

"No!" she shouted. "I've come too far. I am so close to my happy ending."

She began to pace back and forth in front of the mirror, her sister following her movements in silence behind the glass. "Maybe I'm not doing it only for you. Maybe I am doing this for me. But don't I deserve it? For everything that has been done to me. For all the years I lived in silent guilt unable to make amends to you. For all the torment I suffered at the hands of the fairy. For being abandoned by the man I loved."

She stopped and once again faced the mirrored image of Rosslyn. "I have waited a lifetime to be saved. I have waited patiently for my knight to come and slay my dragon. And, what did he do? He left me to rot. I will not wait anymore. I will not leave anything to fate or chance. I have been given . . . no, I have taken the power to set things right, and I am going to use this power, this magic."

Revenge will not bring you the peace you seek, Gwenie. Only true love can do that.

The Princess felt her whole body stiffen in rage. "True love? You speak to me of true love? You who would have married a man that you half-despised . . ."

This time the voice was angry and it roared in her ears. *I MAY NOT HAVE LOVED RUPERT AS YOU DID, BUT I DID LOVE HIM.*

Gwendolyn shuffled back from the mirror.

Her sister's voice softened and whispered now, soothing or trying to sooth. *You saw only what you wanted to see, Gwen. You admitted into your heart only the good things about him. I loved him for the man he was and is. A man, like any other, that has flaws and weaknesses and vices, and, yes, I made fun of him for those. Yours was the love of youth—pure and blind—mine was the love of truth—real and accepting. I know you do not understand, you were, you are, still so young, Gwenie.*

"Stop saying that," Gwendolyn shouted. "You may have been older then, but I am older now. I have lived and suffered like you never did, and I escaped. And I will marry William and we will be happy."

A cloud came over her sister's face. Her eyes grew stern and her voice hard. *Believe what you will of me, but know, Gwendolyn Mostfair, that what you are doing is wrong, and the strength of your convictions cannot make it right.*

Gwendolyn felt the anger rising in her blood. She stood, and her sister stood with her, and the two siblings glared at each other across the barrier of the glass. "I know true love, Rosslyn, and this wedding will prove it. If William and I were not meant to be, then the curse would not allow it. If this is not true love, then how did I cast off the fairy's magic? If this is not true love, then I would still be locked in that accursed spell—half dead."

The sadness came back to the face in the mirror and the voice that spoke was full of grief. *If the spell is broken, if the curse is lifted, then why do you still fear the fairy? If you are free, then cast her and her power away.*

Gwendolyn rose and grabbed the glittering ball in her hands. As she was about dash it to the ground, she stopped and placed the fairy ball back on the table in its cradle of flowers. "No. Not until I am queen. Not until I have shown the fairy that I have won."

The Princess looked back up and her sister's eyes were full of pity. *Oh, Gwenie, I am sorry, I did not know that you were still lost in a dream.*

"NO I AM NOT!" she screamed.

In a fit of anger, Gwendolyn pushed the mirror onto the hard stone floor. It splintered and cracked, and, for a moment, the image of Rosslyn's sorrowful face was duplicated in each of the hundreds of fractured facets. Gwendolyn kneeled to the floor again and a hundred voices, including her own, whispered, "I am sorry."

There was a knock at the door, and nervous voice called out, "Princess Gwendolyn, are you all right?"

The minds that she had been keeping at bay came crowding back in on her thoughts. The shadows that had vanished during her talk with Rosslyn now crowded about, pawing at her. The images of Rosslyn wavered and disappeared, and Gwendolyn found that she was kneeling on the cold stones of the little room staring down now at her own tear-streaked face in the broken glass pieces. She searched for the sad face of her sister in the shattered panes. But Rosslyn was gone. All that remained was Gwendolyn—a haggard, wan, and haunted Gwendolyn, repeated over and over.

"It was nothing," she whispered to herself. "Just an illusion, a trick of the light, and the jitters of a new bride."

"Your Highness? Are you there?"

Her head radiated with pain, and she put a hand to her temple in an attempt to soothe it. She frowned at the closed door and shouted harshly, "OF COURSE, I'M HERE, YOU IDIOT. Where else would I be? What do you want?"

"I beg your forgiveness, Your Highness," came the frightened reply. "Your Highness, I've come to tell you that the guests have assembled. All is in readiness."

The guests have assembled. The pain in her head was momentarily forgotten. She rose to her feet and straightened her dress. *All is in readiness.* She felt a cold confidence fill her body; and when she spoke, it was with the authority that only absolute certainty can provide: "Very well, tell the musicians to begin my march."

She looked back down into the shattered mirror. Her face was a ruin. Her cheeks were sunken and white from lack of food. Her eyes were haunted from lack of sleep. Her face was heavily lined as though the shadows had hidden themselves there. For a moment, her confidence wavered, and she felt the souls she had enthralled pushing back at their bonds, but then she heard her wedding march—the notes rolling and echoing through the stone chapel like a force of nature.

It is time, the cold and confident voice in her head said. *Nothing can stop us.*

"I can't be seen like this," she whispered in horror and growing uncertainty. "They will know."

Don't worry, the voice reassured her, *nobody will see you. They will see only a bride.* Her shaking hand lowered the veil into place, obscuring her face and all the evidence of her grief and doubt and madness. *By the time we are revealed, we will be Queen.*

Beneath the veil, she felt herself smile. The pain in her head was still there, but it was a remote thing and the voices were gone. The cold bodies of the shadow people fluttered about her face, but were obscured by the layers of white cloth. She gathered her bouquet with the fairy glass into her arms, and, fully encased in her lace and silk armor, she strode through the door to the waiting chapel beyond.

CHARMING STOOD AGAINST the wall of the chapel just behind the bridesmaids, one in a row of dozens of fit young men dressed in identical pink uniforms. He was supposed to be watching the gilt door where Gwendolyn would eventually emerge, but he couldn't stop himself from glancing at the line of bridesmaids, studying with particular intensity the two at the end. He was worried about Liz and Elle. The ladies were tense, and Elle had nearly rushed to Will when he and Charming's father marched rigidly to take their place on the chapel's raised dais, next to an expressionless priest. Only a restraining hand, and a hissed "we must wait until the moment is right" had kept her from ruining their disguises.

The notes of the wedding march interrupted his thoughts. He turned his head in time to see light flood through the chapel doors, highlighting the golden rug and mingling with the towering flower arrangements that lined the central aisle. Along with the rays of sunlight came the strong smell of nutmeg, and Charming had enough time to consider that it was an odd choice for a wedding as a phalanx of elfin girls came through the door, dancing with cold perfection and tossing handfuls of rose petals into the air about them. Close on their heels came a quartet of identically stone-faced little boys. Each carried a satin pillow with a jeweled ring. When the children reached their positions on the dais, the music swelled. A massive shadow filled the doorway. Princess Gwendolyn, in a veiled dress that could only be described as epic, strode down the aisle with grace, a glowing bouquet held in her arms. Charming frowned at the shining glass ball half-hidden among the flowers. *There is the source of her power.*

He heard Elle hiss from the far end of the line, "Now?"

He leaned slightly over and whispered, "Not yet. We must wait for the right moment."

PRINCESS GWENDOLYN SURVEYED the church and smiled beneath her veil. It was perfect. The flowers, the afternoon sunlight streaming through the stained-glass windows, the wall of statuesque footmen, the line of bridesmaids on one end of the dais—she was glad to see that they had managed to round up five of the six—balanced by the two kings on the other and the head priest waiting patiently for her before the altar. She frowned at the man's stony face. After a moment's concentration, his mouth turned up into a broad smile. *Better.*

She reached the bottom stair of the dais. Rupert, her former love, stepped forward jerkily, and, putting out a hand, led her to the top of the platform opposite her future husband, King William. She made Rupert bow to her, and then dismissed him to his position several steps below her. Then she turned her focus on Will and nothing happened. He stood absolutely still, his face a blank mask of concentration. Beneath the veil, she frowned. He was being difficult. She focused harder on the commands, and, ever so slowly, he moved forward to stand next to her. In unison, they clasped hands and turned to face the priest. Gwendolyn smiled grimly as she felt William's fluttering pulse through his clammy palm. *He will learn his place. In time, they all will.*

WILLIAM PICKETT HAD never felt more drained. He had tried to resist Gwendolyn's commands with every ounce of his willpower, and still he was here, standing hand-in-hand with her as the priest discoursed on the sanctity of marriage in the strangely stilted monotone of one of Gwendolyn's thralls. The homily ended, and, in a sudden movement, he swiveled to Princess Gwendolyn, her face a collection of shadows beneath the lace veil. Will braced himself, knowing what she would make him do. The Princess ended her recital of the vows and the whole of the assemblage focused on him.

Will felt the words she wished him to say rolling through his head. He locked the muscles of his jaw until they hurt with a painful intensity. With each second that passed, the urge to speak grew, and the words echoed louder and louder until he thought his head must burst. The standoff lasted a few seconds, no more. His strength gone, the words issued from his mouth one at a time—emotionless—until he had spoken them all.

With another rigid swivel he was, once more, facing the priest. He would resist to the end, but he knew that the end was coming, and William Pickett had little hope that he would succeed at anything. His only happiness came from knowing that at least his sister and Elle were well and truly clear of this. He would be a puppet-king for Queen Gwendolyn until she was done with him, and then, perhaps, she would let him die in peace. He tried to smile at the thought, but could not. Even this was not allowed.

BENEATH HER PINK veil, Liz clenched her teeth in rage as she watched the Princess pull the strings on her collection of human puppets. After Collins and Alain, she could spot the telltale signs, and smells at once. The priest thrall was speaking now, explaining monotonously, one last time, that the union they were forming was not to be entered into lightly or under pretenses false. Elle quivered beside her.

Please keep hold of yourself, Elle, she thought with a silent shout to her friend.

Almost in answer, she heard Elle whisper fiercely, "Now! We must move now!"

Charming replied from behind them in a soft calm

tone. "Not yet. The moment is not right. When the time comes, I will distract the Princess. You will seize the bouquet. That is where she is hiding the fairy ball."

Liz heard an echo of that old annoying confidence in his voice. Despite herself, she smiled. She did not know what he had in mind, but she was past doubting. She had entwined her destiny with his, and she would share the consequences if they failed.

The Princess said, "I do."

Liz's throat went dry and she whispered a prayer meant only for herself. *Please let Charming know what he is doing.*

IT TOOK EVERY ounce of willpower in Elle's body not to leap forward as the priest asked King William, her Will, if he would marry Princess Gwendolyn Mostfair. Her whole body quivered in impotent rage. *What are we waiting for? Why am I listening to Charming? The man is a fool, and he ripped out my hair!*

Rapunzel's throat went dry and she whispered an oath meant only for herself, "*So help me, if Charming screws this up I will cut off his . . .*"

"BEFORE-THIS-ASSEMBLAGE-and-knowing-the-vows-to-which-you-have-both-spoken," the priest said, "-do-you-King-William-Pickett-Lord-Protector-and-Dragonslayer-take-this-woman-Princess-Gwendolyn-Mostfair-to-be-your-wedded-wife-till-death-you-do-part?"

King William, stood at apparent ease atop the dais, but in his mind, William Pickett desperately fought the answer screaming "no, no, no and no!" in his mind. He tried to form that simple word—"N-O"—but the Princess's command was an overwhelming force. It was as though everything he had known was wiped from his memory, and all that remained were two words—"I do." Unable to speak, he resolved to keep his mouth shut.

Silence interrupted the ceremony, and the crowd murmured and shuffled. Whispers crept from the back of the chapel. Tension filled the air like a fog. The priest smiled stiffly and asked, "King-William?"

Will felt the Princess's being slip into him like a stain, and heard himself say, "I-do," in a high-pitched voice that was nearly a squeak.

He felt the Princess slip back out the way she had come. He slumped his shoulders and grief washed over him. Despite Gwendolyn's power, a single tear escaped, running down his cheek in impotent rebellion.

"Now!" ELLE HISSED to Charming, and she took a half step forward before Liz's hand clasped on her own like iron.

Behind them, Charming whispered, "Almost . . ."

Gwendolyn and William were facing each other again on the dais. The priest held up his hands, "If-anyone-present-here-knows-of-any-reason-"

Charming whispered, "Almost."

The priest continued, "-that-this-man-and-this-wom

an-should-not-be-joined-by-the-holy-bonds-of-matrimo ny-let-them-speak-now-or-forever-hold-their-peace."

Charming's voice, with a power honed by years of ora- torical training, echoed like a thunderclap through the chapel, "I DO!"

He stepped from behind the bridesmaids and down onto the main floor of the chapel at the foot of the dais. Then, with a movement of pure grace, unclasped his pink demi-cape—and with a swirl of fabric, he shed the footmen's uniform like a cocoon, emerging in a bril- liant blue-and-gold satin doublet and matching breeches that complemented his eyes, showed off his muscular body, and displayed his hair to perfection. The sword remained, a dangerously virile slash of pink and silver against his leg.

Only Liz's very discerning eye caught the little hitch in his unveiling and the gasp of suppressed pain that told the story of what that flourish cost him. Her face curved into a hidden frown, and she added another grievance against the Princess to her growing list.

Stunned silence filled the chapel. Then the Princess, in a fraught voice, a mix of fear, anger, and wonderment, sputtered, "Charming? It can't be. You are supposed to be dead."

Charming kept his gaze on the Princess, but out of the corner of his eye he saw two of the pink puffs slip along the line of bridesmaids toward the back of the altar. His job now, he reminded himself, was to keep every eye in the chapel on him—he had never been more in his ele- ment. Charming took another step forward, ran a hand through his auburn hair, and embraced everyone in the room with his most charming smile. "I cannot die. I am Prince Charming."

There were a few sighs from the ladies, and one even swooned, but on the stage the Princess said, "But you're not Prince Charming, you are just Edward Charming. Seize him!"

Almost as one, dozens of guards clad in pink stepped away from the walls and advanced. He thought about using the sword at his side, but then remembered Liz's admonition at the cottage and took his hand away. In an instant, the guards surrounded him, and two on either side grabbed his arms and forced him to his knees, causing the wound in his side to stretch and tear.

Regarding Charming from beneath her veil, Gwendolyn yelled, "I WILL HAVE YOU SENT TO THE GALLOWS FOR THIS OUTRAGE. YOU HAVE NO AUTHORITY. NO VOICE IN THIS COURT. YOU HAVE BEEN DISOWNED, DISCARDED, THROWN OUT BY YOUR FATHER." She waved vaguely down the stair to where his father, the former King, stood in frozen silence. "YOU ARE NOBODY."

Charming let the words wash over him as he watched, surreptitiously, as Elle and Liz slipped behind the altar. He only needed another few minutes. When the Princess was finished, he smiled even more brightly up at her and said, "But that is why I am here, Dear Lady. I am Prince Charming. I have been destined since birth to marry you, Princess Gwendolyn Mostfair, and to rule this Kingdom." He let the smile fall on the audience again to a chorus of "Ohhhs" and "Ahhhs," and then dropping the smile, he nodded his head over at Will. "I declare that this peasant is not and cannot rightfully be King. That crown is mine, and I am the only one in this land worthy of you, Princess."

"But—but," the Princess stuttered, "what about your peasant girl, Elizabeth Pickett? Have you not declared your undying love for that tramp?"

The attention of everyone in the room, Gwendolyn included, was totally focused on him now. He risked a quick glance at Liz and Elle, who were now, step by ever so cautious step, creeping closer to the Princess. A minute, no more, and they would be ready. "Elizabeth Pickett?" He said the name with derision and prayed that Liz would understand. "She was a tryst, a conquest of no consequence. A man of my position and stature is expected to have many such adventures. True, I thought if I wooed and disgraced her that it would prove once and for all the absurdity of William Pickett's fraudulent claim to nobility, but to believe that she meant anything to me is laughable." He laughed—a playful sound that titillated the assemblage with its delightful wickedness and hidden suggestions.

"I don't believe you," she said harshly. "Take him away!"

The guards seized him roughly and pulled him to his feet. Gwendolyn began to turn back to the priest. He needed more time, just a little more time. A sudden, wicked thought came to him. "Before you throw me in the dungeons," he said in his most Charming voice, "I have a last request."

"And why would I grant a last request to the man who tried to ruin MY wedding?" Gwendolyn asked.

"Because if I cannot have you, then at least I wish to give you a wedding present." He swallowed as the shadowy face beneath the veil stared at him suspiciously. "I wish to grace you with my final couplet."

Elle and Liz were now just behind her.

"Couplet?" said Gwendolyn. "Fine, make a fool of yourself. It will be good to remind everyone of who you really were."

At an unseen command from the Princess, the guards released him and he fell to one knee. He cleared his throat to hide his gasp of pain. He placed one hand over his heart and with the other gestured grandly.

> *"Never have I seen such beautiful eyes,*
> *Or woken to discover such pure bliss.*
> *Not for riches or titles would I exchange,*
> *That timeless moment of true love's*
>   *first kiss."*

Gwendolyn fell silent. "That wasn't couplet."

Charming smiled back, dropped one hand to the hilt of his sword, and tensed his body. "And it wasn't for you. Now!" he shouted.

A screech came from Gwendolyn as Liz and Elle sprang at her, clawing at the bouquet. The flowers flew apart in a rain of pink and red and white, and, for a second, the three women disappeared into a confused wash of pink and cream satin. Charming tried to jump to his feet and felt something tear in his side, and then a brilliant light flared and Gwendolyn's voice rang out, "STOP!"

The struggle was over. A strong smell of burnt spice hung in the air of the chapel. Charming looked about in disbelief. Everyone but he and the Princess had simply frozen. It was as though the entire chapel was a painted canvas that the two of them were walking through. The Princess gathered herself and threw back her veil, revealing a hag's face of creases and shadows, in her hand the fairy ball glittered like a torch. She reached down with her other hand and ripped the veils off Elle and Liz and chuckled to herself. "So, this was your plan—pathetic."

She looked over at Charming as he struggled to his feet and took a step back in horror at the change that had been wrought on the Princess. She gasped. "How? How are you moving?"

Charming wondered that also. He looked at the unmoving guards surrounding him and took a painful step toward her. She raised the glass sphere, glowing now with the intensity of the noonday sun, and again shouted, "STOP!" That same smell of nutmeg hovered about Charming like a cloud, and he felt a chill emanate from the little golden wolf around his neck as she said the words. He sent a wordless thanks through the miles to the Beast and, giving her a predatory smile, took a single step forward. The pain in his side was a burning brand,

and he felt something warm and wet against his skin. He ignored it, gathered his strength, and stepped forward again.

"FAIRY, I COMMAND YOU TO MAKE HIM STOP!"

A voice echoed about the room, seeming to come from all corners at once. *"I cannot fulfill thy desires, Mistress. He is immune to my magicks."*

Her eyes widened with fear. "No, that isn't possible."

"It is over, Princess Gwendolyn," said Charming, drawing his sword. "Release the others and I shall treat you gently."

"Nothing is over until I command it," she hissed. Like a striking snake, she drew a curved black knife out from a fold in her gown—and, far faster than Charming could hope to move, especially considering his current condition, she placed the blade against Elizabeth's throat. "Don't make me hurt her. I don't want to hurt anyone, but I am going to have MY wedding."

Charming stopped as fear gripped his heart.

Gwendolyn said, "Drop the sword and back away. My wedding will continue. I will be queen."

Charming's blade dropped to the ground with a ringing clatter. "Please don't hurt her."

"You are in no position to make petitions. I may choose to be merciful. After all, she is going to be my sister, but if you try anything, you will force my hand."

"Don't. If you are going to kill anyone, kill me. This was my plan. I made them come along. They had no choice. After all, I am, or I was Prince Charming."

"I will be glad to have the guards take you to the dungeons. We can discuss the penalty for your treachery later." Several of the frozen guards stiffly stepped forward.

STANDING JUST TO Gwendolyn's side, Will thought, *It can't end like this. Someone has to do something. I have to do something.*

He could feel Gwendolyn's anger at Charming roil across their bond. She was distracted and her control had slackened a fraction. He shifted his eyes down to the knife in Gwendolyn's shaking hand. The vision of the blade held against his sister's throat, the anger and fear, boiled his blood. He shifted his eyes again, and focused all of his thought, all of his will on one goal—the orb. The magic bond stretched and then something broke, and his hands lashed out like a loosed arrow. He did not see, but felt, the cool of the glass orb against his palms, and with instinctive bestial violence, he ripped it out of Gwendolyn's hand.

In an instant, the thoughts of a hundred minds crashed against him like a wave and then receded as the room sprang back to life. Elle and Liz stirred at his feet, the gathered crowd erupted into noise, the priest and several of the bridesmaids fainted dead away, and somewhere in the turmoil, Gwendolyn screamed.

A musical tinkling voice seemed to float down to Will from somewhere up near the ceiling. *I bid thee good day, King William, and offer unto thee riches beyond thy wildest dreams if thou will free me from this prison of glass.*

He saw a vision of himself sitting atop a pile of treasure surrounded by beautiful courtiers of immodest dress. Will shook his head and whispered, "I don't understand."

I am a fairy Queen. Princess Gwendolyn caught me by magicks dark and powerful and imprisoned me in this bottle. If thou free me, I shall give thee anything thy heart could wish for, and I shall make sure that her punishment is terrible, indeed.

Once more, images formed—unbidden—in Will's head. He saw Gwendolyn locked in a dark place of shadows and specters, wailing in fear and pain, her body twisted and bent, her face an unspeakable abomination. Some part of him thrilled at the idea of her humiliation.

Trust this to me, Great and Terrible King, when I am done with her, no one will ever dare to defy thee.

Will felt a tendril of power reach out from the ball toward the Princess. Though nothing visible happened, Gwendolyn shrieked and fell back as though struck by a whip. Her face was a mask of fear. A half-ring of nobles and footmen, all victims of Gwendolyn's manipulations, surrounded the dais, screaming for her blood. Charming, sword drawn and a trickle of something dark staining the side of his doublet, stood between the mob and the Princess. It was a horrible scene, made worse because it seemed to Will that even the shadows of the room were stretching forward to surround the Princess, pulling at her hair and clawing at her face.

Thou canst do more, Great Lord. I can make her feel anything thou dost desire. Would thou wish for her to burn alive? Gwendolyn screamed again, a long horrifying cry of pain, and collapsed onto the floor

"SILENCE!" Will roared.

A sudden hush filled the chapel. The mob, even Charming, fell to their knees and bowed their heads. Liz and Elle knelt beside Gwendolyn's sobbing body. Will looked about in bewilderment, wondering if perhaps the King had made some signal, but the King was on his right, bowing along with the others.

Finally, Will turned to the King, "What is happening, Your Majesty? Why is everyone kneeling?" There was an uncomfortable silence. "Tell me what is going on?"

"You are our liege, King William," answered Rupert, his head still bowed so that he addressed the carpet at his feet.

Will shook his head and felt the weight of the crown atop his head. He put a hand to his brow and caressed the cold metal of the jeweled circlet, and then pulled it away as if it had burned. "No. This cannot stand." He approached King Rupert, his hands outstretched. "You must not bow to me. The crown was not given willingly. You are the King. The crown is still yours."

Rupert looked up and shook his head. "No, Your Majesty. I have relinquished my rule, and you have been crowned. That is all that matters. There is no requirement that a crown be given willingly. If it were, the history of this kingdom and many others would be far different."

Will spun and rushed to Charming's side. He grasped

the man by the shoulder and tried to pull him to his feet, but Charming would not rise. Will put a hand to his head, removed the gleaming circlet, and offered it to him. "Prince Charming, you are the rightful heir to the throne. The crown should be yours not mine."

Charming, eyes cast down on the stones at his feet, shook his head. "I am disowned, not even a noble, Your Majesty. I am simply Edward Michael Charming, nothing more. I swear my fealty to you, and offer my sword to you in any cause you deem just." With a cough of pain, Charming laid his blade at Will's feet.

Will stumbled away from the sword as though it was a snake. He spun and found himself face-to-face with Liz and Elle. "Tell them, Liz, Lady Rapunzel, tell them that I am not the King. This is madness."

Elle kept her gaze on the floor and would not speak, but Liz raised her eyes to meet his and smiled sadly. Will's legs went out from under him, and he sat heavily on the top stair of the dais. "I don't know what to do. Liz, what do I do?"

Despite herself, she clucked her tongue in irritation. "How should I know? You might give us leave to rise . . . Your Majesty."

"Yes, of course. You may rise," he said. The crowd of nobles stumbled to their feet and the footmen returned to their posts against the walls of the room. He looked back to his sister, "What next?"

Will saw Liz's lips draw into a thin line and waited for a sharp retort, but Elle slipped her hand over Liz's wrist. The two exchanged a glance in the inscrutable way of women, but Will noted that Elle's eyes went to his crown, then Liz's followed. Liz made a quick nod of her head.

Liz looked down at her feet and shrugged. "I have never been anything more than the mistress of a farm, and a poor one at that." Then with a sideways glance at the former king, she added, "This is beyond me."

He followed her gaze, and a sudden light shone in Will's eyes. "King—I mean, Lord Rupert?"

"Yes, Your Majesty?" he said.

Will hesitated, but realized that if he was the King he needed to act and sound like a King. "I seek your counsel. What should my first act as King be this day?" He thought that sounded kingly.

Rupert considered the matter and then glared at the Princess and said, "Your Majesty, it is my counsel that your royal judgment be meted out on Princess Gwendolyn Mostfair, for her crimes against the Crown."

A murmur of assent rose from the gathered nobles.

William looked at the Princess, a dark spot on the floor where the shadows lay most heavily. His heart ached. She was deathly pale and her face was heavily lined with grief and fatigue. In her despair, she reminded him more of the girl he had found in the dark tower than the cold, proud woman who had enslaved him. A deep sadness washed over him.

"So be it," he said. "If that is what is required, then that is how we shall begin."

Chapter 11

A Fairy's Tale

WILL SAT HEAVILY on a high-backed chair, his crown forgotten in one hand, and the glowing glass ball clutched in the other. His face was a blank, but inside his head he was listening intently to a gleeful fairy listing all of the crimes committed by the Princess in her sad life. Somewhere in the distance, he heard Rupert bark, "Seize the prisoner."

Two grim-faced, pink-clad guards grabbed the Princess—a black stain in Will's eyes—and dragged her down to the foot of the dais, holding her arms roughly behind her back. He waved his crown at them. "Release her!"

They released her, but the shadows did not. She stood before him, swaying slightly, her arms still outstretched, suspended by the dark hands. Will chewed on his thumb and stared, lost in the memory of the tower and kissing her. From somewhere behind him, he heard Liz murmur something about his posture. He straightened himself with a start and reluctantly placed the crown on his head.

The fairy spoke to him, whispering royal words in his mind. *Princess Gwendolyn Mostfair stands accused of using dark magicks to bewitch, control, and enslave persons too numerous to mention, and plotting to depose the rightful King of this land. . .*

He almost repeated the words without thinking, but then Gwendolyn raised her eyes to meet his and he saw such despair and hopelessness. He murmured words only he and the fairy would hear: "What are these dread shadows that surround her?"

They are the echoes of her cursed wish, the fairy said with gleeful malice. *She awoke before her time, and now they try and drag her back into their dreams. I can control them, if that is thy wish.*

Without warning, one of the shadows struck Gwendolyn. She convulsed and fell to her knees, gasping for breath. A drop of crimson stained the corner of her mouth.

Will glared at the glass orb, enraged. When he spoke, it was in a thunderous voice. "ENOUGH! Fairy, make them stop. Tell these shadow demons to release her this instant."

The shades withdrew reluctantly, and Gwendolyn took a shuddering breath of relief. Behind him, Rupert whispered, "Your Majesty, are you well?"

"Yes, of course. They were being cruel, and I had to stop them," he said distractedly.

"I beg your forgiveness, Your Majesty, but I see only the Princess."

The gathered nobles stared at Will, shaking their heads and murmuring. He thought, *Fairy, are the shadows visible only to me?*

Yes, Your Majesty came the smug response.

But, why? he asked silently.

Because thee now control the orb.

And why do they torment her? Is she not free from her curse?

No, Your Majesty. Thy kiss only brought her to this half-waking state. The truth is, her current madness is partly of thine own making.

The horror of the fairy's words struck Will like a thunderbolt. His rage at the creature returned, and aloud he shouted, "FAIRY, I COMMAND YOU TO REVEAL YOURSELF."

There was a pause during which the fairy made many excuses for why this was impossible, and the murmuring among the gathered nobility rose and several actually shuffled back away from the front of the room in fear. Will's face grew red and he barked, "I care not for your magical limitations, Fairy, do what you must. It is my command!"

There was a disturbance, like a gentle breeze in the air above the chapel, and the dust motes filtering through the rays of the afternoon sunlight tumbled and spun. The wind increased and they coalesced into the shape of a semi-transparent winged woman whose naked body shimmered with the shifting of the glittering particles.

Accompanied by the distinct smell of nutmeg, she floated down along the slanting beam of light to land next to a now deathly pale Gwendolyn.

There were screams and gasps from the nobles. Will averted his eyes from the fairy's unclad form. "Would it be possible for you to clothe yourself, Fairy?"

The fairy bowed. "As Your Majesty commands." Another gust of wind blew through the open doors of the chapel, pushing before it in a great cloud the flower petals that carpeted the floor. They rose and swirled around the fairy in a multicolored storm, and when the tempest died, the fairy was clad in a flowing gown of pink and red and white petals.

Will looked at her and frowned. "Fairy, explain why it is that the Princess is still cursed."

The fairy hovered a few feet off the ground now, her face alive with mirth. "Because thee did not love her, Your Majesty."

Will paused, trying to recall the curses in every fairy tale he had ever learned. "Tell me, exactly, why did you curse her?"

The fairy smiled at him as though he were a simpleton. "Her curse was borne of her own wish, Your Majesty, or rather, her many wishes. She didst wish that her beloved sister would never marry Rupert, and that he would love her instead. Since I did not have the power to replace Rupert's love for her sister, it was necessary to remove her sister entirely. Death is the only cure for true love."

A sob broke the silence that followed. Gwendolyn

was on her knees crying. From beside him, Will heard Rupert murmuring, softly at first and then with increasing volume, "no, No, No, No, NO! This is why my Rosslyn died, because of you?"

Gwendolyn looked up at him atop the dais, hands outstretched, pleading, "I swear, I did not mean any of this to happen. Rupert, you must believe me, I . . . I was a child, a fool."

Rupert did not seem to hear her pleas. His face twisted with anger, and he rushed down the stairs and drew back his hand to strike her down, but Charming was suddenly at his side. He grabbed his father's arm before the blow could land and pushed him back away from Gwendolyn. "Father, we are in no position to judge her. Our own crimes against the Princess are manifold."

Rupert looked at Charming, and for a moment hatred blazed there and he again drew his hand back, this time to strike his son. Charming did not flinch, nor try to defend himself, and his father's body seemed to collapse in on itself. Rupert dropped his hand, and choked, "I have other wrongs to ask forgiveness for, including those I have committed against you, son."

Charming embraced his father. "We are beyond that now. Your embrace is enough forgiveness for me, as I hope mine is to you." They held each other silently for a time, for the first time.

Embarrassed to witness such a private moment, Will turned his, and in turn the court's, attention back to the fairy. "I still do not understand, Fairy. If Princess Gwendolyn's wish was to replace her sister in all things, then why did you prevent her from becoming queen? Why have you entrapped her in sleep all these years?"

The fairy blinked at him and tilted her head to one side as though confused. "That was but the first wish, Your Majesty. She also wished to be remembered above all other princesses, so I swept her away to become the prisoner of the dragon and the princess of legend. And then there was her final wish"—the fairy giggled, making a sound like tiny bells—"that she would find true love. Alas, true love is beyond the power of a fairy to grant. So, I didst preserve her until true love came, and she must still wait. I cannot help it if an unfulfilled wish has driven her to near madness. Enchantments are trying burdens on mortal souls."

Will furrowed his brow at the fairy's laughter. "Let us return to the question of my kiss. Why was I not able to wake her from this madness?" He gestured at the shadows that were hovering in the darkness of the vaulted ceiling, held at bay by his command.

"As I said, thou do not love her, Your Majesty. Not truly. Without true love, the curse of her wish cannot be broken and she is still under its power."

Will started to protest, but stopped. It was true. He had never really thought for a moment about who Gwendolyn was beyond his imaginings of her from the story. He had loved the idea of the Princess, not the girl herself.

The fairy either read his thoughts or the sadness in his face, because she said in that same whimsical voice, "Do not be disappointed in thyself, Your Majesty. No one has ever loved Princess Gwendolyn, not Rupert, not his son Edward, and not thee."

She made an exaggerated frown at the Princess and said mockingly, "Poor unloved and unlovable little princess, thou would have been better to stay in thy cage."

Something snapped in Will as he watched the fairy mocking Princess Gwendolyn. He stood and bellowed, "THAT IS ENOUGH, FAIRY!"

The entire court, and even the fairy herself, shrank back from the intensity of his anger. He pointed a quivering hand at the sprite. "Your casual mockery of Princess Gwendolyn's suffering and the curse she has been placed under has made clear to my mind one thing: The Princess may have opened the door that allowed you into our fair kingdom, but it is your agency that has caused our suffering."

The fairy smiled mockingly and seemed prepared to argue, but Will overrode her, saying fiercely, "It was your twisting of a young girl's love wish that brought about the death of Princess Rosslyn. It was your cruel trickery that then denied King Rupert and Princess Gwendolyn their own chance to be together, and sentenced her to a life of imprisonment. And it was your callous disregard for all, save your own malevolent amusement, that brought the dragon down upon us to terrorize this kingdom. Princess Gwendolyn may have wronged the Crown and those in this room, but you set upon us a never-ending nightmare, and, as your crimes are the greater, justice demands that you be judged first. After all, it isn't always the man that throws the first punch that starts the fight."

Will heard Liz groan behind him and realized that he had just quoted Prosper's town drunk. He swallowed, trying to compose himself. "So, um, let's begin."

The fairy's elfin features clouded with anger, and the sparkling light in her face darkened as she seemed to draw the shadows floating above into herself. "Judge me?" she shouted. "Thou wouldst dare judge me? Thou, who art King only because of the treachery of this vile woman and thine own lies?"

The court rumbled a protest at this attack on their new King's honor, and the fairy spun on them. "Know, gathered nobles, that thy King, who darest to wear the label 'dragon slayer,' did not raise a hand against the beast."

She spun back to Will and dropped her voice to a hissing whisper that nevertheless carried to every corner of the chapel: "Say that it is not so."

"It is the truth," he said in an even voice. This made the crowd mutter. Rupert gave him a warning glance, but Will stood and looked out over the gathering. "The dragon's death was an accident, but it was a most fortunate accident for this land and its people. I, for one, will accept the providential nature of the beast's passing with gratitude, and I will measure my small contribution to the creature's death against any other's, save, perhaps, my sister's."

A heartbeat of collective hesitation passed, and Will knew that his reign as King would either end here or . . .

Someone in the back, that Will would later swear sounded a bit like the Scarlet Scoundrel, shouted, "We're with you, King William, every man jack of us!" A general roar of approval sounded at this, and the nobles and foot-men stood together and began a chant of "Long live the King! Long live King William . . ."

Will let the warm embrace of the crowd wash over him and smiled, then gestured for quiet again. The crowd settled, and his face grew stern once more. "I have been judged, Fairy, and am pleased to say have been reprieved."

The fairy extended a long glittering finger from be-neath the flowing sleeves of the flowered gown to point at Will. "So, dost thou now consider thyself worthy to sit in judgment of me?"

A flash of inspiration came over Will, and he said with a dangerous smile, "No, Fairy, not I."

But the fairy did not seem to see, or at least did not heed, the warning sign. Instead, she stared hard at him and continued to speak over a rising rumble of voices in the gallery. "If not thee, then who? Sad old Rupert, naughty little Edward, perhaps thy domineering sister, or thy ill-tempered, ill-mannered wench Rapunzel?"

"Be very careful with your next words, Fairy, you tread on dangerous ground," Will said, gripping the chair arm so tightly that the wood popped under the strain of his anger.

"No, Your Majesty, it is thee that treads upon danger-ous ground," the fairy said, her voice dead and hollow. "Thou dost not know what powers thee trifle with. Know-est now that I canst not be bound by any law of man, and I willst not submit to this mortal tribunal."

Will smiled grimly. "You are right, Fairy. I do not know the limits of your powers, or how our mortal judgment might be brought to bear against you. Fortunately, I will not be the one to make those decisions."

He took a moment's pause to calm his nerves and commit himself fully to the course he'd chosen. Then, quietly but firmly, he said, "No, Fairy, the one who will judge you will be Gwendolyn Mostfair."

"Gwendolyn Mostfair!" sputtered the fairy in rage.

"Yes, Princess Gwendolyn Mostfair," he said again, and the word echoed about the chamber. "I appoint you to be this creature's judge."

Several gasps came from the crowd. The Princess looked up at him with wide eyes. "I don't understand."

Will descended the stairs to her. "You have wronged me, my sister, and this kingdom, and by all rights I should hate you. But I do not. I see now how much you must have suffered under the fairy's hand, and I see the temptation you must have felt to lash out against those that failed you. I do not justify your actions, but I understand them. I also know that you are the only person here who has managed to impose your will upon the fairy. Consider it part of your penance to me and to this kingdom to devise a means of enforcing our judgment that will keep future generations safe from the fairy's wrath."

Gwendolyn studied him for a moment and then nodded.

Will let out a breath of relief and asked, "What would you suggest? Shall we lock her away somewhere?"

Gwendolyn and the fairy stared at each other in mutual hatred, but it was the fairy that dropped her gaze first. Gwen spoke.

"No, Your Majesty, a fairy's life is not measured in years. Even were one to devise a prison that could stand the test of time, a thousand years of confinement might pass and still she would learn nothing. The only punishment that she will feel, that she will suffer, is one that removes her ability to impose her will on others."

The fairy smirked. "She speaks nonsense. Thou may keepest me in thy glass cage for a time, but nothing can bind a fairy's magick."

Gwendolyn mirrored the fairy's disdain. "You forget that I already have. To impose this judgment, Your Majesty, we need more fairy gold. Did you keep the dragon's key?"

Will nodded and gestured for a footman. After a brief conference, the servant sprinted from the room.

For the first time, a flicker of doubt kindled in the fairy's eyes. Gwendolyn fixed her with an icy smile. "Where is your defiance now, Fairy? Shall I explain to them the cause of your fear?"

"While I was sleeping," she turned back to Will, "the dragon would talk to me. In those conversations, she explained a great deal about the magic that had entrapped us. As it turns out, a fairy's magic is fixed by gold spun by that fairy's hand. It serves as a connection between the mortal world and that of fairy, and it is the one thing that can be used to counter fairy magic."

There was a gasp of shock from Charming. Will and Liz looked to see him fingering a golden wolf set on a thin chain. Gwen's eyes narrowed. She strode over to him, snatched the medallion from his hand and studied it carefully. "Where did you get this?" she demanded.

He gently extracted the golden wolf's head from her fingers and hid it beneath his shirt. "I was given this by a nobleman in the Northern Woods. Though his true name is Lord Adam, he is better known to the people of Royaume as the Beast."

An astonished buzz rumbled through the gathered court. "You actually met the Beast?" Will asked.

"Yes, Your Majesty. I lived for several days in the home of Lord Adam. And he told me that when he was younger, he had the misfortune of making a fairy wish, and that this fairy twisted the will of his wish so that he was transformed into the horror of our legends. She gave him this golden medallion as a token of her grant."

The Princess threw back her head and laughed. "This is a rich irony, Your Majesty. This same fairy must have cursed the infamous Beast as well, and also spun this gold medallion. While Edward wore the amulet, her magic had no potency on him. I thought it was the fairy's curse that had stopped me."

At that moment, the footman reappeared. Will's face brightened. "Excellent work." When he turned back to Gwendolyn, he was holding the dragon's golden key in one hand and the fairy ball in the other. "Now what?"

She tapped a finger on the glass ball in his hand. "Within this sphere is the golden locket I wore during my imprisonment. We will bind the fairy into a compact between you," she pointed to the key, "and her," she said, pointing to the locket. "So long as you ensure that the key is not lost or destroyed, she will be bound to her word."

Will turned to face the fairy, who was so dark with

rage and fear that the light that touched her melted away until there seemed to be nothing left but the silhouette of a winged shadow.

"Binding a fairy is an abomination," the fairy warned. "If thou dost this today, I warn thee, there will come a day of reckoning, Your Majesty."

Will's body stiffened at the threat. With the key, he pointed to the floor in front of him. "Kneel, Fairy."

She did not move.

"I said kneel." He thrust the glass orb toward her like a spear.

The fairy, pitch-black in her flower dress, floated slowly across the chapel floor until she stood before him. She glowered with eyes that pulsated an infernal red, and then stiffly dropped to her knees.

Despite his brave words, Will felt sweat on his palms. At his side, the Princess said, "Touch her once with the key."

He took a deep breath and gently placed the key on the fairy's right shoulder. She flinched as though burned.

Gwendolyn's voice cut through the silence that had fallen on the chapel.

> "With gold spun from thy hand,
> We do make thee this command:
> Swear with bonds that none can break,
> To abide the vows today thee make."

The fairy did not answer.

Will lowered the glass sphere so that it lay directly in her gaze. "Make your oath, Fairy."

She bowed her head low until she was a black stain on the stones of the chapel floor. When she spoke, it was in a voice as cold as frost. "By the stone of the Earth, I swear, by the eternal fires of the Sun, by the North Wind's might, by Winter's bite, that I will stand fast to the terms I hear thee make."

There was a swirling of air and light around the fairy, and with it again the strong smell of nutmeg. Then all was still. The fairy remained unmoved.

Will looked hopefully back at the Princess. "Now what?"

Gwen smiled at him. "There is one last thing needed before you can seal the compact, Your Majesty."

She took the ball from his hand and threw it to the floor. With a splintering crash, it shattered into a thousand pieces. The light from the globe swirled about and then into the flickering body of the fairy, filling her until she knelt manifest in flesh and blood before them. Gwendolyn bent and plucked out the tiny golden necklace from the shards of glass. She looped it around the fairy's neck.

"Now you must set the terms of the accord, Your Majesty."

Will nodded and turned his gaze back to the fairy. He kept the key on her as he spoke. "Fairy, my terms are that you shall leave the boundaries of Royaume, never to return. And you shall not, from this day hence, use your magic or curses, either directly or indirectly, on any person, noble, or common, or any creature, great or small, of this land. You are banished."

As his final words faded away, the fairy's eyes went wide. A gust of wind raced up the aisle of the chapel, and swept her rose dress away in a cloud of pink and white blooms. Naked, she grasped at the golden chain around her neck.

The wind became a gale and tore at her illuminated flesh, stripping it away in great plumes of dust. She released the chain and stretched out her hands as the tips of her fingers disintegrated.

Her voice, a bestial shriek, rose above the howl of the wind and then was cut off. "I shall return, and all shall suffer—"

The wind became a gentle spring breeze that swept away with it, in dancing swirls, the motes of her body and the last traces of her telltale scent.

All was silent for a time, eventually the courtiers and footmen rose from their places of refuge among the pews and curtains, then the shocked relief of conversation began to fill the room.

Will turned to the Princess as the particles that had once been the fairy mingled with the dust floating in the light of the sun. "Thank you for your help, Princess Gwendolyn."

"I am sorry, Your Majesty," she said, head bowed.

"Sorry for what?" Will asked.

"Sorry that I was blind to the man you were."

He smiled. "If I had been the man I am today, many things would have been different. I am sorry also for what I did, and what I still must do."

"It's okay, Your Majesty," she said. "Whatever comes next, the fault was mine, not yours, and I . . . I thank you for coming for me."

"It was my pleasure." He gave her one last smile, and then his face turned solemn, he climbed the stairs to the throne and once more faced the crowd.

"Princess Gwendolyn," he began in a low voice, "I have banished the fairy from this kingdom. I now must answer the question of what punishment would best serve justice in your case." He sighed. "Your crimes have been well documented to us, and, though I believe that you have been punished most cruelly for your part in the death of your sister, you must still answer for all that has happened since your return."

The Princess smoothed her dress and, taking on the regal mask she wore so well, looked up to Will. "I am ready for your judgment, Your Majesty, and declare myself guilty of all charges."

"You offer no defense?" he asked.

"None, Your Majesty."

"Very well," he said sadly.

Will started to speak and then stopped. He realized that, while the Princess might never be queen, she and the kingdom deserved a moment of dignity. Carefully, he composed in his mind the words she would be required to live by, and he would need to live with. When he was sure of them, he rose and pointed the golden key at her.

"Princess Gwendolyn Mostfair, as your crimes arose principally out of your reckless ambition for high title, so shall your punishment be one of common humility. You are hereby stripped of all possessions and relations and banished from the court. You are"—his voice broke—"to be cast out into the world, friendless, to make your way as you can. To live by the skill of your own hands and the grace of those you meet."

Gwendolyn's face paled, but otherwise she did not flinch. Instead, she made a low curtsy, and then stood and held her head high. Will gestured to two footmen. "Take her at once from this place. Give her two sets of clothes from the servants' quarters, coin in an amount equal to a month's wages for the lowest maid, and then cast her forth."

The men fell into line beside her. The faces in the crowd were black against her, and she looked so small and frail. As the men turned to march her out, Will realized that he could not do this thing, not like this. He raised a hand. "Footmen, wait!"

They paused and the nobles whispered among themselves.

Will crooked a finger at his sister. "Liz, may I have a moment?"

She crossed the dais to stand next to him. They whispered together for a short time, and then Liz nodded and stepped to the side, a quizzical expression on her face. Will looked at Gwen, who had turned at his command. Her face was a carefully constructed mask of dignity, but he could see that it was brittle.

"Gwendolyn Mostfair, I have completed my judgment as King, but William Pickett is not done. It comes to my attention that you may have difficulty in making your way in the world under the King's judgment. Doubtless, many exaggerated accounts of your deeds will spread beyond these walls. I suspect you will have a hard time finding those willing to take you in." There was a general murmur from the chapel. "I, for one, will not be accused of putting a lady out into this world unsheltered. So, my sister and I offer you our old home in Prosper. It is a poor place, made even poorer by the dragon's indelicate touch, but it is yours for as long as you wish it."

Gwendolyn looked at him in stunned disbelief. The mask broke and tears flowed freely from her eyes and down her pale cheeks. "That is most generous, Your Majesty. I accept."

"We shall see if you still think the offer generous after you have lived there a time."

"It is something of my own. For that, Your Majesty, I shall be ever grateful."

She bowed again, then rose and, flanked by the footmen, strode down the aisle out of the chapel and into the world beyond, like a queen.

The entire court watched her leave and then looked once more to Will, who stared after her, a bemused expression on his face. Will realized with a start that the entire court was staring at him. He straightened his shoulders and said, "Yes, well, if our business is concluded—"

"No, Your Majesty," came the answer from Charming. Will turned and saw the former Prince steal a quick glance up at Liz, his eyes filled with fear and regret. "Your Majesty, if Gwendolyn Mostfair is to be judged today for her crimes, then I must also be judged."

Will raised a hand to stop him, but Charming pressed on. "I acknowledge before the entire court that I perpetrated against you a crime most foul. I betrayed you to a violent and dangerous highwayman."

Someone in the rear of the room shouted, "I HEAR HIS NAME IS THE GREY... I MEAN, GREEN TERROR AND HIS MEN ARE THE SILENT SAVAGES!"

Charming looked back for a moment in confusion and then continued. "Yes, well, whatever their name, the treachery was unforgivable, and I beg the King's judgment."

"Codswollop!" shouted Liz.

Will rubbed his temples and braced himself.

Liz faced her brother and he could see that she had barely restrained herself from shaking a scolding finger at him. "There is no judgment to be made against Edward, because . . . well, because he . . . he has changed. I will admit that when I first met Edward, he was a shallow, conceited man who thought only of women and wine and song and horses and—"

Will took pity on Charming, who was flinching at every word, and said, "Your point, Liz."

She frowned. "Yes, well, my *point* is that he has changed. I won't go so far as to say that he is humble. I mean, it is shocking how much time he spends on his hair in the morning, and his penchant for bursting into verse is maniacal, but—"

Will closed his eyes and put up a hand to silence her. "You were explaining how Charming had *changed*, Liz."

She thinned her lips at him for the interruption, but

then her eyes fell on Charming and her face softened. "Yes, I was." She drifted down the stairs to stand next to him. He looked at her with an ashen face. "I believe Edward has become a man that I can be proud of, and if you cast a judgment against him, then you are casting it against me as well." With this, she grasped his hand in hers.

Will and Rupert looked at the two of them with wide eyes. "Wait, you mean you . . . and Charming?" Will asked incredulously. "And, Charming, do you return my sister's affection?"

The crowd murmured and Liz blushed, but Charming raised his chin and looked up at Will in his high throne. "Yes, Your Majesty. I love Lady Elizabeth with all my heart, and have from the moment I first saw her."

Charming looked at Liz and smiled lovingly, but his eyes were full of regret. He pulled his hand from hers. "However, I know that I am unworthy of her, and, if our positions were exchanged, I would deny her to me without hesitation."

Liz opened her mouth to say something, but Charming did not give her the chance, instead he fell to his knees. "So, I do not ask for your approval, or for her hand. All I ask . . . no, all I beg is that you let me put the question to her. If she says no, then I will leave this castle and kingdom forever."

"And if she says yes?" Will asked.

"Then nothing else that happens will matter," he said quietly. "I will be content."

Will turned to Liz, who returned his gaze with a tight,

thin-lipped smile. Will gulped. "Um . . . well, Charming, if you know my sister at all, then you know that I would never presume to answer for her. Liz?"

"Your Majesty, you should know that I do . . . do love Edward Charming, and have already promised him my hand."

"You did?" both Will and Charming said together.

"Yes," she said defensively, "I did."

Rupert looked down at his son and Liz, shaking his head and said gravely, "But, Your Majesty, this cannot be allowed." Both Gwen and Liz started to say something, but he raised his hand to stop them. "This is not a question of honor, a subject, I am understanding more and more, that I am ill-equipped to make any opinions on, in any case. No, it is a question of the law. I regret to say, Your Majesty, that the law states that the sister or daughter of the King must marry a landed man of title. Edward has neither, and the power to grant either is now beyond me."

Will grinned at Liz and Charming. "A problem easily fixed. What is the point of being king if you can't hand out land and title?"

He rose and walked down to where the couple stood. "Edward Michael Charming," he began, tapping the golden key on his right shoulder first, "I dub thee Lord Protector Edward Michael Charming," he tapped his left shoulder, "and charge thee with defending the subjects of this kingdom and this court against all threats internal and external, and of course making my sister happy." He tapped his right shoulder again.

There was a warm huzzah from the crowd as Charming stood next to Liz. They clasped hands. "Thank you," Charming said. "I don't deserve it."

"Maybe not," Will said with a sly grin and then, seeing the sharp glance from Liz, quickly added, "but my sister thinks so, and as you will soon learn, her rule is always final."

Will hurried on to the next topic. "Now, as for the land—"

A gruff voice rose from the back of the room. "They can have our place." Grady marched forward with five of the other dwarves behind him. The audience in the chapel all turned to look.

Liz looked at the dwarf. "What are you doing here?"

"Nice to see you too, Lady Pickett," he growled.

"What about the guards?" she persisted.

He waved dismissively. "Oh, those guys? Sloane is watching them."

"Sloane?" Liz shouted. "But he's a narcoleptic."

"He'll be fine," Grady said.

Dorian smiled and said, "Yes, he's a very light sleeper."

Will looked between the six little men and Charming and his sister in confusion. "I'm sure there's an explanation"—Liz started to speak and he waved it off—"but I don't want to hear it. Now, what is this about a place for them to live?"

"We're going on the road," Dorian said, "so they can have our cottage, if they want."

"Well, that changes everything," Will said. "In that case, I see no impediment to this union."

"But, Your Majesty," Rupert started.

"Are you still protesting this marriage, Lord Rupert?" Will asked with a hint of irritation.

"No, no, Your Majesty," he said. "But you are a wealthy man, and this is your sister. You could give her an estate that befits her station, a manor house, a small castle, perhaps a tower with some land."

The idea seemed to strike Will by surprise, and he grew silent and thoughtful and began unconsciously to chew at the side of his finger.

"Your Majesty?" Rupert asked after a time.

"Yes . . . yes . . ." he said haltingly. "My sister shall have whatever she desires."

"I desire the cottage," she said. "I don't want a manor house to run, or, forbid the thought, a castle." She shuddered. "All I want is a quiet place in the woods where Edward and I can be together."

Will nodded. "If, dear sister, you are satisfied, then so am I." He turned to Rupert. "Any additional business that I must attend?"

"None, Your Majesty, except that I wish to say something to my son, if it is permitted." Will waved him on, feeling a little uncomfortable that the man had thought the need to ask permission, and wondering what other bizarre new rituals he was going to have to be responsible for.

Rupert turned to Charming. "Edward, I am . . . I am very happy for you, and very proud."

Charming, for once in his life, was speechless and said nothing, but his eyes grew shiny with emotion.

Will coughed to draw the court's attention away from

Charming, who clearly needed time to compose himself. An idea struck him. "Lord Rupert, you have very decided opinions on what is proper for a king to do."

Rupert's face paled at the suggestion that he might have overstepped propriety, and he threw himself down onto one knee. "Your Majesty, I apologize for my behavior today, it was inexcusable. I have no right to question your judgment or authority, and I submit myself to your will."

Will beckoned him to rise. "Your actions may be inexcusable, but I will excuse them anyway. It is my hope that you will do me the honor of being my advisor and steward, and of second-guessing me for as long as I remain on the throne."

Rupert raised his eyes and gasped something incoherent.

"Is that a yes?"

He placed a palm across his chest. "It would be my deepest honor to serve you, Your Majesty."

"Excellent," Will said, as he climbed back up the stairs to the throne with Rupert at his heels. Then lower, he added, "Now, come stand on my right and make sure I don't do anything hideously idiotic. For instance, I'm at a loss as to what I should do now?"

Rupert whispered discreetly, "I think your guests are getting restless, My Liege. If the court business is done, you should dismiss them."

"Ahhh, but it is not," Will said with a twinkle in his eyes.

He stood and, gesturing broadly about the chapel with his golden key, announced, "The fairy is banished,

Gwendolyn deposed, and Lord Charming restored to your ranks. However, there is one more piece of business to which the Crown must attend."

Will stepped down from the throne, took a few steps across the dais to Elle, and bent down on one knee. "Lady Rapunzel, I wish to openly declare my love for you, and beg you the honor of allowing me to court you and, perhaps one day if I prove myself worthy, to agreeing to be my queen."

A collective gasp escaped from the watching nobility, and fans fluttered at double speed in irritation at the premature loss of such an eligible bachelor. Neither Will nor Elle heard the commotion below. They stood atop the dais of the chapel and gazed into each other's eyes—alone for a moment. Then Elle bent down and kissed him gently on the lips.

"I accept," she said.

Chapter 12

Happily Ever Afters

ALL TALES MUST eventually come to an end. The book is closed. The candle doused. Kisses are given and received. The children rest their heads on their pillows, close their eyes, and sleep. But the best tales never truly come to *the* end. The author may have dotted the last period, the telling may have passed, and the reader may have fallen silent, but those special stories linger on, weaving themselves into the heart and mind so that they may live, for a time, beyond the confines of the page, in dreams.

The tale of King William and Lady Rapunzel, of Prince Charming and Lady Elizabeth is such a story for the people of Royaume, and it continues to weave its magical spell over the children of the land, in one form or another to this very day. And, perhaps because it is so well known, the broad arc of the story has not changed much with the telling and retelling. It starts with a dragon, ends with a wedding, and has trolls, dwarves, and bandits sprinkled here and there as necessary to keep the children spellbound and, more importantly, quiet. But the story of Will and Liz and Charming and Elle did not end with the banishment of the fairy, or the march of Princess Gwendolyn from Castle White, or even with King William pronouncing his love for Lady Rapunzel before the whole of the court. Those all might have been *an* end to the story, but they were, none of them, *the* end.

Nor did the end come in the hours following the dramatic conclusion to the grandest wedding that never was, when the noble courtiers of Castle White, in a fit of mad exuberance or some say collective hysteria, did, as one, strip off their finery and go splashing—quite naked—into the intoxicating waters of the moat. And though it can be imagined that the nobles might well have wished it to end there, it also did not end, shortly thereafter, when the Scarlet Scoundrel and his Marauding Men made a most dramatic and lucrative raid on their discarded garments. It did not even end moments after that, when the courtiers, still recovering from the Scoundrel's daring act of banditry, found themselves face-to-face with a gruesome boulder-sized troll with long daggerlike talons, great glowing googly eyes, a maw of bone-yellow pointed teeth dripping with fetid dark spittle that oozed and stank, and mottled green-and-black scaled flesh, who lumbered up to the moat, took a look at the fishless, mossless, golden bubbly water, shook its head, and slowly shuffled back into the night with a muttered, "It's just not right."

Even weeks later, it had not ended when Will, in one of his first ever Royal Proclamations, declared, to the puzzlement of everyone in Royaume but Charming's former squire, that a certain field bordering on the Northern Forest was to be set aside for the permanent use of a family of goats.

And though Will may have wished it to be so, it certainly wasn't over when Gretel released her extremely unauthorized, but incredibly well-received, tell-all book, *Prospering with the Lord Protector: My Saucy Times with King William*.

No, the story came to, if not *the* end, at least a proper end a month or so later—after the now-Lord Charming had been sewn up again by the Royal Chirurgeon and given a chance to heal under Liz's watchful eye. After Tomas had been rescued from the dungeons and raised to the position of Grand Marshall by the now-King William in apology for his having been thrown in the dungeon in the first place. After Lord Rupert was officially sworn in as Steward Rupert, Royal Advisor, much to the relief of Will, who was beginning to understand that it wasn't always good to be the King. And, perhaps most notably, after everyone— Edward and Liz, Elle and Will, Rupert, Tomas, Elle's former footman-cum-huntsman-cum-valet and now Master of the Royal Hunt, Collins, newly promoted General of the Royal Guard, Alain, and of course a heartbroken Royal Tailor— had returned to Castle White after a small ceremony in the courtyard of

Lord Adam, where the seven dwarves, in one of the most contentious weddings ever witnessed, had married the now Lord and Lady Charming.

The friends had spent a happy week together in the castle. Charming and his father had finally had time to have that talk they had always meant to have—this time unburdened by title. Will and Liz had a few moments to be brother and sister again, during which Liz had not tried to mother him even once—well, okay, maybe once . . . or twice. Tomas had a chance to give Charming an earful, as had Elle, as had Will, as to exactly what would happen to him if they ever heard that he was not treating Liz properly. And then it was time at last for goodbyes.

Under the pure pale blue of a late afternoon summer sky that stretched from horizon to horizon unstained by cloud, Lord Charming and Lady Elizabeth rode out from Castle White. Liz looked over at Charming. He gave her that disarming smile of his, and she felt her heart melt as they stared into each other's eyes. "I love you, my Edward Charming," she said, leaning against the neck of her horse and running her fingers through its fine mane.

"And I love you, my Lady Elizabeth." He swept his arm out toward her.

They both laughed.

"Edward . . ." Liz started, ". . . what do you think will happen to everyone?"

Charming straightened in his saddle and thought a moment. "Let me see. My father, the Steward, will fill your brother, the King's"—Charming paused, smiled as if enjoying an inner joke, and shook his head before continuing—"head with how important and grand it is to be King, and Tomas"—he chuckled aloud this time— "Grand Marshall Tomas, I should say, will make sure the King is properly grounded and never forgets what a fool he really is. Between the two of them, he will be confused enough, that it will be a relief when he finally convinces Lady Rapunzel to marry him, because then she can make all the decisions."

Liz pursed her lips and narrowed her eyes in a way that Charming was beginning to realize meant he was on dangerous ground. He cleared his throat. "Um . . . Alain will stay captain . . . er . . . General of the Guard. The man has fantastic skill with the sword, as I can attest." He put a hand to his side and grimaced at the remembered pain. Then he shook a finger at her playfully. "And despite the gossip of some ladies that insist he has maudlin tendencies—

Charming cut himself off as Liz arched an eyebrow. "Hmmm . . ." continued Charming. "Well, the dwarves . . . I mean the Seven Players"—he looked around anxiously as though fearing one might spring at him— "their fame is all but assured. I know that they will perform that play about your life in every hall across the kingdom, to stirring reviews."

Liz sighed and rolled her eyes. "They embellished everything."

"My dear, there is something to be said for artistic license. Now, where was I? Oh, right. The Royal Tailor will certainly enjoy his position for years to come. In time, I suspect he'll break your brother, the King's, rather bad habit of slouching . . ." Charming put a hand to his chin. "Maybe some boning in the doublet."

"There you're wrong," Liz interrupted, and smiled. "I've been trying to do that his entire life. Will is stubborn."

"Maybe you are right," he conceded. "But the fellow is a genius and tenacious. After all, he got me into blue, and, for years, I stubbornly believed I was an autumn. Just the thought of all that time wearing orange and brown makes me . . ." He trailed off as Liz playfully rolled her eyes at him. "Right, so, who is left? Of course. My father, Lord Rupert, will stay on as an advisor until the end of his days. I can't see my father leaving the vicinity of the throne for anything."

Liz pursed her lips and furrowed her brow. "What about Princess Gwendolyn?"

Charming opened his mouth to say something and then shrugged. "That I'm not sure about. Having been where she is, albeit briefly, I can only say that I hope she finds someone with a generous heart to help her." Charming's eyes misted and he had a distant look.

"What are you thinking?" asked Liz, drawing her horse closer.

"I was thinking about Lord Adam, who taught me how to listen to my own heart." Charming's voice was soft, and he gazed deep into Liz's eyes.

"Just so you know," said Liz, "I heard the poem you delivered to Gwendolyn. I loved it."

They were entering the shade of the forest now and shared a smile as the sunlight danced through the leaves to dapple the ground around them.

Liz spoke. "One last question for you, my prince."

"You know, I'm no longer a prince."

"You will always be my prince, and it is precisely your name I have a question about. Will is called King William, and your father was King Rupert. Shouldn't you have been Prince Edward? Why did everyone call you Prince Charming?"

Charming reached out and took Elizabeth's hand, then pulled it gently to his lips. "Milady, I may have experienced victories and defeats, received praise and endured insults, but I don't believe that anyone in this kingdom could possibly deny that I am charming." His eyes sparkled as he released her hand and a broad grin that was pure Charming lit his face.

"Now," he said, straightening himself up in his saddle, "I have a question for you, Lady Charming."

"Yes, Lord Charming," Liz responded with a flickering smile.

"How many children shall we have? Because, I assure you, I intend to start immediately." He gave her a rakish grin.

Despite herself, Elizabeth Pickett blushed.

"Two? Three?" prompted Charming with a wink.

Liz recovered and gave him an impish smile in return. "You underestimate yourself, Lord Charming. I want at least a dozen children."

It was Charming's turn to blush, and he obliged. They

reached out and held hands. She gazed at him and felt herself fall deeper into Charming's impossibly beautiful brown eyes. He smiled back, a pure smile, a smile free of artifice and practice. She opened her mouth to say she loved him, madly, deeply, perfectly, but a movement over his shoulder drew her gaze to the trees along the side of the road. A line of maddeningly adorable creatures—two deer, four rabbits, a squirrel, and an impossible collection of birds—were shadowing them, following alongside in the undergrowth. Liz, feeling her mouth draw into that dangerously thin line, narrowed her eyes at the creatures and said acidly, "And I want all our children to learn to hunt." In a twinkling, the creatures melted away into the dark of the forest.

Charming drew back a little at this unexpected pronouncement. His eyes widened in surprise and his smile broke a little. "I don't understand."

She silenced him the only way she could. She leaned across the saddle of her horse and she kissed him. For the first time in her life, Elizabeth Pickett was well and truly content.

FROM THE BATTLEMENT of Castle White, King William and Lady Rapunzel watched Charming and Liz depart.

"So, Your Royal Majesty, what do you think will happen to your sister?" asked Elle.

Will was quiet as he watched Charming and Liz ride toward the distant trees. "I think only one thing could happen."

"What?" asked Elle, smoothing her dress.

"All fairy tales that I have ever been told end the same way. They will live happily ever after, of course," said Will.

He raised a thumb up to his mouth, but Elle intercepted it, slipped her hand into his, and leaned her head against him, discovering to her delight that it fit perfectly on his shoulder. "Your Royal Majesty, don't think that this means you shan't have to court me," she said.

"Lady Rapunzel, I wouldn't dream of failing you in that."

And so, King William and Lady Rapunzel watched Lord Charming and Lady Elizabeth ride away until they disappeared beneath the shadowed canopy of the forest, and, remaining on the battlement, they enjoyed the sunset and each other. And of course, all of them, each in their own way, lived happily ever after.

Epilogue

Wishing, Well

GWEN SAT HEAVILY on the low stone wall that surrounded her well and mopped her brow with one of the headscarves she had taken to wearing. She looked about at her new home from the vantage of the small hillock on which the well was situated. It really wasn't such an unpleasant place. The King had sent his men to repair the little house so that it was livable, and she found the valley enchanting. The air was clean and rich with the smells of earth and growth. Because the land had been allowed to lie fallow, the rains of late spring had brought forth a brilliant mixture of multicolored wildflowers and exuberant weeds, interspersed here and there by the occasional deep green of a rogue stalk of corn. The effect was wild and beautiful, if not very productive. She would need to find a way to till those fields, but for now, she would enjoy the flowered needlepoint of the land. Maybe she could be content here.

She unlatched the winch and dropped the bucket down the well. After a slight delay, she heard a distant, echoing splash. She waited for the bucket to sink and began winching the vessel back up from the cool depths. Her muscles were still unaccustomed to the exercise, and she distracted herself from the effort by thinking of the pleasure of the cool water to come. "Perhaps I shall treat myself to a wash this evening."

The bucket came into sight. She caught hold of the handle and pulled it onto the wall of the well. She plunged her cupped hands into the water for a drink. There was an initial glorious cool and then something slimy brushed against her fingers and started to slither up the wrist of her right arm. She got an impression of something small and green, and then shrieking, jerked back in shock, sending whatever it was flying back into the bucket.

"A SNAKE! A SNAKE!" she screamed, and leapt off the well, flapping her arms in alarm.

From a safe position, several strides away, she watched the bucket for any sign of life. Nothing stirred. "Maybe it was just your imagination," she suggested to herself. "You always have been a little hysterical."

In answer, something moved and a splash of water sloshed down the wooden side of the bucket. "And that was my imagination also, I suppose," she hissed. "This is not a matter of hysterics. There is a snake in there, and why not? Of course, there would be snakes in the well, and just when I thought I might be able to tolerate the place."

Gwen stared at the bucket. She considered retreating back to the house and letting whatever it was lie. But she couldn't bear the thought of a night spent with no tea and no bath. "It's my water, and I'm going to have it, snake or no."

She picked up a good-sized rock and cautiously approached the bucket. As she got closer, she could see ripples on the surface of the water. She sucked in a few gulps of air to try and calm her shaking hands, and then rushed forward. A small green head appeared above the edge of the bucket along with a pair of black eyes rimmed in yellow. The eyes widened in alarm as they saw her and the rock, and disappeared again.

"Please, spare me, gracious lady!" came a voice from within the bucket. It had a foreign accent and a creaking quality, but the words were most definite.

Gwen stopped in midstride, her mouth held open in stunned silence. She looked around to see if there was someone hiding nearby, playing some kind of cruel trick on her. The children from the village did like to taunt her and throw mud clods at her back whenever she went to market. Gwen supposed that they, not unreasonably, thought she was a witch.

But she saw no one. She was alone—at least alone, save for the creature that had taken up residence in her bucket. She steeled herself. "Show yourself."

That strange, deep voice answered back, "Do you still have the rock?"

"No," she said brightly, and hid the stone behind her back.

The top of the head popped over the edge of the bucket, and those strange black eyes peered at her suspiciously. "You are lying," said the creature, and it disappeared again.

"No, no, I dropped it," she said with a shake of her head.

The eyes appeared again and then narrowed. "You are hiding it behind your back."

She blushed at being found out. "I will drop it if you show yourself."

The lumpy green head shook back and forth. "You drop your rock and I'll climb out."

"You don't trust me?"

"No," the creature croaked.

She pursed her lips in irritation. "Fine, but you are being childish." She extended her arms out wide and dropped the rock.

The little green head looked back and forth between Gwen and the rock and then nodded. "All right, I'm coming out."

There was a splashing noise and a flurry of tangled green limbs, and then, between one blink and the next, a frog was sitting on the lip of the bucket. Its body was only about the size of one of her open hands, vibrant green, and smooth as wet glass.

"You are a frog," she said in disbelief.

"Ah, my nature is revealed," the frog responded with humor. It stood and took a quick bow. "Please allow me to introduce myself. My name is Montaigno Ricardo, Esq., and I am—"

Gwen's eye caught the glint of something golden around the frog's neck. She took a couple of quick paces until they were only an arm's-length apart. She squinted. There it was, a golden necklace with a frog-shaped amulet in miniature. She laughed and said in a dry monotone, "Let me guess, you are a prince who made a fairy wish ages ago that ended with you being turned into a frog, and now you need to find love's first kiss to break the spell."

The frog blinked up at her in surprise. "It is just so, milady!" And then added quickly, "More or less. You . . . You read my mind. Are you a sorceress?"

Gwen shook her head. "No, I'm not a witch," she said, and then added under her breath, "anymore." She smiled grimly at nothing and addressed herself to the frog. "Fairy wishes and curses are more common than you would think."

The frog made a movement with its eyes that, had it had hair, would have resulted in a magnificently arched eyebrow. "I see." It cocked its head to the side and studied her as she contemplated the ground at her feet, lost in thought. "Are you quite all right, fair damsel?" it said. "You seem preoccupied."

"What?" she asked, looking up. "Yes, yes, I'm fine."

"Yes, well, this is not the usual reaction I receive from the ladies."

She looked at the little green frog with a thin smile and an arch of her own eyebrow. "And, what is the 'usual' reaction?"

The frog gave a Gallic shrug. "Well, usually there is a lot of screaming, and maybe some fainting, or if not that, then there is certainly the throwing of the shoes, which, to be honest, I thought was the direction you were taking at first."

"I admit I was tempted," Gwen said dryly. "But I only have the one pair, and you are such a handsome frog."

"You mock me," the frog said with an exaggerated frown. "I don't blame you. I am repulsive, it is true, but," he raised a finger and gave her a sly grin, "there was a time when the maidens, well, I don't like to speak out of turn when I am with a lady, but suffice it to say I was quite popular."

Gwen favored the frog with a sour smile. "In my experience, when men talk like that, it can mean only one thing. They have been behaving very badly."

The frog dropped his head and frowned, this time with genuine sorrow. "You are right, of course." He hopped down from the bucket and paced gracefully back and forth across the stone wall, gesturing here and there with his painfully thin green arms. "I was the worst sort of rake. I was a scoundrel, a Lothario, constantly trifling with the hearts of the ladies. And now?"—he made a sweeping gesture with his arms—"and now, I serve a penance most fitting. I am made to be forever repulsive to the fairer sex. Unless . . ." He suddenly jerked his head up and gazed hopefully at her.

She shook her head. "No."

He fell to his knees on the stones, flippered hands

held in supplication before him. "Please, fair one, you are a lady."

"Nice of you to notice."

"No! No!" he said so loudly that he croaked. "Excuse me, it happens when I get excited." He shook a flipper at her. "I think you are making of me the fun perhaps? Let me put it to you as best as I can."

He dropped to one knee, and, placing his fore-flippers over his heart, said, "You are a beauty for the ages. You are fair as the rising of the sun. Truly do the heavens blush in shame that they cannot crown you with the glory befitting your grace."

She held up her hands to stop him. "You should stop while you are ahead, Frog. I think I get the idea."

"But, no," he said earnestly, "you do not. You see, when the fairy put the curse on me, it said that I must receive the kiss of love most true to break the spell, but that was not the only condition. No!" He rose and crossed until he was as close as the wall would allow. "The fairy also said that the kiss, it must come from a princess."

"Why?" Gwen blurted out.

The frog smiled sadly. "The fairy said that I might be able to convince a . . . well a . . ."

"Farmer?" she offered.

"I think *peasant* was the word the fairy used," the frog said apologetically. "The fairy said that I might be able to convince a peasant to kiss me with promises of riches to come, but for a princess to do so would mean that I had been able to woo with the earnestness of my request alone, for what could a frog possibly offer a princess to induce her to kiss it?"

Gwen nodded. "Yes, that sounds like the fairy."

"But let us cast that aside for the moment," he said in a bright voice. "Here I find in you a beauty that outshines even the most noble of ladies in the grandest of courts." He stopped to trace the curved outline of Gwen's body in the air with one of his flippers in a way that made her wish for a moment that he was a man. "Surely, a kiss from your glorious lips, from a lady with your beauty and virtue, would match anything that might be bestowed by a lady of the court."

At the word *virtue*, she felt shame well up in her breast. She could not meet the frog's eyes and instead found herself talking to the ground. "I am sorry, Montaigno."

"Please, call me Monty, fair lady."

She looked at him, but her voice was heavy and slow with sorrow. "I am sorry, Monty, but if you are looking for a lady of virtue, then I am the last woman in Royaume that you should wish to have kiss you."

"I don't understand. I know you are not a princess, but I am willing to take that risk. You must believe me when I say that I have never met a maiden fairer than you, or that carries herself with greater nobility. If you are not a princess, it is merely an error of birth and not character."

"It won't work," Gwen said, shaking her head. "Trust me, Monty, if anyone would know what it takes to break a fairy's curse, I would, and I am not what you need." Tears glistened in her eyes, and she dropped her gaze back to her feet.

"Dear lady," he said in a voice soft as rain and filled with concern, "I can see that you are suffering. If I can help?"

"Stop," she shouted. "You don't know me, Monty, and to understand why I refuse, you must." Gwen inhaled deeply, trying to keep the bitterness from rising again, and when her eyes rose at last to meet his, they burned with intensity so much so that she seemed to be staring through him. "Monsieur Montaigno Ricardo, I will tell you the truth of myself. I am a wicked and wretched woman. I am accursed, and it has been ordered that I should be shunned for my deeds. That is what I am. That is why my kiss would be no boon to you. That is why it would be better if you found your way to some other well, where a woman of true virtue might find you and lend you her favor."

At the end of her speech, she fell to her knees as though struck down. Apart from her dreams, which were always troubled, the shadows had not returned for some time, but Gwendolyn felt them now—very close. She looked about nervously and saw that a thin black fog seemed to be rising from the depths of the well. A shuddering sob escaped her and she scrambled backward in the dirt, away from the sudden menace.

In an instant, the frog was beside her on the ground, his outstretched flipper resting on her hand. "Please, fair lady, you must not torture yourself this way. My presence has caused you distress. I will take my leave, but before I do, let me tell you this. It is true we do not know one another, and I do not know what it is you may have done in your past, but I do know remorse most true when I see it. We, each of us, have a past. I am not proud of who I was when I was a man, but I yearn every day for the chance to prove that I have changed. Perhaps you, in your mercy, can grant me that chance. And, maybe, in helping someone even more desolate than yourself, you can also find the grace to forgive yourself."

Gwen looked up at this, her eyes still wet with tears. "I am afraid, Monty."

"But why?" he asked. "If the kiss does not work, I am still a frog and you are still a woman most beautiful. I will withdraw from this place forever and never again darken your door, or well for that matter. I am willing to take the chance of failure, why are you not?"

"Because I am, I was, a princess," she whispered.

His eyes widened in surprise, but he said calmly, "And this is a problem because—"

"Because, I was . . . I am Gwendolyn Mostfair," she said so softly that it might have been a prayer.

Monty's eyes widened even further until they seemed to fill his face. "You are the Princess of the story? Then this is destiny. If you will but grant me the favor of your kiss, all will be well. I will, once more be a man."

"But if we fail . . ."

"We won't, fair one. There can be no lady in any land more noble than you."

"You still do not understand," she said, the anger returning in an instant.

He bowed and spread his hands wide in a gesture of

surrender. "Forgive me. I am being pushy, and nobody likes a pushy frog. Please, explain to me your fear. I assure you that there is nothing that is more important waiting for me at the bottom of that well."

Gwen smiled, but then just as quickly, a shadow of grief passed over her face. She straightened herself. "I may have once been known as Princess Gwendolyn Mostfair, but I lost everything. Even my name. Today I can delude myself that something of what I was still remains, and that there is hope. But if I kiss you, and you remain a frog, then this really is all that is left. This life. This loneliness. I am not sure I would survive."

Monty nodded gravely. "I see." He sat down cross-legged next to her. "Let me tell you something, Gwendolyn Mostfair, that I have learned while sitting at the bottom of very cold, very damp, and very lonely wells for the last few dozen years. Many things can be taken away from you in this life. You can lose your riches, your title, even your body"—he gestured to himself— "but no one can take away your soul."

He put a flipper on her hand again. "In your heart, you are a princess, no, you are *the* Princess, the Princess of fairy tale. That is something no one can ever take from you."

Their eyes met. They gazed at each other as the wind whipped about the top of the hill, and the crickets began their evening song in the field below, and the clouds passed overhead, until, at last, some silent agreement passed between them. She bent down toward him. He spoke as she drew near. "Wait. Gwendolyn, I have a confession to make. I am not a prince, just the son of a . . . farmer. I am sorry I lied to you."

Gwen laughed softly. "Have you seen where I live, Monty? I don't need a prince. I need a farmer."

"But I will never be able to give what you once had, Gwendolyn."

"I do not want what I once had, Monty."

He leaned forward. She spoke as he drew near. "Is this true love, Monty?"

"What is love, but the selfless need of one person and its answer reflected in another. This may not be full love, but what is there could not be more true. In time, who knows? Is that enough for you, Gwendolyn?"

She closed her eyes. "I am willing to take the chance."

They kissed, and an electric wind swirled about them. She felt hands, human hands, a man's hands, cupping her face. She let the feeling linger and then, at long last, Princess Gwendolyn Mostfair opened her eyes.

AN END

Acknowledgments

AS ALWAYS, WE would like to acknowledge everyone who has helped us on this long journey to making this book a reality. Inevitably, someone will be forgotten in this list, but this won't be the last book. We'll fix it.

First, to Taba and Heather who always had faith and love to spare even when we faltered. You gave this book life as much as anyone. Happily ever after.

To the members of the Paragon City Writers: Dara, Wayland, Brad, Anna and Jon. Keep writing.

All of our beta readers: Anthony, Bill, Cathy, Chris, Dorothy, Kayla, Kim and Oliver. This doesn't happen without you. Thank you so very much.

To our families, including parents, in-laws, uncles, cousins, grandparents, brothers, sisters and fairy godmothers. We love you all and appreciate the inspiration, support and understanding.

To everyone at Estes Express, thank you for believing.

A special mention to Rasheen for the music and the breakfast walks. Thank you.

To our fellow Harper Voyager authors, thanks for the friendship, community, and support.

From Harry to Dad, you have always believed in me. Thanks for the bedtime stories.

From John to Dad—*Tout passé, tout cassé, tout lassé.*

Finally, again a big thanks to Kelly and Jessie and everyone else at Harper Voyager.

About the Author

JACK HECKEL's life is an open book. Actually, it's the book you are in all hope holding right now (and if you are not holding it, he would like to tell you it can be purchased from any of your finest purveyors of the written word). Beyond that, Jack aspires to be either a witty, urbane world traveler who lives on his vintage yacht, *The Clever Double Entendre*, or a geographically illiterate professor of literature who spends his nonwriting time restoring an eighteenth-century lighthouse off a remote part of the Vermont coastline. Whatever you want to believe of him, he is without doubt the author of *A Fairy-tale Ending*. More than anything, Jack lives for his readers.

www.jackheckel.com